ELMO'S FIRE

A DERRICK ANDERSON ADVENTURE

MATTHEW GUNNOE

TWISTED SKIES
PUBLISHING

Elmo's Fire: A Derrick Anderson Adventure
Copyright ©2024 Twisted Skies Publishing

Trade Paperback ISBN: 979-8-9903356-0-8

Published by Twisted Skies Publishing
Wichita, KS 67220

DEDICATION

To Mom and Dad:
Who passed before ever getting to read this story.

To my wife:
For putting up with me. She truly is a saint.

CHAPTER 1

Sitting in the left-turn lane, waiting for the light to change, Derrick could hear his heart beating over the sound of the signal clicking.

"I never dreamed I would even see this place, let alone be sitting here waiting to get in," he thought, excitedly.

The green arrow appeared, and as the line of cars started to turn, he was taken over by the signs that met him: *Restricted Access. Government Installation. No Trespassing.* He was finally here.

As the other vehicles continued straight towards an ominous gate ahead, he made a right turn into the Visitor Center lot. After parking, he sat for a minute watching car after car pass by, going into this mythical location. Thinking about the day he would join them, he made his way to the Visitor's Center and was amazed that you couldn't see anything on the inside from the lot. There was only treeline after treeline around him.

He opened the old, heavy door into the center and noticed the building looked to be an original fixture from when the complex was built. While pondering the age of the building, a voice broke the silence.

"Can I help you?"

It was in a gruff New England accent. Coming from Texas, he was surprised by the curtness of the greeting. Turning his gaze towards a line of bank teller-like stalls, a middle-aged woman stared at him with a scowl.

"Hi! It's my first day!" he replied with his usual enthusiasm.

"Driver's License," the clerk spouted in the same apathetic voice as a seasoned DMV employee.

His smile beamed as he handed it to her. It was met with a glare as she went about her work on the computer. He started thinking, "How could anyone working here be this…" His thoughts were interrupted by the gruff voice again.

"Here's your badge and instructions on where to go. Show it to the guard on this side of the building." With that, she pointed away from the main entrance where all the others were going.

He thanked her and went back out through the large, heavy door.

After climbing back into his car, he proceeded to the secondary gate. There he met two guards in black police gear.

"Morning," said the first officer.

Derrick showed him his newly received badge.

"Ah, first day?" the officer asked.

His demeanor was a continent away from the old lady inside the building.

"Yes, it is!" he replied as he noticed the second officer was looking into his passenger side windows.

The first officer handed him back the badge.

"Well, congratulations! You may proceed… and welcome to CIA."

He froze as goosebumps covered his entire body. Thanking the officer, he retrieved his badge and proceeded down the two-lane road leading into the grand complex. As soon as he cleared the gate, the trees ended, and there before him was the massive building known as Headquarters. It was bigger than he had ever imagined.

He started looking for a spot in the copious acres of land designated for parking. He had gotten there two hours before orientation was supposed to begin, but after a frustrating twenty minutes, he thought it might not have been early enough. He made it out to the purple lot where, back in row XX, he finally found a spot. After pulling his shiny, red Mustang into the parking spot, he found he only had mere inches to get out because of its large doors. Rolling down his window, he climbed halfway out of it trying to get his feet on the pavement before his butt did.

Looking at the map to see which part of the campus he was supposed to go to, Derrick found that it was on the exact opposite side from where he was standing.

"Now I know why they said to wear comfortable shoes."

He started the mile-long trek to the "Bubble" where orientation was to be held. Being used to the low sixties for this time of year, Derrick quickly realized he wasn't in Texas anymore. The bitter wind blew the twenty-degree morning air across his now numb face.

"How is it even possible to be this cold," he thought.

Of course, being decked out in a suit, Derrick didn't see a reason to have brought a coat too.

"This jacket will be plenty warm," he thought back in the hotel.

He made it to one of the bus stop huts and took shelter from the wind for a few minutes. Maybe he would get lucky and the shuttle would come by and take him the rest of the way. The shelter blocking the wind did little to warm him up, so he trudged on, realizing he had not seen a shuttle the entire 30 minutes he had already walked.

As he slowly shuffled, pondering his poor choice that morning, he looked up and was suddenly unaware of the cold temperature around him anymore. He had heard about it, but now he was staring frozen nose to nose at the Oxcart on display. The proud aircraft that made so much of this agency's legend possible was now greeting him on that freezing Monday morning.

"Such a beautiful aircraft, isn't it?"

Turning around, he saw a friendly face standing there beside him wearing an oversized fur-lined coat.

"Hi, I'm Tae. Is this your first day too?"

Surprised by the pleasant greeting from the obviously smarter new acquaintance standing before him, he replied with a shiver,

"Yes. I'm just trying to survive to get to the Bubble."

Tae replied, "I'm on my way too. Let's see if we can find it together."

Making their way towards the Bubble, Tae asked,

"What will you be doing here?"

"I'm in IT. Commo," replied Derrick.

Tae's eyes widened, "So am I! I'm starting the communications program too!"

Looking around at what had to be close to a million cars in the parking lots surrounding them, Derrick couldn't help but think, "What are the odds?!?"

Finally, making it to the Bubble, they walked in to find the lobby filled with people surrounding several tables.

"Welcome! What's your name?"

"Anderson, Derrick Anderson."

He giggled as he said it that way, thinking it was only appropriate now that he was standing INSIDE of the CIA... well, in the Bubble lobby at least, but to him, it still counted.

He was handed his folder and directed to take a seat inside the auditorium. He walked up to the entrance where there were three large double doors with a marquee sign above them that scrolled "Unclassified".

"That seems a little cheesy, but okay," Derrick thought.

Just then, he felt an arm land on his back.

"You want to sit together?"

Looking to his left, he found Tae standing there with that weird smile of his.

"Yeah, that sounds good. Maybe it will keep us awake," Derrick replied.

They both took a spot in the middle of the left-hand side and started talking.

Tae was a Tar Heel from North Carolina where he had worked for an electric company for many years. Before that, he was in both the Army and the Air Force. The confused look on Derrick's face must have been obvious, but as Tae tried to explain, another person sat down next to Derrick and interrupted.

"Hey, you guys seem to be having a good time over here. I'm Richard Turner, but my friends call me Richie!"

He was a tall, well-tattooed guy who smelled of cigarettes. Everything about this guy screamed military, except for the well-tailored gray suit he was decked out in.

"I hate these monkey suits, man!" he continued.

Piping up, Tae asked, "Were you military?"

"Navy, seventeen years!" Richie replied, proudly.

Derrick was intrigued. "Seventeen years?!? Why did you get out and come here?"

"Long story," replied Richie, and he left it at that.

"Tae here was in both the Army and the Air Force," Derrick said as he introduced him.

"BOTH?" Richie questioned.

"Yeah, well, I started in the..."

Tae tried to explain, but Richie cut him off.

"Man, I got to whiz! Anyone seen the head?" and he jumped out of his seat and took off on a mission to find the bathroom.

"He's kinda strange. Do you play Magic?" Tae looked perplexed as Derrick laughed at his question.

"You just got finished saying Richie was strange and then asked if I play Magic."

"Yeah... and?"

"Never mind," Derrick resigned.

As time grew near for orientation to start, the auditorium filled in. Richie finally made his way back from the bathroom.

"Hey, I forgot to ask, what are you guys going to be doing here?"

Derrick replied, "Tae and I are both commo."

"WHAT? Same here! Small world!" Richie exclaimed.

About that time, the announcer stated, "Can I get everyone to take their seats?" as the large doors in the back clanged as they closed. He continued greeting everyone, "Welcome to CIA! We hope you will have a long and productive career here, but first, we need to take care of some preliminary information and then we will take you over to the great seal where you will be sworn in."

The great seal! The one that you always see in the movies that is synonymous with CIA Headquarters. This was the moment he had dreamed of.

Nudging Derrick, Tae said, "How cool is that? We get to swear in on the great seal! I hear that is in front of the wall of the fallen officers."

Derrick leaned over and whispered, "Wall?"

"Yeah, there's a wall where they carve a star for each officer that is killed in the line of duty. It's amazing, I hear."

Hours passed as the presenters went on and on with the standard boring presentations about benefits and policies like any new hire orientation does.

Derrick had almost nodded off when Tae elbowed him. "You think they will ever get around to telling us where they keep the aliens?"

Derrick could barely keep himself from laughing out loud. Thankfully, Richie piped in, before he could embarrass himself.

"You think they will ever shut up? I have to take a whiz again!"

This Richie guy was an interesting creature. He was probably six feet, three inches of slim, military muscle. He had a buzzed haircut and his eyes were so dark, it looked as if you were looking into Hell itself. If you met him on a street at night, you would likely want to walk on the other side. With all these ominous features, he couldn't stay out of the bathroom.

Before Derrick could reply, the speaker announced that, after a quick break, they would all be going to the lobby to take the Oath of Office on the great seal... in front of the wall of stars! Derrick felt goosebumps crawl down his arms and legs as Tae nudged him. Derrick turned to his right to talk to Richie only to find him halfway out of the aisle, running for the bathroom.

Tae quietly yelled, "You know they make medicine for that!", but it was clear Richie didn't hear him... mostly because Tae was still alive. He was a funny guy, but clever. He made sure he said it quietly enough that Richie wouldn't be able to hear.

After the short break, they instructed everyone to the lobby. Tae, Richie, and Derrick made the short walk out of the Bubble and towards the row of doors with *Main Entrance* etched in stone above them. Derrick was surprised that it had warmed up beyond butt-numbing cold in the three long hours they had been there. Making it to the door first, Richie held it open for the other two. When Derrick walked in, he froze. Before him was a vast lobby with the massive seal stretching out on the floor.

Tae nudged him and said, "Look at that! We made it!"

Walking to the rows of folding chairs, Derrick noticed the white marble wall on the right. It was full of black stars with flags framing it on the sides and a small podium with an opened book.

"That is the wall of fallen officers", remarked Tae. "A master carver comes in and hand carves each of those stars when someone dies in the line of duty."

"There's a lot more than I expected," Derrick said as his mind started drifting...

He could suddenly see the old carver scratching away at the wall as four new stars slowly formed. The environment changed from excitement and anticipation to that of mourning. He walked over to the book that was by the wall and saw four very blurry names. As he squinted to make them out, they disappeared, one by one.

★★★

Four stars among many. Four empty spots in a book.

★★★

Snapping Derrick out of his daymare, the Director asked them all to raise their right hands and repeat the oath:

"I, Derrick Anderson, do solemnly swear or affirm that I will support and defend the Constitution of the United States against all enemies, foreign and domestic; that I will bear true faith and allegiance to the same; that I take this obligation freely, without any mental reservation or purpose of evasion; and that I will well and faithfully discharge the duties of the office on which I am about to enter. So help me God."

***

Back in the Bubble, orientation dragged on. Speaker after speaker and lecture after lecture. It was getting so monotonous that Derrick nodded off...

"6-8, need you for an MVA in Barberville." He *woke from his sleep and was sitting in the driver's seat of an ambulance. Still trying to get his bearings, he reached for the radio....*

Tae whispering to him again woke him from his dream. "I think it's almost over."

As orientation was finally concluding, the speaker ended it with, "And once again, Welcome to CIA! You're going to love your time here."

Derrick murmured under his breath, "THE... Welcome to THE CIA." The omission was starting to grate on his nerves.

As they gathered their things to leave, Tae, chipper as ever, asked Derrick where he was staying.

"I'm at the Marriott in Tyson's Corner."

"How cool, I'm just a block down in the Spring Hill Suites," Tae replied. "I just went to an Applebee's last night that's within walking distance of both of us. Wanna go for dinner?"

Derrick would find out that Tae had an unhealthy obsession with Applebee's. "Sure, why not?"

Overhearing their dinner plans, Richie chimed in. "Applebee's? Hey, I love Applebee's! They have great wings and brewskies!"

"Why don't you join us?" Tae asked.

"Already there mate!"

As they left the Bubble together and started the long walk back to their cars, Tae was excited about the next day. "I can't wait! We get to head down to the school in the morning and check it out!

Derrick listened as Tae rambled on with all the excitement of a kid on Christmas morning when they finally made it back to the Oxcart on display.

"Well, I guess this is where we part for now. I found a spot right over there. Lucky, huh?" Tae exclaimed, smiling.

Derrick glared at him in disbelief. Knowing his car was still a good mile away, he was really glad it wasn't still horribly cold out. "So I guess we will meet at Applebee's shortly then?"

Tae's eyes lit up thinking about that place. "Indubilly! How about in an hour? That will give us time to change and freshen up."

"An hour it is then," remarked Derrick, still pondering what *Indubilly* meant.

Just then, Richie passed by with his abnormally quick gait. "I'll get us a table. Anyone mind if I start without you?"

Before either of them could reply, Richie kept talking, "Okay, sounds good! See you there..." as he strolled out of voice range.

"That is one strange character," Tae remarked.

With Derrick nodding in agreement, they parted ways.

Derrick wondered if he was even going to make it to his car in an hour... or, for that matter, actually find it again. As he walked through the parking lots, a police car passed him for the third time. This time the officer rolled down his window and asked, "Still haven't found it yet?"

"I think it's just around the corner," Derrick replied, noticing the officer unsuccessfully trying to hold back his laughter.

"Oh, please let it just be around the corner," he whispered, walking down yet another aisle.

After 30 long minutes of scouring the parking lots, he saw the shiny, red bumper sticking out from between two cars... and, of course, they were still too close to easily get in. Derrick stood for a second staring, sighed, and then started crawling through the driver's side window.

***

The Marriott was one block down from Applebee's and, since it was noticeably warmer than this morning, Derrick decided to walk.

He was almost to the restaurant when a police car went by running its lights and sirens. The ambient sounds started fading…

…*He opened the door to the ambulance. Stepping out into the darkness, there was a smell in the air that made his nose retract. It smelled of a weird combination of antifreeze and…*

"Derrick!"

Hearing his name snapped him back to reality.

"Derrick! Over here!" Tae called out to him again.

The waitress showed them to their table where Richie was watching the game and three beers deep.

"I hope you guys like your wings hot!" Richie exclaimed.

"I'm more of a…" but before he could finish, Tae piped in. "The hotter the better!"

Feeling his stomach already rumbling, Derrick thought, "This is going to be a long night."

The evening was pleasant as they were making small talk about the weather and the game on the TV beside them, when Tae, who had been pondering Richie's reply earlier of "long story", decided to ask him again why he chose to work here.

After slamming back what was left of his 5th beer, Richie answered, "Seventeen years in the Navy. I needed a change."

Derrick could tell from his answer that Richie didn't want to go into more details, so he redirected the conversation. "Tae, you never did explain how you were in both the Army and the Air Force."

"Yeah, I did my four years in the Army, and I decided to switch over to the Air Force. So, I did another four years with them for fun," Tae explained.

Dumbfounded, Richie interjected, "Said no sane person ever. Dudes, I've got to hit the head again. Order me another beer while I'm gone."

"Well, if you'd slow down, you wouldn't have to go so much." Tae quipped, once again making sure Richie didn't hear it.

"Do you have any military, Derrick?"

"No, I was a medic for 8 years."

Tae's eyes lit up. "That must have been exciting getting to drive with a siren."

Derrick's disposition dropped. "Not as much as you would think."

Thankfully, the server showed up about then with a fresh platter of wings and Richie's beer before Derrick had to explain

---.

Richie and Tae swapped "war" stories for the rest of the night as Derrick sat and listened.

After a couple of hours, Derrick was getting rather tired. "Guys, this has been fun, but I think I'm going to head back to the hotel and turn in. We have a bit of a drive tomorrow."

Richie, now a bit tipsy, gave Derrick a good ragging. "Okay, Grandma. You go get your beauty sleep while the real men sit up and talk business."

Derrick shot back with a smile. "Let me know how that works out for you in the morning."

CHAPTER 2

...He had just crawled into the rear window of the car. The old gentleman in the front seat was in critical condition. The car had rolled so many times there was no other opening large enough to crawl through. He put his hand down into the back seat to regain his balance. The LifeEVAC helicopter was landing nearby. Its landing lights suddenly illuminated the inside of the car. He looked down and saw...

Derrick jerked straight up in bed, gasping for air. The sunlight streamed through the hotel room window. He contemplated going back to bed for a few more hours, but since sleep only allowed the nightmares time to wage war on his brain, he decided it was best to just get ready and head south.

***

Lynchburg was more than 120 miles west of Richmond. It was home to an old community college that the government purchased for interagency technical training.

After the long, four-hour drive, Derrick pulled into the parking lot at the dorm hall on the campus. The two-story, brick structure would have been at home on any college campus in the country.

He sat for a minute in his car thinking about the flashback earlier in the day. On the passenger seat of his Mustang was the suitcase that contained everything he owned in the world.

As he was about to get out, a large Toyota Tundra 4x4 pulled up beside him. He had to look up to even see the windows. It was Tae. They both went down the breezeway to the main doors where they checked in.

"Ah yes. Hello, Mr. Anderson," said the housing director. "Your room is 223. Second floor, all the way down the hallway on the right," as he slid him the keys.

He made his way up the stairs and to his room. It was small, only being big enough for a full-sized bed, chair, and a small work desk. "At least it has a bathroom," he thought as he placed his bag on the floor.

He had just plopped down onto the bed when Tae knocked at his door. "Hey, ya! I'm hungry. You want to grab something to eat?"

"Sure, I'm starving. Where you thinking? I have no idea what they have here."

"I wonder if they have an Applebee's!" Tae didn't have an unhealthy relationship with Applebee's. He had an outright obsession.

"Sure, why not? Anything sounds good right now," Derrick said as he grudgingly rolled out of the bed.

Tae volunteered to drive, so Derrick walked over to the passenger side and looked up at the door.

"How do you get into this thing?!?" he asked Tae.

After arriving at Applebee's, Derrick did his best to get down out of the truck without ending up on the ground. "You sure you're not from Texas?" he asked.

After entering, they were shown to a table and Derrick started checking out the menu. Looking up, he found Tae smiling with his hands folded, already knowing what he wanted.

Glancing over Tae's left shoulder, Derrick noticed a lady sitting by herself on the other side of the restaurant. She was mid-twenties, slender build with long brown, curly hair. His stomach did a flip.

"Oh, wow," he said under his breath.

Tae, hearing him, discreetly turned around to see what he was looking at. "Hey! Why don't you go ask her to join us?"

Derrick's face flushed. "Dude, she's WAY out of my league."

Even still, he couldn't keep his eyes off her.

While he was staring at her, she glanced over his way and smiled.

He quickly turned his head, trying to act cool. "Oh crap, she saw me! Why is she sitting alone? Is she waiting for someone? Is she lonely? Maybe I SHOULD ask her to join us?" Derrick's mind raced with questions.

Having built the courage to go ask her to join them, he slid out of the booth and stood up when a well-built military-looking guy came back and sat down across from her. Derrick's heart sank. Sitting back down, he looked at the food before him and realized he wasn't hungry anymore, knowing he missed his chance.

A couple of minutes later, he glanced back in her direction to find what looked like them arguing. She finally got up and left in a huff.

Derrick had no clue what Tae had talked about the rest of the evening or, for that matter, what he even ordered.

As they were walking out, Tae elbowed him. "You're still thinking about that brunette, aren't you?"

Derrick looked over at him as if he had just woken from a daydream. "Huh?"

Tae grinned. "That's what I thought."

***

Stumbling out of bed the next morning, Derrick felt like a zombie. Today was orientation for the school, but he didn't get much sleep last night because faces from his past wouldn't leave him alone.

As he was throwing on some clothes, Tae knocked on his door. "Hey, ya! You ready?"

It was bordering on annoying how energetic he was so early in the morning.

While they were talking, the door across the hall from them opened and out walked the girl from Applebee's.

"Dude, isn't that the..." Tae started until Derrick elbowed him in the stomach, hushing him. She was having trouble getting the zipper on her coat to work.

Building courage again, Derrick asked, "Want me to give it a try?" He reached down and pulled the zipper up with no problems.

"Oh, thank you so much! This thing always gives me trouble."

She looked up, and they made eye contact. Derrick froze. The deep blue-gray shade of her eyes was the most astonishing color he had ever seen before.

Struggling to remember how to formulate words, Derrick was still stammering when a Latino girl walked up and said, "You ready to go, Lydia? We're going to be late."

Derrick and Tae headed over to the administration building, which was a three-story brick structure with double glass doors in the front. Upon entering, there was a sign directing all new students to the conference room that they used as an auditorium. In front of the doors to the room was a lady sitting behind a folding table.

"Welcome! Last names please?" she asked.

Derrick was staring off, daydreaming about Lydia as Tae finished checking in.

"How about you, sir?" the lady inquired.

Derrick snapped back to reality and realized he had no idea what the lady wanted.

"Seven!" he said instinctively.

Staring at him, confused, the lady asked again, "Uh... Your last name?"

"Oh! Anderson. Derrick Anderson, ma'am."

"Okay, we have you all set. Take a seat and we will begin shortly."

Derrick walked in and found Tae had saved him a spot... directly behind Lydia and her friend.

Tae whispered with a grin. "I figured these were the ones you wanted."

Before Derrick could reply, Richie walked up behind them and grabbed their shoulders. "What up, dudes?!"

This made the two ladies turn around. Sticking out his hand to them, Richie introduced himself. "Hey ladies, the name is Richie."

The Latino girl shook his hand, "Well, hello Richie, I'm Izzy. This here is Lydia. It's nice to meet you!"

Lydia shook his hand and then gave Derrick a side grin before turning back around.

Tae leaned over and whispered, "Duuuude!"

The dean started the morning with a brief history of the school, followed by an introductory activity.

"I'm sure some of you have already met, but we like to do a little icebreaker where we go around the room and you tell us about yourself. We'd like to get your name, where you're from, what college you went to, what you studied, and three interesting facts about yourself. Who wants to go first?"

Being the first to raise her hand, Izzy started off. "My name is Izzy and I'm from Phoenix, Arizona. I studied Electrical Engineering at UCLA and my three interesting facts are: I love to surf, I've been to Machu Picchu, and I was trapped for three days after the 2018 earthquake in Los Angeles."

"Oh my," said the dean, "That had to be scary. I hope everyone was okay after."

Izzy replied, "It was me and my brother. We were home alone when it hit and the stairwell collapsed in our apartment. The fire department finally was able to get to us through the window."

Looking at Lydia, "Wow! You want to follow up after that intro?"

"Sure, but mine isn't nearly as exciting. My name is Lydia and I'm from a tiny town in southeast Iowa that no one has ever heard of called Bloomfield. I went to the University of Iowa and studied Computer Science. My three facts are: I worked at the Blank Park

Zoo as a penguin keeper for three summers, I'm a panhead, and I got lost in a corn maze overnight."

"A panhead?!?" inquired the dean.

"Yeah, someone who likes the band Skilett," she said with a smile.

Tae interjected, "I think we are a little more interested in the corn maze debacle than being a pancake... head... whatever."

Lydia blushed a little.

The dean continued on. "Well, that will give you guys something to talk about later. Next," as he pointed at Derrick.

Lydia turned around to listen, which caused him to stumble at the beginning.

"I'm... um... Derrick and uh, I'm from Elmo, Texas. I went to MIT where I dual majored in Electrical and Computer Engineering and minored in Chemistry. I chased the 1999 Oklahoma City tornado, flew an air medical helicopter for eight years, and received third-degree burns from a crash."

"So you went to MIT and then spent eight years working on a helicopter?" asked the dean.

"Not exactly. I started working on the bird while I was in college and continued afterward."

"You worked there AND dual majored at MIT?"

Being slightly confused, Derrick replied, "Yeah... doesn't everyone work somewhere when you're in college?"

A snickering came from the back of the room.

Turning around, Derrick saw the guy that was with Lydia at Applebee's, lounging in the corner with his chair tilted back and feet propped up on the desk.

"Did you say you were from a town called 'Elmo'?!? He paused a moment for effect. "Did Sesame Street run through the middle of it?"

The room filled with laughter as even the Dean let out a chuckle.

"Okay, sir..." the dean started before being interrupted.

"The name's Obadiah."

"Fine... Obadiah, why don't you go next?"

Obadiah, Richie, and Tae went on to detail their military careers and their experience with communications. Tae ended his intro with his last interesting fact.

"And I once punched a shark in the face."

Derrick glanced over at him, intrigued yet confused.

"It was trying to attack me at the aquarium, so I punched it," Tae expounded.

His explanation heightened Derrick's confusion, but he wasn't able to ask him about it as the dean quickly moved on to far more boring topics.

After orientation, they were heading back to the dorms when Derrick heard Tae's stomach growl.

"Man, I'm hungry. You up for Applebee's again?

"Dude... we just had that the last two nights in a row! How about we order some pizza and watch a movie?"

"Sure, why not? That sounds good too. I've got the perfect movie too!"

They were sitting in the common room, watching some movie Derrick had never heard of when Lydia walked by.

"Hey, Lydia!" Tae called. "You want some pizza?"

"Is that where that smell is coming from?!?" she exclaimed. "Oh yes, please! I'm starving!"

Grabbing a slice off the counter, she sat down next to Derrick on the couch. His stomach got a little queasy as he looked over at Tae, who had a smile growing on his face.

"So, tell us about that corn maze," Tae inquired.

While Lydia was elaborating on how she kept getting turned around and the owners of the maze didn't know she hadn't left with her group, Obadiah walked up.

"Why are you out here with these losers? Come on, we'll go have some fun," he said to Lydia

Summoning his courage, Derrick stood up, demanding, "Who do you think you are talking to her like that?"

Obadiah's ire grew as he started walking towards Derrick.

"She's my girlfriend, you son of..."

Lydia jumped in between them and shouted, "I am NOT your girlfriend, you slimeball. All we did was have dinner that one time and it certainly wasn't a date... or fun."

Obadiah reached out to grab Lydia's arm, but it was swatted away by Derrick.

"Oh, you're going to regret that..." Obadiah growled pushing Lydia out of the way and approaching Derrick.

Richie heard the commotion and popped around the corner.

"Hey folks, what seems to be going on? Oh, Obi, you making friends?"

Obadiah stopped and scowled nose-to-nose at Derrick. "This isn't over," he snarled and then left down the hallway.

After the movie finished, the three of them sat around chatting for a few hours. Knowing why Derrick was there, Tae asked Lydia what caused her to apply.

"Well, my daddy was a Marine and did communications in the Gulf War. He caught me playing with one of his radios and instead of getting mad, he taught me how to use it. Ever since then, I've been in love with them."

"If you were legacy, why didn't you join the Marines too?" Tae inquired.

"I thought about it, but I have this incredible fear of getting shot at. I figured this would be a safer option. Oh, speaking of radios, is anyone else taking the class tomorrow?"

Derrick raised his hand.

Smiling, Lydia asked, "Hey, cool! You want to grab some breakfast beforehand?"

"Yes, ma'am. That sounds like a plan."

"Well, thank you guys for the pizza. This was fun, but I think it's time to turn in for the night," she said as she stood up.

Looking at Derrick, she gave him a grin as she headed back towards her room.

Tae was unable to keep his ear-to-ear grin from beaming.

CHAPTER 3

After breakfast, Derrick and Lydia walked into the classroom. There were four rows of tables, each with two stations for them to choose from. Derrick picked the station in the first row against the left wall, while Lydia chose the one on the right in the second row. He wished Tae was taking the class too, so he would have someone to help him. Derrick was great with electronics, but he was horrible at radios.

Obadiah squeaked in just before class started and sat down next to Lydia. To Derrick's surprise, he heard her exclaim, "I don't think so, slimeball." She then walked up to his row and asked if she could sit beside him.

"Why, yes. It would be nice to have a friendly face to sit by," he replied, unsuccessfully restraining his nerves.

Derrick did his best to concentrate on the lecture, but he was so distracted by Lydia sitting there, that he didn't comprehend anything that was said.

"The cables on your desks run to the antenna on the roof that is pointed to the communications satellite over the Atlantic. So, everyone, grab your radios, connect the cable to the radio, and input the frequency for the Atlantic bird," the instructor directed the class.

Derrick started looking through the manual to figure out how he was supposed to enter the frequency since he wasn't listening.

"Come on Derrick. You did this all the time in the helicopter. It's the same thing here."

As he fumbled through the manual, he happened to glance over at Lydia, who had already finished and was waiting for the next step. "Wow, she smells good. Dude, focus. The teacher is staring."

Lydia, seeing he was having problems, asked, "Do you need some help?"

"I used radios all the time on the helicopter, but these are completely different."

"Here, let me show you." Rolling over beside him, she showed him how to turn the knob on top to the "load" position and then scroll down on the screen to the "A" bank. "And this is where you type the number in," she explained.

"Thank you so much! I appreciate it," Derrick exclaimed, breathing a sigh of relief.

Smiling, she slid back to her side of the table.

The teacher did a test call to demonstrate the style they should use when calling in:

"Overwatch Center, this is Train 1. How do you copy?"

"Train 1, Overwatch. Have you loud and clear."

"Overwatch Center, this is Train 1. Have you loud and clear as well, over."

After he finished, he had everyone try a call for themselves. Derrick listened to Lydia's. It sounded like she had been using the radio all her life.

When it was his turn, Derrick followed the script for the first call and Overwatch replied. However, this time, he couldn't make out what they said. Knowing everyone was watching him, he panicked.

"Overwatch Center, this is Train 5. Have you loud and clear but unreadable, over."

The room fell silent as the teacher scratched his head in amazement.

"Did you just say loud and clear, but unreadable?"

"Yeah. The call was loud and there was no static. I just couldn't make them out," Derrick explained.

There was some snickering in the back of the room.

"Amateur hour up there. It's like working with Elmo from Sesame Street," Obadiah jested.

Derrick could have dissolved into his seat. Not because of Obadiah, but because he just did that in front of Lydia.

"Not heard that one before," the teacher explained, "but the correct reply should have been 'could you repeat?' I think we need to take a break after that one."

Lydia rolled over to Derrick who was still frozen in his chair.

"Derrick. Hey, come on. We are all going to make mistakes in the class. You just got yours out early. How about we go take a break, laugh about it, and then come back and forget it ever happened?"

Derrick and Lydia walked out of the classroom and headed down to the water fountain.

"Your call sounded great," Derrick complimented.

"Well, thanks. Like I said before, I played a lot with my dad's when I was younger. I don't mind helping you with them. Maybe you could help me with the electrical classes we have. I don't know anything about those."

Returning to their seats in the classroom, Derrick still seemed nervous. Lydia reassured him, saying, "Don't worry about Obadiah. He's a jerk."

Curiosity getting the better of him, Derrick inquired, "What happened at Applebee's on Tuesday night?"

Lydia squinted and grinned a little, realizing that it might not have been Obadiah making him nervous.

"He asked if I wanted to grab some dinner and no one else was here yet, so I said sure. I didn't consider it a date, but apparently, he did."

The class progressed without Derrick embarrassing himself again. Right before they were dismissed, the teacher gave a rundown of the next day.

"Tomorrow, we will be practicing setting up the portable antennas and making calls to Overwatch. Whenever you're ready, you can take the practical, and then you are free to go."

Looking at Derrick, "Some of you might need more of that practice time than others."

Derrick was packing up his radio bag when Lydia slid over.

"You want to practice tonight? I can show you some tips," Lydia offered.

"That's really nice of you, but I don't want to take up your free time. You probably have plenty of other things you'd rather do."

"Actually, I don't have any plans tonight and enjoy talking about radios... especially with new friends."

"Well, if you insist. I do need all the help I can get. This isn't anything like the ones I've used before. Do you want to meet on the porch after dinner?"

"How about we just eat together and then stroll back to the porch afterward?"

Derrick wasn't sure if she had seen him catching his breath.

Realizing that might have sounded a little forward, Lydia added, "Oh, and we can grab Tae too if you want. I'd hate for him to have to eat alone."

At dinner, Izzy grabbed a table while the three of them got in line to get their food. Tae paid for his and made his way to their seats. When Derrick walked up with Lydia, he gave Tae a look of disbelief. He had taken the seat beside Izzy, leaving the remaining two chairs beside each other. Tae smiled at Derrick with his goofy, mischievous grin.

Derrick didn't eat much that evening. Having spent the entire day with Lydia, the butterflies hadn't left his stomach. On their way back to the dorms, he headed to his room, grabbed his radio bag, and met up with Lydia on the porch. She went over the process of putting the radio together, setting up the antenna, and entering the frequencies a couple of times before having him try on his own.

Derrick pulled the sections of antenna from the bag and started to put them together when he felt a presence to his left. He looked and Lydia was hovering over his shoulder, watching. He couldn't help but stare at her face, especially with it being so close to his.

After a few seconds, she whispered, "You're supposed to be putting the antenna together."

Blinking, he went back to work, except his hands were shaking, making it hard to assemble the small pieces.

"Am I making you nervous?" she asked playfully.

"What, no... I mean... I burned my hands a few years ago and the nerve damage makes them do that sometimes."

While technically it wasn't a lie, Derrick knew better. Lydia was taking over his thoughts.

"Oh, I'm sorry! What happened?" Lydia asked, worriedly.

Derrick paused, reliving the accident. "I was trying to rescue someone from a burning vehicle..."

She noticed his gaze trailing off. Her voice softened as she asked, "Were you able to get them out?"

He lowered his head and went back to work.

***

The next morning in class, Derrick was sitting in the grassy field near the classroom practicing for the final. Lydia took the test first thing and, after passing it with flying colors, came over to see if she could help him.

"Hey, Sparks! How's it going?" she asked excitedly, kneeling down beside him.

He gave her a puzzled look. "Sparks?!?"

"Yeah! That's what they call radio guys in the military. At least that's what they always called my dad."

Derrick chuckled. "I think there might be more to the story than that, but I like the nickname."

After a few practices, Derrick decided he was ready to take the test. When he informed the teacher, Derrick could see the skepticism on his face.

"Are you sure you don't want to take a few more... days?"

Going through the process, Derrick did everything perfectly, to the amazement of his teacher.

Well, even seeing it, I still don't believe it. You passed!"

Seeing Lydia watching from a distance, he walked over and told her the news, to which she gave him an enthusiastic high-five.

"YES! I knew you could! We should go celebrate! Let's go get some ice cream from the cafeteria."

Derrick loved the chocolate ice cream they served. He still wasn't sure what they added to make it so good, but he always found himself getting one after dinner. Lydia grabbed a double scoop of their strawberry and the two of them went out and sat on the Administration building's steps.

As they were enjoying their cones, Derrick turned to Lydia with a question. "If you could go to one place in the entire world, where would it be?"

She didn't even have to think. "London. I want to see Big Ben."

"That is a good one," Derrick agreed.

Turning the question back to him, Lydia asked, "Okay, Socrates... what's yours?"

Thinking for a moment, imagining all the places he would like to see, Derrick kept coming back to one spot.

"The Maldives. The pictures from there are breathtaking."

Lydia smiled, imagining the sunset reflecting on the water. "That's a really good choice too, but it's not one of those places you want to go by yourself."

Looking into her eyes, his mind drifted. "No... it's not."

CHAPTER 4

Derrick stood at Lydia's door. He had almost knocked three times now. Seeing him in the hallway, Tae came to see if he could help.

"What are we doing?" he whispered.

"I'm trying to ask Lydia to a movie, but can't get the nerve to knock," Derrick explained.

"Oh... well that's... odd. Here, let me help." Tae reached up, knocked on her door, and then walked away. "Thank me later."

Derrick, still in shock, was contemplating running when she opened her door.

"Oh, hi Derrick. You need something?"

"Uh... um... no... well, yeah. I was thinking about going and seeing the new *Spy of the Eclipse* movie, and it's not that much fun to go alone," Derrick clumsily explained.

"*Spy of the Eclipse*! I've been wanting to see that! What time are you looking at going?"

"I was thinking about the 9:15 showing tomorrow night."

"Oh, perfect! We can grab some dinner beforehand. You like Chinese?" Lydia asked.

"Of course."

"Great! It's a date... I mean, see you then... oh... you know what I mean," she said with a grin before closing her door.

Derrick slowly walked back to his room and sat numb on his bed. Tae poked his head in.

"Does that look mean it went good or bad?"

"We are going out tomorrow for dinner and a movie."

Tae giggled as he left the room. "You're welcome!"

***

The next day in class, Derrick couldn't concentrate. They were all taking *Electrical Standards* and were going over circuit wiring. Being an electrical engineer, this was all basic to him, leaving ample time for his mind to wander towards Lydia.

After a lunch break, he and Tae went to the lab to work on their projects, which consisted of repairing an air handler and rewiring the outlets in a room.

Derrick was finishing up when he accidentally crossed one of the 220-volt hot wires from the handler with a 110-volt neutral from an outlet. Not catching his mistake, he flipped the master switch on the breaker panel. It exploded into a fountain of sparks, knocking him to the floor and lighting his shirt on fire.

While rolling on the ground trying to extinguish his clothing, Derrick missed the smoke coming out of the outlets and the paint on the wall above them discoloring.

Lydia and Izzy were down the hall working in the second lab when the fire alarms went off, followed by an announcement overhead.

CODE RED, CODE RED—ELECTRICAL LAB ONE. SUPPRESSION SYSTEM ACTIVATED!

PLEASE LEAVE THE BUILDING VIA THE NEAREST EXIT!

Derrick sat on the floor of the classroom, leaning against the wall while the fire department was cleaning up. Monoammonium phosphate from the fire suppression system floated through the air. He was almost completely covered in the white powder, while black soot contrasted the parts that weren't. Stepping out of the lab, Tae sat down beside him, shaking the powder off his clothes.

"Um... I don't think that was wired right."

Derrick slowly turned his head and glared.

"Just saying. It's not supposed to do that."

Lydia and Izzy navigated their way through hoses and overturned chairs to reach them.

Seeing Derrick completely covered in the powdery residue, Lydia questioned, "Oh, Derrick. What happened?"

Having already figured it out, Izzy answered instead. "I've seen this before. You mixed up the hot wire from the handler with a cold wire from one of the outlets, didn't you?"

Derrick took a deep breath and sighed an unenthusiastic, "Yeah."

Concerned, Lydia asked, "Are you okay?"

He looked at her and managed a smile. "Yeah. I'm good."

"Are you still up for the movies tonight?" she asked hopefully.

Their teacher walked out of the lab and said, "Yes, Lydia. I think he needs supervision tonight... and pretty much every night from now on. Please take him... FAR... away from here."

***

Derrick spent forty-five minutes in the shower trying to get the electrical smell off his body. After drying off, he stood looking into his closet.

"I have no idea what I'm supposed to wear tonight. Is it a date? Is it not?"

He finally settled on a polo shirt and jeans. He had just finished tying his shoes when there was a knock at his door.

<Knock, knock, knockity knock>

He opened his door and there stood Lydia in a white sleeveless sundress with red flowers all over. Of everything in her wardrobe, that was easily becoming his favorite.

"You ready to go, Sparky?"

"Sparky, huh?"

"Yeah, I thought it was kinda fitting. At least you don't smell like an electrical fire anymore. You actually smell... nice."

He reached for his keys, but Lydia interjected. "Oh, don't worry about those. I'm driving!"

Derrick climbed into the passenger side of her white Volkswagen Beetle. Having never seen the inside of a newer one before, he found it was a little roomier than his Mustang. His favorite part, though, was that it smelled just like her—like freshly picked strawberries.

They drove into the nearby town and pulled up to the Chinese restaurant.

"I love this place," she said. "It has a great buffet."

Since he opened the restaurant's door for Lydia, she was the first one to reach the counter.

"Two for the buffet, please," as she slid her card to the lady.

"You're not supposed to pay!" Derrick objected.

"Fine, you can pay for the movies then," she teased, winking at him.

They were shown to a cozy table for two where Derrick, being a gentleman, pulled out the chair for Lydia. To his surprise, she had already made her way to the buffet. Derrick filled his plate as well and headed back to the table. Lydia, already seated, was waiting for him to start eating.

Sensing his unease, she asked, "What's wrong, Derrick? Are you not enjoying yourself?"

He hesitated briefly. "Um… I guess I'm just going to say it. I don't know if this is a date or not."

"Do you want it to be?"

Derrick saw his way out of the awkwardness, but deep in his heart, that was really what he wanted. "Actually, yeah. I do."

"Good. Then it's a date. Now enjoy your food, silly," she declared with a grin.

Later, at the movie theater, after buying the tickets, Derrick walked with Lydia to the concession stand.

"What would you like?" he asked.

"You have to have popcorn! Especially for a movie like this," she exclaimed, excitedly.

Approaching the counter to place their order, Derrick said, "I'd like two popcorn and two drinks."

"Two?" Lydia questioned. "We can share one. Remember… it's a date now," she added with a smile.

"Okay, I'll take two drinks and ONE large popcorn then."

Making their way into the theater, they found a couple of seats right in the middle. While they waited for the previews to start, Lydia was going on and on about how she loved the other two movies in the series and how she wouldn't even watch the trailer for this one to keep from having it spoiled. Derrick could tell she was nervous for some reason, so instinctively, he reached over and placed his hand on hers. She stopped mid-sentence and they both froze looking at each other.

The lights dimmed as the movie started. Derrick withdrew his hand and focused his attention on the screen.

It was a couple of minutes into the show when he felt something touch his leg. Lydia had reached over and was feeling around for his hand.

"Is this really happening?" he thought.

Finding it, she turned his hand sideways and interlaced her fingers with his.

"I guess it is."

Derrick struggled to pay attention to the movie after that. Most dates he had been on never went that well. His mind raced as he sat there, hand in hand with this beautiful woman.

However, he did manage to catch Lydia whispering, "That is so romantic."

In the movie scene, Dominic knocked on Madeline's door and asked, "Have you ever seen the sunrise?" Taking her hand, he led her to the beach, where he had laid out two blankets for them in the sand. They sat together, watching the sun rise above the horizon.

After the movie, Lydia finally let go of his hand. The thought crossed Derrick's mind to suggest watching another movie, any movie, just so the night wouldn't end. But since it was already 11pm, they headed out of the theater and to her car.

Derrick was about to get in when Lydia surprised him with a question, "It's a nice night tonight. Do you want to go for a walk?"

She led him to a nearby promenade with several late-night shops. At the beginning was a Starbucks, where Lydia HAD to stop and get a coffee. Derrick, sensing an opportunity, suggested he stay outside since it was rather busy.

While she waited in line, Derrick slipped into the store next door, having seen something he wanted to get for her. When she came out with her drink, she found him sitting on a bench holding a mysterious bag.

"What's in the bag?" she inquired.

"Sit down and find out," he replied with a mischievous smile.

"Ooooh. Is it for me?"

Derrick's grin widened as she took a seat. Inside was a fluffy, stuffed dolphin. She pulled it out and began squeezing it.

"I love dolphins! Thank you! I think I will name her... Madeline."

After finishing her coffee, they got up and resumed their stroll. Derrick offered to put Madeline back into the bag, but she refused, squeezing it tighter. Derrick's wish also came true when she reached down and took his hand again.

As they meandered along the promenade, lost in conversation, Derrick noticed that some of the stores had turned off their lights. Glancing at his watch, he was surprised that it showed 2:10am.

"Wow. We've been talking for over three hours."

"I guess we should probably head back to the dorms then," Lydia reluctantly admitted.

Pulling back into the dorm parking lot, Lydia heard the exact words she was hoping for all night.

"Would you like to go out again sometime?" Derrick asked.

"Oh, I guess." She said flirtingly while screaming "YES!" on the inside.

***

Derrick lay on his bed, staring at the ceiling. It had been an hour since they had come back to the dorms and said goodnight.

"I don't know who I'm kidding. There's no way I'm going to be able to go to sleep after a night like this."

He decided that if he was going to stare at something, it might as well be the stars outside.

He headed down the breezeway and out onto the porch. The night was unusually warm for Virginia at this time of year, so he thought about lying on the swing and watching for meteors. When he stepped around the corner, he was surprised to find Lydia was doing that same thing.

Derrick softly spoke. "You had the same idea?"

Lydia screamed and fell out of the swing, flailing her limbs.

"Where did you come from?!?!" she asked in shock from the ground.

"Texas."

"Ha-ha, Mr. Funny Guy Who Sneaks Up On People and Makes Them Wet Themselves."

"Wow... that's a long name," Derrick joked as he helped her up off the ground. "I couldn't sleep so I decided to come out and watch for meteors. Do you like the stars?"

Lydia settled back into the swing. "In Bloomfield, there were hardly any city lights to ruin your view, unlike here. I would sneak out, lay a blanket down in the field, and watch the Milky Way for hours some nights."

"That sounds amazing. I've never seen it in person."

"Keep playing your cards right and maybe I'll arrange it for you," she said with a grin as she laid back down on the swing.

Derrick grabbed a chair, reclining it as low as he could.

"Do you have your own star?" Lydia asked. "You know, like your favorite?"

Derrick thought for a moment. "Polaris."

Surprised, Lydia asked, "The North Star? Why's that your favorite?"

"Because it's always there for you. It may not be the brightest out of all the others, but they move throughout the night and even disappear with the seasons. But not Polaris. It's like that one special friend who will always be there no matter how bad things get or how lost you are."

Derrick couldn't see it, but a delighted smile had crept onto Lydia's face. She quietly whispered to herself, "That's mine too."

Their conversation drifted from stars to reminiscing about childhood memories of their hometowns, and eventually to their future aspirations and goals. Derrick noticed that he was able to see Lydia clearer now than he had remembered when he came out.

"Are my eyes just getting more adjusted to the darkness?" he thought.

The number of stars he could see now was far fewer than before as well, but there was a distinctive shape of the tail of a stuffed dolphin lying beside her on the swing. Derrick realized it was almost dawn.

"We've been out here all night," he said with shock in his voice.

"What?!? What time is it?" Lydia gasped

Derrick looked at his watch, which read *6:53am*. "It's almost seven!" he exclaimed.

Lydia sat up, almost losing her balance again. "I'm supposed to meet Izzy for breakfast at seven! We are going shopping and she wanted to get there early."

Derrick walked her back inside to her door. "Thank you for keeping me company last night. I had a really good time," he expressed warmly.

Lydia responded with a shy grin, saying, "Me too."

As he turned for his room, he noticed Izzy slowly walking down the hall toward him. "Morning Izzy. She should be ready shortly," he informed before entering his room.

Knocking on Lydia's door, Izzy's eyes grew when she answered.

"Girl... isn't that the same outfit you were wearing last night when you left for your date?!?"

***

It was 2am. Derrick awoke to a storm outside and a frantic knocking on his door. Answering it, he was blinded by a flashlight and someone bursting into the room. They jumped onto his bed and wrapped themselves up, head to toe, in his blankets.

"Come on in," he said sarcastically. Derrick tried to find his way back over to the bed, but tripped over his shoes, still not being able to see. "You, uh, comfortable in there?" he asked the blob that now resided on his bed.

"Hi. I was just checking to see if the storm woke you up, too. You want to hang out until it's over?" Lydia said frantically.

Derrick peeked under the blanket. "I take it you're not a fan of storms?"

"It's not that I don't like storms, it's just I don't like being ALONE in storms!"

Lightning then lit up the room and a large crack of thunder interrupted their conversation. It shook the floor, causing Lydia to let out a scream.

"I can make some room in here if you want to get under, too," she offered, nervously.

Derrick giggled a little. "No, it probably wouldn't look right if I did. I'll just sit over here in my chair.

The thunder and lightning continued outside when a bolt struck the woods behind the dorms, causing the entire room to shake.

Lydia screamed once again. "Are you sure you don't need to get under the blanket?"

This time Derrick heard a faint, desperate plea after the question. "Please?"

Getting up from his chair, Derrick sat down on the side of the bed. Lydia scrambled across to him with the blanket still over her head and climbed onto his lap. He could feel her whole body trembling as he put his arms around her.

The storm continued to rage outside, but after a few minutes, he noticed she was no longer shaking.

"You doing okay?" he asked.

"For some reason, it's not as scary now."

"You want to come out from under the blanket, then?"

"NO!" Lydia said emphatically.

Derrick thought the storm was calming down when a blinding blue flash was immediately followed by a loud bang, and the power going off.

Lydia let out her biggest scream yet. "No! No! No! Not the power! It's a tornado, isn't it?!"

Derrick hugged her even tighter. "Calm down, it's not a tornado. The transformer outside blew. You're safe."

"How do you know it's not a tornado?"

"Because I used to chase them in Texas. Would seeing the radar help?" Opening his weather app, Derrick slid his phone under the blanket to her.

"It looks like Christmas with all that red and green."

"Yes, but as you can see, there's no rotation. It's a quasi-linear complex with a strong gradient," Derrick tried to explain.

"English please!"

"No naders."

"Are you... sure?" Her voice broke as she asked.

"I'll tell you what, maybe you should spend the rest of the night here just to be safe."

"In the same bed?" Lydia asked with playfulness in her voice.

"Noooo. You can have the bed and I will sleep in my chair."

"Can I hold your hand at least?"

"If that's what you need, I can pull my chair up beside you." Derrick saw the blanket bob up and down in agreement.

He brought his chair over and laid his hand on the bed. Lydia reached out, snatched it, and pulled it under the blanket with her, almost dragging Derrick out of the chair.

"You good now?" he said, injecting a hint of sarcasm.

"Much better!" came the muffled reply from under the blanket.

Lydia's flashlight happened to shine on Derrick's arm allowing her to finally notice the scars from the skin grafts he received after the burns. They were slightly discolored, and the edges were barely visible. Oddly though, some appeared newer than the others. Those were more straight lines than large sections.

"Are these scars from when you tried to rescue that person?" she delicately inquired.

There was a momentary pause before Derrick replied with a distressed tone.

"Something like that."

Contrary to popular belief, sleeping upright in a non-reclining chair isn't exactly comfortable.

Derrick watched out the window as dawn began to break. Having been awake for most of the night, he headed to the common room and brewed a pot of much-needed coffee.

The power had been back for about an hour, but since it was almost morning, he figured there was no point in waking her now.

The sunlight was shining brightly through the blinds when he came back to his room.

Sitting down in his chair, Derrick gently whispered her name to wake her up... but she didn't move.

Peeking under the blanket, he found her still sound asleep in her matching red and white PJs. She was hugging Madeline so tight it looked like that poor dolphin's eyes were on the verge of popping out of its head.

He said her name again a little louder and shook her a bit. This time, she started to stir.

"It's morning. Go ahead and start waking up. The coffee is almost ready.

Lydia was sitting up on the side of the bed holding Madeline when he came back in carrying the cups of coffee.

"You let me sleep all night in your bed while you slept in a chair? All because I was scared? It's almost like you are MY Polaris."

Handing her the cup of coffee, Derrick responded casually, "It was no big deal. I enjoyed the company."

Lifting the cup to her mouth with both hands, she tried to hide the smile that was growing on her face. "I kinda hope we have another storm tonight," she mused.

As Izzy came to get Lydia for breakfast she noticed Derrick's door open and Lydia sitting on his bed in her PJs.

"Oh, I'm sorry. I feel like I've interrupted something," Izzy said surprised.

Lydia hopped off the bed. "Don't be silly, Izzy. Give me a minute and I'll be ready to head over."

She gave her a suspicious grin and went back to the common room to wait.

"Thank you for being there for me last night. You made me feel... safe," Lydia said while sheepishly hugging Madeline.

"It was my pleasure. It's been a long time since I've had a... sleepover."

Lydia grinned as she turned to walk out of the room. "You want to go to breakfast with us?"

"Sure. Save me a seat. I'll grab Tae and meet you there."

Lydia went to her room and quickly changed. She was skipping when she went to get Izzy.

Seeing Lydia's unusual excitement, Izzy knew her suspicions were right. "Something DID happen last night, didn't it?"

"Yes... but not what you think."

Derrick texted Tae, "Come to room. ASAP."

Tae came running into his room moments later. "What? What's wrong?"

"Something happened last night..."

CHAPTER 5

Derrick and Tae were in the same *Mechanical Functions* class. This was Derrick's dream class, where seemingly random parts were assembled to create something useful. In fact, that was their final exam.

Derrick was working on a four-legged robot that could gather specimens from dangerous locales. He attached a camera to the robot and rigged up the joystick from an Xbox system and an old smartphone. The camera would send the image back to the phone, allowing him to steer it from a distance. The only problem he was having was getting it to walk. He couldn't find a motor that was strong enough to move the legs but light enough to not cancel the force out.

Then, one night, he had an idea from one of his dreams. He snuck into the common room, disconnected the DVD player, and took it back to his room. Taking it apart, he removed the motor that ran the disk drive and attached it to his robot. Surprisingly, it worked perfectly! He put the DVD player back, planning to keep the motor until he could order a replacement. No one used that old thing anyway... he thought.

The next evening was the weekly dorm dinner. Everyone gathered for a meal on Thursdays and usually played board games afterward to release some stress from the week. Derrick could hear Obadiah down the hall; it was obvious he wasn't too happy, but he was always complaining about something.

He sent the robot out his door and down the hallway towards the common room where he knew Lydia was. In the hand, at the end of the robot's arm, he placed a rose that it was going to deliver to her.

The robot slowly walked down the hallway and made the turn into the common room. Moving the camera around, he found Lydia sitting on the couch, talking to Izzy. Steering the robot toward her, he tapped her leg with the arm. She looked down and was surprised to see this little spider-like contraption lifting a rose to her. When Izzy saw it, she let out a squeal of excitement.

"That is SO nerdly romantic!"

Lydia bent down, took the flower, and looked into the camera.

"Derrick, you are so darn cute, you know that?"

The robot shook its head up and down, causing the girls to laugh.

He turned it around and started walking it back to the hallway. Obadiah, not seeing it on the floor, stormed out of the common area after his attempts to make his movie work had failed.

"Why does this piece of..." *<crunch>*

Derrick lost the signal.

"What the?!? Is that a bionic spider?!?" Obadiah exclaimed.

Lydia jumped up and shoved him out of the way. "Why are you such a jerk?!? That was Derrick's class project you crushed."

Derrick ran around the corner to see Lydia holding the pieces to his robot. "I'm sorry, honey, Obadiah stepped on it. Can you fix it?"

Taking the parts, Derrick examined them. "I don't think so. The frame is snapped in three places."

Obadiah, not even pretending to feel bad, came over and snarled, "You shouldn't have had it on the floor in the first pla... wait... is that a motor from a DVD player?"

Derrick had an overwhelming sense of fear fill his stomach.

Obadiah's face started turning a deep red as his eyes locked onto Derrick. "Did you take the motor out of my DVD player, and that's why I can't watch *13 Hours* right now?"

Derrick was slowly walking backward while trying to formulate a response. His retreat became hasty when Obadiah started coming toward him. Running down the hallway, Derrick was able to get his door closed and locked before a loud bang came from it as Obadiah slammed into it.

"You little piece of chicken... Open this door now and take your beating like a man!"

Richie walked down the hall with Lydia in tow behind him. He approached Obadiah, stopping within inches of him. Richie's intense gaze bore into

Obadiah's soul as if daring to pluck it out through his nose.

"You have a problem with my friend?" Richie asked, his voice carrying a subtle intensity.

Obadiah backed up a little. "Come on Richie, you know I'm just messing with him."

Richie's gaze was undeterred. "How about you grab your little DVD, put it in the PlayStation there, and we can all enjoy a good movie?" His eyes added the threat of a lengthy hospital stay if he declined. "Deal?" Obadiah walked back to the common room, muttering.

Lydia knocked on Derrick's door. "Honey, it's me."

Unlocking it, Derrick cautiously opened it to let her in.

She met him with a hug. "That was the cutest thing I have ever seen, you bringing me a rose with your homemade robot. Thank you! I'm going to put this on my dresser so I can wake up to it every morning. "Walking over to his desk, she saw the ruins of his robot. "Are you sure you can't repair it?"

Derrick picked up the now destroyed DVD motor and sighed. "I could build another one, but not by the deadline."

"What are you going to do, then? Can you explain what happened to your teacher and show him the pieces?"

"Possibly, but thankfully, I have another idea that I've been working on."

***

While waiting in the dining hall for Lydia and Tae to finish class, Derrick worked on his new design. It was a small, portable device that would emanate an infrared beam up into the sky. Only those with IR goggles could see the beam, allowing for safer rescues. He also rigged it with a frequency generator that would cause a burst of static to pulse S.O.S. in Morse code.

Class finally ended, and they met Derrick at his table. Lydia came around and sat down next to him.

Tae, who was looking a little troubled, asked, "Lydia, what did you get on question 12?"

"31.26. You had to solve for F and then multiply it by the displacement."

"They wanted a number?!? I wrote green," Tae said, dejected.

Obadiah saw the three of them and walked over. "What's up, nerds? Doodling again, Elmo?"

"It's a portable IR emitter for rescuing troops behind enemy lines. It's my replacement project for the one you smashed."

"I swear, Elmo. If you take apart the DVD player again..." Obadiah threatened.

Lydia started digging her nails into the table as she growled, "You'll what?"

Seeing her reaction, Obadiah chuckled. "Oh, needing a girl to fight your battles now?"

Derrick leaned back in his chair, smiling. "Nope, but it's going to be fun watching her kick your butt."

Looking at Lydia, Obadiah smirked. "I knew she still wants a piece of this fine…"

Lydia had just launched out of her chair as Richie walked up to the table. He motioned for her to sit back down and he greeted Obadiah, "Hi, Obi."

He knew Obadiah hated that name. "How about we don't finish that statement and you just be on your way?"

Clearly agitating Obadiah, before leaving, he snarled, "Play with your junk then, Elmo. Leave my DVD player alone."

Sitting down beside Derrick, Richie started looking through his notebook.

"If you ever get this working, I want one."

Derrick's eyes widened with surprise. "You understand it?"

"Nope, but it looks cool," as Richie flipped the page. He found it full of chemical formulas and calculations. "Why are you working here?!? Why aren't you at NASA or something?"

Derrick laughed a little. "I wanted to, but they wouldn't let me near any of their rockets."

"Well, at least there is still some intelligent life left on this planet. What is all this?"

Derrick pointed to one of his newer drawings and proudly proclaimed, "I call this one 'Go Away Juice'. It's stored inside a ball with a switch on it. Flip the switch and put it on whatever you want to go away."

Rolling his eyes, Richie groaned. "Ugh, I'm going to regret this, but... what do you mean by 'go away'?"

"It's a combination of thermite and white phosphorus. It... 'dissolves' whatever it gets on."

Richie got up and started walking away, mumbling. "Great. Now I'm an accomplice. Why do I ask these questions?"

***

Derrick rarely had any classes on Friday, so he usually spent the morning working on some of his designs in the lab. The parts he ordered from eBay had come in yesterday and he was eager to start on his IR emitter.

He had an old iPhone, a small frequency generator, and the laser assemblies from both a DVD and a Blu-ray player. For power, he had an old laptop battery. It wasn't ideal because of the size, but it would do for now.

Only needing the case and the screen, he removed the components of the phone. Then, detaching the lasers from the player assemblies, he soldered them into the case.

Finding a toy at the Goodwill store that had a blinking light on it, he took the flashing module and attached it to the Blu-ray laser.

Next, he ran the power wires through the speaker hole. All that was left was the frequency generator. That was the part he couldn't figure out. Radios weren't an area he was great at, but he knew someone who was.

As if on cue, Lydia stopped by after class.

"Hey, sexy Einstein, whatcha working on?"

"I'm trying to get my emitter to work, but I can't get this frequency generator to modulate."

She walked over to the cabinet of parts and started digging through it, coming out with three small chips and a crystal with leads.

"That's because you need these. Know how to solder them together... correctly?"

Derrick knew she was messing with him, but somehow it only made her cuter.

"No, I probably don't, and since I spent around $500 on these parts already... do you mind?"

Lydia shook her head in disbelief as she grabbed some goggles. "I'll pretend like you didn't just say $500."

After she had finished installing the modulator, Derrick put the screen back on and closed up the case.

"There, perfect! Except I forgot the battery back in my room."

"Well, grab it after lunch. I'm hungry and have generator class in an hour."

They started out the room door when Derrick remembered he left his Swiss army knife behind.

"Oh! I almost forgot it!"

As he was closing it up, Lydia noticed that the well-worn knife had the tip of its large blade broken off.

After finishing lunch with Lydia, Derrick headed back to his room. He set the emitter onto the battery so the wires could reach the terminals and connected them. A clicking could be heard from the flashing module as the emitter powered up.

He could also hear Obadiah from down the hall... and he wasn't very happy. "What is wrong with this stupid...? ELMO!!!! I know it's you that's making my TV flash S.O.S. at me!"

***

It was Saturday afternoon. Lydia and her friends went shopping on a "girls' day out" and Tae had flown back home for the weekend.

Derrick was bored.

He had ordered some white phosphorus from the internet, and it came in a few days earlier. So, he decided to test out his "Go Away Juice" concoction.

Taking the phosphorus package, thermite ingredients he acquired throughout the campus, and a metal trashcan he found at a thrift shop, he went outside to the basketball court. He mixed the thermite compound but was going to leave the phosphorus out until he was ready to test.

Richie was walking back from the dining room when he saw Derrick playing around in a trashcan and his curiosity got the better of him. Walking closer, he asked,

"What are you doing?!?"

Derrick turned around wearing a full face shield, goggles, elbow-length gloves, and an apron.

"Never mind. I don't want to know," Richie resigned as he walked away.

Derrick added the phosphorus into the mixture and it began to smoke and heat up.

Richie found Obadiah sitting out on the back porch having a drink and started telling him about the Commanders game he went to earlier in the week. Derrick ran by, catching their attention. He was carrying the trashcan, which now had a brilliant white beam of plasma shooting up into the air and smoke pouring out behind him.

"DON'T BLOW, DON'T BLOW, OH PLEASE DON'T BLOW!"

They watched in disbelief.

"Well, that can't be good," said Richie.

"You saw Beaker running by with a flaming trashcan too? Good. I thought I had finally snapped... You think we should move?"

"Probably, but I'm curious to see what he's going to do with that oversized lightsaber."

They watched as Derrick chucked the trashcan into the lake and then dropped to the ground. Before they could react, the lake erupted into a geyser of smoke and water. Fish started hitting the roof of the porch and Richie ducked a trout as it flew past his head.

"He just assassinated that entire lake full of fish."

When he heard no response from Obadiah, he looked over to find him sitting there with a bass stuck on his face. Its tail was still flipping, smacking him every time it moved.

"Um, Master Jedi Elmo... a word?"

The girls came home to find several firetrucks and police cars outside the dorm. They could see the lake out back was smoking and dead fish lying all over the parking lot.

Izzy looked at Lydia. "Well, what did you expect? We did leave him unsupervised."

"You don't know Derrick had anything to do with this."

Izzy gave her a look.

"Well, we don't know for sure!"

Lydia went upstairs to Derrick's room, passing a police officer who was trying not to laugh as he was finishing his report. Sitting at his desk, still wearing all of his protective clothing, Derrick was muttering and writing in his notebook.

"Too much phosphorus…"

"Oh honey, please tell me you didn't kill all those fish."

From out in the hall, Obadiah yelled, "Oh yes, he sure did! He blew up the whole freakin' lake with a trashcan lightsaber!"

Later that evening, as Lydia and Derrick walked toward the dining hall for dinner, she reached down and grabbed his hand.

"So this is a conversation I never dreamed I was ever going to have, but we won't be blowing up any more lakes, right?"

"In my defense, it wasn't supposed to do that."

"Derrick."

"No more lakes."

Lydia glared at him.

"Fine. No more blowing stuff up."

Patting his hand, she said, "That's a good boy."

When they entered the dining room, Lydia looked at the entree for the day that was written on the board: Blackened fish.

She turned to Derrick. "Feel like Mexican?"

***

The next weekend, Derrick stumbled to the common room in hopes of finding a cup of coffee.

As he was pouring a large mug full, Richie and Obadiah came in, arguing about who was going to win the Army/Navy game that afternoon.

"Army is going to stomp all over you seaman! The Navy is nothing but a bunch of squid-eating swabies!"

"Nice," Replied Richie. "Strong words coming from a dog face ground pounder. Oh... and who's won the game more often?"

Obadiah let out a growl.

Derrick was trying to be invisible as he stood next to the counter. "Please don't drag me into this! Please don't drag me into this!" he thought.

Richie noticed him standing there and asked, "Hey Derrick! Who are you rooting for?"

Derrick's face turned white, not knowing much about either team. "I'm just hoping both sides have a good time."

For the first time, Derrick was able to unite the Army and the Navy into equally hating the same thing.

He slowly backed out of the room while being glared at by Obadiah and Richie when he ran into Lydia, who had been watching the train wreck from the hallway.

"Stuck his foot in his mouth again, didn't he?"

"Save me!" Derrick whispered to her.

Lydia laughed and went to the cabinet to get a mug.

"Come on, guys. You know Derrick is a dork and wouldn't know the difference between the line of scrimmage and the end zone."

Richie spit out the coffee he had in his mouth.

"Dude! You're going to need some aloe for that! You just got BURNED by your own girlfriend!"

Derrick sat at his desk as Lydia walked in with her coffee.

"Honey... why can't you just play nice with others?" she said, laughing.

"I tried!" he exclaimed. "All I wanted was some coffee! They came in and trapped me."

As she walked over and sat down next to his desk, Izzy came to the door.

"Hey, Lydia! The guys had a great idea. We're going to have a cookout and watch the game together. Want to go to Walmart with me and get some stuff?"

"That sounds great!" Lydia agreed. "Hey Derrick, you want to go with us or would you rather stay here and spend some more time with your... 'friends'?"

Derrick jumped up and headed for the door. "Who's car we taking?"

Lydia parked and looked into the back seat at Derrick. "Izzy and I need to grab something from the *Lady's section,* so how about you find us some good steaks so we can try that 'special seasoning' you keep going on about?"

"Oh, you guys won't regret this!" Derrick exclaimed excitedly.

The girls were on the other side of the store when Lydia turned towards the camping section.

Confused, Izzy asked, "I thought we were going to the feminine aisle?"

Lydia giggled. "I just said that so he wouldn't follow us. I'm getting his Christmas present. He's going to love this!"

Derrick was looking at the steak selection, trying to find just the right ribeyes for everyone to try his seasoning on.

"I can't wait for her to taste this! She keeps going on and on about the steaks out in Iowa and how perfect her dad makes them."

While he was engrossed in thought, Lydia snuck up behind him and grabbed his sides. "Hey, cutie!"

Derrick jumped half out of his skin.

Izzy, having been a witness to the show, walked away shaking her head. "You two are embarrassing."

He noticed that Lydia didn't have any items in her hands after her special trip. "Did you not find what you were looking for?"

Lydia blushed a little trying to come up with a story that wouldn't sound like a blatant lie. "Oh...uh... I was embarrassed and took it out to the car already," she said shyly.

Derrick realized this was probably not a conversation he wanted to continue so he went back to looking at the steaks.

"Did you find us any good ones?" Lydia asked being relieved her diversion worked.

"I did," as he picked up the four packages in front of him. "I'm going to blow your socks off!"

Derrick could almost read Lydia's thoughts as a grin grew on her face. "That's some big promises there, Cowboy."

As they walked past the soda aisle, Izzy asked, "Oh! Do we have any drinks?"

Feeling a bit overconfident now, Derrick said, "I'll get them."

Lydia, who was pushing the cart, suggested he take it with him.

"Don't you worry, little ladies. I've got this," he said in his best cowboy impression.

Izzy looked at Lydia with the cringiest look she could make.

Lydia blushed. "Well, at least he's really cute."

Grabbing a couple of two-liter bottles, Derrick noticed a tag showing that they were on sale. "5 for $6? That's a good deal!" he thought.

He grabbed two more putting one under each arm, but he realized the fifth one was going to be a problem.

"Hmmm. I've got this. I can just tuck it here on the left beside this other one..."

Seeing the disaster about to happen, Lydia yelled at him. "Derrick! Hold on. I'm bringing the cart."

He finally got the fifth one secure enough to start walking down the aisle towards her.

When she was only a few yards away, Derrick felt one of the bottles starting to slip.

"Uh oh."

He tried adjusting to stabilize it when the lone bottle on his right side slipped. It fell and started bouncing around on the floor. In the process of trying to catch it, the second bottle on his left side fell as well.

When it hit the ground, the cap broke, and it took off down the aisle like a rocket... right over the ducking head of Lydia. It continued on its trajectory down the aisle and into the clothing section.

Obadiah was looking through a rack of shirts, trying to find a replacement for his favorite one that now reeked of fish. He heard a commotion to his left and turned to see a two-liter bottle streak by his face... spraying cola all over him, the clothes, and the floor.

His flinching from the close proximity projectile made him lose his footing and land flat on his back in a puddle of the liquid.

Lydia popped her head back up over the top of the cart and glared at Derrick... who now had a sheepishly painful grin on his face.

"Maybe we should get you out of here before Obadiah finds a rope. Whatcha think, Hoss?"

Derrick put the three bottles he still was holding into the cart. He grabbed another off the shelf as Lydia picked up the one that was on the floor.

She started to say, "I think we should open this one las..." when the bottle exploded in her hand.

Derrick couldn't look. All he heard was silence from her direction other than cola dripping off her onto the floor.

Izzy yelled down the aisle, not wanting to be within arm's reach. "How cute is he now?"

***

Back at the dorms, Derrick sat alone at his desk, thinking of their first date and all the wonderful times he had spent with her. Tears filled his eyes.

"I've ruined the greatest thing to ever come into my life," he said under his breath.

From behind him, he heard, "Did you break something else, because everything looks okay to me?"

He turned around to see Lydia behind him, smiling with her hair wrapped up in a towel.

"I ruin everything. I was just trying to impress you."

Lydia knelt beside him and started wiping his face with her hand.

"Honey, you are the most amazing person I have ever met, but you try a little too hard sometimes. Relax. I'm not going anywhere."

He went to hug her, but since he was still covered in sticky soda, she pulled back and laughed.

"Not so fast, Sticky Man. Why don't you go clean up a bit first? I'll be waiting here when you come out."

Derrick was preparing the steaks with his special seasoning when Lydia came back inside from the porch looking frustrated.

"I can't get the grill to work. Does anyone know the trick?"

Obadiah quipped from the couch, "Yeah, you let a man do it!"

Richie, who happened to be sitting on the other side of the couch from him, jumped up and went into the hallway. "Nope! I'm not getting blood on me today!" he exclaimed.

Derrick grabbed Lydia by the shoulders and turned her to look directly at him. "Honey... Let's go check it out together."

"But he makes me SO angry!"

"I know, I know. He's just pushing your buttons. Ignore him. He's not worth it."

Lydia led Derrick out onto the porch to the grill.

"So, I've turned the gas on and when I push the button, I can hear it clicking, but there's no fire," she explained.

"Okay, so let's think about this methodically. The gas flows from the tank, through the regulator, up the hose, and into the extremely rusted pipes leading to the burners."

Derrick leaned down into the grill and sniffed. "I don't smell any gas flowing so I would expect the issue to be these rusted parts."

The connection where the hose goes from the tank to the burners was rusted and crumbling beyond repair.

"Well, that's no good. We can't have a grill out with this. Let me see what I can rig up," he said as he headed out to the old maintenance shed nearby.

Finding a lawn mower, Derrick exclaimed, "Ah, yes!" as he started taking the handle apart.

Lydia sat on the swing and watched as he came back with what appeared to be an armful of random junk.

"Tell me you know what you're doing?" she said, worriedly.

"Well..." Derrick tried to explain when Lydia interrupted.

"Stop! I don't want to know. Just do your thing and don't blow up. I'd like to at least get past our honeymoon before that happens."

Derrick fumbled everything he was carrying.

"Oh, my bad," she said. "That was my inside-the-head voice."

He worked on the grill for about fifteen minutes when he finally stood up and said, "I think we are ready to test!"

Turning on the gas, he waited a few seconds and pressed the igniter. The grill erupted to life.

"Yes! We have fire!" he exclaimed.

Lydia walked over and grabbed him by the sides of his head. "You are so cute, Mr. Anderson. Do you know that?"

Derrick's legs started to become jelly. "Oh, really Ms. Evans... and what are you planning on doing about that?"

She gave him an evil grin. "Patience, Cowboy. We have food to grill," and she let go and headed back inside.

Having a rush of hormones flowing through his body, Derrick thought, "Nope. We have a cold shower to take is what we have."

After cooking the steaks, Derrick and Lydia were prepping the tables outside for the food to be placed on when Obadiah came out with some hotdogs.

"Hey! Who turned off the grill?!?" he grumpily inquired as he checked the tank.

His presence made Lydia's blood start to boil again until Derrick grabbed her hand and said, "Calm down... it's okay."

But then his face turned from comforting to confusion. "Wait... didn't we leave the grill on?"

He barely finished his statement when Lydia's nose retracted. "Eww, what's that smell?"

Derrick's brain finally connected the pieces when he saw Obadiah reaching for the ignitor. He screamed, "NOOOOO!!!!!!!" as Obadiah pressed the button.

Fire erupted from the grill and the fireball rolled down the porch.

He pushed Lydia to the ground and, spreading his coat out as wide as his arms would go, leaped onto her, wrapping her upper body as the fire flowed over them.

After what seemed like an eternity, Derrick felt the immense heat die down.

"Are you okay? Are you burnt? Where does it hurt?" he inquired of Lydia in a panic.

"I'm fine. What about you?" she replied.

"Oh... I don't know. I guess I am," he said, not having considered his safety.

He was finally able to let out a sigh of relief knowing they both were safe.

"You know Derrick, you really... light up my life," Lydia joked.

Giggling, Derrick took a couple more deep breaths to calm himself down.

A few seconds later, Lydia grinned and said, "Um... Derrick?"

His eyes widened, realizing he was still lying on top of her. "OH! I'm so sorry!" he said, rolling off.

Now staring up at the roof, Derrick was reliving everything that happened when he heard a resoundingly loud, "ELMOOOOOOOOO!!!!!" come from the other end of the porch.

He sat up and his face turned to terror when he saw Obadiah glaring at him, holding a large knife... and he was missing his eyebrows.

Lydia knocked on Derrick's door. He had been in his room for most of the afternoon.

"Are you not going to come watch the game with us? I'm all alone out there," she said with a pouty lip.

"I think it's safer if I stay in here. Obadiah wasn't too happy with his new look."

CHAPTER 6

<Knock, knock, knockity knock>

Derrick knew exactly who it was just by that knock. He opened the door and found Lydia all beaming with excitement.

"Are you doing anything special for Christmas?" she asked.

"I don't know. Had nothing planned I guess. Why?"

"Now you do. You're flying to Iowa with me to spend Christmas with my family. Sound exciting?"

"Uh... No."

Derrick meant to hold his reaction firmly within his head. Before he could conjure up a nicer response, Lydia interjected.

"I already have the plane tickets, so you can't say no. You can see where I grew up and meet my friends. I can show you the stars from my field like we talked about and take you to my favorite restaurant. There's the zoo where I worked in the summer. Oh! You can meet Fred, my giraffe."

Derrick stopped her on that one. "Um... hold on. You have a giraffe?"

"Well, he's not really mine, silly. He was my friend at the zoo. I would feed him every day and he would lick me in the face."

"Ew," he thought, failing to see the excitement about that part.

"And you can meet my parents!"

"I think I am going to go back to 'No'. You have told me stories about your Dad."

"Oh, Daddy is a big softie. He will love you!" Lydia excitedly explained.

Derrick's face showed a different emotion while his brain questioned, "But isn't that how most horror movies start?"

***

It was the day before they would leave for Iowa and Derrick was getting ready. He was very calculating when he packed and tried to get away with as few items as possible. He counted out four shirts, four pants, underwear, socks, and a belt.

"Probably should take something nice to wear on Christmas Day, just in case. Could probably use the same outfit for church as well. Need some nice shoes, though."

Derrick hated packing shoes with his clothes as, inevitably, they would get dirt all over the nicest thing he had in the bag. He felt like he was missing something, though.

"Ugh... Christmas gifts."

He didn't know what her parents liked to even begin searching for theirs. Grabbing his keys, Derrick took off for the only store in the area: Walmart.

As he was standing at the front of the store trying to figure out where to even start, Tae walked in.

"Hey ya! What are you doing here?" he asked.

"Lydia is taking me to Iowa to meet her parents for Christmas."

"What?!? Look at you, man! Getting to meet the parents already? Think you will make it to graduation before you two are married?"

Derrick laughed but then caught himself contemplating that thought.

"What does she like?" asked Tae, bringing Derrick back to reality.

"Do what?"

"Lydia. What does she like? What are you getting her? This is a big milestone: Your first Christmas... and with her parents, no less."

Derrick froze in fear. "Oh, crap. What am I getting her?!?"

Tae saw the deer in the headlight look he caused Derrick to have.

"Oh. Sorry, dude. I didn't mean to freak you out. I'll leave you alone for a bit to think. If you're still standing here when I get ready to leave, I'll come over and help you to a chair or something."

Tae left half giggling from his attempt at a joke.

Derrick didn't hear a word he said.

"Maybe if I walk around, I will see something that makes me think of her."

He went by the jewelry counter and saw a necklace that caught his eye.

"You know, she does have a nice neck. Maybe this would look good on her. Wait... a nice neck? Seriously?!?"

He looked again at the necklace. It was a 14kt gold chain with a heart pendant attached.

"You know what, I like this."

He motioned for the lady behind the counter who came over to help. When he pointed at the pendant, she smiled and reached into the display case to retrieve it.

"Got someone in particular you are thinking of?"

"Yeah. My girlfriend is taking me to meet her parents in Iowa tomorrow," Derrick replied.

"She sounds rather special, then. I think this pendant would be a nice present for her. I know I would love it if a young man gave it to me."

Derrick reached out to take a closer look. He loved how the lights from overhead reflected on it and bounced in different directions.

"I'll take it... and thank you."

Derrick's head was spinning a little, thinking of Lydia wearing that new necklace. He had never bought a gift like this for a girl before, having no girlfriends growing up. He was always more interested in trying to figure out how his computer worked so he could put the one back together that he took apart because it was raining outside.

"Hey ya, man! I see you finally can move again. Did you find something?"

Derrick pulled the pendant out and showed him. Tae's eyes grew to almost double their normal size.

"Dude! Very nice! She's going to love that! Did you figure something out for her parents?"

Derrick's elation vanished. His face must have dropped because Tae then stated, "Oooooh. I guess not. So you said they are from Iowa, right?"

"Yeah. The only thing I know they have there is... corn."

"Yeah, but they also like their BBQ. Don't you have a supply of your 'special seasoning' that you put on the steaks when we grilled a couple of weeks ago?"

"Had to bring that back up again, didn't you?"

Tae looked at him with his goofy grin and gave him a nod.

Derrick pondered how that was a horrible idea, but as he tried to come up with something better, he had nothing.

He finally made his way back to the room where he wrapped the pendant with some wrapping paper he picked up while at the store. He lucked out to find some that had dolphins wearing Santa hats, which reminded him of Madeline.

"Hopefully, she'll like the paper," he thought.

Still not sure what he was going to do for her parents, he grabbed two bottles of his seasoning, wrapped them, and placed those in the suitcase as a last resort.

While he was making sure he had everything, there was a knock at his door again.

<Knock, knock, knockity knock>

He closed up his suitcase so she wouldn't see the present he had put in there.

"Hey, cutie!" Lydia said as he opened the door.

"I was just making sure you were ready for tomorrow. I don't think I can sleep tonight. You wanna go grab something to eat?"

"Sure. What are you thinking?"

"Chinese! I have been craving some egg rolls. Let's go! You can finish going over your suitcase for the third time when we get back. I'm driving!"

Derrick usually enjoyed driving, but he still loved riding in her car. It smelled just like she did... strawberries.

"Wait... I don't go over it three times!"

Lydia laughed as she was waiting for him to close his door. "I know. It's usually four."

CHAPTER 7

Lydia pulled into a spot in the long-term parking garage at Dulles International. When he opened his door, he was amazed at how much larger the parking spots were here compared to Headquarters. Her white Volkswagen Beetle was a little narrower than his Mustang. "Even so," he thought, remembering how he had to crawl out the window just a month ago.

He walked around to the front and opened the lid to get the luggage. Lydia had loaded the car at the dorms while he went back in for the phone charger he had once again forgotten.

She started laughing at his puzzled face.

"The engine on the new versions is in the front, silly!"

Derrick played it off as if it was a joke, but the red slowly creeping up his face gave away the truth.

As they made their way into the terminal, Derrick's nerves were ramping up into overtime about the flight. Having flown helicopters, the fear of flying was rather weird to have, but at least he was in "control" then.

They were greeted as they approached the counter to check-in.

"Hello, Mr. Anderson and Ms. Evans. How has your day been so far?"

Lydia smiled and replied, "Doing good, but he's a tad nervous about meeting my parents."

Derrick's eyes must have grown a bit because the lady behind the counter let out a short laugh.

"Well, I'm sorry, sir, but Delta can't help you with that. Good luck!" as she handed him his license and claim tag.

They made it through security with no issues and then headed for their gate. As they approached A12, Lydia saw a Starbucks and was off.

"Got to get a coffee, be right back!" she yelled as she sprinted away.

Derrick walked over and found a pair of seats near the window. A few minutes later, she came back with the biggest cup of coffee he had ever seen.

"Is that normal?" he inquired.

"No! It's a DOUBLE Venti", she replied.

"Oh, boy. This is going to be an interesting flight."

"*Ladies and Gentlemen, we will now begin boarding for flight 1482 to Kansas City.*" They had to make a connection in Missouri because apparently, nobody in their right mind flies to Iowa. He was going to let her go first so she could have the window seat, but she declined.

"I like the aisle so I can get out to the bathroom easily."

Derrick sighed. "Oh goodie, I get to watch all the moving parts outside that are thirty thousand feet in the air," he groaned.

They made their way down the aisle of the plane until they came to row 18. Their Airbus was in a two-seat by three-seat configuration.

"I tried to get one where we could sit by ourselves," she told him with an almost expectation in her voice.

"What's she thinking we are going to do on an airplane?" Derrick didn't have to wonder long.

Lydia loved to sleep during flights and as soon as the plane left the ground, she leaned over onto his shoulder and was out cold. He put his arm around her so she could be a little more comfortable and not lying on his bony shoulder. Lydia wasn't the only thing that fell fast asleep. His arm soon followed, though strangely enough, he didn't mind.

"I have a beautiful woman lying on my chest comfortable enough with the situation to be sound asleep," he thought. "And then there are the strawberries...."

Derrick usually couldn't wait for a plane to land so he could get off of it, but this time, he wished the flight would never end. He loved the feel of her soft, brown hair lying on the parts of his arm that still had feeling.

Since he couldn't really move, he had plenty of time to contemplate Tae's joke. *"Think you will make it to graduation before you two are married?"* He never really had thought about getting married... ever. He just didn't think it would happen. But he couldn't help but let his mind wander this time. "What would it be like having her lay on me for the rest of our lives? Why is she taking me to meet her parents when we've only been dating a little over a month?"

He was imagining what life would be like with her when the pilot came on the overhead with the announcement that they had started their approach into Kansas City.

He gave her a light nudge, hoping to stir her from her sleep. She didn't move. He then nudged a little harder. "Nothing? Really?" He took his other hand and shook her a bit, calling her name. "Lydia. We are landing. You need to sit up now."

She groggily sat up and started getting her bearings. He tried moving his arm back over to his side, but it completely ignored his request. He had to reach around with his other hand to physically move it back over. When he was putting his hand down, he realized something else about Lydia. She drools when she sleeps. His shirt had a three-inch wet circle right in the middle, but he didn't mind so much seeing where it came from.

"You know, this would be a totally different feeling if this flight was with Tae and that was his drool," he thought.

Having awoken from her nap, she laid her head back down on his shoulder, which now had pins and needles running through it. She smiled a little as she said, "You smell good."

They had about forty-five minutes in Kansas City before the next flight left for Des Moines. Derrick disembarked the plane and stopped for a second when he reached the concourse to find which direction their next flight was.

"Looks like we are about twenty gates away," he said to no one.

Looking around, he realized she wasn't there. Off in the distance, he saw her in a dead sprint to the Starbucks two gates up from where they were.

He walked towards the coffee shop and found a seat in the concourse to wait for her. After a few minutes, she came walking up with a smile on her face.

"Lady, you have a problem, you know that?"

She winked at him and said, "Yeah, but I'm your problem."

When they made it to their next gate, he looked out the window at the plane.

"Um... did they leave our plane out in the rain too long and it shrunk?"

Lydia laughed. "No, silly. Des Moines is a small airport, so they don't use the big jets like at Dulles. You'll be fine."

When they were boarding, Derrick didn't know the door was smaller than the last plane and hit his head on the frame.

"You know, you're supposed to duck under hard metal objects, right?" He turned to find her with a huge grin.

"Says the person who can't outsmart her own clothing."

"Oooooh. Shots fired," she said, laughing.

He started down the aisle towards their seats and was still concerned about the size of the aircraft.

"You know, I've been in bathroom stalls bigger than this plane."

"Yeah, but it didn't fly in the air at 400mph."

A cold chill went up his spine. "How is that helpful?!?"

Upon arrival at the Des Moines Airport, Derrick stopped in the bathroom to dry his shirt again before heading to the baggage claim. He met back up with Lydia and wondered where the screens were that showed which baggage claim was for which airline. He quickly found out why.

"There's only one conveyor belt?!? For the whole airport?!?" he said in disbelief.

"Geez, you weren't kidding when you said you didn't fly anywhere."

They grabbed their bags and walked over to the rental car counter. Derrick asked the representative about getting a vehicle when Lydia piped in, "Already taken care of, stud." She handed the guy her reservation number, and he slid her the keys.

"You know I can help pay for some of this trip, right?"

She flashed him a grin as she walked for the exit.

Once they found the SUV, Lydia hopped into the driver's seat.

"I'm not going to get to drive at all this week, am I?"

"Do you know where you're going?"

"Well, no, but you could always tell me."

Starting up the Tahoe, she looked over at him and said, "Pass".

They drove for over an hour, passing cornfield after cornfield before approaching a small town.

"You know, I thought Texas was flat."

"Oh, you get used to it. Doesn't seem as flat when there's corn growing."

Lydia pulled up to a large farmhouse with a stereotypical white picket fence out front.

"This is home!"

"Wow. Your house is enormous."

Derrick saw an older lady step out onto the porch.

"MOMMA!"

Lydia skidded the Tahoe to a stop, jumped out, and rushed up to her mom. He could make out her mom asking her a question when she turned around and pointed to the SUV.

Derrick's heart stopped for a second when a grizzly bear-looking man stepped out from behind them.

"Uh, oh".

He looked over at the ignition, hoping to make a quick escape.

"She took the keys with her?!?! She barely put it in park!"

Through the closed doors of the vehicle, he overheard Lydia say, "Now Daddy".

Derrick grabbed his phone and started texting Tae his location and what he wanted put on his tombstone.

Lydia ran back over to the SUV and opened his door.

"Come on, come on! Come meet my parents!"

"I think I'd rather be back on the airplane and have one of its wings fall off instead," he said.

Lydia kept tugging on his arm.

He slid out of the SUV and walked up to the porch. Her mom came closer and hugged him.

"Well hello, Derrick. She has not stopped talking about you for the last month. I'm glad you came."

"Well, at least her mom is nice," he thought before glancing back at her dad who had begun to growl.

"Eeeeeh!"

Lydia led him up to her dad and introduced him.

"Daddy, this is Derrick. The guy I have been telling you so much about." Leaning up to his ear, she whispered, "I really like him, so be nice."

His glare didn't waiver.

Derrick stuck his hand out and said, "Good evening, sir. It's an honor to meet you."

He didn't budge.

"Daddy..." Lydia told him.

Finally sticking out his hand, he met Derrick's with a vice-grip handshake and then turned around and went back inside. Lydia came back over to Derrick.

"See, he's a teddy bear."

Still being unable to close his hand from the pain, he replied, "Yep, big fluffy teddy bear. Do you happen to have any ice?"

They headed back to the SUV to get their bags. Derrick grabbed her three and went to carry them in when she grabbed his bag and shut the trunk.

"Oh, you don't need to take that in. I'll get it when I get to the hotel."

"Silly boy, there are no hotels in Bloomfield. You're staying here."

Derrick stopped dead in his tracks. "Say what now?"

"Yeah, you're staying here with us."

"WITH THE GRIZZLY BEAR?"

She started laughing, "Of course! Momma fixed up the guest bedroom for you. How are they going to get to know you if you're not here?"

Derrick felt a pain start in the back of his head that he only assumed was the beginning of an aneurysm.

She showed him into the house and towards the grand staircase that led upstairs.

"Come on, your room is up here."

He followed her up the stairs and into the hallway to the third door on the left.

"Here's your room," she said as she opened the door for him.

His mouth dropped open at the sheer size of the room. "Are you sure this isn't the master bedroom?!?"

"Silly, this is the small one."

She set his bag down near the bed and went to take hers that he was still carrying.

"No, I've got them. Just lead the way."

She walked out of his door and opened the one across the hall.

"Here's my room!"

He froze. "Wait... my room is across the hallway from yours... in the same house with your mom... and the grizzly bear?"

Her dad walked up the stairs and Derrick could have sworn his life flashed before his eyes.

"Just put the bags down in there. It will be fine."

"Um... you want me to go into your room with your father standing right there?" He whispered to her.

"Don't be silly. He's not going to do anything."

Derrick tried not to make eye contact as he slowly started walking towards her door. A growl could be heard from down the hall.

"Man, I wish I wasn't such a bleeder," he muttered.

Lydia walked down to meet him.

"Daddy! Stop it. He's a nice boy who's trying to help."

"Dinner is in 15 minutes."

She got up on her tippy toes and kissed him on the cheek. "Thank you, Daddy," as she sauntered back down the hallway.

Lydia drug Derrick downstairs for dinner.

"Come on, now. What happened to my brave CIA man? I saw him about an hour ago. Where'd he go?" as she playfully lifted one of his arms and pretended to look.

"That guy had the largest man in the world growl at him... not once, but twice!"

"Well, Daddy doesn't like new people. Especially if they are dating me. He'll warm up," and she turned around to go downstairs.

"Yeah... so does napalm," Derrick said quietly.

He followed her through the gigantic house to a table that probably could seat everyone in town. Her dad was seated at the head along with two other younger men who appeared to be in their mid-teens. Lydia came up beside him and introduced them.

"Derrick, these are my two brothers: William and Caleb."

"Hello, gentlemen," Derrick said elegantly.

"I heard you were a CIA agent," Caleb said.

"It's officer, not agent."

"You kill anyone?"

"What? Uh... No."

"I bet he's lying," piped in William.

"I seriously haven't killed anyone."

Lydia came to the rescue. "He was a medic before he came to the Agency. He saved people's lives instead of taking them."

William was still skeptical. "Yeah, but now he's a G-Man. Things are different."

Derrick thought, "G-Men are FBI, you idiots," but he figured it was best to drop it.

Her mom came in with a ham and placed it on the table. "Momma, let me help you while the men get acquainted," Lydia stated as she followed her mom back into the kitchen.

Her dad and brothers kept staring. He knew this was probably not going to end well, but it was better than silence.

Looking at her father, Derrick asked, "Sir, what would you like me to call you? Daddy just doesn't feel right."

"Sir works."

He realized now that silence WAS actually the better option.

"Sir, it is then, Sir."

Derrick made it through the rest of the dinner and then asked Lydia to go with him on a walk. It was freezing outside, but she agreed and bundled up in her coat.

They went out onto the porch and she asked, "Where do you want to go?"

Derrick replied, "Anywhere but in there."

"It's not been that bad, has it?"

"Well, your mom is lovely. I see where you get it from."

He couldn't tell if she had blushed or if her face was just freezing from the cold.

"Your brothers... well... they are... inquisitive. Your dad, though, is possibly the scariest thing on the face of the planet."

She smiled at him. "I know he can be overbearing, but I wouldn't have introduced you if I didn't think it would be useful down the road." She then gave him a slight, playful grin and then turned, walking down the stairs.

"What exactly did she mean by that?!?" Derrick pondered.

Lydia showed him around their property and the old tree that she used to swing on growing up. She told him about the time the rope broke and she flew off, hurting her knee and having to go get stitches.

Then she took him to her favorite spot to look at the Milky Way.

"I have never seen so many..." Derrick said as his voice faded off in amazement.

"I told you! Isn't it beautiful? I used to sneak out on warm summer nights and lay out for hours gazing at them.

After about thirty minutes, their hands and faces were numb from the cold, so they went back inside and turned in for the night. Tomorrow was Christmas, and she loved waking up early and opening presents.

***

Derrick waited until he was sure everyone was already asleep, and then crept downstairs with his gifts. He made it to the tree without making a sound. He bent down and placed them with the rest of the presents. When he turned around to go back upstairs, he saw her dad sitting in his chair and almost screamed.

"Some situational awareness you have. You didn't even see the Sasquatch sitting there watching you!" he thought in disbelief.

"Boy, have a seat," boomed Lydia's dad.

Derrick made his way over to the couch near him and sat down.

"I found it strange that she would bring you here after only dating for about a month and wanted to find out what exactly was going on. What are your intentions with my daughter?"

Looking him directly in the eye, Derrick replied, "I like your daughter very much. She makes me a better person and my life feels brighter when she is around. I hope she can say the same for me."

Her father looked at him for a minute. Just long enough for it to make Derrick a little nervous. "Tell me about yourself."

"Yes, sir. I was born and raised in a small town in east Texas. Once I graduated from high school, I went to college and pursued electrical and computer engineering. While in college, I worked in EMS where I served for eight years as a medic and pilot on a medevac. Two months ago, I joined the Agency where I met your daughter."

"What college did you go to?"

"MIT."

"As in 'The Massachusetts Institute of Technology'?" her dad asked, surprised.

"Yes, sir."

"Why did you stop EMS and flying?"

"I sustained an injury on a call, sir, which ended my career."

"Helicopter crash?"

Derrick paused for a second and swallowed hard. "Something like that."

Picking up on the distress in his voice, Jeb pondered Derrick's response, but decided to address it later. "Thank you. That's all for now. You can go back upstairs."

Derrick stood up and said, "Good night, sir," as he made his way back to his room.

CHAPTER 8

He had just fallen asleep after his encounter with her father when he felt something land right beside him on the bed.

"Wake up, sleepyhead! It's Christmas! Time for presents!"

Trying to figure out what just happened, Derrick slid over to the side of the bed as she ran out of the room.

"Did Santa forget one of his elves when he came last night?!?"

He heard another knock at his door as her mom stuck her head in.

"You better head downstairs before she comes and does that again."

Derrick stumbled downstairs and was making his way to the living room when Lydia came running and jumped into his arms.

"It's Christmas!!!!" She hadn't even bothered to change out of her red flannel penguin pajamas.

"Yes, I believe you said that at least once already today."

While Lydia took another lap around the living room, Derrick made his way to the couch. Before he could even get seated, she jumped over the back of the couch and landed right beside him.

"How much coffee have you had today?!? Wait, let me guess. You have a Starbucks in the barn."

"I'm on my third cup!" she said, jumping back up and heading over to the tree.

"Must be a pretty big cup."

Watching her sprinting up and down the stairs from waking the rest of the family up, Derrick thought, "Science needs to study how to harness that energy she's got right now."

After everyone had made their way downstairs, Lydia started passing out the presents. Her mom walked up behind Derrick and whispered into his ear,

"She's like this every year. Just warning you... every... year."

Derrick giggled a little inside watching this normally composed woman turn into a six-year-old wanting to know what Santa brought. She flew back and forth around the room delivering presents to each person. He was surprised when she slid over and handed one to him.

"This is for you, cutie," she said with a grin before she was off again.

Derrick never really had a big Christmas growing up, since it was just him and his parents. He enjoyed watching the excited faces of her family as they tore into their gifts.

Lydia plopped back down beside him.

"Open yours! Open yours!"

Looking at the label, it read, "To my guy." He carefully started to unwrap the present when he heard a booming voice come from across the room.

"You better rip that paper, boy!"

Derrick instinctively replied, "Yes, sir!" and ripped the rest of the paper off.

He held in his hand a brand-new red Swiss Army knife.

"I saw that yours was worn out and had a broken blade, so I thought you could use a new one."

Being a little overwhelmed, he smiled at her and said, "Thank you," as his voice broke a little. She hugged him and then was off again.

The sound of the room started fading into the distance as he looked at his knife.

"It was the perfect gift," he thought as he opened each blade.

He snapped back into reality when he heard Lydia yell, "Daddy! This one is from Derrick."

Her dad tore through the paper and looked at the two bottles of seasoning. Lydia clapped with excitement.

"Oh wow, Daddy! You've got to try those on your steaks! Derrick made some for us with it and they were amazing."

Her dad looked at Derrick and just said a matter of fact, "Thank you". Derrick had no idea if he liked it or not, but was relieved that it went better than he had thought. His relief turned to anxiety as Lydia grabbed his other present from under the tree. "There's one present left!"

"Oh, how cute! I love the paper. Let's see who it's to." Reading the tag aloud, "To Lydia from..." she grinned, glancing up at Derrick. All Derrick could think as she hopped back onto the seat beside him was, "Incoming!"

To his surprise, she started slowly opening the present. He could see her dad's irritation. "What is up with this dude and ripping stuff up," he thought.

Looking at Derrick, she said, "I love the paper. I want to keep it." After removing the paper, she held the box out and slowly lifted the lid.

This hyper, excited girl... froze.

Derrick saw the reflection of the gold dancing in her wide-open eyes. A tear started to roll down her face. He reached over and wiped it away. Still, not even breaking eye contact with it long enough to blink, she asked him, "Will you help me put it on?"

He took the necklace out of the box as she lifted her hair. Placing it around her neck, he latched the clasp. Her eyes widened as she stared at it resting against her skin. Whispering so only Derrick could hear, she said, "I love it."

Then, in one fluid motion, she spun around, grabbed the back of his head, and pulling him closer, laid a huge kiss on his lips. This was their first kiss... and right in front of her entire family. Derrick swore someone set off fireworks in the house because he could see them all around.

He wasn't sure how long that kiss lasted, but he was pretty sure it was probably going to be his last thanks to her dad. She then hugged him, which placed him in direct sightline of her dad. Derrick felt his skin sizzling from the lasers coming out of his eyes.

Finally breaking the tension, her mom asked, "Alright everyone, who's hungry?"

Derrick started to pick up the paper that was around him when Lydia grabbed his hand and whispered,

"Leave it."

She pulled him towards one of the side rooms. He wasn't exactly sure what was going to happen next, but he was pretty sure it was going to disappoint her father.

Once they were in the room, she pushed him up against the wall and kissed him again. This time longer and more passionate.

"I love the pendant. Thank you so much. It's beautiful!"

"Just like you," he replied.

She gave him another quick kiss and then flashed him her playful grin as she went back out into the living room. Knowing her dad was fully aware of what was going on, Derrick really wished there was a back way out of that room.

***

After breakfast, her dad and brothers went back to the living room to watch TV. Luckily for Derrick, Iowa State was in a bowl game and they weren't going to miss it. Her mom went into the kitchen and started cleaning up.

Derrick grabbed a few plates and followed to help.

"Oh, honey, you don't need to help me. I've got this. Why don't you go watch football with the boys?" Lydia's mom suggested.

"Because I'd rather go run my foot over with the car right now," he thought. "That's okay, ma'am. I don't mind helping out with the cleanup."

Lydia nudged her mom and whispered, "See?"

When they finished, she told her mom that she was going to take Derrick for a drive so he could see the town. They both went back upstairs and before she went into her room to change out of her PJs, she pushed Derrick against the wall again and got nose-to-nose with him. Pressing her body up against his, she gave him another long, passionate kiss.

"Thank you again for the pendant, Mr. Anderson," as she turned and walked across the hall.

Derrick went inside his room, shut the door, sat down on the bed, and replayed the last hour. Her kisses felt amazing. They made everything bad with the world suddenly right again. He cherished his knife, but the present that he loved most that year... was her kiss.

After changing into some warmer clothes, Derrick went back into the hallway to wait for Lydia. A few minutes later, she stepped out of her room and apologized.

"Sorry, my sweatshirt got stuck."

"Got stuck?!? On what?" he asked.

"My head."

Derrick received a light smack across the arm as he struggled to contain his laughter.

Lydia drove down the main street of Bloomfield showing Derrick all the sites the town had to offer.

"Here's where they set up the Farmer's Market. Momma and I would always come here to get our fruits and vegetables. They had the biggest zucchini you could imagine. Momma would buy me a container of strawberries to keep me busy while she shopped. I would eat the entire thing before we even made it back to the car."

Rounding the corner, they passed a row of old-style downtown businesses.

"Oh, and that's Miller's Old Store, where we used to go and stock up on candy to sell at school."

"Wait... you used to smuggle contraband into an educational facility? Does work know this?"

"Haha, funny guy. Candy wasn't banned in schools back then."

A building with a large marquee hanging off the front caught his eye.

"Is that a theater?!?"

Lydia's face beamed with pride. She loved that Derrick was taking delight in her town.

"That's our *Iowa Theatre*. It usually has two or three showings a day of some of the 'newer' movies. We never got to see any on their release day, but the positive side was it was only a dollar to get in."

Her eyes lit up with every "landmark" they came across. Derrick realized this was more than a tour of the town, but was a tour of her memories.

"This is probably all boring to Mr. Big City Texan, isn't it?" Lydia asked, almost sounding a little embarrassed.

"Sweetie, I grew up in a town with barely 1,700 people in it who never locked their front doors. On Friday nights, the entire town was empty because everyone was at the football stadium. You could have robbed any house you wanted except the robbers were at the game as well. I understand about small-town memories... and how they aren't the same now."

She pulled over into the park on the outside of town.

"Do you miss your hometown?" she asked him.

"Sometimes. Especially when I'm in DC, but I don't think I would ever go back there. It's just not the same once you leave."

"You don't miss your parents?"

Derrick sighed. "I miss them every day."

"Well, why don't we go see them sometime? I'd love to meet them!"

His shoulders dropped some.

"I wish we could. About five years ago, they were driving home one night after a football game and another car crossed the center line..."

Lydia gasped as she leaned over to hug him. "I'm so sorry!"

"It's okay. It was hard at the time to get the call because I was up at MIT. The last time I was down there was when I flew in for the funeral. There's just nothing left for me there now."

***

Later that day, they headed back to the house. Her dad and brothers were still glued to the TV. The game had just started after the hours-long pre-game interviews. Lydia headed for the kitchen to assist her mom with dinner.

Derrick tried to help as well, but her mom chased him out with a towel. "Git! Git! Go do football things or something. We got this!"

He wasn't much of a football fan, but it was better than getting whacked with a wet dish towel. When he sat down on the couch, he was sure he heard her dad let out a slight growl.

"Don't move. He can't see you if you don't move," Derrick joked to himself.

Starting again, William asked, "So you're saying you've never killed anyone?"

"Yes, that's what I'm saying."

Caleb joined in, "So you're saying you've killed someone before then?"

"Wait what? No. That's not what I'm saying."

"So what are you saying? Get your story straight!"

"I have NEVER killed anyone!"

"Are you lying to us?"

"No!"

"How do we know you're not lying?"

"You're just going to have to take it on faith."

"That's not good enough. Show us some proof."

"Proof of what?!?!"

"That you've never killed anyone before."

"And how exactly do you suppose I show you proof of something I've never done?!?"

"Where's your gun?"

"What gun?!?"

"The one every agent is issued."

"It's 'officer' and not everyone is issued a gun."

"Did they issue you one?"

"No!"

"I think you're lying. It's back in your office, isn't it?"

"Oh, my stars. I don't have an office."

"You don't, then where do you work?"

"I can't tell you."

"Why not?"

"It's classified."

"What would happen if you accidentally told us?"

"I'd have to kill you."

It was at this moment that Derrick realized he messed up.

"Then we would be your first kill. Is that what you are saying?" asked Caleb.

"That'd be cool!" exclaimed William.

Lydia walked into the middle of this head-dizzying conversation.

"I think I'm going to go outside and sit on the swing," he told Lydia.

"Honey, it's 34 degrees outside."

"Yeah, I know. I'm hoping a polar bear comes along. I'd have a better chance of surviving against those two."

Derrick could hear Lydia and her dad arguing. He couldn't quite make out what was being said, but he was pretty sure it wasn't about the weather. He hung his head and contemplated how coming here might have been a mistake.

After a few minutes, the front door opened and Lydia came out with her coat on. She sat down beside him and rested her head on his shoulder. For ten minutes, they sat in silence until she convinced him to come back inside.

"Well, I guess I can always get my shower before dinner," he rationalized.

Derrick headed upstairs and into the bathroom in the hall. The shower was a walk-in with rainfall heads built into the ceiling.

"You know, I'm starting to think the Evans's are better off than I had imagined."

Turning the faucet on, he was startled as ice-cold water sprayed out. Letting out a yelp, he jumped out of the shower and waited for it to warm up.

"Well, I knew this house had a flaw somewhere," he thought, shivering.

The water finally warmed, and he stood just letting the rain soak his body.

"I could get used to this."

After finishing his shower and drying off, Derrick got dressed and put on some of the cologne that Lydia loved.

He stood at the top of the stairs hoping to come up with any reason not to go back down.

"Hmm... the front door is right there. I bet I can get out of it and halfway down the driveway before anyone even knew what was going on." He thought better of it when he remembered there was nothing for miles in every direction.

Her dad and the twins were still glued to the TV, watching the game. He tried to sneak through the living room and get to the kitchen without having any more stupid questions asked. He almost made it there when Caleb saw him.

"What kind of gun do you have?"

"There's no gun!!!"

Lydia turned around and laughed as he entered.

"Your brothers are pure evil, you know that?"

"Never said they weren't," she said with a grin.

"Why don't they annoy you about whether you've killed anyone?!?"

"Because I told them yes the first time they asked." She winked and then went back to finishing the mashed potatoes.

Her mom approached and suggested, "If you would like to help, you could carve the turkey for us."

Derrick responded, "You sure Smokey wouldn't think I was overstepping?"

Her mom didn't miss a beat. "Nope, he doesn't like burning his paws."

Rather impressed, he thought, "Okay... so now I know where Lydia gets her witty banter from."

He helped Lydia carry the turkey and sides out to the table, but every time he would go out there, one of her brothers would fire another question at him.

"Do you know James Bond? Do you have a gun like his? Have you ever made out with one of those Bond girls?"

He tried ignoring them, but he finally snapped. Knowing this would gross them out enough to get them to stop asking so many questions, he answered, "Yes, James and I are friends. No, his Walther PK is only a .380. My Glock is a 9mm and yes, I've made out with one of those beautiful Bond girls. It was your sister."

The two of them gasped.

It was at this moment that Derrick realized he messed up again. He refused to look up when Lydia placed her hand on his back.

"He's not looking at me, is he? Please tell me he had to go to the bathroom or something and isn't there."

"Nope, he's there... and he's getting out of his chair."

Derrick didn't have much of an appetite at dinner. He honestly was surprised he was still allowed in the house at that point. Thanking her mom for the lovely meal, he excused himself to go hide in his room for the rest of the night.

Lydia came up shortly after.

"Not your night, huh, slick?"

"Your dad hates me."

She sat down on the bed next to him and put her arm around his waist.

"Don't let him stress you out. He'll come around once he realizes that he's not the only one who loves his baby and wants the best for her. You're the first one that has even made it through the front door. If it helps, my mom adores you. She's already told me to marry you."

"If you did, could we move far away from your brothers?"

She leaned over and kissed him, but then stopped.

"Yes, I put my cologne on after the shower."

She gave him her mischievous grin and moved back in for a second kiss.

"Come here, stud!"

He stopped her after a few seconds. His brain threatened to punish him for it, but he knew that if her dad caught them kissing in his room, there would be a real possibility he would not make it out of Iowa alive.

"I know... but save it for when we are back at school."

Lydia understood and started for the door.

"Good night, Derrick. I love you."

"I love you more," he replied.

He could see her face light up into a smile as she went across the hall to her room.

CHAPTER 9

...Derrick pulled up to the scene and blocked the road with his car. Before him was a downed helicopter on fire. He jumped out and ran up to the cabin. It was a medical helicopter. He saw the tail number. It was HIS medical helicopter. He could see the medic and flight nurse in the back unconscious. He tried opening the doors, but they were too damaged. He pulled on the left pilot's door. It was locked tight as well. He made his way to the other side, where he found the pilot bleeding profusely. He tried to break the window in the door, but the fire grew higher. It engulfed the inside of the cabin. He kept trying and trying but couldn't get the glass to break.....

His alarm woke him up. It was 7am the next morning. Trying to shake off his latest nightmare, Derrick sat up on the side of the bed when he heard a soft knock at the door.

"Come in."

Lydia opened the door and sat down next to him. "Another bad dream?"

"Yeah. I'm fine though."

Derrick noticed her PJs. She was wearing a tank top and shorts set that had a scene from Lilo and Stitch on the front. It was Stitch holding a piece of paper that said, "Badness level" with the scale colored in red almost to the top.

Before he could mention them, Lydia asked, "Who's Emily?"

Derrick closed his eyes. A tear formed in the corner of his left one.

"You were screaming her name just a bit ago," Lydia elaborated.

"She was my flight nurse at LifeEVAC. Emily was part of my team for 8 years. She was my friend. I knew her family. Her husband Jim. Her kids: Amy and Terrance. We hung out every weekend when we weren't on shift.

She decided to take another shift to have a little extra money for Terrance's upcoming 9th birthday. I was packing up my stuff that morning when Stefan came to relieve me. We did the handoff briefing and then I went to the crew area. I hugged her and told her to have a good shift as I left. She invited me over the next day because Jim was smoking some ribs. We were going to take Amy and Terrance to the park and have our annual *Start of the Summer* football game.

I had just made it out to my car when they walked out to the helicopter for a transfer. I watched them lift off before getting in my car and starting home.

About two miles down the road, there was an explosion up ahead. When I got there, I saw the helicopter on the road. They had hit a new power line that had been installed after a recent storm that wasn't on the maps. The tail had broken off and the rotor blades were in pieces laying everywhere. There was an oil leak, and the engine was on fire. I ran up and tried to open the doors, but the crash jammed them shut.

I could see Emily and Frank in the back. Frank was unconscious, but Emily was moving around a bit. I went around to the front and Stefan was still in the pilot seat with the cyclic in his hand. He was unconscious as well and bleeding badly from his head. I tried breaking the windows, but they wouldn't break. I grabbed part of the metal skid that broke off and rammed it repeatedly into Emily's window. It just wouldn't break. The shatterproof windows were an upgrade the company did a month earlier to protect from bird strikes.

The casing of the engine on top of the crew compartment was cracked and had been leaking oil inside. The oil ignited and the inside of the cabin erupted in flames. Emily was banging on the window, begging me for help. I kept punching the glass as hard as I could. I couldn't get her out. I watched as her uniform igni..."

Derrick's voice broke.

"That's how I got the third-degree burns and broke three bones in my hand. I just couldn't save her."

Tears started running down Lydia's face as she pulled him close to her and let him grieve. After a few minutes, Derrick tried to compose himself.

"That's why I never flew again. Every time I went to get into the new helicopter, I saw Emily's face. I did my best. Jim even came to the burn ward to thank me. I know in my heart I did everything I could and more, but that doesn't mean you can forget. I went back to their house one more time. Amy answered the door and started crying. It was when she said, 'Why didn't you save my mommy?' that I realized that it might be better off for the kids if I just went my way."

They didn't know Lydia's dad was standing outside the door, listening.

***

Derrick got dressed in the nicer outfit he brought and headed downstairs. Hearing some commotion coming from Lydia's room made him giggle a little. "Her dress must be fighting back."

When he got downstairs, her parents and brothers were waiting in the living room. Her brothers didn't dare ask him questions after last night.

"Well, at least there was some good that came from that train wreck."

He went over and stood near the door, as it was going to be less awkward than looking her dad in the eye. Unfortunately, her dad had other plans. As he started walking over, Derrick couldn't help but ponder where they found a suit to fit a 6'10" 350lb grizzly bear. Having walked up right in front of Derrick, he stuck his hand out.

"You can call me Jeb."

Derrick met his hand and said, "Thank you, sir... I mean, Jeb."

Seeing motion at the top of the stairs, Derrick looked as Lydia was descending towards him. She was wearing a beautiful knee-length, long-sleeved, navy blue dress.

"You are gorgeous!" he exclaimed.

"Why thank you! You clean up nice yourself."

Everyone started filing out the door to their cars. Lydia and Derrick got into the Tahoe and started down the long gravel driveway.

Being concerned about having left him alone with her dad, Lydia placed her hand on his leg and asked, "How are you doing, honey?"

"I'm doing great now that you're here."

She blushed a little. "I'm sorry you were alone down there with him. I tried to hurry, but…"

"Let me guess, you got into a fight with your dress?"

She gave him a playful slap on the arm. "Hey!"

"Well, did you?"

"Of course I did!" she said with a little huff. "I hope my dad didn't give you a hard time when you came down."

"You mean, Jeb? Nah, we had a pleasant talk."

Lydia skidded the SUV to a stop in the middle of the road. "HE TOLD YOU HIS NAME?!?!"

They finally made it to the church building. Derrick was thankful they made it there alive after her reaction to him calling her dad, Jeb. Lydia stopped her mom before she went into the building,

"Momma! Dad told Derrick his name?"

"Yes, dear. He went up to him, stuck out his hand, and asked to be called Jeb. He was very civil and didn't even growl once."

Lydia was in shock as she walked back over to Derrick.

"You ready?"

"For church?" Derrick asked, confused.

"No... for my friend."

As they walked into the building, Derrick heard, "Lydia!!!" A young lady ran up to her and they both started screaming.

"Odd. Maybe Tae and I should try that to see what people would do," he thought.

The young lady then looked over at Derrick and asked, "Who's this fine piece of work?"

Derrick started looking around until he realized she meant him.

"I believe that's the first time I've ever been called that," he thought.

Lydia rushed over and put her arm through his. "Olivia, this is Derrick. He's mine!"

"Oh girl, don't you be playing with me now!"

Showing her the shiny new necklace, Lydia boasted, "Nope. He's off the market. See this pendant?"

"You're engaged?!?" Olivia jested as they both started laughing.

"Derrick, this is my best friend, Olivia! We have known each other since we were both three."

"It's very nice to meet you, Olivia," Derrick said.

"Oh girl, and he's smooth too. If he won't, you propose to him!"

Derrick heard the bell for class to start and he thought it couldn't come soon enough. Walking into the auditorium with Lydia, they found a pew about mid-way up the aisle. He assisted Lydia in and took a seat.

After class had ended, the preacher walked up and greeted them.

"Welcome back, Lydia. Who's the young man with you?"

"Adam, this is Derrick. He came up with me for Christmas," she proudly stated.

"Ah, the fiancé."

Confused, Derrick thought, "Did I miss something here?!?"

"Nah, he's not my fiancé... yet," Lydia remarked with her mischievous grin.

"Well, it's nice to meet you, son," Adam said, extending his hand.

"Thank you, sir. It's great to meet you as well."

Lydia took him around and introduced Derrick to what felt like everyone in the building. As they were heading back to their pew, a little girl came up to him.

"Excuse me, sir, are you the secret agent?"

Derrick kneeled to her level, stuck his index finger to his lips, said, "Shhhhh," and then gave her a quick wink.

The girl hugged him and ran back over to her mom.

As he sat back down next to Lydia, Derrick resigned, "Yeah, and apparently the worst one ever since even a random five-year-old knows."

Lydia chuckled. "That's Ava. Isn't she so cute?"

Jeb and Lydia's mom came up and sat down in the pew behind them.

Leaning over, Derrick whispered, "It's behind me, isn't it?"

Lydia couldn't contain her giggling.

"Out of every other pew in this place, they chose that one!" he exclaimed.

"It's their normal seat."

He gave Lydia a side glance as if to say... "You knew that and still picked this spot?!?"

She shrugged innocently.

As he was glaring at her, Adam walked up to her parents and greeted them as well. "Jeb, Mary. How was your Christmas?"

Derrick leaned over to Lydia again. "Who's Mary?"

"That's my momma."

"Your mom's name is Mary?"

"Yes."

"Why didn't you tell me?"

"Because we always call her Momma."

Her logic was hard to argue with.

Services started with the singing of a few songs. Derrick loved to hear Lydia sing. She had the most beautiful voice and wasn't afraid to belt the lyrics out.

Derrick, on the other hand, was tone-deaf as a skunk. Unfortunately, no one ever really told him.

After the service, Caleb came up to him. "Were you singing that way on purpose?"

"What way?"

"All goofy and such," he explained.

Derrick glanced at Lydia. "Goofy?"

Caleb continued, "Yeah, you were way off-key for that last one."

Derrick stared into Caleb's eyes, pausing for a second. "I think you're going to be my first."

Caleb's eyes grew. "Excuse me," he said and took off for the door.

Derrick leaned over to Lydia, "You know… this could actually be fun."

As they were heading out, Lydia stated, "Olivia wants to know if we would come over to her house for lunch."

"I'll follow you anywhere you want to go. I've come to realize it's probably the safest practice around here."

Lydia smiled. "Great! I'll let her know. She's invited some of my other friends as well. I can't wait for you to meet them too!" she said as she walked away to tell Olivia.

"Uh… Can I change my mind?" Derrick thought. "I'd probably have better chances with the grizzly bear and the psycho twins."

CHAPTER 10

Lydia pulled up to Olivia's house, whose driveway was full of cars.

"How many friends do you have, exactly?"

"I don't know. Eight... Nine..."

Derrick blinked in shock.

"Oh, you'll have a good time. Come on!"

Olivia answered before she could knock. "Hey, girl! The gang's all here. Come on in!"

Lydia stepped into the house to the greetings of her old friends. Derrick hung back on the porch, a little hesitant.

"Well, a 2022 Tahoe can't technically be hotwired..." he thought, but Lydia grabbed his arm and pulled him inside.

Mia yelled, "A BOY!!!!"

Lucy followed by exclaiming, "Lydia! You didn't tell me you were engaged!"

Derrick glanced at Lydia and asked, "What is with everyone in this town thinking we are engaged?!?!"

Lydia cautiously explained, "Well, it's kind of tradition here that when you get engaged, you're supposed to bring your fiancé to meet everyone in town."

Derrick's face dropped in puzzlement and she shot him back a sheepish grin.

A tall, attractive lady walked up to Derrick and started checking him out.

"What do we have here? So this is what the boys in DC look like? Any chance you still have that link where you applied for that job?"

"Down, Hailey," Lydia said. "We just work together in DC. He is actually from Texas."

"You got yourself a cowboy? Oh, girl, you have got to tell him about Larry then."

Confused, Derrick thought, "Larry? What kind of cowboy name is Larry?!? Hoss, John, George… even Derrick make good cowboy names… but Larry?!?"

He didn't have to wait long until Hailey asked, "Lydia, you remember that time you tried to ride Larry at work?"

This caught Derrick off guard. "Say what now?"

Hailey clarified, "Larry is a llama at the zoo we all used to work at."

With his interest now piqued, Derrick glanced at Lydia. "Larry the llama, you say. Oh, do tell."

"Didn't happen," Lydia said bluntly, refusing to look at him.

Hailey insisted, "Yes, it did! You didn't tell him about Larry?"

Shaking her head, Lydia replied firmly, "Nope. No clue what you're talking about."

"We dared Lydia to sneak into the llama pen and try to ride him. He wasn't very happy after she jumped onto his back, and he threw her off into the mud. She was covered head to toe in that stuff!"

Derrick grinned as Lydia turned beet red. She was right about one thing, though; he was going to have a good time.

The doorbell rang. Derrick figured he should get it since the girls were having such a good time reminiscing... and the fact that none of them even acknowledged it. Derrick opened the door to find a delivery guy holding eight pizzas.

"Good night!?!" Derrick thought, "How many do we need?!?"

Derrick took the pizzas about the time three of the girls ran up and relieved him of the aromatic pies. He pulled out his wallet and gave the delivery guy a $100 bill and went back inside to see if there were any pieces left.

After grabbing their slices from the kitchen, everyone congregated back into the living room. Derrick came in and stood against the wall like he usually did, hoping to avoid chaotic conversations. He failed as usual.

Mia immediately noticed him and dragged him over to the couch where she and Natalie were sitting. "Has she told you about the time that she fell down the stairs in high school because she was trying to take her jacket off?"

Derrick chuckled. "No, hadn't heard that one, but I am fully aware of her ongoing war with killer clothing."

Lydia let out a shocked, "HEY!"

Looking at Mia, Derrick admitted, "I've said too much."

Natalie quickly changed the subject. "So what do you do for a living?" she asked while lightly rubbing his arm.

From across the room, they heard, "NATALIE, I WILL END YOU!" as Lydia leaped from her chair.

Derrick glanced at Mia and Natalie and said, "Is it okay with you two if I go over there and sit with Lydia?"

Mia replied with a simple, "Sure," but Natalie had a different answer. "No... No, it's not."

Derrick got up and headed over to where Lydia was sitting. She glared at him while pointing at the chair. As soon as he sat down, Lydia plopped onto his lap. Then, at her friends, she declared, "We clear?" The room erupted with laughter.

Continuing with the conversation, Zoey asked, "Hey, Natalie brought up a good point. Where do you work, Derrick?"

"I work for the government doing IT work."

"Oh, so you're a spy?" said Mia.

"Um, no. I work on computers."

Natalie inquired, still giving him an "I want you" look. "You ever kill anyone?"

"Oh, here we go again," Derrick thought. "How about we tell more Lydia stories? Those are more interesting anyway."

He received a slap on the arm for it, but that was far better than having to go down that rabbit hole again.

"Did Lydia ever tell you about the time she saved someone from drowning?" Zoey asked.

"No, she has never mentioned she was a hero," Derrick said while looking at Lydia. He expected her to blush but instead noticed she shied her eyes away from him.

Zoey explained how Lydia had been walking on the Hwy 63 bridge just north of town when a car ran off the road, crashing into the water. She jumped into the water and pulled the unconscious driver out just as the car began to sink. Noticing that he wasn't breathing, she performed CPR until he revived.

"Well, technically, it wasn't CPR, it was just rescue breaths," Lydia quietly corrected.

"Wow! I never knew. That's amazing, honey," Derrick exclaimed, unsuccessfully trying to cheer her up.

Zoey then added, "The plot twist was it was her boyfriend that she just broke up with. He made a move on her a few minutes earlier and she was walking home. He ran off the road trying to hit her with his car."

Lydia started crying.

Pulling her in close to his chest, Derrick embraced her, causing her to cry even harder. He stood up with Lydia in his arms and took her to another room in the house.

Natalie leaned over to Mia and said, "That is SO hot!"

Looking back at Natalie in disbelief, Mia asked, "Have you been drinking again?"

Derrick set her down on the edge of a bed. "So you risked your life to save somebody who tried to take advantage of you and then kill you moments earlier," he restated.

Through her tears, Lydia explained, "I couldn't just let him die. I wanted to. I so badly wanted to stand there and watch him drown, but I couldn't do it. It was the hardest thing I have ever had to do. I felt so horrible afterward for thinking that way. I hope you don't think worse of me for it."

Derrick pulled her in tight. "Lydia... It only goes to further prove how wonderful of a person you are. I'm not sure I could have made the same decision. I'm not sure many people would have. I love you dear. I wake up every morning trying to imagine how I could love you more and every day you continue to show me."

Her tears flowed even harder.

Olivia peeked around the corner.

Derrick silently mouthed to her, "She's okay. Give her a second."

Nodding understandingly, Olivia retreated back to the living room.

After finally calming down, Lydia was ready to rejoin the others. The mood of the room had changed, though... except for Natalie. "So, have you guys set a date yet? 'Cause if she won't commit, I will!"

"No, we aren't engaged," Derrick politely explained.

"Is that because you are always traveling to dangerous places, saving the world with your big, muscular arms?"

Derrick looked at Lydia, "What is wrong with the people in this town?!?"

"They don't get out much," Lydia joked through her sniffles.

Mia chimed in. "What is the time you were the most afraid?"

That one came easily to Derrick. "I'm going to go with the Bond girl comment I made yesterday in front of her dad."

It was getting late when they left Olivia's house. Derrick offered to drive since Lydia still wasn't feeling great.

With some skepticism, she asked, "You sure you know how to get back?"

"No problem!" Derrick replied with confidence. "This town isn't that big!"

"Do you still want to go to the zoo tomorrow?"

Derrick tried hard to cover his giggling. "Of course I do! I wouldn't miss the chance to meet Larry!"

This time, Lydia smacked his arm with force.

"Ouch!"

Sarcastically, Lydia mocked him, "Oh, that hurt Mr. Big Bad Secret Agent Man... Huh?"

Derrick couldn't help but laugh as he continued down the road.

Looking around, Derrick started to wonder where he was going. He thought their house was this way, but now he wasn't entirely sure. All the buildings started disappearing and the speed limit went up to 70mph.

"Where are we going, stud?" Lydia asked, smugly.

"Well honestly... I don't know anymore," as he turned the car around.

"Would you like some hints?"

They finally arrived back home... with a little help from Lydia. Okay, a lot of help from Lydia.

He parked the car and asked, "You okay?"

"Yeah, I'm fine."

"Liar."

Lydia looked back as she was getting out of the Tahoe, "Yep, certified professional one."

Opening the front door for her, Lydia headed for the kitchen. Derrick watched as she tried to take her coat off. "Oh, this could get interesting", he thought, but Lydia gave up and left it on.

He hung his coat up on the tree by the door, and when he turned around, William and Caleb were walking toward him.

"Do those two not have anything better to do?!?"

Derrick darted up the staircase and without breaking his gait shouted, "If either one of you asks a single question, I swear I will do to you the same thing my team did to that Russian General last week."

Both of them stopped in their tracks.

After changing into more comfortable clothes, Derrick headed back downstairs and made his way to the kitchen. He saw the psycho twins on the couch. Caleb looked like he was almost going to say something.

Derrick stuck his index finger up and said, "Eh!" and kept walking, to which Jeb let out a chuckle.

As he entered the kitchen, Lydia and Mary were sitting at a small table.

"I think I just heard Jeb let out a giggle…" Derrick stated, visibly shocked.

Mary looked confused, "Come again?!?"

"I know, right?"

He walked over to where Lydia was sitting and kneeled beside her.

"You sure you're okay?"

She reached out, kissed him, and said, "Yes. I am fine. Honestly."

"Well, if you're sure, I guess I will go back out into the living room and torture your brothers for a bit to relax some."

Mary looked at Lydia and asked, "Did he just use the words 'relax' and 'torture' in the same sentence?!?"

"Yep, that's my man."

CHAPTER 11

The next morning, Lydia snuck into Derrick's room and woke him with a kiss.

"Well, I have to say that is my new favorite way to wake up."

"Get dressed! It's an hour and a half drive to the zoo."

"What time is it?"

"It's 5am!"

"Are you insane?"

"I want to get there early so we can see it all. We can stop by Starbucks on the way."

"By any chance, are you a paid spokesperson?"

"No. Wait... do you think they'd hire me?"

"No," he said matter-of-factly. "You'd drink them out of business."

Derrick got dressed and stumbled his way downstairs. He found Lydia struggling to get her arm through the sleeve of her coat.

"Need some help?"

"No! Well... maybe."

Derrick grabbed her sleeve and pulled it out straight, which allowed her to slide her arm through.

"Thank you."

"It's what I do. I pull sleeves and kill people."

On the drive to the zoo, they talked about school and the places they would like to go.

"I hear Somalia pays the best," Derrick offered.

"Uh, that's a war zone post. You'd never get me to one of those. I like the beach, but I love the water more."

"Well, Somalia has water... and pirates."

"The rum drinking kind?"

"Noooo. More of the board your boat by gunpoint kind."

"Eek!" she exclaimed.

"I think I'd like London. You would go to work and then be able to go see the sights in the evening," Lydia explained.

"I've always wanted to go to London."

"Do you think they would send both of us to a place... you know... together?" Lydia asked with hope.

"I believe the only time they do that is if you are married and then I'm still not sure how that would work."

Lydia paused for a second and suggested, "Well, we could always just do TDYs."

Derrick looked at her inquisitively.

"You know, backfills and quick trips. The 8-10 day kind of stuff. I hear they bring home good money and that way we wouldn't be gone for large periods."

"That's not a half bad idea," Derrick said, "but a lot of those types are to the beaches without water."

"Yeah, but wouldn't it be more tolerable if it was only for like a week versus an entire year?"

"You ever thought about after work? Like if you could create your perfect place, where would it be? What would it look like?" she asked.

"I see a modest house sitting on the water. The Gulf. It would have a small pier that stretched out over the sand beneath it. There would be rocking chairs on the porch to watch the sunset every day."

"That sounds beautiful," Lydia said, wondering how he described the home she had been dreaming about.

"Oh... but there would be one more thing. I could have the rest of that, and it still wouldn't be home without this one thing."

"What is that?" she asked.

"You don't already know? That one thing... is you. You standing there on that pier. Watching the sunset with your hair blowing in the breeze. THAT would be my paradise."

***

They arrived at the zoo just as it was opening. Derrick went up to pay, but the guy in the ticket booth recognized Lydia and gave them some passes.

"Hey, Lydia! It's been a bit. You coming to visit Fred?"

"Of course! Also, showing my boyfriend around my old haunts."

Derrick piped in, "Oh, and don't forget Larry!"

Lydia was getting great at smacking him on the arm.

She first took him to their indoor penguin exhibit. Derrick loved penguins. She told him all about the species they had there. He knew most of the information already but loved hearing her talk so passionately.

They came out of the exhibit and Derrick noticed the sign that said, "*Llamas*" and an arrow to the right.

He grabbed her arm and said, "Look, Llamas!" and started heading towards the exhibit.

They arrived to find there were five llamas out in the pen. Derrick couldn't tell which one was Larry and Lydia wasn't telling.

"Larry! Larry! If you're Larry, raise your hand, er foot... hoof?"

The teenager running the exhibit came up to them.

"Hello! My name is Wyatt. Welcome to the Blank Park Zoo."

"That's still the dumbest name for a zoo," Derrick thought, but would never say that to Lydia.

"Are you interested in feeding a llama?"

Derrick announced overenthusiastically, "Why yes Wyatt, we are!"

Lydia covered her face in embarrassment. "You having fun?"

"Oh, I'm having a blast!" Derrick replied, laughing.

Wyatt brought up a llama and a bucket of food. Grabbing a handful, Derrick handed Lydia some. "Here, sweetie. Go ahead! It looks hungry."

Lydia was fighting hard not to crack a smile. She thought he was funny, but wasn't about to give him the satisfaction.

"What's this one's name?" Derrick asked.

Stroking her on the head, Wyatt stated, "This one is Matilda."

"Well, hello, Matilda. It's nice to meet you."

Lydia let out a quick giggle.

"Wyatt, I remember that there used to be one named Larry here a ways back. Is he still around?"

"Why yes, Larry is right over here."

Wyatt turned to get Larry and Lydia smacked his arm again. Derrick looked at her, laughing.

"What? I figured you would like to see your old friend again."

Wyatt walked up with Larry, who appeared to be giving Lydia the stink eye.

"I wanted to show the lady here my old friend. I loved coming here feeding him year after year."

Lydia gasped in disbelief. "Liar!" she said under her breath.

"I remember going to a zoo in Texas one time that had a place where you could actually ride the llamas. Do you guys do that here?"

"No, unfortunately, we don't. They even added a policy in the employee handbook specifically prohibiting it a few years back after one employee tried to ride one."

"Somebody just up and jumped on one here? What were they thinking?!?"

"I'm not sure, but some people are a little crazy," Wyatt said.

"Well, thank you, and Larry, It was nice to see you again, old buddy."

As they walked away, Lydia swatted at him, but this time, he expected it and dodged her.

Derrick couldn't stop laughing. "What? It had to be done. That was hysterical!"

She then led him to the giraffe exhibit. It was closed for the season, but the attendant recognized Lydia and asked if she was there to say hello to Fred.

"You know it, Ollie. How's he doing?"

"Oh, Fred is doing great. He even fathered a little one last May. We named him Fred Jr. because we figured you would have. Who's this gentleman with you?"

Lydia smiled and put her arm around Derrick. "This is my boyfriend. I brought him home for Christmas."

Surprised, Ollie asked, "And Jeb didn't scare him off?!?"

Lydia chuckled. "Oh, he tried to run, but I got the handcuffs out."

Ollie nodded his head. "Yeah, that sounds about right. Come on in."

Derrick's head snapped to look at Lydia. "Sounds about right... for the handcuffs?!?"

She winked at him, grinned, and went inside the building.

Derrick walked in and found Lydia already hugging this gigantic beast who had lowered his head down to her level.

"Oh, Fred, I've missed you so much. How are you doing, pal? I hear you have a little Fred now. You hungry?"

Derrick walked up as Lydia grabbed the feed bucket.

"Fred, this is Derrick. He's my man." Then looking at Derrick, Lydia asked, "You want to say hi to him?"

"Well, if he's that special to you, of course I do."

Derrick started to address Fred, but Lydia stopped him.

"No, put your hand out like this. That is the signal I taught him to lower his head so we can pet him."

Derrick stuck his hand out like Lydia had shown and Fred started lowering his head. Ollie almost said something, but Lydia shot a glare at him. Ollie kept quiet and stepped back.

Fred lowered his head until it was right in front of Derrick. As he reached out his hand to pet him on the head, Fred stuck his tongue out and licked him from his neck to the top of his head via his face.

He never heard Lydia laugh so hard in her life. He stood there with his face dripping on the floor.

"What? It had to be done," Lydia laughed as she replied mockingly.

Derrick watched this laughing, gorgeous woman who had just played the best prank on him and realized that she might be the one.

Ollie took Derrick to their employee washroom so he could get cleaned up and then Lydia finished showing him the rest of the park. A lot of the exhibits were closed because of the time of year, but he had a great time, anyway. They went back to the Tahoe and headed to Bloomfield.

Derrick was rather quiet on their drive back. Lydia finally asked if there was something wrong.

"A huge, long-necked mammal licked three layers of skin off my face with its black tongue," he said emotionless.

Lydia started laughing so hard, she swerved onto the shoulder and partly into the grass.

"Would you please stay on the road?" Derrick pleaded, holding onto the door handle.

"I can't! I'm dying over here! That was so funny!" she exclaimed.

Finally composing herself, Lydia looked over at Derrick, who was still staring at her with a squinted glare. She lost it again.

When they arrived back at her parents' house, Lydia noticed Derrick had that look on his face like he was trying to process something.

"You're not still mad about the giraffe, are you?"

"What? No. I never really was mad. It was hilarious. I was thinking about something. Remember when we were in the radio class and had issues with the antenna reaching the satellite? I think I just figured out a way to amplify the signal."

"Derrick Anderson! You promised me you wouldn't be blowing up any more fish!"

Derrick helped Lydia with her coat. While it would have been funnier to watch her struggle with it, he was a little too tired to enjoy it.

"Dinner is probably almost ready. I'm going to go see if Momma needs any help."

"Okay, sweetie. I need to find some paper..."

Derrick picked up the newspaper from the coffee table and began sketching his idea. Jeb watched as Derrick's wheels turned until it appeared he ran into a problem.

"Whatcha thinking so hard about?"

Still scribbling down formulas, Derrick explained. "I'm trying to work out an idea I had for an antenna shield that would amplify a signal by accelerating it through reflection, but I can't find the right incident angle. Something is missing."

"Did you take into account the medium thickness?" Jeb suggested.

It was as if a lightbulb had switched on in Derrick's mind. "That's it!" The ladies walked in with the food as Derrick was finishing his last formula.

After dinner, William and Caleb sat at the table staring at Derrick.

"Do you ever get to work with bombs?"

Derrick knew where this was going, so he decided to have a little fun with it. "Why, yes, I do. I have built many," he replied with a smile.

"You ever set one off?"

"Of course."

"Did you kill anyone when you did?"

Leaning back in his chair, Derrick proudly said, "Yes."

Their eyes grew. "How many did you kill in your biggest one?"

"The one a couple weeks ago killed 352 with a flick of a switch. It even took out one of our own guys who was sitting too close to the explosion."

The twins were completely engrossed now. "What kind of bomb was it?"

"It was a *phosphamite* incendiary."

They gasped.

Lydia and her mom walked out of the kitchen and were listening from the doorway. She leaned over to Lydia and asked, "Did he really blow up 352 people?!?"

"Fish... 352... fish. He blew up the lake behind the dorms with an exploding trashcan. Those poor fish went everywhere. They didn't stand a chance."

Mary burst out laughing. "Why did he blow up a lake?!?"

Lydia sighed. "We left him unsupervised for a few hours."

"Oh honey, even I know better than that, and I've just met him!"

***

As Derrick was getting ready for bed, Lydia knocked on his door.

"My brothers loved your 'fish' story."

Derrick grinned. "Hey, I told them a good story and didn't tell a single lie in it."

"Then what exactly is *phosphamite*?!?" Lydia said, suspiciously.

"A combination of phosphorus and thermite that I came up with on the fly. You like it?"

Lydia walked over, shaking her head slightly.

"My handsome assassin. What am I going to do with you?"

"Oh, I could think of a few things, but that's for a later time," Derrick said with a smirk. "What are the plans for tomorrow?"

"I'd like to take you to my favorite Chinese restaurant, but other than that, I was going to see if there was anything you'd still like to see."

Tapping his chin with his finger, Derrick contemplated, "With all the attractions in this town, it would take me a while to narrow it down to one or two."

"Now listen here, mister!"

Derrick laughed. "You know how cute you are when you get all feisty like that? We can just play tomorrow by ear and then finish with a wonderful dinner."

"I love you; you know that, Mr. Anderson?"

"For as much as you put up with me, you'd have to."

Lydia gave him a kiss goodnight and headed off to her room.

CHAPTER 12

...Derrick was being chased down a gravel back road by two black SUVs who were matching his every move. The speeds approached 80mph when he lost control in a curve and went tumbling over and over. When the car finally came to a stop, the SUVs were right beside him. Two gray figures with large, black, oval eyes stepped out and approached his door. He tried to get out to defend himself, but his legs were trapped. The two figures leaned down to his window. Derrick swung at one of them...

POW! THUD! GASP! He woke and in one fluid motion had punched Caleb in the face and pulled William into a chokehold. After falling backward off the side of the bed and onto the floor, Caleb staggered to get back up. He then jumped onto Derrick's back and tried to set William free. Without breaking his hold, Derrick lunged backward off the bed and landed on the floor on top of Caleb, knocking him out cold.

Lydia heard the scuffle and barged into his room to find both of her brothers unconscious on the floor, and Derrick sitting on the side of the bed.

"Uh... One too many questions?" she asked.

He explained what happened as they tried to bring them both back around. "I'm sorry, honey. I thought they were a couple of big-headed freaks from another planet... well, I mean actual aliens."

Lydia was laughing when her parents came to the door.

Jeb looked at the scene and said, "I don't want to know. They probably deserved it," and headed back downstairs.

Derrick felt a little uncomfortable at breakfast since William and Caleb would not stop glaring at him. Caleb's eye had swollen shut by this point and was turning purple.

"What were you two thinking?!?" Lydia asked.

"We wanted to see if he really was a secret agent."

"Well? Convinced?"

Acting like he felt sorry, Derrick suggested a peace offering.

"How about I show you guys how to make a small explosion after breakfast?"

Lydia didn't know where he was going with this but feared no good could come from it.

"Honey?"

Looking at her with an evil smile, "It's okay. After the incident this morning... they deserve it."

Derrick grabbed the ingredients he would need: hydrogen peroxide, dish soap, and yeast. He put everything into a small trashcan he found in the half bathroom, walked to the door, and gestured for the boys to follow him.

Mary nervously looked at Lydia. "Honey... he has a trashcan and an evil look in his eye."

Placing her forehead on the table, she asked, "Is the number for the fire department still on the refrigerator?"

Derrick placed the trashcan on the ground and removed the ingredients. He instructed the two on the proper way to mix the substances.

Mary, Jeb, and Lydia came out onto the porch with a fire extinguisher and a first aid kit.

Derrick's last instruction was for the boys to put the yeast into the mixture. As William and Caleb poured it into the can, they were too engrossed with the potential of causing an explosion to notice Derrick had taken many steps away from them and pulled out his phone to record the event. A violent reaction occurred shooting the elephant's toothpaste straight up into the air and all over their faces.

The two of them stood there in shock, covered head to toe in the sticky foam substance. From the porch, a visceral laugh echoed, but Derrick noticed it wasn't a female voice. Turning around, he found Jeb laughing so hard he could barely stand.

Derrick was cleaning out the trashcan when Lydia came up and hugged him.

"I have never heard my dad laugh so hard before. I sent him the video you recorded, and he's in the house right now, watching it on repeat. I think he might pull a stomach muscle before the day is over."

After finishing outside, Derrick went back in and took a seat on the couch. Jeb was still watching the video over and over, laughing hysterically.

Mary whispered into his ear as she was heading back into the kitchen, "I have NEVER heard him laugh this much in all our years."

When the video ended this time, Jeb looked over at Derrick.

"That is still the funniest thing I have ever seen in my life!"

Just then, William and Caleb walked into the living room having taken showers to clean off the sticky goo. Every hair on their heads was standing straight up.

"Daddy, we washed, but our hair is still sticky. I tried brushing it, but it won't lie down!"

Jeb almost fell out of his chair, laughing. "I stand corrected! THAT is the funniest thing I have ever seen!"

Derrick couldn't hold his laughter in anymore, either.

Mary came running out to see what was going on. "Oh... My... Stars..."

About an hour later, Lydia walked into the living room and sat down next to Derrick, who was watching the football game Jeb had playing on the TV.

"What's that look for?" he asked.

"Well... We were able to get the twin's hair to finally lie back down... after four more showers."

Jeb started giggling again.

"Daddy!" Her reaction made him switch from giggling to laughing.

"It was like they saw a ghost!"

Derrick apologized. "I'm sorry, sweetie."

"Oh, don't apologize. They totally deserved it."

He leaned over and hugged her. "That's why I love you."

Derrick finished getting ready and stepped out into the hallway to hear a commotion coming from the bathroom. Lydia yelled from behind the door. "Ewww! Why is the shower so sticky?!?! TWEEEEEEBS!!!!!!!"

She met him downstairs, and they headed out to the Tahoe.

"So... what happened in the bathroom?" Derrick asked.

Lydia growled. "Those tweebs got that goo all over the floor! I had to wash my feet three times to get it off."

Derrick covered his mouth and whispered to himself, "Don't laugh, don't laugh, don't laugh."

Turning onto US-63, he looked at her funny as they drove past the Bloomfield city limits.

"Sooo, where's this place at?"

"Ottumwa."

"And what language was that you just spoke?!?"

"You goober. It's a city north of here. Doesn't Texas have some funny sounding town names?"

"Depends what you call funny."

As she pulled into the parking lot, she proudly proclaimed,

"Here it is! *The Jade Palace.*"

Derrick looked suspiciously at the building. "Well, I bet it has a great personality."

She smacked him on the arm as she was getting out. "Hey now! Don't knock it till you try it!"

The inside was decorated in typical Chinese restaurant fashion with two jade colored floor to ceiling dragons bracketing the entrance. Scrolls with Chinese letters adorned the walls, and red lanterns hung from the ceiling.

They were shown to a corner booth with large, plush benches.

"You were right. This place looks a lot nicer on the inside."

Her smile grew. "I knew you'd like it!"

The server came by and delivered their menus. Derrick was looking over it when Lydia interjected.

"I know, it's all in Chinese, but I can interpret it for you, though."

"Wait, you know Chinese?"

"Well, no. But I've been here enough that I know what the dish is by the picture."

"What do you recommend?" he asked Lydia as he leaned back in his seat.

"My favorite dish is the General Tso's. It is flat-out amazing here!"

He closed the menu and placed it on the table. "Alright. I'll take that then."

During the meal, Derrick heard what sounded like someone panicking. He looked over and saw a lady had gotten up and was shaking her child, yelling, "Are you choking? Breathe!"

Running over to the table, Derrick picked up the child and began performing the Heimlich maneuver, while Lydia called 911. After a couple of thrusts, he was able to dislodge the food but noticed she was still not breathing. He laid the girl on the floor and started rescue breaths as Lydia helped those in nearby booths to clear the area. The girl finally took a breath and started crying for her mother.

A few moments later, the ambulance arrived, and as they wheeled the girl out on a stretcher, Derrick returned to his seat and continued eating.

Lydia sat in disbelief. "How are you hungry after that? I'm still shaking!"

He shrugged. "When you've done it enough times, it doesn't bother you that much anymore."

On the way back to Bloomfield, Lydia was rather quiet. Even though he felt a strange tension in the air, Derrick couldn't stand the silence any longer.

"You were right, that place was amazing! We need to go there again the next time we come."

She turned her head towards him and questioned him in an angry voice. "Okay... so we aren't going to address what happened?"

Derrick's mouth dropped open as he looked around. "Um... what happened?"

She continued to glare at him, flabbergasted.

Derrick, realizing what she was referring to, "You mean the kid? What's there to talk about? She's fine."

"You saved her life! You're a hero!"

Derrick shied his head, looking away. "No, I'm not. I just did what I was trained to do."

When they got back to the house, he helped her off with her coat and then said, "I'm going to go up and start packing."

Lydia smiled. "Make sure you check it three times."

Derrick lightheartedly glared at her and fake laughed. "Aren't we a cute one?"

Before he could turn around, William came up and started questioning him again. Derrick wasn't really in the mood for the games, so he reached up and squeezed a spot on William's neck and he collapsed to the ground.

"DERRICK!" Lydia exclaimed.

"He's fine. He'll come around in a few seconds," Derrick nonchalantly stated.

Lydia made sure William was okay and then headed to the kitchen. "Momma!"

Mary turned around from the sink where she was washing the dishes. "Oh, hi honey. How was your dinner?"

"You're not going to believe this one!"

CHAPTER 13

Derrick was sitting on the bed, waiting for Lydia so they could start their hour-long drive to the airport for their early flight.

Poking her head into his room, she asked, "You ready?"

"Yes and no."

Smirking, Lydia suggested, "Well, I guess you could always stay here with my brothers."

Standing up, Derrick grabbed his bag and hurried towards the door. "Which way is the car?"

Jeb and Mary met them at the bottom of the stairs, and Lydia hugged her mom.

"I love you, Momma!"

Derrick stuck his hand out to Jeb. "Thank you, sir, for letting me stay here and enjoy your family's company for Christmas."

He reached out and took his hand. "I told you to call me Jeb."

"Yes, sir, Jeb."

***

Snow was falling as they landed in Kansas City and rumors were spreading around the plane that flights were being delayed due to the weather. When they entered the terminal, Lydia headed for the restroom while Derrick found the status of their next flight on the screen. It read, *"DELAYED: NOW 3:31pm"*.

"Wow. That fourth coffee went right through me," Lydia explained as she met back up with Derrick in the terminal.

"Our next flight is delayed... for three hours."

"Three hours?!? Well, I guess it could be worse. It could be canceled," she said with positivity.

Derrick rolled his eyes, "Uh, don't give them any ideas."

They headed over to a row of seats by the window and settled in for their long wait. Lydia broke out her phone and started playing whatever new game she had found that week in the app store while Derrick watched the snow fall outside the window. The peacefulness of the gently falling flakes made it hard for him to stay awake.

"I'll just close my eyes for a few minutes," he thought, and within seconds, he was sound asleep.

Derrick was awakened a few moments later by an announcement from the gate agent.

"Ladies and gentlemen, we are getting word from the tower that the weather has gotten worse and we are now forced to cancel flight 556 to Washington Dulles. Please see one of our representatives for rescheduling options. Once again, we are canceling flight 556."

After waiting an hour in line, it was finally their turn at the counter.

"Hello. Just the two of you today? Let's see what options we have." The agent said as she was typing away on her computer.

"Our next direct flight isn't for three days, but I can get you on a connection through Los Angeles tomorrow morning. It departs here at 8:25am."

Derrick looked at Lydia for confirmation as a grin started to grow on her face.

"I think that means we will do the LA flight then," he told the agent

After getting their new tickets, Derrick checked his app and found that there was a Marriott on the premises, but even with his Bonvoy status, it was completely booked for the night.

"Looks like we are sleeping here in the terminal."

As Lydia went down to the BBQ restaurant to get them some dinner, Derrick convinced a Delta agent to let him have a blanket to use for the night.

It was a little after 10pm when they finally finished eating, and Derrick could tell she was getting tired. He found an empty gate where the overhead lights were subdued and set up his backpack against the wall so he could lean on it. Lydia and Madeline nestled up beside him. She laid her head on his chest, and he spread the blanket over her.

"Aren't you going to be cold, though?" she asked.

Smiling, he kissed her on the head. "Nah, you're a nice little heater."

He put his arm around her as she snuggled up a little closer and fell asleep.

Derrick usually could sleep in just about any position he was in, but this time he was only able to catch a few catnaps. Every time he would drift off, he would catch himself flinching from a dream and was afraid he would scare Lydia.

"Who needs rest when I can sit here and watch her sleep so peacefully?" he tried to convince himself.

***

As the sun rose outside, activity started to pick back up in the terminal. An overhead announcement woke Lydia from her slumber.

Seeing her eyes open, Derrick quietly greeted her to the new day. "Good morning, beautiful. Did you sleep well?"

Lydia wasn't much of a morning person until she got her caffeine, but she was able to give him a short grunt before wrapping the blanket tighter around her body and snuggling back up for an extra bit.

Ten minutes later, the overhead lights at the gate turned on to her annoyance.

"Well, I guess I'm up now. I'm going to grab a coffee. You want one?" she asked, wobbling as she stood.

"That sounds great. I'm going to pack everything up and I'll meet you over there."

Derrick didn't want to tell her that the real reason he was taking a bit longer was that both of his legs had fallen asleep hours ago and he couldn't feel them at all right now.

As soon as she was out of visual sight, he crawled over to a bench where he rode out the waves of paresthesia. Before they could wake normally again, she came back with the coffee.

"Your legs are asleep, aren't they?"

"A little." He could tell she didn't buy that answer. "Okay, a *lottle*," he resigned with a grin.

"Thank you for being my pillow last night. I don't remember the last time I slept so well. It was nice having someone to go through this with," as she lay her head back on his shoulder.

***

Derrick loved their three-hour flight to Los Angeles. He was finally able to get some sustained sleep, even with Lydia cuddled up on him. The flight attendant's arrival announcement finally woke him a few minutes before touchdown. He had never been to California and enjoyed the view of the skyscrapers downtown as they came in for the landing.

When they got off the plane, he pointed to the Starbucks a few gates down, knowing that would likely be the first place Lydia would look for. To his surprise, she didn't take off running.

"I need a picture of us with the *Welcome to L.A.* sign! Momma has always wanted to come here and has yet to make it."

The selfie she took of them became Derrick's phone background. The excitement in her face quickly made it one of his favorites.

While their flight to LA was smooth and relaxing, the five-hour flight to Dulles was anything but. The winter storm system that canceled their trip the day before caused turbulence throughout this flight.

Derrick tried to catch some sleep, but he would inevitably be dreaming about being in a helicopter. Every time they would hit a rough patch, he would jolt awake thinking he had fallen asleep flying. The jerking would then cause Lydia to wake up in a panic.

Launching upright in her chair, she exclaimed, "Ah! What? Are we crashing?"

"I'm sorry, sweetie. I fell asleep again."

They finally arrived at Dulles and headed back to the school. Lydia pulled into the dorm lot, and putting the car into park, turned to Derrick.

"I had a great time."

"Had? I hope this adventure is only beginning," Derrick offered.

Leaning over, she gave him one of the kisses that he was growing to love.

Grabbing their luggage, Derrick followed Lydia as she led the way up the breezeway to their rooms. She opened her door and then stepped aside, allowing Derrick to put her bags down in the room.

She shot him a wink as he started to close her door. "I'll be dreaming of you tonight, stud. Make sure you save me a seat in networking class tomorrow. I'd hate to throw Tae out of it."

Derrick acted aghast. "No goodnight kiss?"

His face turned to shock as she started running towards him. He dropped his bag just in time for her to leap into his arms. Grabbing his head and wrapping her legs around his body, her kiss made Derrick's legs turn to jelly.

After a good minute, Lydia finally unwrapped herself from him and sauntered back over to her door.

Derrick had difficulty articulating sentences, but was able to get out, "Wow... kiss... good..."

He stood in the hall for a moment as the blood started flowing back into his legs when he noticed Tae by the elevator. From the look on his face, it was obvious he had just seen everything that had transpired. Derrick walked towards him and went to hug him.

"Hey! How was your Christmas?"

Tae stood frozen and could only reply, "Something happened, didn't it?"

CHAPTER 14

Derrick had been watching the weather all week. There was a winter storm heading towards the east coast and it was predicted to hit two days before New Year's. They were forecasting an accumulation of over a foot of snow.

Lydia, being the only one who was familiar with that type of weather, suggested they get some sleds and have some fun on the hill near the dorms.

"I can't believe you three have never been sledding before!" She said as the group sat in the common room.

Richie added, "I'm from Hawaii. I've never even seen snow."

"That's it. Everyone to my car," Lydia ordered.

Derrick and Tae sat in the rear and Richie hopped upfront since he would have had to dislocate a few joints to get in the back. She drove them all to Walmart and led everyone to the seasonal aisle.

"Look at all these choices!" Tae exclaimed.

Derrick found a toboggan-style sled he was interested in, as it looked fast and would keep him off of the snow most of the time.

Richie came up behind them and put his arms over their shoulders. "Dude, tubes are the way to go. We used to tube the river all the time."

Tae, feeling braver than he was in orientation, "What the crap does tubing rivers have to do with sled riding?"

Lydia reassured Richie, "Tubes are a good choice, especially for someone as tall as you."

Pulling it down from the shelf, Richie made sure to bounce it off of Tae's head as he walked by.

"What kind are you getting?" Derrick asked Lydia.

"I'm more of a classic disc kind of girl," she said with a grin, reaching for a strawberry-red circular sled.

As they were about to leave, Tae was still staring up at the shelf. "Can't decide, buddy?" Derrick asked.

"No... I'm in love."

Tae was staring at an inflatable sled that looked like a jet ski.

Derrick checked the price tag. "That one is $50!" he exclaimed.

Being mesmerized by its design, Tae replied in a trancelike manner, "Yeah... but it's SO cool!"

They headed back out to her car and, after everyone else took their seats, Derrick carefully fed the four sleds in. He then maneuvered through the back door and closed it behind him. It was so packed that he wasn't even able to turn around from the way he got in and rode home backward.

***

Derrick was awakened the next morning by a knock on his door.

<Knock, knock, knockity knock>

He was going to ignore it and keep sleeping, but since he knew it was Lydia, he stumbled out of bed.

"Hey, sleepy head! You look outside yet?"

"No. I was being a normal person and sleeping," he mumbled, trying to get back into his bed.

Lydia grabbed his arm and led him over to the window. She flung back the curtains and, after his eyes stopped being blinded by the light, he stood in awe. There was a blanket of white covering everything in front of him.

Jumping excitedly, Lydia exclaimed, "You were right, it snowed! It looks like a least eight inches and still falling!"

"Woo," Derrick replied unemphatically. "You know what that sight makes me want to do? Curl up under my blankets and go back to sleep."

He turned and tried again to get back into his bed. But once again, Lydia stopped him.

"Nooo. It makes you want to put your coat on and go play in it."

"Nope. No, it doesn't."

Lydia persisted. "Ah, come on. Please go out and play with me in the snow?"

"Can we at least go get some breakfast first?"

Running out of the room to grab her coat, Lydia replied, "Sure! I could use a third cup of coffee!"

Derrick yawned. "Ugh. If she wasn't so cute."

After breakfast at the cafeteria, the group trudged back to the dorms through the thick snow.

"What do you even wear to go sled riding?" Derrick asked.

"I've got my big, puffy coat and a couple of pairs of fleece-lined leggings I usually use," Lydia explained.

Richie nudged Tae. "I'd pay $100 to see you in a pair of those."

Tae blushed. "I couldn't get a pair of hers over my right leg."

Richie persisted, "It's $100, man. Find a way."

Ignoring the weird conversation Richie and Tae were having behind them, Derrick asked Lydia, "I have a pair of jeans and a coat. Will that be enough?"

"You're gonna get cold, but I guess I could always warm you up afterward," shooting him a quick wink.

"Can we just skip to that part?" he said, half-joking.

Everyone trudged to the top of the hill through the deep snow carrying their sleds.

"First, you have to make a path. Since I have the widest sled, I'll do it."

Lydia started slowly pressing the snow down with her sled into a straight path that led down to the dorm parking lot. When she was finished, she yelled up the hill for someone to try it out.

Richie threw his tube down and hopped on, shouting, "See ya later, girls!" He did his best to get moving down the path but wasn't having much luck.

Mockingly, Tae yelled, "Planning on going sometime today?"

Spinning around, Richie gave him a rude gesture as he finally started to pick up speed.

Tae put his snow ski down and waited for Richie to clear the path. Taking a running start, he jumped onto the sled. He was picking up some good speed when he lost control and flew off the path, ending up headfirst in a snowbank.

Richie and Lydia were walking back up the hill when they passed by Tae. "Hey, look! A snowstrich!" Richie said, laughing.

Lydia smacked him on the arm. "Be nice!"

Derrick put his toboggan down and climbed onto it. He tried pushing with his hands but didn't get very far before Lydia ran up behind him and gave him a shove.

Even with the help, Derrick only slowly slid down the hill. "Well, that was anticlimactic."

Getting an idea, he headed towards the classroom building with his toboggan.

Yelling from the top of the hill, Lydia asked, "Hey, where are you going?"

"I'm going to fix my sled!"

Richie looked at the other two. "Anyone else worried about that?"

Derrick scribbled some formulas on a classroom whiteboard and figured out that by combining propylene glycol with some sort of lipid, he could produce a super slick, hydrophobic substance. He hurried over to the cafeteria and persuaded them to give him some grease from their grill.

Lydia watched as he excitedly ran back towards the classrooms, carrying a coffee can. "Okay, now I'm worried," she sighed.

He mixed the propylene glycol with the grease and tested its viscosity.

"Perfect! But how do I get it to stick to the sled now?"

Looking through the cabinets in the lab, he found a spray can of lacquer.

"Hmmm, that might work."

Spraying the lacquer on the bottom of the sled, he then smeared the mixture on, letting it dry. While waiting, he calculated the speeds he could expect to achieve.

His mechanical teacher saw the light on and found him working on the equations.

"Dear sweet Ayesha, Derrick. What are you doing now?!?"

"My sled was too slow, so I'm trying something."

The teacher looked at the calculations. "Oh my. Yeah, that'll work, but good luck stopping."

Realizing that having a way to stop would be helpful, he cut up an old tarp into the shape of a parachute and affixed some strings to it and the sled.

As he headed back up the hill, he passed two legs sticking out of a snow bank.

Offering assistance, he tapped Tae on the foot. "You need help getting out, buddy?"

"Nah, I'm good. It's comfy in here," Tae replied

Seeing Derrick's sled, Richie jested as he slid by. "Should I go ahead and call 911 to get them started?"

"Haha, funny guy," Derrick sarcastically replied.

Finally reaching the top, Lydia was waiting for him with her hands on her hips.

"Derrick."

"What? I just polished it a little."

"Then why is the bottom glowing, and what did you get from the cafeteria?"

Dismissing her concerns, Derrick responded, "If it works, I'll let you try it next."

"Just don't hurt yourself."

He took a running start and jumped onto the sled. "You know me!"

Lydia replied dejectedly, "That's what I'm afraid of."

Derrick picked up speed quickly... and was still accelerating halfway down the hill.

Richie was on his way back up and watched as he flew by, screaming.

"AHHHHHHHHHHHHHHHHHHHHHHHHH!"

Seconds later, he saw Lydia go by on her disk in pursuit. "I'm on it!"

Derrick reached the bottom of the hill and continued across the parking lot without losing any of his speed. He deployed the parachute which, to his horror, fell straight to the ground and flopped behind him.

"Well, that's not good," he thought as he slid through the breezeway of the dorms.

Obadiah was on the porch, enjoying the quietness of the falling snow when he heard a noise from the breezeway that quickly got louder. He poked his head around the corner just in time for Derrick to go flying by— still screaming. The parachute finally caught a gust of air and opened with explosive speed, wrapping around Obadiah's face and knocking him to the ground.

Thoroughly secured around Obadiah, the parachute string grew taut on the sled. Since the laws of physics were still in effect, the sled stopped, but Derrick did not. He continued off the front and flew through the air for about twenty feet before touching down on the edge of the frozen lake. He rolled a few times and slid out to the center.

Running through the breezeway, Lydia passed Obadiah lying on the ground screaming, "It's eating me alive! Someone get it off!"

Seeing Derrick lying flat on his back on the lake and not moving, she went to step out onto it when she heard him yell, "OWWWWWWW!"

"I'm coming, honey!" She called out to him. "Hold on!"

Feeling the ice starting to give, Derrick warned, "No don't! It's already cracking under me!"

As it gave way, Derrick thought, "Oh crap!" as he fell into the ice-cold water.

Derrick's brain shorted out with pain. Even though the lake was freezing, it felt like he had fallen into a vat full of lava. Struggling to reach the surface, he realized something wasn't right with his left arm. After managing to get his head back above water, he tried everything he could to get onto the ice surrounding him, but it broke every time he tried.

Lydia looked for something to throw out to him as he worked his way to the edge.

He finally got close enough for Lydia to step out into the lake and grab him by his left arm, causing him to scream.

Unzipping her coat, she pulled him in as close as she could, then wrapped it back around him. Derrick, shivering heavily, suggested, "I hear... the best... way to warm... someone up is... skin to skin..."

"Don't push your luck, cowboy."

Rushing back to the dorms, they passed Richie. He had his phone out, recording Obadiah, who was still flailing about on the ground, completely entangled in the parachute.

"Are you gonna help him out?" Lydia asked as they went by.

"Nah. I actually think he's winning."

Opening Derrick's door, Lydia had him sit down while she turned on his shower.

"Any chance you need to get warm too?" he said with a grin.

Just then, Tae popped around the corner.

"No, I asked Tae to help you in the shower, while I get changed."

Derrick's shoulders slumped.

Lydia headed to her room, while Tae helped Derrick get his shirt off.

Cocking his head sideways, Tae asked, "Has it always stuck out like that?"

Derrick looked in the mirror, confused at what prompted the question. He saw a large lump protruding out from the front of his shoulder.

"Ugh... it's dislocated," he groaned

"How do we fix that? Do I need to get a hammer?"

Derrick was hoping Tae was kidding, but he couldn't tell for sure by the scared look on his face.

Stepping into the shower, Derrick instructed Tae, "Just let Lydia know that I will need a ride to the doctor."

***

She slowly traversed the snowy roads towards the urgent care.

"How is that not hurting you?"

"It did when I landed on it, but I think it's still numb from falling in the lake. I'm not complaining, though."

Derrick entered the urgent care, holding his shoulder. Walking up to the triage desk, the nurse greeted him. "Hello, what seems to be the problem today?"

"I had a minor sledding accident."

Walking up beside him, Lydia exclaimed, "Minor?!? You fell through a frozen lake after supercharging your sled!"

Derrick turned towards Lydia, and the nurse let out a gasp, seeing the bulge protruding from under his shirt.

"Oh, uh... Hold on. Let me find you a room."

The doctor helped Derrick take his shirt off and handed it to Lydia before beginning his examination.

Lydia sat, biting her finger trying to hide her growing smile as she tried to not stare at his muscles.

"Well, it's definitely out of place," determined the doctor. "Let's get an X-ray to make sure it's not broken."

Derrick was certain that the x-ray technician thought he was a pretzel with all the positions he put him in. When he was taken back to his room, Lydia could tell that he was in a lot more pain now. She wanted to hug him, but the doctor came back in before she could.

"Well, it's definitely dislocated, but there is also a hairline fracture on the head of the humerus. We are going to carefully put it back into the socket and then take some more X-rays to make sure the crack didn't get bigger. Do you need anything for pain before we start?"

Derrick was trying to act like a tough guy to impress Lydia. "No. I think I'm good."

He grabbed her hand as the doctor and nurse lifted his arm, pushing it back into place with an audible pop. They placed it in a sling and led him back to the X-ray room.

Derrick didn't show that he was in any pain, but Lydia knew better by the throbbing in her hand from being squeezed so hard. Guilt raced through her head.

"I just wanted to show him how I used to have fun as a kid, and he ended up getting hurt."

Derrick was wincing when he came back into the room.

"That tech is crazy. Doesn't he know the human body doesn't bend that way?"

Lydia hugged him as she apologized, "I'm sorry."

"You're sorry? For what?"

"It was my idea to go sledding," she explained.

"Yeah, but it was my idea to smear that mixture on the bottom of the sled. You didn't do anything but try to show me a good time. I'm the one that should be sorry. I stopped you from being able to sled anymore today."

The doctor returned and gave the test results. "Okay, so the crack didn't get any bigger, but you will still need to wear the sling for four weeks and then follow up with an orthopedist to check the progress. I'll give you a script for some pain meds. You're going to need them tonight."

***

Derrick left his door unlocked so Lydia could get in if he needed some help. At 3am, she decided to sneak over and make sure he was sleeping okay. Slowly, she opened the door and poked her head in to find him sitting up in his chair, wide awake.

"What are you doing up? I thought the doctor gave you some meds to sleep tonight?"

"No... he gave me meds to help the pain... doesn't help enough to sleep."

She pulled up a chair beside him. "Can I do anything to help?"

Derrick smiled. "You already are."

Grinning, she laid her head on his right shoulder.

Since they were both wide awake now, Lydia suggested they watch a movie. Derrick got the player ready as Lydia ran over to her room and grabbed Madeline. He moved his chair over to the end of the bed and took another pain pill to help him relax. Running back over, she hopped up onto the bed and crawled down next to him.

"What are we watching?" she asked excitedly.

"*Spy of the Eclipse: Hunt for Xerxes Eye.*"

"Oh, that's my favorite out of the series!"

She laid her head on him, and as the opening credits finished, Derrick heard snoring coming from his shoulder.

***

...The night was silent and cold. Strobe lights flashed all around. He maneuvered through the mangled vehicles that littered the road. A bystander pointed to a coat lying on the ground with legs sticking out. They were the legs of a child. He walked over and lifted the coat...

Derrick flinched hard, waking himself up. Almost immediately, he felt something impact his right temple, causing everything to go black and almost knocking him out of his chair. It took a moment for him to regain the vision in his right eye. When he finally could see again, he found Lydia sitting up in the bed with her fist balled up.

"OH HONEY! I'M SO SORRY!" Lydia adamantly apologized. She had forgotten that she was in his room and thought he was an intruder.

"OWWW! Where did you learn to do that!?!"

"It was just a reaction. Are you okay?"

Coming back into the room with an ice pack, Lydia apologized again, "Here, I got this for your eye. I'm really sorry. Are you sure you're okay?"

"I'm fine. I'm just glad it wasn't my shoulder, or I might have cried in front of you."

She smiled slightly with a touch of embarrassment as she applied the ice pack to his eye.

Derrick headed out to the common room to make some coffee, while Lydia went to her room for a quick shower before starting to cook. Today was New Year's Eve, and the dorm had a large get-together planned. After starting the coffee brewing, Derrick turned around to find Obadiah standing behind him.

"Thought the parachute prank was funny, didn't you?"

"No. How would I have even known you would stick your head around the corner?"

Pointing to Derrick's eye, Obadiah smirked. "I see Lydia has been making nice to you, too. Did you smart off to her or something?"

"I'm done, Obadiah. When you can talk civilly, come find me."

As Derrick turned to walk away, Obadiah reached out, grabbing his left shoulder and squeezing it tightly.

"Don't you ever turn your back on me, Elmo."

Through the pain, Derrick couldn't resist making a snarky comment.

"I can see why Lydia chose you, oh wait..."

Obadiah's blood boiled, and he threw a punch at Derrick's left shoulder. Not even flinching, Derrick walked back towards his room. He wouldn't let Obadiah have the satisfaction of knowing there was a white-hot pain searing through his brain. Entering his room, he shut the door, fell face-first onto his mattress, and released the scream he had been holding in.

Luckily, he had a few pain pills left and took a couple before his shower. Removing his arm from the sling, he noticed that his shoulder now had bruising around the socket that wasn't there before.

"Well, that's not a good sign," he thought.

After showering, Derrick headed back down to the common room where Lydia, Izzy, and Tae were cooking. Tae saw his eye, which was now turning a mixture of dark red and purple, along with the grimace on his face.

"Rough night, buddy?"

Lydia turned around, giving Derrick a sheepish grin.

"Something like that," he replied.

After finishing lunch, Lydia suggested they all play a game of Pictionary. Once everything was set up, they split up into teams. Lydia, Izzy, and Derrick formed one team, and Richie and Tae were the other.

Derrick was first, drawing a square with a couple of triangles and a jagged line on the other side.

Izzy excitedly yelled, "That's the electrical circuit diagram for a Caterpillar D175 generator!"

"Yes!" exclaimed Derrick. The rest sat dumbfounded.

"What the crap was the word?!?" Richie inquired.

"It was *caterpillar!*"

"Yeah, I'm out. Should have known better than to play against a bunch of nerds," he said as he got up to get some more finger foods.

Later that night, everyone was gathered around the TV to watch the ball drop.

"3... 2...1... Happy New Year!" the group yelled out.

Lydia grabbed Derrick and drew him in close for a kiss when they noticed everyone was staring at them.

"What?!? You looking for a show?" she asked, sarcastically.

Tae looked away sheepishly, "Well... kinda."

Derrick grabbed Lydia's head and planted a big, showy kiss on her lips, causing Izzy to turn away and close her eyes.

"Ewwww. That's gonna be burnt into my brain for a while."

Standing up, Richie announced, "Enough of that gooiness. I'm going to go outside and set off some fireworks. Who wants to join me?"

Derrick's eyes widened. Immediately regretting asking, Richie pointed at him.

"No! You stay here and make out with her or something. No fire for you!"

CHAPTER 15

Friday after classes, Derrick and Tae had just walked back to the dorms when Lydia and Izzy met them in the breezeway.

"Hey, Sweetie!" Lydia exclaimed as she ran up and pressed Derrick against the wall.

Izzy rolled her eyes. "I'm already regretting this."

"Regretting what?!?" Tae asked as he turned to Derrick, who was preoccupied with a long, epic kiss.

Richie, hearing the commotion in the hallway, popped his head out to see what was going on.

"Ewwww! Get a room!" he exclaimed as he quickly shut the door.

Izzy explained to Tae their plans. "Tomorrow is my birthday and I thought we could all head over to Virginia Beach to have fun for the day. Lydia was supposed to be organizing it, but I guess we will have to wait until Derrick gives her tongue back."

Derrick looked around Lydia's head in a daze. "Huh? I heard my name."

Looking rather disgusted, Izzy growled, "Well, if you two are done now... Tae and I are over here planning a day trip to the beach."

Lydia backed away from Derrick, blushing and wiping off the corner of her mouth with her hand. "Sorry about that... he just smelled really good."

Derrick quickly regained his senses. "The beach? It's January."

Lydia laughed. "No one said anything about getting in the water, silly! There are a bunch of good restaurants and arcades on the boardwalk. Besides, it's Izzy's 21st birthday, and well, you know..."

"Sure, why not?" Derrick agreed. "As long as she's not driving, I'm good."

"Ooh, Ooh! I'll drive!" Tae excitedly volunteered.

The three of them turned to Tae in unison with terrified looks on their faces.

"Ah come on! Anyone could have mistaken that for a speed bump!"

<Knock, knock, knockity knock>

Derrick opened the door to find Lydia bundled up in her puffy coat and her hair pulled up.

"Wow!" he exclaimed in amazement. "Your ponytail is really cute."

Lydia's unamused look confused him. "Where's your sling?" she snarled.

"It's right here on the bed. I took it off to get dressed," knowing full well he hadn't worn it since last evening.

Her eyes were like laser beams burning a hole through him.

"Fine. I'll put it on," he resigned.

"The doctor said 'all the time'. If you don't, that crack is going to break and then you will have to get a cast."

Derrick lightheartedly played it off. "Cool! Then I could get the girls to sign it." He quickly realized that might not have been the safest thing to say.

"I'm... dead... serious... Derrick."

Feeling like a dog that had just been scolded and was running away with its tail between its legs, Derrick apologized as he put it back on. "Okay, Okay. I'm sorry. It's just horribly uncomfortable."

Lydia leaned over and kissed his shoulder. "Thank you. I just want you back to full strength. How else are you going to catch me when I jump into your arms?" she asked grinning.

***

The group was sitting on the porch of *Chix on the Beach* enjoying the crisp air and some fruity drinks. Lydia and Derrick both ordered strawberry lemonades while Izzy and Tae were indulging in a couple of margaritas.

After finishing his third, Tae announced to the group that he was going down to the water and see if he could find a shark to punch.

"What is it with you and punching sharks?!? What happened in your life for such hatred?" Derrick joked.

Stumbling onto the boardwalk, Tae explained, "Well... they have all them teeth... and no toothbrushes... they're the devil."

Derrick rested his face into his hand debating his life choices. "I guess I'm going to go with him and make sure he doesn't drown or anything stupider."

Lydia laughed, "Okay sweetie. Have fun!"

Izzy giggled and slurred, "Yeah, sweetie!"

Annoyed, Lydia glared at Izzy. "You better not throw up in my car."

Derrick was freezing as he walked with Tae along the water line.

"You know, buddy... I don't see any sharks out here. How about we head back to the restaurant with the girls?"

"Those smug sharks... they know better than to face their ugly shows... I'll... punch them right in their... liver," Tae proudly slurred.

"Yep... they're scared of ya, buddy. Let's go back up where it's warmer."

Derrick turned to start walking back when he noticed Tae taking off his shirt.

"Dude, what are you doing?!? Put your clothes back on!"

"I wanna get in the water!"

"No, no you don't."

"Yeah, I do. The SEALs do it all the time. It's invigorating!"

"And seals get eaten by sharks..."

"Not those seals... You know... the ones with flippers."

Tae stepped out into the water and then, to Derrick's shock, dove into the frigid waves. He stood watching as Tae flopped around in the water seemingly impervious to the freezing cold water that kept washing over his head.

After a couple of minutes, Derrick yelled out to him, "Alright, come back in, buddy... you're going to get hypothermia."

To Derrick's horror, Tae walked back onto the beach with his right arm covered in jellyfish.

At first, Tae thought the goo covering his arm was funny, but that quickly changed.

"Uh... Derrick... the slime hurts," he said calmly before letting out a loud scream.

Derrick quickly led Tae back out into the water where he wiped off the tentacles that remained and then rushed him back up towards the restaurant.

"Oh, no. This is where you pee on me, isn't it?" Tae asked in fear.

"What? No! That doesn't work" as he pushed him into his chair. Derrick grabbed Izzy's margarita, which had just been delivered, and poured it onto Tae's reddening arm.

Izzy protested. "Hey! I'm legal now! Use his!"

Derrick sat pouting in Lydia's pink puffy coat. She insisted he wear it while they waited for the check since his was soaking wet. On the positive side, the frozen sling was helping with the pain and swelling of his shoulder.

"You hurt it, didn't you?" Lydia scolded.

"I left the sling on like I was told though..."

As they were getting back into the car, Tae opened his door and then giggled when he looked at Derrick. "You look cute in that coat."

Lydia grabbed Derrick, holding him back, as he tried to climb across the roof to get to Tae.

"Let me at him! No judge would convict me!"

***

The next morning, Derrick had just poured a cup of coffee in the common room when Tae stumbled around the corner.

"Oh! Hey buddy! How are you doing today?" he exclaimed loudly as he gave Tae a rather stiff slap on the back.

Tae grimaced in pain and grabbed his head.

Derrick whispered, "I'm sorry... do you have a headache this morning? Think it had something to do with the..."

Derrick switched from whispering to yelling again, "GALLON OF TEQUILA YOU DRANK YESTERDAY?!?!"

"Dude! I said I was sorry!"

"No, you told Lydia you were sorry for throwing up in her car... twice."

Tae groaned, "Uhhh... that wasn't a dream?"

Laughing, Derrick shook his head. "Nope! And neither was the whole shark wrangling fiasco... idiot."

Lydia walked around the corner carrying a bucket and a mop. "Ah! Just the person I was looking for. Let's go, Jellyman!"

CHAPTER 16

Derrick and Tae had just finished breakfast and started their walk to the driving track.

"This is going to be so much fun! I've always wanted to take someone else's car onto a track and drive like a madman," Tae announced.

"I was thinking about asking if I could bring my Mustang out here instead of their Chargers. After dealing with DC traffic, this should be a cakewalk."

"Ya might not want to do that. They are going to be PITing us as well."

Derrick's face retracted. "Uh... yeah. Let's leave the 'stang far away from here then."

As they got closer, Derrick started removing his sling. Tae looked confused.

"Aren't you supposed to be wearing that all the time? Lydia's going to be mad."

Derrick stuck his finger up to his mouth. "Shhh. Don't tell her. They won't let me drive with one on."

The first half of the day was full of boring classroom lectures and videos teaching them how to handle the vehicle in various situations.

Derrick looked over at Tae and rolled his eyes up in his head. "This is SOOOO boring! When do we get to go crack up some fenders?!?"

Tae tried to hold in his laughter.

After lunch, the instructor took the class out to the track and led them to a row of vehicles. They would have thirty minutes to drive around to get used to the course before moving on to maneuvers.

"Hey, you wanna ride together?" Tae asked.

"Dude, of course! My luck, I'd get stuck with Obadiah if we didn't."

Tae jumped into the driver's seat and fastened his belt. He turned the key to start the car, but nothing happened. He tried this a couple more times with the same result.

"Dude, I think we have a dud."

Derrick leaned over and whispered, "You have to push the clutch in to start it."

Tae jerked back, looking at him. "What's a clutch?!?"

Derrick stared at him for a second and then said, "Get out."

After the warmup, the instructors took the groups out and demonstrated what to expect if they were ever PIT'd.

Just before the instructor made contact with their fender, Derrick told Tae, "Make sure you push the clutch in! You want to keep that engine running or they have you."

As he finished his statement, a thud was felt on the rear of the car, and they started spinning clockwise. Derrick mashed the clutch in and as soon as the car stopped spinning, he jammed the gas down, shooting off in a cloud of tire smoke.

"Just like that!"

Later in the day, Tae and Derrick watched some of the other students chasing each other, practicing their pursuit and evading techniques.

Obadiah was on the track, spinning anyone he could get within range of. Derrick studied his technique carefully and nudged Tae.

"Watch Obadiah. He only PITs when they are going into the curve."

Their turn to take the track came and Derrick pulled the stock Charger out of the garage and onto the front stretch. Tae was punching Derrick on the arm and psyching him up like it was the pep rally before a big game.

"It's the Derrick and Tae show! They aren't gonna know what hit them! All they are going to see is smoke and burning rubber on the ground!"

Derrick stopped adjusting his mirror just long enough to glare at him.

"Did you take your medicine this morning?!?"

The chase car dropped in behind them, and three flashes of their headlights signaled the start of the pursuit. Derrick floored the gas pedal, leaving a streak of black rubber behind them.

The course they were on was the replica of a city about a half-mile square with multiple side streets in between the outer roads. By the time they reached the end of the north side of the track, they were doing well over 80 mph. Derrick looked back to find he had over a twelve-car length lead, catching the chaser off guard.

As they approached the turn, Tae started holding on for dear life. He let out a scream that sounded like an eight-year-old girl in a dark, werewolf-infested forest.

"I wasn't aware the human voice could hit that octave, especially from a full-grown man," Derrick thought.

He made a quick jug to the left and swung the car into a hard right turn. Derrick rode the power slide through the corner and lay back down on the gas.

At this point, the screaming had stopped. He looked over and Tae had passed out cold. Grabbing the radio, he called,

"Real life, real life, real life!"

The chase came to an instant stop. Derrick slowed his car down to a more reasonable 50 mph and drove back to the command tent.

As he was stopping, Tae regained consciousness, and another unworldly scream resonated through the car as he unbuckled his seat belt. He bolted from the vehicle and didn't even break his stride when he jumped over the low safety wall in the pits, making off down the road leading back toward their dorms.

"Someone grab a car and go bring him back, please," the instructor said, wiping his hand down his face.

Another voice spoke up from behind him. "Your stupid antics are going to get someone killed, Elmo."

Derrick didn't need to turn around to know who spoke.

"If you have a problem with the way I drive, why don't you show us how it's done then, Obadiah?"

"With pleasure," he snarled back. "Since the only thing Elmo is good at is running, I'll take the pursuit car."

Derrick walked up to him until their noses almost touched and said, "Let's dance."

Obadiah gnashed his teeth together so close to Derrick's face, that some in the class thought he had bitten his nose.

"You know the rules," the instructor announced. "You have four minutes to either evade or disable the other vehicle. PIT maneuvers are only allowed on the inside of the pursuit vehicle."

Derrick climbed into his Charger. Having watched Obadiah's moves earlier in the day, he knew his skills with the PIT, but he would only try to turn him in the corners.

The instructor grabbed his radio and announced, "Your four minutes begin in three... two... one... GO!"

Derrick once again shot off the line like a rocket. He looked up to see where Obadiah was and, to his shock, he was right on his bumper...*<thud>*...and apparently close enough to hit it. He expected Obadiah to try to spin him out in the first corner, so he thought of a new tactic.

As they approached the last inside street before the end corner, he spun the steering wheel to the right and gave the emergency brake a quick yank. The jerk was enough to lurch the car sideways, and then Derrick floored the gas.

In a move straight out of a video game, his car shot sideways and streaked down the side street. Looking in his mirror, he saw Obadiah fly past on his original trajectory. He could almost make out the profanity-laced tirade coming from his lips as he went by.

Derrick tried to use his sudden advantage to burn some time off the clock, but within seconds, Obadiah was right back on his tail.

With two minutes left now, they both rocketed towards the southwest corner. This was when Obadiah made a strike. He drove hard into the inside of the corner, catching Derrick's right rear fender. His car lurched hard to the right, but he recovered and sped away.

Obadiah tried the same maneuver twice more, with each time Derrick breaking free.

Now, with only thirty seconds left, Obadiah knew this was going to be his last shot. If he tried the same old PIT again, Derrick would steer out and scamper away, winning the bragging rights of being the best driver. He wouldn't allow that to happen... even if it meant he had to cheat.

They both drove hard into the last turn, but instead of ducking to the inside like before, Obadiah faked inside and then cut to the outside.

He clipped Derrick's left fender at the same moment he started his right turn. Derrick's vehicle broke to the left, and Obadiah then powered hard to the right, sending Derrick sliding toward the outside safety wall at full speed.

The right front of his Charger impacted the wall at 70 mph, causing the vehicle to launch into a counter-clockwise spiral through the air. After two full rotations, the driver's side door impacted the base of an oak tree causing the vehicle to shatter into pieces.

"*Real life! Real life! Real life!*" rang out on the radio. "*Dispatch, Track Command. Major MVA on Track 3. Send Fire and EMS!*"

The instructor jumped into a car and made for turn four. Skidding to a stop, he exited the vehicle and ran for the safety wall. Looking over it, he froze in horror.

The radio keyed up to a siren wailing.

"Rescue 12, en route to Track 3. Can we get number of vehicles, number of souls, and any other scene information?"

His voice breaking, the instructor responded. *"One car, one soul, and, dear God..., it's... everywhere!"*

***

Lydia and Izzy stepped out of the cafeteria and were heading back toward their dorms when they noticed several emergency vehicles on the main road. While it wasn't unusual to see an ambulance and fire truck responding somewhere, the third one caught Lydia's attention. She read the side of the massive truck as it roared by.

"Heavy Rescue? That can't be good. I wonder where they are going?"

A couple of minutes later, as they were about to step into the dorm hall, Izzy pointed at the sky. A medical helicopter flew low over the buildings and started circling. Lydia's heart sank when she saw it make its landing approach toward the area of the driving track.

***

Derrick had a searing headache and a high-pitched whining felt like a red-hot knife being stabbed into both of his ears. He tried opening his eyes, but they wouldn't respond. Matching the whine in volume was also a deep thumping whose source he could almost make out.

"I've heard that before, but whhhhhheerrr....."

The sounds started fading away and Derrick was out again.

CHAPTER 17

After what felt like only seconds, but oddly also like days, Derrick began to hear sounds around him again. The thumping was gone, but his head was still throbbing. Also, his left shoulder felt like it was strapped down, and random sharp pains shot through it.

Even through all the pain, Derrick could still make out some of his surroundings. Distant voices were muffled by a rhythmic beeping, making them hard to understand. There was also a soft, sniffling sound… almost like someone had been crying a lot.

A distinct smell lingered in the air.

"Strawberry-scented industrial cleaner?!?" he pondered. "That's not a product that will catch on."

He tried opening his eyes again, but still, they wouldn't respond.

"Where am I?!? What is going on?!? AND WHAT IS THAT INFERNAL BEEPING?!?!"

He tried moving his legs.

Nothing.

He tried moving his arms.

Nothing.

Nothing worked.

Even his brain wasn't working.

He tried to remember what happened, or where he was, or, anything for that matter. Nothing would come to him except the HORRIBLE pounding headache.

Something then touched his right hand and lifted it slightly. It was soft, warm... and trembling. A quiet voice that was much closer than the others he'd heard caused a warm wave to wash over him.

It said, "Derrick. I love you."

"I wonder who this Derrick guy is. He sure is a lucky man," he thought.

The voice continued.

"Please come back to me."

An even softer feeling touched him on his lips.

His brain raced, trying to piece together what exactly was going on. The soft hand. The soft lips. Strawberries.

"LYDIA! Hey! I'm that Derrick guy! But why is she begging me to come back? Where did I go? Why can't I open my eyes? Why can I feel things, but not move anything?"

Derrick racked his brain for any of his medical training he could still remember through the throbbing pain.

"Coma. I'm in a coma... What am I doing in a coma?!?"

***

A couple of weeks went by and Derrick was getting restless.

"I've always wondered if people in comas would get itches on their nose and they weren't able to scratch them. The answer is yes. Yes, they do."

Then he heard someone enter the room.

"Hello, Dr. Adkins," Lydia said.

"Morning, Lydia. How are you holding up?" a male voice responded.

Derrick's heart sank when he heard the pain in Lydia's reply.

"I'm okay. Just wish he would show some signs of getting better."

The doctor pulled out his stethoscope and lifted the edge of Derrick's hospital gown.

"Well, let's look and see where he is today."

Derrick could feel something cold moving around on his chest, followed by a couple of thumps on his elbows and knees.

Then the doctor checked his eyes.

"Holy crap, Doc! Could you use a brighter flashlight? I have a headache, you know! Oh wait, you probably don't. Well, could you at least scratch my nose? It's driving me crazy!"

When the doctor was finishing the checkup, he reached out and scratched Derrick's nose.

"Oh, thank the maker!.. wait..."

The doctor explained to Lydia, attempting to lighten the mood somewhat.

"I always scratch my coma patient's noses just in case they can still feel and have an itch. So, things are progressing. His brain is still very swollen, but his eyes do show some signs of internal pressure lowering. The bruises are also changing to that delicate shade of dark purple, so there's no new bleeding."

Derrick heard Lydia's worried voice again.

"Do you think he will be okay?"

"He still has a ways to go, although, after an accident like that, he's making great... " Dr. Adkins's voice faded as he paused. "Say that again."

Being thoroughly confused by the doctor's sudden reaction, Lydia asked,

"Um, say what again?"

Dr. Adkins's eyes widened and he exclaimed, "Look at the monitor! His pulse and respirations increase when you talk."

She leaned in close to Derrick and whispered in his ear, "Derrick, I love you so much."

Derrick felt that warm wave wash over him like before, and his pulse jumped.

"He can hear us, and he's responding to your interaction. You may very well be the key to his recovery."

Lydia whispered again. "I'm not going anywhere. I love you and want my Derrick back." She gave him another kiss; this time longer and more passionate.

She paused as if expecting to hear those words reciprocated. She longed to hear those words again but to her dismay... there was nothing but silence.

***

Another week passed and Derrick was getting horribly bored. He had always imagined being in a coma was like sleeping, and when you came out, it would have been like time had just passed. He tried keeping occupied by working on new ideas or theorems.

"Eureka! I just figured out P vs NP! Now if I only had a scratch pad... and a pen... and a hand that worked."

He also enjoyed it when Lydia had the TV on so he could at least imagine what was taking place on the screen. She loved watching cooking shows but they would inevitably cause Derrick to want to eat what they were making.

"I could so tear up some of them meatballs right now! Pretty much anything would be better than the crap they are putting down this NG tube though."

***

A month passed, and Derrick was showing some slight neurological improvements, but he was still deep in his coma.

Tae visited a couple of times, having been the one who rushed to the dorm and got Lydia right after the accident. His classes would only allow him to come over on the weekends, where he would bring Lydia some fresh clothes and the occasional fast food burger to break up the hospital food monotony. He also tried teaching her how to play Magic but Derrick could tell that she was more interested in the company than the game.

***

One night, Lydia was painfully lonely. After the nurses had made their rounds, she snuck over and climbed into the bed with Derrick. It had been so long since she had been able to hold him and feel his arms around her.

She knew it was against the ICU rules, but she couldn't take it anymore. Placing her head on his chest, she could hear his heart beating. Closing her eyes, she let the rhythm soothe her.

...Derrick was lying on the beach, relaxing in the sun, when suddenly he saw a huge crab start crawling towards him. He tried to swat it away, but his arms wouldn't move. Just as it was about to crawl up onto his arm...

He felt something creeping up onto the bed. It lay down beside him and put its arm around him. He then realized it wasn't something, but someone. It could only be Lydia!

Having the warmth of her body against his made him try everything he could to break out of the darkness that engulfed him, but he just couldn't wake up. Feeling her fighting back tears as she held on so tightly was the worst pain he had ever felt in his life.

"Something! Just move something to let her know you're here! ANYTHING!!!!"

Derrick screamed inside his brain.

***

Lydia jolted awake about two hours later, not realizing she had fallen asleep. She had a blanket over her now and the blinds had been pulled.

Crawling out of his bed, she snuck back over to the cot an aide had found for her a few weeks back. As soon as she was getting settled, Derrick's nurse stuck her head around the corner.

Lydia offered an apologetic smile. "I'm so sorry. I know the rules, but I just had to hold him for a bit."

The nurse grinned sympathetically. "I know, honey. I was the one who put the blanket on you and pulled the curtains. Dr. Adkins mentioned that Derrick was responding positively to your presence, so we talked while you were asleep. We agreed that it might be in his best interest if you spend some close time together... and for yours as well. A little later today, we are planning to move the lines from his right side over to his left so you can get in and out freely without the fear of pulling anything out or hurting his broken shoulder."

Lydia's smile grew so big it lit up the room.

Derrick listened in on the conversation. It wasn't like he could do anything else.

"Broken shoulder? Is that why it hurts so badly? I guess if it was a big accident, then that would make sense. Man, I hope it wasn't in my Mustang. I love that car. The fact that it smells like strawberries now makes it even more special."

***

Weeks went by with the same routine. Lydia would lie beside him throughout the night, make the bed for him in the morning, freshen up, and then turn on the Travel Channel. She talked to him as if they were embarking on a journey to all the destinations featured.

"Hey, Derrick. We are going to your favorite place today: the Maldives. You wouldn't believe how crystal clear the water is! We have a cute little bungalow that sits out over the water..."

Derrick especially enjoyed the Maldives episode. Since their trip to Iowa, he had dreamed of seeing her swimming with all the beautiful fish in those waters. He also imagined her standing on a pier that extended out into the bay as the sun set around her. The water reflected the beautiful colors of the sky as the wind gently blew her white sundress that he loved so much.

"If I make it out of this, I think I know the perfect place to take her for our honeymoon..."

***

The next morning, as the sun was rising, its rays gently peeped in through the window blinds. The light kissed Lydia's eyelids, causing them to flutter before she opened them.

There was Derrick, right beside her, looking like he was sleeping peacefully except for the two black eyes and the bandages on his head.

Carefully getting up, Lydia folded her blanket neatly at the bottom of his bed while still holding onto Madeline. She loved that dolphin and slept with it every night.

Walking over to the window, she opened the blinds to invite more sunlight in. Derrick liked the sun. They both did. She dreamed of the day that they could go back together to the beach.

Leaning onto the bed, she whispered in his ear, like she did every morning.

"Derrick, I love you."

But this time, Derrick mumbled a response.

Stunned, Lydia took a step back.

"I heard that, right? I didn't make that up. He tried to say something," she thought

Leaning back in, she spoke normally, her voice having a glimmer of hope in it.

"I love you, Derrick."

He replied clearly this time, "I love you too."

Lydia let out a squeal of joy so loud that the nurses heard it at their station and came running.

When they entered, Lydia was lying on the bed, squeezing him, crying uncontrollable tears of joy.

"Where am I? What happened?" Derrick inquired, but she was too excited to answer. She kissed him, which left his face covered in her tears, and went back to hugging him.

Dr. Adkins was making rounds when he received a page from the nurses and hurried to Derrick's room.

"Well, I was coming to check on you, but it seems like you have better company. How do you feel?"

"My head hurts and I've never been more confused in my life, but if all I have is her, I've never been better," he replied.

"Well, you are at Richmond General after having an accident at work. You've been in a coma for the past two months, but don't worry about that right now. I'm going to finish up with the other patient, and then when I come back, we can go over everything."

"Thank you, doc," Derrick said, "oh... and thanks for scratching my nose."

***

Over the next few weeks, Derrick's recovery continued, and with the help of physical therapy, he could now move around with little difficulty. After one of his sessions, Dr. Adkins came in and gave Derrick a thorough physical.

"Looks like our most beloved couple is finally getting to go home tomorrow. First, though, the nurses have requested that I make you take one last walk around the floor to say goodbye to everyone. I will see you tomorrow morning for the discharge."

As soon as the doctor left, his nurse entered with a big smile.

"Alright, time for your walk."

"Okay, but only if Lydia comes with."

"As if you think I would leave your side around any one of those nurses," Lydia smirked at him.

The nurse's grin grew, and she gave Derrick a quick wink.

"See, I'm watching you!" Lydia joked as she pointed to the nurse.

***

As Derrick was wheeled through the front doors of the hospital, Lydia pulled up in her Beetle.

"If it's not bad enough that I have to go back to school all beat up and face Obadiah again, I have to do it in a Beetle?!?" Derrick joked.

"Keep it up, smart aleck. You know the ER is right there… you don't have far to go back… anyway, you don't have to worry about Obadiah."

"You killed him, didn't you?"

"No. I didn't get the chance. He was 'dismissed' from school after the incident. I hear he even left the Company and works for a contractor now doing overseas security."

Back at the dorms, Lydia helped him out of the car and then up to his room. After opening his door, she led him over to his bed.

"Oh, sweet cloud from Heaven! I never dreamed I would have missed this lumpy mattress."

"You should probably try to get a nap before dinner time. Is there anything I can get before you drift off to la-la land?" Lydia asked.

"I'm sure gonna miss you snuggled up against me all night. I never felt more at peace."

Lydia was very confused.

"How did you know I snuggled with you in the bed? I only did it when you were in the coma."

"I could hear and feel everything going on. I heard you whispering in my ear, telling me you loved me. I felt the kisses on my lips. I could hear you crying as you hugged me, telling me to come back to you. I knew you never left my side. I heard you and Tae talking about how you went on leave from the school and now wouldn't be graduating with your class. I heard it all. I tried so hard to reply. I wanted you to hear 'I love you' again so much. My heart broke every time nothing would come out."

Lydia started crying.

"I couldn't leave. I had nowhere else to be. I didn't care about school, work, or anything... anything but you."

CHAPTER 18

Lydia had just completed her networking final and went downstairs to the lab to find Derrick.

"Hey! How did it go?" he asked.

She stared back at him with an unamused glare.

"Oh... that good, huh?"

"I need a break from this place. Do you want to go do something this weekend?"

Derrick's eyes widened with excitement.

"Oh, that can't be good," she thought.

He got up and ran over to her, banging his arm on the table.

"Ow ow ow ow!" Derrick cried.

Lydia, reaching out to his good arm, "Honey! Are you okay?"

"Yeah, don't worry about that. I have an idea. Go back to your room and start packing. I will arrange everything."

"Derrick, I wanted less stress. What do you mean, '*start packing*'?"

He excitedly put his hand on her shoulder and explained.

"Go grab what you need for a weekend getaway and pack a bathing suit."

Lydia folded her arms and glared at him.

Derrick sighed. "How does a weekend in Virginia Beach sound?"

Her frown perked right up. "I'll be right back!" and she ran out of the room.

He finished up what he was working on and started towards the dorms. Lydia met him halfway there with her suitcase and Madeline in hand.

"I'm ready! Let's go! I'm driving!"

"Give me a second. I have to grab my stuff. I will meet you in the car."

"Hurry up, Grandpa!" she yelled as she scampered towards the parking lot.

He was finishing up packing when he began to hear honking coming from outside.

Shaking his head in disbelief, Derrick thought, "Wow! She's impatient."

Derrick was walking down the hallway when he ran into Tae.

"Dude... Lydia is in her car freaking out. What's going on?"

"I'm taking her to Virginia Beach for the weekend. I guess she's excited," Derrick explained.

Nodding his head, Tae gave him a sly.

"Not like that. Just a fun getaway... in separate rooms."

Tae started smiling, "Right... so that's the story we're going with?"

Derrick got into her car, and she started backing out before he could even close the door.

"Excited much?"

"I want to get there to get some sun time in before we have to make the trip back tonight."

"Weekend trip... we aren't coming back until Sunday."

She smiled at him all innocent-like. "A hotel room?!? Why Mr. Anderson! I'm not that kind of girl!"

He looked at her rather suspiciously. "Yes, you are!"

After receiving a firm smack on the leg, he clarified, "I booked TWO rooms for the weekend. One for me... one for you... and neither the twain shall meet."

Lydia did a facepalm in disbelief. "I think you forgot your handkerchief."

When they arrived in Virginia Beach, Derrick guided her onto Atlantic Avenue, leaving Lydia a bit perplexed

"Are we heading straight for the beach? I figured we'd drop our bags at the hotel and change into our swimsuits," she inquired.

Derrick clarified, "We ARE going to the hotel. Take the next left."

"Left into what?!?" Lydia asked in confusion.

"The hotel. The *Fairfield Inn*... you know... right there!"

As she stared up at the eight-story building, her mouth hung open. "But that's on the beach... like ON the beach!"

Derrick, still unsure about her astonishment, replied, "Yeah... and?"

"You got two rooms for the weekend... THERE?"

"Yeaaaaah. Is there a problem?"

Lydia unintentionally put her foot into her mouth as she pulled into the parking garage. "You don't have that kind of money... I mean... it's so expensive."

He glared at her and said bluntly, "I used points."

They walked into the lobby, and Derrick made his way to the counter. Lydia dropped her bag and ran to the back glass wall, exclaiming, "IT'S SO BEAUTIFUL!!!!"

His face blushed a little as he said, "I have reservations under the name Anderson," and slid his ID across the counter.

The front desk agent nodded, "Ah yes, we have two rooms beside each other for you as requested. I'm assuming the other one is for that lovely lady?" as he gestured towards Lydia, who was still gazing at the view outside.

Derrick rubbed his forehead. "Yeah... she's with me."

The agent chuckled and slid the keys to Derrick. "Enjoy your stay, sir. I think she already is."

Having settled into their rooms, they decided to take a stroll on the boardwalk. Lydia heard live music coming from the *Oceans 14* restaurant, so they stopped for dinner.

Being shown to their table, Lydia thanked Derrick. "This place is just what I needed to de-stress after these last few weeks."

Derrick noticed an arcade as they were leaving the restaurant and asked, "You up for a little skee-ball competition?"

Lydia's face lit up. "Oh, you're SO going down!"

After a couple of "friendly" rounds, he found out she could probably have gone pro on the skee-ball league... if they had such a thing.

***

The next morning before sunrise, Derrick knocked on Lydia's hotel door. After a couple of tries, she finally answered. "Come with me," he whispered.

Grabbing her room key, she followed him down the hallway to the elevator. He led her to the beach, where two towels were waiting.

"Have you ever seen the sunrise?" he asked.

About twenty minutes later, the sun started to creep above the horizon and Derrick heard Lydia gasp. She didn't move her gaze as the sun crested and rose above the outstretched ocean that was turning multiple shades of pink and blue. She carefully pushed him onto his back and ensuring she didn't hurt his arm, she planted a kiss on him that put the one at Christmas to shame. While he recovered, she lay on his chest and watched the waves caressing the shoreline.

Derrick put his good arm around her, admiring how, even at six in the morning, she still smelled like strawberries. They sat long past his legs going numb, not wanting the moment to end. Eventually, a seagull decided his toes looked like some form of food and started to peck at his left foot. Since he had lost the ability to move them about forty-five minutes ago, he was at the mercy of the now-laughing Lydia to shoo it away, which she did... eventually.

Derrick stood up, trying to gain feeling back in his legs and feet. He suggested that they grab some breakfast and then come back out for some sun time.

Derrick was in his room getting dressed when he paused for a second.

"I've never seen her in a bathing suit."

Having no idea what to expect, he went to her room and knocked again. Answering, she wore a neon pink and black tankini with her hair pulled back by her sunglasses. All he could do was stare.

As she strolled by, she remarked, "You know, you would have seen a lot more than this already if you weren't such a boy scout!"

Derrick watched from shore as Lydia played in the water. He wished he could join her, but with his arm still in a cast, he couldn't.

As Lydia bounced around in the water, she turned back towards land and waved at him. Unaware of the large wave forming behind her, Derrick frantically pointed towards the ocean, but she didn't understand in time.

When she finally turned around, the wave had already begun to crest at head level. It took her underwater backward and washed her towards the shore.

Derrick rushed toward the waterline when she finally stood up, clumsily waddling to shore with a large clump of seaweed in her hair, which hung down into her face.

"Are you okay... uh... Swamp thing?"

"Haha, very funny guy. Can you help me get this thing off my head?"

Derrick carefully removed the wads of wet grass from her hair and body.

"There, pretty much clean. Now... you okay?"

"Yeah, except I have half the beach in my shorts still."

His smile grew. "You need help cleaning that out too?"

Being irritated at his sudden playfulness, "Oh, now the boy scout wants to be naughty... well... no. You don't get to play until there's a ring on my finger."

After spending most of the day enjoying the sun, they decided to head back in and get ready for dinner. Derrick looked over at her as she was opening her door.

"It still amazes me how you could be covered in sand and seaweed and still look that beautiful."

She smiled at him. "Swampy is going to go get a shower now... oh... and... thank you."

They found a cozy local pizza shop across the street from the hotel. While they were waiting for their dinner to be prepared, Lydia noticed Derrick looked a little red.

"You got a little sun today," she said, pointing at his forehead.

"Yeah, I noticed that too when the shower started. I think I forgot sunscreen this morning."

She gasped. "Derrick!"

"I know. I know. I usually remember, but the thought of you in a bathing suit distracted me."

She looked at him pitifully. "What am I going to do with you?"

As they were leaving the pizza shop, Lydia spotted an ice cream parlor a few stores down.

"Ice cream? Don't mind if I do!" she said, grabbing his hand and heading that way.

They got their cones and strolled over to the boardwalk. Derrick took a lick from his and ended up with ice cream on his nose. Lydia laughed as he failed to lift his left arm high enough to wipe it off.

"Let me get it."

Leaning over, she kissed it off his nose. They resumed walking, and Derrick lifted his cone again, purposefully sticking his nose into the ice cream this time.

"Uh, honey... a little help?" he said, smiling.

Lydia admired the colors of the sunset reflecting off the ocean.

"This place is so beautiful. Thank you for bringing me here. This was exactly what I needed. A short getaway with the greatest guy in the world."

Derrick looked at her in surprise. "What?!? You met someone else?!?"

After laughing sarcastically, she noticed he was squirming a bit on the ride up in the elevator.

"Something wrong?"

"Yeah, my back is starting to sting. Would you be willing to put some aloe on it for me?"

Lydia gave him her mischievous grin. "You'd have to take your shirt off..."

Back in the room, as Lydia was helping him out of his shirt, she suddenly let out a gasp.

"Derrick! That has to HURT!"

Looking in the mirror, he found *most* of his body was a very bright red. "Ugh," he thought.

When she undid and removed his sling, she couldn't help but laugh. Contrasting his bright red torso was a pasty white line where the strap had been. She started fighting back the chuckles.

"I'm not laughing... really..."

"Can you just put the aloe on, Swampy?"

"OH! For that..." She flicked him lightly on his neck.

"Oooooow! Okay! Okay! I'm sorry... Sweetie... not Swampy."

Derrick sat on the balcony listening to the waves crashing onto the shore and watching the lightning from a distant thunderstorm. His infernally burnt back wouldn't allow him to lie down to get some sleep. Reminiscing over the last two days, he couldn't help but think... "This really was a good trip."

***

On Friday morning, back at the school, Derrick stood outside the auditorium, looking through the doors, thinking about how he and Lydia should be graduating as well.

A voice from behind him said, "I don't regret it. Not one minute."

Lydia had managed to walk up without him knowing.

"Your life shouldn't have been put on hold because of me," Derrick mourned.

She stepped in front of him and got up on her tiptoes to look him directly in his eyes.

"Derrick, when will you realize I didn't put my life on hold? You ARE my life."

The ceremony was rather short for a graduation. They gave a quick introduction and then had the graduates walk across the stage and officially receive their posts. Tae was going to Botswana, Izzie to Sydney, and Richie would be doing TDYs to the "less than desirable" places.

Derrick met up with Tae afterward.

"Congrats, man! Have they told you when you head out yet?"

"Yeah, I leave Tuesday morning."

"Three days?!?"

"Yep! They said they were hard up and needed me right away."

Derrick patted him on the back. "We need to go out and celebrate before then."

Tae's eyes lit up. "Applebee's tonight?"

Derrick laughed. "Of course."

Catching Richie in the hallway back at the dorms, Derrick stopped him.

"Hey! I have something for you."

Reaching into his bag, he pulled out the IR emitter. He had figured out how to power it off a battery pack the same size as the phone.

"Oh wow! You got it working?" A scared expression crossed Richie's face, and he took a step backward. "It's not going to... like... blow up or anything, is it?"

Derrick laughed. "No! It's very stable. I just hope you never have to use it."

Richie reached out and took the gift. "Dude. Thank you so much! I appreciate it."

CHAPTER 19

The lady behind the counter greeted them with a large smile.

"Welcome to the Fairfield Inn, checking in?"

"Yes, ma'am. The name is Anderson. Derrick Anderson. There should be reservations for two rooms."

"Thank you and good evening, Mr. Anderson. I see your reservation right here. Oh, wait. It only shows one room. Did you say there should be two?"

"Um… Yes, ma'am. I reserved two on my app a couple of days ago."

"Hmmm… Let me grab my manager. Just one second, please."

Lydia leaned over and said, "This could be an interesting weekend."

Derrick, not exactly sure what she meant by that, just nodded.

The lady came back with an older gentleman whom Derrick presumed to be the manager.

"Good evening, Mr. Anderson. I'm sorry for the confusion. Do you have the reservation numbers with you? We can try looking up the second room with those."

Derrick pulled out his phone and showed him the app with the two numbers. The manager tried looking up the other one, but the computer returned nothing.

"Unfortunately, I'm not showing that the second reservation reached us, and even more unfortunate, we are completely full tonight. I presume the second room was for this lovely lady?"

Lydia blushed a little.

"Yes sir. I know it's old-fashioned, but since we are only dating, we didn't want to share a bed yet," Derrick explained.

The manager nodded his head. "I understand. I see you stay here frequently with us and I know this is an inconvenience for you. Let me offer this. Of course, we will completely refund the second room since we don't have that one. How about I comp the first room as well for both nights? I believe it was a double full room, correct? I don't want to disrupt your weekend any further, so I will throw in free dinners at our restaurant for tonight and tomorrow as well. Will that work?"

Derrick wasn't sure what to do. He looked over at Lydia, who had a grin on her face.

"That could work. I know you aren't the type of guy to pull any funny business... unless it's not you that you're worried about," she said with a sly grin.

"Okay, I think we can make that work. Thank you for your generosity," Derrick replied as the lady slid him the key cards.

They headed towards the elevator and pressed the button for the fifth floor. On the ride up, Lydia could tell Derrick was a little tense.

"Honey, you know us. We already live across the hall from each other. If we were going to do something, we would have done it by now. I respect you. You respect me. We'll be fine. Let's just enjoy the weekend at the beach... Just don't mention it to my dad."

Derrick's face changed from tense to terrified.

As they walked up to the room, he slowly swiped the key to unlock the door. He always wanted to be the first through the doors into unknown rooms. Call it chivalry. Call it training. Either way, Lydia found it cute. Derrick flipped the light on, walked in, and froze.

She came up behind him. "What's wrong?"

The manager was mistaken about the room. It was not a double full, but a single king room.

"Uh... Ummm. This isn't going to work," he stammered.

Lydia reassured him, "We'll find a way. There isn't another room available in the city for tonight, and look at this view!"

She stepped out onto the balcony, admiring the ocean down below them with the moon reflecting off the water.

"I guess I can always go sleep in my car. I've done it many times before when I arrived early for a shift."

"Don't be silly. It's fine." Lydia was trying to be positive but had some apprehension herself. She was only half kidding when she said Derrick should be worried about her.

Derrick paced around the room trying to find a solution. "I have an idea. The chairs on the balcony fold out to loungers. I've slept on many chairs worse than that in my day. I can curl up on the balcony and fall asleep to the sounds of the ocean and nature."

Lydia tried to think of a better option. "No, we will make it work. There's no need for you not to get sleep."

He walked over to her, took her hands, and explained purposely, "Sweetie, this will make me comfortable enough to spend the night here with you. Please let me."

Lydia cracked an adorable, but grateful smile. "Okay. Thank you. I love you, Honey."

Derrick did his best Han Solo impression, "I know."

***

Back in the room after dinner, Derrick pulled out a few pillows and the spare blanket from the closet and headed toward the balcony. As he drew the blinds, she grabbed his hand.

"The waiting will all be worth it."

"I know," Derrick replied.

"No, uh, that actually was a question. You were supposed to talk me out of it," she said sheepishly.

"Good night Lydia," he said leaning in to kiss her on the forehead. Lydia grabbed his face and exclaimed, "Don't go cheap on me now, cowboy!" before planting one right on his lips.

Derrick settled onto the balcony, finding the cool night surprisingly comfortable. The sound of the waves crashing on the beach made him quickly drowsy.

As he began to drift off, he heard a commotion come from inside. While he couldn't see directly into the room, he found he could see a reflection in the door's glass. He could just make out Lydia struggling to get out of her shirt. He giggled inside. She sure was a brilliant lady but had horrible trouble with clothing. Derrick continued to watch as she flailed around for a moment, finally freeing herself from the shirt. Before her hair fell back down, he caught a glimpse of her bare back.

Derrick thought, "Wow!" but quickly looked away. He felt guilty for looking, but couldn't stop thinking about what the future might have in store.

He whispered to himself, "You were right. This truly will be an interesting weekend."

***

Derrick was awakened by a ray of sunlight shining directly into his left eye.

"Well, that's annoying," he grumbled.

Figuring Lydia was still asleep, he tried to figure out how he could sneak into the bathroom without waking her. To his surprise, when he opened his eyes, he found her standing on the balcony soaking in the sunrise.

"Mornin' Cowboy!" she greeted.

***

As they strolled down Atlantic Avenue toward the pirate mini-golf, Lydia playfully teased Derrick.

"We could always go back to the arcade and play some skee-ball again. Don't you want to defend your honor?"

Derrick shot her a glare. "What honor?!? I left that place with my tail between my legs! At least with mini-golf, I stand half a chance."

"We'll see," she laughed.

Derrick was leading by two points at the twelfth hole. He was lining up the shot when Lydia walked up beside him and blew into his ear. He over swung the club and the ball went flying off the back of the course.

"Jezebel!" he yelled.

"I believe that's an extra stroke," Lydia calmly remarked.

"Nuh-uh! You cheated!"

Trying to look innocent, she replied, "I did not! I saw a bee on your ear and tried to get rid of it."

On their way back from the game, Derrick was staring off to the west with a concerned expression on his face.

"What's that look for?" Lydia inquired.

He pointed to a small area of wispy clouds. "See that area of convection?"

She squinted. "No."

"It's going to rain tonight... a lot."

Derrick grabbed his pillows and blanket, preparing to turn in for the night. When he opened the door to the balcony, the sky outside lit up, followed by a loud boom.

"Sweet!" he exclaimed. Excitement grew on his face as the rain started to pour down.

From under the blankets, Lydia protested. "Honey, you can't sleep out there!"

He looked at the bump in the bed. "Why not? That looks like fun!"

Lydia poked her face out, glaring at him as the wind picked up, driving the rain onto the balcony.

"How about now, Aquaman?"

"No big deal, it will let up soon."

An hour and a half later, Derrick sat gazing out the window. The thunder and lightning had subsided, but the rain was still falling in torrents.

"Anyyyy minute now..."

Lydia got up from the bed, walked over to him, and lightly smacked him on the head.

"Listen up there, SpongeBob. It's not going to let up anytime soon. It's 1 am, and I want to go to bed. You're sleeping in here tonight. Get over it."

Returning to the bed, she made room for him beside her and forcefully pointed at it.

"Sweetie... I'm not sleeping in the same bed as you. It's not that bad out there."

"Not that bad out there?!? Derrick... the hurricane center just named it. Besides, we already have slept in the same bed before... Back at the hospital."

"That didn't count! I was unconscious."

Glaring at him, Lydia growled, "You're about to be unconscious again..."

Staring at the bed, he fought conflicting desires. On the one hand, the idea of sleeping with her warm body against his was appealing... but he also knew that wasn't how he was raised.

"I just can't do it. It's against my conscience."

Lydia empathically stated, "I'm not going to let you sleep out in that storm, either."

After thinking for a minute, he suggested, "How about I curl up here in this chair?"

Lydia was tired of fighting it. "Sleep in the bathtub for all I care. Just be quiet about it and turn out the light!"

***

On the way home, they discussed their future plans.

"I know we have a bit of time, but have you thought about what we are going to do for housing after graduation?" he asked.

Lydia pondered for a moment. "I had always assumed I would just get an apartment somewhere in the DC area. Did you have other ideas?"

"Well, from what I've heard, anything in that area is pretty pricey. What do you think about getting one to share?"

Lydia's eyes widened, and a smile spread across her face. "Mr. Do Good Boy Scout wants to share a room now?!?"

"No. A two-bedroom apartment. That way, we will each have our own room and share a common living room. It's essentially what we have now at the dorms. Doesn't that sound like a great idea?"

Lydia slumped back into her seat and pouted. "NOOOO!"

CHAPTER 20

Having just returned from Richmond after picking up her present, Derrick knocked on Lydia's door, his stomach tied in knots.

Lydia smiled when she opened it. "Oh! Hello you,"

Derrick found it difficult to talk with his mouth being so dry. "So... your birthday happens to be next Friday...."

"Wait, it is? Who knew?" she said jokingly.

He grinned a little, his stomach still in his throat. "I just happen to have two tickets to the Skilett concert that Friday night. Front row. Would you like to go with me?"

Her mouth dropped open. "Skilett!!! Live?!?! Of course, I would! I love you!!!!"

He almost hated to mention the next part. "The concert starts at 7pm... In Bonaire."

Derrick could tell Lydia hadn't fully processed the conversation yet.

"Bonaire?.. I've never heard of that town. Is it very far away?" she asked.

"It's not too bad. It's only about eighteen hundred miles south of here."

Her eyes widened. "Come again?"

"Yeah, it's in the Leeward Islands."

Lydia still was very confused.

"It's one of Carnival's 'Live' concert cruises. We leave Sunday out of Cape Canaveral. Me... you... seven days cruising the Caribbean. You in?"

She finally understood and screamed, "YESSSSS!!!"

***

After an early morning flight to Orlando, Derrick and Lydia boarded a Carnival shuttle bus headed for the Cape.

"I can't believe we're almost there! What do you want to do first?!?" she said excitedly, looking at the humongous ship outside her window.

"Well, after we drop off our bags in the room, maybe we could go find a secluded little spot to ourselves while we pull out of port."

It was obvious she didn't hear a word he said.

"Me too! I hear they have quite a sail away party!"

"Or there's that," he muttered under his breath.

Derrick was regretting suggesting they take the stairs up to their room on the eleventh deck. Finally reaching the room, he dropped his bag on the counter and plopped down onto his bed by the window.

"Ah! Maybe we should take a quick nap before we set sail," he said as he curled up with a pillow.

Lydia, having none of it, grabbed his foot and started to pull. "Get up, lazybones! It's party time!"

Stepping out onto the pool deck, they realized the celebration had just started. Lydia jumped into the dance line and started the *Cha Cha Slide*. Derrick grabbed a cola from the bar and found a lounge chair to sit and watch her having fun. To his horror, she started waving for him to come join. He shook his head and took a sip of soda.

Running over, she grabbed his arm and exclaimed, "Come on! Have some fun! Let's celebrate you getting out of your cast."

"Lydia, I dance like I sing. I have no coordination, you know that!"

"At least try!" she said as she continued to drag him onto the deck.

Derrick did his best to follow the moves, but he was always a second or two late with each one, causing some minor collisions. He had almost finished the song when he stepped on the foot of his neighbor, causing him to roll his ankle. He fell, taking out three other people.

Lydia rushed over to his side. "Derrick! Are you okay?"

He lay on the deck looking up at the sky. "Did I have enough fun to be able to go back to my soda now?"

Derrick sat with Lydia at the back of the ship, watching the sun and the coast both disappearing over the horizon.

"That never gets old, does it?" he asked. "You ever notice how much we take the sun for granted? We only truly appreciate it when it's either going down or coming back up."

***

Derrick stood on the balcony mesmerized by the sunrise. Lydia joined him with her cup of coffee after finishing a run on the track.

"There is nothing like being on the water. No traffic. No horns honking. No cell phones. Just the sound of the waves and the ocean's vastness all around," he admired.

After breakfast, they headed out onto the upper deck. Lydia had spotted a ride she wanted to try while out on her morning run.

"They have a roller coaster that takes you out over the water sideways! Sound like fun?"

Derrick watched in horror. "Looks like an OSHA violation to me."

She grabbed his arm and pulled him towards the line. "Stop being such a coward!"

Lydia went first and screamed with enjoyment the entire way. Derrick contemplated not doing it, but before he knew it, he was buckled in and the car was about to launch.

"What am I doing?!?" he thought as he sped out of the station and onto the track.

He kept telling himself, "It's almost over... it's almost over..." when he felt a grinding sensation come from underneath the car. It slowed quickly and came to a stop... while hanging off the side of the ship. He looked down all one hundred eighty-seven feet to the water and closed his eyes tight. "And so is the passing of Derrick Anderson."

One of the operators shouted out to him, "Just stay in your car. We will get you off shortly."

Derrick yelled back, "WHERE DO YOU THINK I'M GOING TO GO?!?"

Fifteen minutes later, the car jerked a little and then started slowly crawling back towards the ship and to the station.

Not knowing exactly what to say, the operator apologized. "I'm sorry, sir. We here at Carnival hope you have an exciting rest of the day!"

Derrick looked at the guy and replied sarcastically. "You hung me off the side of the boat on a broken ride. I can't wait to see what *Carnival* has planned for me next!"

He walked down the exit ramp to find Lydia waiting for him holding a bowl full of frozen yogurt.

"You went and got ice cream?!?"

"Well, you were up there goofing off and I was hungry. Can you believe they have strawberry here?!?"

After Lydia finished her frozen delight, she could tell Derrick was still a little on edge. "Honey, I have just the thing to help you relax."

Derrick could only see the bottom part of the window while he lay face down on the massage table, but it was enough to watch the water calmly going by. Lydia was right. The hour-long massage was just what he needed after his stressful morning.

Afterward, they headed out onto the Serenity deck to bask in the sun for a bit. He was thankful it was right outside the spa because his legs were still jelly from the massage. He sat down on one of the padded lounge chairs and was out within seconds.

Back in the room, Derrick had crawled into bed among his pile of pillows and was adjusting them just right into the proper sleeping position when he heard a series of loud bangs come from the bathroom. Lydia stepped out in a tizzy.

"How can anyone change in that tiny closet?!?"

Derrick smiled a little. "You can always change out here."

Lydia's mouth dropped open in disbelief. "Why I never!"

Her response made Derrick laugh. "I'll pull the blanket over my head so I can't see."

Making sure he couldn't see her anymore, he gave her the go-ahead. He heard another round of commotion and a couple of thuds coming from the wall.

"You okay out there?" he asked.

"Oh, hush you!"

Something then hit his bed and he heard, "Ow! Ow! Bedframe!"

Finally, she said, "Alright, I'm done."

Pulling the blankets back down, he started to chuckle. "Um... you know your shirt is inside-out, right?"

While getting onto her bed, she replied, "I don't care anymore."

***

After spending the day on the beach in Bonaire, Lydia went back to the room while Derrick headed up to the burger joint to grab them some lunch.

On his way back, he was riding down the elevator with their burgers and bottles of water when it stopped on the fourteenth floor. The doors opened, and he was shocked to see Ron Kooper, the lead singer for Skilett, getting into the car with him.

"Hello, mind if I ride with you?"

"Not at all, Mr. Kooper," Derrick replied.

The doors closed, and the elevator descended a few feet before it jerked to a stop with a bang.

After calling for help on the elevator phone, Ron hung up and turned to Derrick. "Looks like we might be in here for a bit."

After a couple of minutes of silence, Derrick finally initiated the conversation.

"My girlfriend and I love your music. It's her birthday today. I brought her on the cruise to see the concert as a present... and then I planned on proposing to her afterward."

Ron gave him a grateful smile. "Well, it's nice to meet people who appreciate the songs. So, you're going to propose to her tonight? Want to do it DURING the concert?"

Derrick's mouth dropped. "That would be AMAZING! How could I ever repay you?!?"

"Well, if we're in here much longer, I might be asking for one of those burgers. They smell great!"

They sat down and started planning out the details as they ate their hamburger lunches.

After about thirty minutes of being trapped in the elevator, Derrick started sniffing.

"Do you smell that?"

"Yeah. It smells... electrical," Ron replied.

Derrick contemplated how it was likely the brakes beginning to fail. Looking up, he saw the maintenance hatch on the roof of the car and thought, "If I jumped off this wall, I think I can reach it."

He envisioned the whole scenario in his head. He'd sprint towards the wall, leap off it about midway up, and that would spring him high enough to pop open the hatch. Grabbing the top of the car, he would pull himself up onto the roof. Then, reaching back in, he'd assist Ron up. Together, they would both pry open the door with their hands, leaping to safety as the brakes failed, and watch the car crash down 14 floors.

Not having shared his plan, Ron watched as Derrick ran across the car, jumped off the wall, and landed flat on his face, missing the hatch by a good two feet.

"OWWW! Well, that didn't go as planned," Derrick said, regretting his decision.

Ron reached down and helped him back onto his feet as the maintenance crew opened the doors of the car.

"Lydia is a saint, isn't she?" Ron asked while trying not to chuckle.

Derrick sighed. "Yeahhhh."

Derrick took the stairs the rest of the way to their stateroom. Upon entering, Lydia asked, "Where have you been?!? Did you get lost?" She then noticed he had nothing in his hands. "Wait... where's my burger?!?"

"You would not believe what just happened!" he said as he began to tell her about his adventure.

"You gave Ron my burger?"

"Yeah! Isn't that cool?"

"NO! I'm hungry!"

"Oh! I'm sorry dear. Wait right here. I'll go grab another."

She popped up off the bed. "I'll go with you this time... just in case we meet Ron again!"

***

Derrick and Lydia stood in line, waiting for the doors to open to the auditorium on the ship. Lydia couldn't contain herself and was jumping up and down with excitement.

"Derrick!!! I can't believe it! Skilett!!! Best birthday present ever!"

He pulled out his phone to record her excitement... more of a distraction to himself than anything. "If she only knew what was going to happen in about an hour..."

After performing their hit *Overdose*, Ron took a break to talk with the crowd. From the front row, Lydia yelled out, "You owe me a burger!!!"

He looked down and spotted Derrick standing by a lady clearly enjoying herself.

Ron smiled and then announced, "There is a special young lady in the crowd tonight celebrating her birthday, and since I owe her for the burger she shared with me, how about we bring her up on stage and sing her favorite song?"

Ron walked over, helped Lydia up onto the stage, and led her over to the chairs arranged in front of the instruments. He showed her to the middle seat and the other band members took their places beside her. The dazzling flashing lights and strobes dimmed, leaving only the spotlights on the five of them.

As Ron began an acoustic rendition of *Searching for Comets*, a stagehand guided Derrick up a set of stairs on the side of the stage, out of sight.

They reached the bridge of the song, and Lydia soaked in the lyrics. This was her favorite part, and she had hoped to see Derrick when they sang it, but the spotlight made it almost impossible to see anything.

As soon as Ron finished the last note of the bridge, the music dropped out, and the band's spotlights dimmed until only Lydia's remained. She started looking around, confused when a familiar voice came over the speakers and Derrick walked out.

"I was once a storm-tossed soul lost on a dark, vast sea until you came into my life and became my Polaris. My North Star. My *comet*. I don't dare close my eyes because even a second not gazing into your beautiful soul is a second lost to all eternity. I need you as my guiding star through the trials of life. Lydia Annabelle Evans... will you marry me?"

The entire hall gasped and then fell into a hushed silence. Lydia slowly rose from her seat and said, "What took you so long?"

The hall erupted in applause as the stage lights flickered back on, revealing the band had returned to their instruments. Ron re-started the song from the beginning as Derrick slid the ring onto Lydia's finger.

The two of them danced as the song played on. When the bridge came back around, Lydia's heart melted as Derrick serenaded her with the lyrics in his charmingly tone-deaf way.

The rest of the concert was a blur. Afterward, they went for a walk on the deck and stopped at the back. She pushed him up against the railing and kissed him.

"Thank you for the best night I have ever had."

"It was a really good concert," he replied.

She glanced down at her ring and added, "I wasn't talking about the concert."

Back in the room, they sat on Derrick's bed, snuggled up, watching a movie on the TV. He had just about nodded off when Lydia stuck out her hand to look at her ring.

"I have dreamt about this day ever since that night with the thunderstorm and yet, for some reason, it was still a surprise. The best surprise I've ever had! I love it so much!"

Derrick pulled her closer and kissed her head. "It pales in comparison to you, my dear." Blushing a little, she smiled as she snuggled back up to his chest.

***

With all the thoughtful gestures Derrick was showering her with, Lydia wanted to get him something, too. Derrick loved watches, and he had been eyeing one since before they had met, but he never bought it. Every time she tried to get him to, he would just reply, "I'm saving up for something else at the moment." She didn't realize until tonight that he meant her ring.

The next morning, while Derrick was taking a shower, Lydia made a "candy run" and stopped at the watch store in the Fun Shops. She searched for a minute until, sitting before her, was the very Omega Seamaster Derrick had been dreaming about.

The salesman took it out of the case and placed it in her hands. Trying it on, Lydia immediately understood why Derrick loved that model so much. The bracelet felt as smooth as velvety butter, and the crystal glistened in the store's lights. "I'll take it! Can you wrap it up?"

Lydia returned to the room with a bag of strawberry Sour Patch Kids. "Can you believe they make these?!?" she exclaimed.

At dinner, Lydia slid the small, wrapped package across the table to him.

"I got you an engagement present," she said with a smile.

"What? No. That's not how it works."

"It does in my world and besides, I can't take it back, so you're stuck with it."

Derrick objected, but Lydia gave him one of her looks.

"Okay, fine, but I officially protest," he said.

"Your protest is acknowledged, and I still don't care. Open it!"

Derrick carefully unwrapped the package and saw the Omega symbol on the top of the box. In disbelief, he looked up, only to find her smiling from ear to ear.

"Honey..." he said gasping.

"Open it! Open it!"

Derrick slowly lifted the lid and saw the gleaming watch shining back at him. He caught his breath.

"I hope you like it!"

He was still too stunned to speak.

Lydia couldn't take it anymore. She slid over and took the watch from the box, latching it onto his wrist.

"That looks amazing on you!"

"But honey, it's too much."

She took him by the hand and looked him in the eye. "I want you to have it."

CHAPTER 21

After the cruise, Lydia spent the following week researching apartments in Reston. She came across the Cosmopolitan at Reston Town Center and arranged a viewing for the Saturday before graduation. As they approached the towering fifteen-story building, Derrick expressed doubt about being able to afford such a fancy place.

Lydia was undeterred by his hesitance. "Let's at least go look. It looked so pretty on the webpage and wasn't that expensive."

Upon meeting the manager, they were led to a two-bedroom, two-bath apartment on the fourth floor. Opening the door, Lydia immediately fell in love with the living room and all the sunlight that poured in from the floor-to-ceiling windows.

"This is exactly what I was imagining! The two bedrooms each having their own bathroom, divided by a living room."

"This plan is $2,050/month, utilities included," the manager said, but she could tell Derrick was not entirely sold on it yet.

"Would you like to see the rooftop pool?"

"Pool?" Derrick questioned.

They were taken to the roof, and as the elevator doors opened, a stunning, heated pool with a panoramic view of the surrounding skyline unfolded before them.

Lydia turned to Derrick with excitement. "Oh honey, please, please, pretty please!"

"If only there was a hot tub," Derrick added.

The manager walked them around the corner. "Unfortunately, we don't have one… we have three."

He stared in disbelief. "Where do I sign?"

Lydia hugged him, giggling with glee.

On their way back down, they came across an elderly lady trying to open her door while juggling groceries.

"Ma'am, let me help you with that," Derrick offered, taking her bags.

"Oh, thank you so much, Sonny!" the elderly lady exclaimed.

The manager introduced her to Derrick. "This is Mildred Lowell. She's one of our sweetest residents."

"Are you new to the building, dear?" Ms. Lowell inquired.

"Why yes, ma'am. It looks like we will be moving in shortly."

"Oh, that's nice! What do you do?"

Derrick gave his usual vague response, avoiding going into details. "I work with computers."

"Fantastic!" Ms. Lowell said. "It will be nice having someone from the Geek Squad living here."

Lydia struggled to contain her laughter.

Turning her gaze, Ms. Lowell said, "You have a pretty wife."

Lydia smiled and replied, "Why thank you, but we aren't married yet."

"Hussy," She remarked as she turned and headed into her apartment.

Lydia's face dropped in shock.

Upon returning to the car after signing the rental agreements, Derrick looked at Lydia and asked, "Where do you feel like grabbing lunch from, Hussy... I mean, Honey."

She punched him in the arm this time instead of her normal smack. He fought not to show that it actually hurt.

***

Today was finally graduation. Derrick stood in front of the mirror in his new black Armani suit.

Lydia always complained that he never dressed up for anything, so a couple of weeks ago, he went into Richmond and got fitted for it to surprise her. Even though he abhorred wearing suits, he had to admit that he looked sharp in this one.

He fastened his new watch onto his wrist and smiled when he thought of when she gave it to him. After adjusting his pocket square and putting on his sunglasses, he headed across the hall to shock his lady.

Knocking on Lydia's door, he took a step back. She opened the door and let out a joyful squeal.

"That suit looks AMAZING on you!"

Expecting to be the one delivering the surprise, Derrick found himself utterly speechless when he saw her. She was wearing a formfitting red sheath dress with a black suit jacket that looked as if it was made specifically for her.

"Uh... hmm... Wow."

She posed for him to get a better view from the side. "So, I take it you like this outfit?"

He looked up at her face and could only get out, "huh?"

She smiled as she went back into her room to get her purse. "That would be a yes."

Derrick entered the auditorium with Lydia, her hand snugly tucked into the crook of his arm. Their *Electrical Standards* teacher approached them and saw the shiny, new ring on Lydia's finger.

"I was going to tell you both congratulations on graduating, but it looks like there might be something bigger to celebrate. Lydia, I don't know how you do it, but you really are a saint. Keep him supervised."

Lydia looked at Derrick and grinned. "Oh yes, sir. I plan to keep my eye on him."

The teacher looked at Derrick. "Alrighty then. Derrick, don't lose her. She's something special... oh...

and don't let anyone try to stifle that brain of yours. You have a gift. Use it for good now."

He looked at him, puzzled. "Now?"

Even with the ten people graduating today, the ceremony was rather short. They announced where everyone was going and then, this time took a poll for what each person was most likely to do. Derrick was voted most likely to blow up a lake and Lydia was voted most likely to have to rescue Derrick.

She leaned over to him and whispered, "Well, they're not wrong."

After the ceremony, Derrick caught up with Mike. "You excited for Peru? I hear they have some great food there."

"I can't wait!" replied Mike, "but I still have some hurdles to clear with medical first. It seems like there's an issue getting my asthma medication there, so while they're working that out, I'll be in Overwatch helping with the radios."

Lydia chimed in, "Just remember what I told you... count to two after you key up."

Mike smiled at her. "Of course! Thank you for helping me in the class. I don't think I would have passed without it. I was excited to hear that they talked you into teaching the refresher courses at Headquarters."

"Ah, thanks!" she replied, slightly embarrassed. "I'll still get to take the occasional trip, but honestly, I'm glad they offered it. Now I get to spend more time with Derrick in between his tours.

As everyone was filing out after the ceremony, Lydia revealed her surprise for Derrick.

"You ready for a little adventure?"

Feeling a tad apprehensive, he replied, "Not with that look."

She enthusiastically explained. "I booked a hot air balloon ride over the Virginia countryside, ending up at the beach. It's been a bucket list of mine. Doesn't that sound like a great time?"

Derrick felt a sudden rush of terror coursing through his body.

"You mean flying a few thousand feet in the air in a basket made of wicker attached to a flamethrower? Sounds... life-altering."

Lydia's face dropped. "You don't want to?" Her eyes seemed on the verge of tears.

"No honey. It sounds like fun."

She leaped into his arms, giving him a tight hug. "Go get changed then! We launch in two hours."

***

Lydia pulled into a field in Appomattox, where their bright purple and green balloon was already being filled.

"Well, that's very 1980s," Derrick remarked.

The crew gave them a quick overview and before he knew it, the time to fly had come. Lydia made him get in the basket first because she didn't trust him not to run.

The pilot pulled down on the burner handle and they started rising. "Here we go!"

Derrick bent down below the railing, so he didn't have to watch, but Lydia grabbed him by the shoulders and pulled him back up.

"Quit being a coward!"

"What? I was just tying my shoe," he replied.

"Riiiiight. The laces on your sandals?"

As they were passing through one thousand feet, Lydia noticed Derrick had his eyes tightly shut.

"I'm going to throw you over if you don't open your eyes!" she playfully threatened.

It took Derrick almost thirty minutes to finally start calming down. Looking out, they could see the coastline, so Lydia had the pilot take a picture of them with the ocean in the background.

"Smile!" the pilot said, pausing. "Um, Mr. Anderson, you should smile."

"I thought I was."

Lydia smirked, "Hold on..."

Reaching behind Derrick, she grabbed his butt.

"Whoa!" Derrick exclaimed.

"There we go. Cheese!"

Two-thirds of the way into their hour-and-a-half flight, the pilot announced that he was going to start the descent. They were both looking out over Virginia Beach, pointing out their favorite spots.

"There's *Chico's Pizza*!" Lydia exclaimed.

"Oh, I loved that place. We need to go back!"

While they were talking, Derrick heard the burner ignite and run for what he thought was an unusually long amount of time for a descending balloon.

He turned around and saw the pilot slumped over the console, pulling the burner handle. Derrick lowered him to the basket floor, checked his pulse, and upon finding none, started CPR. Lydia grabbed the radio.

"Mayday, Mayday, Mayday! *Adventure* hot air balloon to anyone out there."

"*Chase team to balloon. Go for your mayday.*"

"The pilot has collapsed and is receiving CPR. Need assistance to land this thing!"

"*Stand by. Clearing the air space with air traffic control and then we will guide you down.*"

A few moments later, the chase team radioed back. "*Chase team to balloon. Our safest bet is to have you land in the ocean. Do you see the handle that says 'Vent'? Give it a pull for fifteen seconds. We will call it for you.*"

"Yes, have the handle and ready," Lydia relayed.

"Pull now."

She pulled the vent handle, and the air started escaping from the top of the balloon. *"Thirteen, fourteen, STOP!"*

"Okay, vent closed," Lydia radioed.

"Great, this sets you up for a landing in about thirty minutes. The Coast Guard has a helicopter en route and will be handling the rescue from here. Switch Com2 to 156.525."

Lydia could tell Derrick was wearing out.

"Do you think he'll make it?"

"No... I don't," he said solemnly.

Just then, the radio crackled to life.

"Distressed balloon, this is Coast Guard Helo 6024 approaching from the north. When you have a moment, can you report on how many souls are on board?"

"Coast Guard, we have visual and there are three souls onboard. CPR in progress," Lydia replied.

"6024, good copy. We will dispatch the swimmer once your basket touches the water. When it does, pull the vent handle and lock it open. Stay inside if safe to do so. We will extract the CPR first."

Derrick, almost out of breath now, complemented Lydia. "I'm really glad you are the one on the radio. I'd probably be telling them they were unreadable."

As they approached the water, Lydia started audibly calling out the distances so Derrick could prepare. "Fifteen feet... ten feet... brace, brace!"

Lydia opened the vent when they hit the water, causing the balloon to deflate rapidly, but not before it tipped the basket over filling it with water. Derrick was no longer able to keep doing CPR, as he didn't have a hard surface for the pilot to lie on anymore.

With his arms feeling like jelly from sheer exhaustion, Derrick fought to keep his head above the water. At one point, a wave tried to sweep him away from the basket, but Lydia grabbed him and pulled him back to the rail.

"Get back here! You're not getting away that easy."

Within minutes of the helicopter arriving overhead, the rescue swimmer approached the basket. Lydia directed him to the pilot, who was promptly loaded into the awaiting litter.

As it was being lifted to the helicopter, the swimmer came back to the basket to prepare them for the next extraction.

Lydia tried to convince Derrick to go next, but he wouldn't hear of it.

"Women and children first. I'm okay. I'll meet you up there in just a second," he reassured her.

Lydia was led to the litter that had just descended and the swimmer helped her strap in.

As she was being lifted, a large wave came through and submerged the balloon basket. When it resurfaced, Derrick was no longer in it.

"DERRICK!!!!!" Lydia screamed over the noise of the rotor blades.

After recovering himself, the swimmer rushed back over and started searching, but couldn't find him anywhere. Diving under the water, he finally spotted Derrick unsuccessfully fighting to untangle himself from the balloon's ropes. Struggling against the sudden strong current, he finally reached Derrick and started cutting the ropes away with his knife.

Derrick was no longer moving as the last rope was cut, and the swimmer pulled him back to the surface. Lydia's legs went weak, and she cried, "NO, NO, NO, NO, NO, PLEASE NO!" as she saw his lifeless body loaded into the litter, with the swimmer giving rescue breaths as they were being lifted.

The technician pulled the litter into the helicopter and Lydia yanked Derrick out and onto the floor. Through her tears, she continued the rescue breaths while the technician secured the door.

On the fourth breath, Derrick spit up the water from his lungs all over her and began coughing violently.

She rolled him onto his side until he was breathing normally again and then buried her face into his chest, crying uncontrollably.

As he held Lydia tight against him, Derrick's heart sank as the pilot was placed on the monitor.

"Asystole," the swimmer said dejectedly and restarted CPR.

Back at the air station, Derrick sat in the doorway of the helicopter and watched as they continued CPR on the balloon pilot while loading him into the awaiting ambulance. Lydia, still with her face buried in his chest, was refusing to let him go. He fought his emotions hard, but a single tear escaped and rolled down his cheek when he realized just how close that was for them both.

CHAPTER 22

Derrick finished putting his spare parts into a box and he zipped up his suitcase. Today they were moving out of the dorms and heading up to their apartment in Reston.

He carried his things down to the car and loaded them into his trunk. As he was shutting it, he saw Lydia coming down the breezeway with three suitcases and a couple of garment bags with dresses.

"Let me help you with those," he offered.

"Oh, thanks! Can you load them into my car while I go back for another load?"

"Another?!?" he thought.

After loading her items into the trunk, he headed back up to her room. When he walked in, she asked, "How much space do you have in your car?"

Lydia stared at the dorm hall and her eyes started to well up. Derrick came up and put his arm around her.

"What's wrong?" he asked.

"So many memories here. This is where we met. This is where we had our first date. Our first storm. Our first trip to the hospital... and second... and third..."

"Oh, haha, funny girl."

Derrick was cruising up I-95 with his speed set at 70mph. Traffic was abnormally light for being just north of Richmond on a Tuesday.

He was enjoying the peaceful drive when a white beetle pulled up next to him on the left. *Meep Meep.* Lydia honked her pitiful horn and motioned for him to roll down his window. She yelled out her passenger side loud enough for him to hear her over the road noise.

"Get off the road, Grandpa!" She was laughing as she sped up and started leaving him.

"Oh, no, she didn't!" Derrick wasn't one to speed, but he wasn't allowing that level of disrespect for the Mustang.

He accelerated until he was right beside her again. After shooting her an eyebrow flash, he downshifted and slammed the accelerator. As he shot away, the roar of his exhaust made her visibly jump.

His phone rang shortly after and all Lydia said before hanging up was, "Uncool!"

Derrick pulled into the parking garage for their apartment complex and found their designated spots. Lydia got out of her car and saw him climbing out of his window.

"Why did they have to give us the spots with a pole beside them?!?" he murmured.

"Ha, serves you right! Mr. Noise Pollution Driver... Person You."

"Got that?"

"I'm not the one about to fall from their car window onto the pavement." Her comment was dripping with sarcasm.

As if on cue, Derrick lost his grip and slid down the side of the car onto the concrete.

"Seeeee," she said smugly.

After Derrick's third trip from the garage to retrieve her bags, they finally were unloaded and officially moved into their apartment.

"I can't believe it! Our own place!" Lydia exclaimed.

"Yeah... with no furniture."

"We're gonna take care of that tomorrow when we go to IKEA!"

"But what about tonight?"

Lydia hadn't thought that far. "Um... huh... I don't know."

Pulling out his phone, Derrick said, "Find us somewhere yummy for dinner, and I'll take care of tonight."

"Ooooh. I like the sound of that," she said, winking at him.

"I'm going to find a hotel nearby."

Lydia's eyes grew even more excited. "Well, helloooo!"

After finishing their subs from Santini's, they made their way to the Springhill Suites off Herndon Parkway, where Derrick was able to get rooms beside each other.

He swiped his card and was about to enter the room when Lydia approached from behind.

"If you need anything, I'll be next door... by myself... all alone in that scary room..."

He kissed her on the forehead. "Good night, honey. I'll see you early tomorrow morning."

Dejected, Lydia turned and headed back to her room. "Man, you're such a boy scout."

***

They drove down Fairfax County Parkway towards Woodbridge, which Derrick's GPS said was the closest IKEA.

Lydia was bouncing with excitement.

"*I-Keaaaa, I-Keaaaa, I,I,I, I-Keaaaaa!*"

"Whaaat are you doing?"

"I'm singing my IKEA song," Lydia explained.

"Yeah, caught that from the lyrics... I reiterate... WHAT are you doing?"

She reached over and pinched his cheek. "Mmmm, my little grumpy bear. No one can be a grumpy bear in IKEA."

"Wanna bet?"

Derrick tried to find a parking spot in the garage that was out by itself... mainly to have the ability to get out without having to crawl through the window. He didn't even get the car into park before Lydia bolted out the door and took off running for the entrance.

"I'll meet you upstairs!" she yelled from across the parking lot.

He sat for a minute contemplating his life choices. "I have a feeling I should have just ordered online."

As he was riding up the escalator, he could see her at the top with a Cheshire cat grin. Not only did she have a cart, but it was already half full.

"How is that even possible?!?!" Derrick pondered.

"Let's go look at beds!" she exclaimed as she took off again.

"You know, after all this moving, I could go for some 'bed testing'," he thought.

Within fifteen minutes, Derrick had picked out his mattress, bed frame, and dresser. It took him another fifteen minutes to find Lydia in that maze.

She was bouncing between three different beds, unable to decide which one was the most comfortable.

"You're done already?!? Did you just pick the first one you came across?"

"Well... kinda. It was affordable, and it was comfortable. Then I just had to pick a cheap frame and dresser. Done."

"Was the frame pretty?"

"What? Um... No... er, yes... um... it's a frame. It's just a metal frame. I guess you could call it pretty if you were into that stuff."

"You have to get a pretty frame! That's the bed my parents are going to sleep in when they come to visit after we are married."

"What?!?" Derrick's face scrunched as if he had just smelled something horrible. "Ewwww! There's an image I'll never get out of my head now. Thanks a lot!"

Derrick headed over to the living room section and found a couch that looked comfortable. He knew she was going to be a while with the beds, so he made himself at home. A few moments later, he was fast asleep

---

...He watched as fire shot out of every window of the two-story house in front of him. He placed the oxygen tank and med bag back on the stretcher as he heard over the radio that no survivors had been found. A shadow caught his eye at the front door. Out walked an object that vaguely looked like a man except it was completely covered in fire. He grabbed the blanket off

the stretcher, ran to the figure, and tried to smother the flames. When he placed the blanket over the figure, it crumbled into a pile of ash...

Derrick woke with a slight scream to find a small boy standing in front of him, staring. The boy didn't move for a few seconds and then burst out into a loud cry and ran away.

"I guess that will teach you to stare at someone while they are sleeping."

Lydia walked up, having caught the back part of that scene.

"Making friends again, I see?"

"Are you finally done so we can go home?" Derrick said exasperated.

"No, silly! We need to pick out a couch now."

"What's wrong with this one?"

"It doesn't match my bedframe and dresser."

"Why does the couch have to match your bedroom furniture?"

"Well, if someone comes in from the living room to the bedroom, they will notice they don't match," she explained

"Who's going to be going from the living room to your... never mind. I'm going to lose this anyway. Lead on."

They walked across the aisle to another grouping of couches when an older lady huffed up to him.

"What did you do to my kid to make him scream like that, you pervert!"

"I didn't do anything to your brat. I was taking a nap and when I woke up, he was staring at me. Maybe you should teach your kid it's not polite to stare."

"I'm reporting you to security!"

"Go for it. See if they can help me find the exit."

Derrick stood against a post and watched as "they" picked out a matching couch when he heard a commotion behind him. He turned to find the lady dragging a security guard towards him.

"That's him, officer! Arrest him!"

"Ma'am, I explained to you, I'm a security guard, not police. Also, we looked at the tapes, and he didn't do anything to your kid."

"I don't care! I want him kicked out!" she screamed.

Derrick looked at the guard and mouthed, "Help me!"

The security guard replied to the lady, "Ma'am, the only one acting disorderly around here is you. Maybe you should find your way to the exit."

The lady huffed in disgust and left the area.

Derrick looked at the guard with disappointment. "Dude, I asked for rescuing! Bro code, man!"

The guard chuckled. "Sorry, sir. We aren't allowed bro code here."

Hearing the commotion, Lydia walked up behind Derrick and put her arm around him, giving the guard a big smile.

Derrick facepalmed. "She paid you, didn't she?"

Three naps, two meatball trips, and a bathroom break later, Derrick heard the most beautiful words Lydia had ever said to him: "Okay, I think I'm done."

They took their carts and all their tags down to the checkout, where she asked him for his items.

"No, I'm going to pay for my own. We aren't married yet."

"Just put it on mine. I want the points. Most of this is 'ours' anyway. We can sort it out later," as she yanked the tags out of his hand.

"Can I at least pay for my own water?"

Being the first thing he had drunk in hours, Derrick was downing the bottle of water when the cashier read the total.

"Okay, so that comes to $11,785.48."

Water sprayed from Derrick's mouth, soaking Lydia. "Oh, crap! That was probably like fifty bucks worth of this fancy water!" he thought.

Lydia slowly turned her head to look at him.

"Oh! Sweetie! I'm sorry! Um... you wanna try out one of your new towels?"

As Derrick was cleaning up the counter, Lydia handed the cashier her card.

"Wait, you have that much available on your card?!?"

She looked at him with an innocent grin. "It's daddy's card."

Derrick got choked up and started coughing.

He had just finished stuffing the last bit of the items she bought into the trunk of his Mustang when Lydia walked up, rolling the receipt.

"The delivery is all set. Our stuff will get there tomorrow."

"But what about tonight? I guess I will book us some more rooms."

Lydia grinned as she climbed into the car. "Ever been camping?"

Derrick stood at a loss. "No."

***

Back at the apartment, Lydia was unboxing the tents she purchased as Derrick brought the rest of their items in.

Watching in surprise, he said, "I thought you were kidding."

"Come on, you can't tell me this isn't exciting? Camping in our own living room! OUR...OWN... LIVING ROOM."

Still confused, Derrick inquired, "But why tents? We are indoors. Shouldn't we just have air mattresses or something?"

"Don't be a spoilsport! It will be just like when we were kids and camping out with our friends." Lydia could tell from Derrick's face that something wasn't right. "You've never been camping, have you?"

Derrick hemmed and hawed a little but finally admitted, "No."

"How can you be from Texas and never been camping?!?"

Not wanting to be outdone, Derrick did his best at a comeback.

"Well, how could you be from Iowa and never..." He racked his brain the best he could to find something to finish that with, but nothing came. "Yeah, I don't know where I was going with that."

Lydia started chuckling. "Come here, stud. Look at it this way, we get to sleep in the same room and it not be awkward. I'll be in my own place and you'll be over there in your own uncoordinated tent with clashing furniture."

Lydia had her tent set up in less than five minutes and was looking at the menu from the local Chinese delivery on her phone.

Derrick, on the other hand, was struggling to put the poles in the right slots.

"Come on, Derrick. You graduated second with honors from MIT. You once fixed an electron microscope with duct tape and a shoelace. You can figure out a simple tent."

He finally threaded the poles through the right loops and placed them into the anchor points on the ends. Climbing into the tent, he proclaimed loudly, "You can call me *Master of the Tents* from now on!"

Hearing a creaking sound coming from the peak, Derrick wondered if that was normal. He got his answer a few seconds later when the pole buckled and shot out across the room. The tent fell, covering him.

He lay there listening to Lydia, who was now rolling around on the floor, laughing to the point of having trouble breathing. "Hey Tent Master! Is that a new 'slim' model you are sporting there?"

Once Lydia stopped laughing, she came over and released Derrick from his plastic entrapment.

"How about a little help there, Tentman?"

She retrieved the poles from the kitchen where they flew and had the tent back up in no time.

Derrick was setting up his TV on the floor while Lydia answered the door for their food delivery. He loaded one of her DVDs into the player and they had their own little camping movie night.

When the credits started rolling on the movie, Derrick noticed Lydia was sound asleep, curled up with Madeline. He took her new "ocean" blanket she bought, placed it over her, and gave her a light kiss on the cheek.

Taking his pillow and blanket, he groaned as he crawled into his tent. "Ugh, this floor is so hard."

That night, a thunderstorm rolled through. Derrick was already awake with his back on fire from the floor when he heard something knocking on his plastic walls. He unzipped the "door" to find a furry blob of sea animals.

"Come on in," he said as she crawled in and lay down.

Derrick's back was killing him when he woke up with the sun the next morning. Lydia was still bundled up in her blanket burrito, sound asleep. Their items from IKEA were coming today, so he thought it would be a nice treat for them both if he went and got them breakfast before their hard day.

After heading to Chick-fil-A and Starbucks, Derrick made his way back up to the apartment.

Walking down the hallway, he passed several moving men coming from the apartment. When he entered the apartment, he found the dining room stacked halfway to the ceiling with boxes.

"Our order came!" Lydia said with glee.

Derrick spent the next twelve hours putting together the two bed frames, end tables, dressers, couch, and coffee table. He was trying to get everything finished before he would leave in a couple of days for Tripoli on his first tour.

He was down to the dining room table but was starting to get loopy. Lydia had already gone to bed as she was teaching a class early the next morning. She was woken up a couple of times when Derrick would slip with the hammer and end up smashing one of his fingers.

"OWWWW! That's gonna leave a mark!"

Lydia rolled over and noticed it was quiet out in the living room. The clock read 2:13am. She tried to go back to sleep, but curiosity got the best of her.

"I wonder if he got it done or just gave up?"

She carefully turned the knob and cracked the door open. The sight she saw almost made her burst out in laughter. Derrick was sound asleep lying on the upside-down table. He was intertwined in three of the legs that were attached... and they each were pointing in a different direction. Lydia placed her new fuzzy sea animal blanket over him and kissed him on the cheek.

CHAPTER 23

Derrick sat down on one of the rock-hard seats in Terminal D. Even though he would travel business class, Dulles was not known for its comfort. Looking up at the gate board, he double-checked the departure time.

"5:15, good." He always made sure he was very early for any flight. "That gives me two hours to relax."

Propping his bag up on the armrest, he laid down for a quick nap.

...Derrick looked around. He couldn't see anything. There was just a dark gray cloud surrounding him. His lungs felt like they were on fire. He trudged on. The cloud parted and he could see the source. It was a car fire. Smoke was pouring out of every window. He ran closer. A person was in the driver's seat... a young lady. She looked at him. The fire then shot up around her. She let out a horrific scream....

He jerked awake so hard the lady sitting across from him gasped. "Sorry about that," he apologized.

Before she could acknowledge it, the intercom came to life. *"Good evening, passengers. We would like to begin pre-boarding for flight 12 to Frankfurt."*

The flight attendant showed him to his single window seat at the front of the aircraft. Derrick stowed his bag under the TV and kicked back in the plush, oversized chair. He pulled his phone out and texted Lydia to see how she was doing.

"The friendly skies are much better when your butt doesn't go numb."

"*I picked up Olivia at Reagan and we went to that Thai restaurant in town,*" Lydia texted back.

"I see you're already missing me."

"*Of course, I'm missing you. I even cried when I saw you took your credit card with you. Lol! We are going shopping for wedding decorations and cake testing in Tyson's after.*"

"I thought we were supposed to do that together?"

"*You want to go flower shopping with me?*"

Derrick cringed. "Noooo."

"*Then take the win!*"

Derrick grinned. "Wish I was with you on Virginia Beach instead of going to Libya right now."

"*It's only for 10 days, stud. We will have plenty of time before my Baghdad trip. If it makes you feel better, schedule it for when you get back and I'll pack =)*"

"It's a date!"

Derrick was checking for rooms when the flight attendant started the safety briefing.

After dinner, Derrick reclined his chair, took his shoes off, and flipped through the catalog of movies. He found a couple of adventurous ones he hadn't seen before, but nothing really caught his interest.

Turning the TV off, he pulled out his phone. While he was flipping through pictures of Lydia, he found a video that she snuck into it. He hit the play button and there she was, wearing his favorite sundress.

"Hey, honey. I just wanted to record you a little message to watch for when you get lonely..."

Derrick watched the ten-minute video over and over again until he finally drifted off to sleep.

***

...He and Lydia were over in New Baltimore at a pick-your-own strawberry field. Derrick's basket was nearly full when he heard his name called from behind. "Derrick!" He turned around just in time for Lydia to tackle him to the ground. Straddling his abdomen, she held him down by his shoulders. Her long, brown hair fell around them, blocking out everything but her face. As she leaned in for a kiss, the scent of strawberries engulfed his sense, and her soft lips met his..."

Derrick's eyes popped open to find the flight attendants making their rounds.

"Hello sir, are you ready for breakfast?"

"Uh, almost ma'am, thank you. Give me a couple of minutes to wake up."

He sat his chair up, and after putting his shoes on, headed to the washroom. Upon returning to his seat, he pulled his phone out once more. As he watched the video, the flight attendant brought his breakfast and placed it on his tray. Looking up, he smiled when he saw one of the bowls was full of strawberries.

Derrick had never been to the Frankfurt airport and, even worse, he didn't speak a word of German. Using the translator app on his phone, he was able to find his way to baggage claim. Upon retrieving his bag, he called the number for his transport to the military connection flight. He gave them the exit he was at, and they notified their driver.

He was standing outside the terminal by the pickup lane texting Lydia when an SUV pulled up. The front passenger window rolled down, revealing a familiar face. "Get your scrawny butt in the car, Elmo," Obadiah ordered. Derrick's heart dropped.

They drove him to another part of the airport where a C-17 was in the process of being loaded with supplies.

"That's our ride," Obadiah remarked.

"Our?"

"Unfortunately. I'm the lead for your security detail while you're here. Which reminds me, how's Lydia? She find someone better yet?"

"We're engaged," Derrick said proudly.

"So that's a no, then? Unfortunate… for her."

Obadiah led Derrick up the ramp of the aircraft and to the seats within the cabin.

"What's on the menu tonight?" Derrick joked.

Throwing an MRE at him, Obadiah snarled, "Get used to them, Elmo. That's considered gourmet dining where we are going."

Their six-hour flight was almost done when Obadiah leaned over to check Derrick's seat belt.

"Get ready to pucker up. We are about to drop out of the sky for landing."

Derrick had no clue what he meant by "drop out of the sky." A few moments later, he fully understood.

The pilots put the engines into idle reverse, and the plane went into a 45-degree dive. Derrick started floating, only being held in place by his seatbelt. He glanced over and Obadiah had his hands up and was laughing manically. "Don't crap on me now, Elmo!"

They fell for what felt like hours when the aircraft finally leveled back out and made a smooth landing.

Derrick kissed the ground as he got off the plane. "You are such a wuss, Elmo. I can't believe you even made it to graduation."

"No thanks to you," Derrick replied. "I'm sorry I missed yours... oh... wait."

He could tell that comment stung a bit.

Obadiah led him to the operations building where he introduced him to the base commander.

"Chief, here's the new commo guy, Elmo."

Derrick snapped to attention. "Sir, the name is Anderson. Derrick Anderson."

Excusing Obadiah, the chief remarked. "At ease, son. So, Derrick, I've heard a lot about you."

"Sir, you can't believe everything Obadiah has said about me. We've... had a history."

"Yes, I'm aware of the incident at the driving course. No, I was referring to the memo I received about... an exploding lake... is that true?"

"Well, it wasn't on purpose," Derrick said, blushing.

Chief Henderson showed Derrick around the base and finally to the IT room. Tripoli was a forward operating base, so it lacked a lot of the amenities that a normal post would have... like individual housing, high-speed internet, and working air conditioning.

"You are our only commo guy this week. We have the occasional op that needs radio or IT support, so make sure you attend the daily briefings."

After the chief left, Derrick headed straight to the AC unit to see if he could figure out what was wrong.

A couple of hours later, Henderson opened the IT room door and was met with ice-cold air flooding out.

"My stars! It's freezing in here. How did you fix it?"

Derrick was kicked back with his feet up on his desk. "Nothing that a little silicone and tinfoil couldn't fix."

Shaking Derrick's comment off, he explained why he was there. "We have a mission in an hour. I need you in the SITROOM in ten minutes. Bring your radio bag and some of that tinfoil, too."

Derrick stepped into the Situation Room and was surrounded by a group of hardened military operatives.

"I think I'm in the wrong room," he said feeling a little overwhelmed.

Then from the corner, Obadiah piped up, "Elmo, you ready to get your butt wet?"

"Ugh, how is that even a saying?!?" he thought.

The Ravens Team Leader started briefing the team on the mission details.

"We have an evac of a local from the medcenter in Garyan. Obadiah, Samir. You will be in the follow helicopter providing cover while supplies are offloaded. Take the new guy with you for coms support. Dismissed!"

Obadiah walked up and smacked Derrick on the back. "Well Elmo, it looks like you are our little..."

Samir interrupted him. "*'Ello Derrick, de name is Samir. 'Appy to meet you.*" Samir was a native Libyan who immigrated to the U.S. at a young age.

They took Derrick to the armory to get him outfitted for the mission. Obadiah threw some body armor at him while Samir brought him an M4.

"Hey, nobody said anything about giving Elmo a weapon. Freakshow here probably would find a way to shoot himself with it."

"*Everyone is armed, Ob. You know dat.*"

Obadiah growled and then walked outside. "Hurry up, Elmo. We won't wait for you."

Derrick strapped on his vest and then the radio pack over it. All the gear added at least another fifty pounds and was a little difficult to walk with. He headed out with Samir and climbed into the second Black Hawk.

He was having trouble getting the helmet to fit his abnormally large head. Even back at LifeEVAC they had to specially order him one. Obadiah enjoyed watching him struggle until Samir reached over and pounded Derrick on top of the head popping the helmet into place.

"Thank you, Samir," Derrick said gratefully.

Obadiah was visibly annoyed. "It's like taking the Queen of England into a warzone except she'd probably smell better."

Derrick watched out the door as they lifted off and flew low over the city. He could see children playing on old, rusted military vehicles from a long-gone war. Obadiah saw him staring off outside.

Obadiah rolled his eyes. "I really hope you're not coming up with another one of your inventions, Elmo."

Derrick continued to stare at the city passing by in disbelief. "People back home have no idea how good they have it."

"It's a different world here, man."

After twenty minutes of flight time, they were finally over the makeshift medical center. Eagle 1 would be flying out a local to the trauma facility in Benghazi and Derrick's team, Eagle 2, would be providing support and delivering supplies.

The pilot keyed up on the headsets to give instructions for arrival. "This is going to be a hot load, so watch your heads when you are under the blades."

Obadiah looked at Derrick. "Make yourself useful, Elmo, and help carry those boxes in."

As the helicopters touched down, Obadiah and Samir deboarded and took up defensive positions around the landing zone. Derrick grabbed a stack of supplies and followed the others into the medical tent.

He struggled to keep everything in his arms as he departed under the still-turning rotor blades.

There were rows and rows of cots, and each one had someone sick or injured on them. The crew met up with the doctor and was led to a head and torso lying on a table.

"He stepped on a landmine and had both his legs and arms blown off. We've stopped the bleeding the best we can..."

They loaded the patient onto their stretcher, and Derrick helped carry him to the helicopter. He had been in this position several times before where the patient was looking to him for hope. Trying to hide his real thoughts, Derrick helped load the man and then retreated to the med center with the stretcher. He watched as a cloud of dust rose when the helicopter lifted off.

He was still thinking about the poor guy they just sent off as he climbed back into the second helicopter and onto his seat. Obadiah and Samir returned as Derrick was staring off at the nearby buildings.

A young girl, wearing a cream sunflower dress, emerged from an open door and started walking toward them. She only looked to be about five years old.

Derrick peered through his rifle scope to get a better look at something. She had stopped and then looked back towards the door that she came from for a moment. Her eyes were filled with tears as she turned back around and slowly continued toward the helicopter.

Obadiah saw Derrick with his rifle raised. "Elmo, what do you see?!?" He spun around and saw the girl. "Are you stupid?!? What are you doing!?! Put your gun down! It's just a kid!"

To Obadiah's horror, fire flashed out the end of the barrel.

Derrick fired two quick shots, and time stopped. He could see the bullets slowly flying towards the little girl, who was staring at the ground.

He watched in horror as she looked up just in time for the first round to enter the center of one of the sunflowers on her chest. It blew out the other side of her tiny body and a red mist sprayed in all directions behind her. He saw the light in her eyes dim as the second round struck a few inches lower. The skin on her face started melting off the bone and then disappeared as a tremendous explosion vaporized her existence.

The blast wave shook the helicopter and knocked him back into real-time. He almost fell out of his seat as the pilot jerked the chopper up off the ground.

"Tripoli command, Eagle 2, proximity explosion. Lifting to a safe distance."

Derrick kept his eyes closed and his head hung on the way home.

Obadiah finally broke the silence. "How did you know she had a bomb, Elmo?!?"

He took a deep breath. "I didn't... at least not for sure."

Obadiah's face turned white as a ghost. "You shot a kid without knowing?!?!"

Trying to explain, he kept having to stop to compose himself. "She was terrified... You could see it in her face... Kids who run up to helicopters are excited... Not... Not crying... Then she turned back as if she didn't really want to go and I saw what looked like an antenna sticking out from under her dress. It was as if someone in the house told her to keep approaching us..."

For the rest of the flight, Derrick didn't know if anyone even said a word. He couldn't even hear the noise from the engines anymore. After landing, he headed for the IT room.

"Elmo, we have debriefing. It's this way," Obadiah barked.

"Tell me how it goes. I don't need to be there."

He sat alone for about an hour before Chief Henderson knocked on his door.

"You alright?"

Derrick sighed. "No."

"Well, your sharp instincts saved the entire crew. You should be commended."

"What evil in this world would send a five-year-old girl to blow up a helicopter?" he asked, still staring off in a daze.

"Unfortunately, Derrick, it's all too common. No one expects them and even if they do, most won't pull the trigger."

Turning his gaze to the chief, "You ever seen someone's life disappear from their eyes?"

"Yes... I know exactly what you mean. You never unsee that. You just have to live with the fact that she was going to die either way. It was just a question of how many of your team were going with her. So, if you need to cry, do it. If you need to scream, do it. If you want to talk to the doctor, do it. No one here will think less of you for it."

***

Derrick didn't sleep much that night. Memories of the girl kept playing through his head, so he got up and started work on a design he had. He was still working on the diagram as the sun started to peek through his window. After making his way to the mess hall for breakfast, he sat down with his tray and noticed the table legs. An idea popped into his brain, and he pulled out his knife.

"Hmmm... that just might work," he thought.

Samir and Obadiah stopped into the IT room to do their hourly checkup on their protectee but Derrick wasn't there.

They heard some thumping on the roof and went up to find him working on the satellite antenna. He had placed some kind of dish on it that made it look like a *Jiffy Pop* ball.

"*Derrick, wat are you doin'?*" Samir asked.

"Oh, hey guys. The internet here sucks, so I was trying to boost the gain on the antenna."

Obadiah sounded impressed. "Now that's something I can get behind. Just don't electrocute yourself, Elmo. I don't want to have to carry your charred body down those rickety stairs."

After working on the roof most of the day, Derrick headed over to the commons. He'd heard the mess hall would bring over some wings and popcorn every Tuesday evening for movie night.

He took up a seat by the wall and watched as Obadiah frantically looked for something. "It was right here this morning. Has anyone seen the remote for the TV?"

Derrick's phone started vibrating and he heard the FaceTime incoming call jingle from his vest pocket.

Checking the screen, he saw Lydia's face. He tried to sneak out into the hallway, but not before the guys gave him some grief.

"Ooooooooh! Elmo, Sesame Street is calling!"

"Oh, maybe it's that Nina girl! Hey, can I get her number? She's so hot!"

"Hey honey, how's it going?" Lydia asked from the screen.

"It's been really busy—Lots of broken things. We had a medflight earlier today." He paused, trying not to break down.

Lydia's excitement faded to worry. "Are you okay, honey?"

He craftily changed the subject. "Obadiah is my overwatch." He was pretty sure he heard a growl come from Lydia.

"Watch your back then. Only six more days and I get to have you in my arms again."

His radio keyed up and Chief Henderson's voice said, "SITROOM—FIVE MINUTES!"

"I'm sorry, honey, but I have to run. We have another mission brief in five minutes."

"Make me proud, stud! I love you, Derrick."

"I love you more, Lydia."

Chief Henderson walked in and started the briefing.

"Mateo is in possession of a hard drive with high-value intel. The mission is to extract him and the drive for examination. Derrick, are you good to go?"

He nodded.

"Excellent! Everyone... get in, get the assets, and get out. We leave in five. Dismissed!"

Derrick climbed into the second to last Humvee of the convoy and the group took off for the location Mateo had sent. Obadiah could tell that Derrick was distracted as he stared out the window.

"Elmo, tighten it up! Your head is going to need to be in the game for this one."

They arrived at a large building nestled among many factories. The extraction team unloaded and made their way through the side entrance. Derrick, Obadiah, and Samir waited outside, providing cover for the vehicles.

"I can't believe we've got valet duty. It's all thanks to you, Elmo. You shouldn't even be here."

Derrick was starting to agree with him.

Ten minutes had passed since the team made entry when Obadiah walked over to Samir.

"Something just doesn't feel right," Obadiah remarked.

Agreeing, Samir added, "I feel it too."

The hair on Obadiah's arm started to stand up. "It's almost like... we are being watched."

As if on cue, gunshots rang through the night. Obadiah and Samir ducked behind the Humvee as rounds pinged all around them.

Derrick felt an impact on his chest, as if he had been hit with a sledgehammer. He dropped to the ground, gasping for air. Looking down, he saw a smoking hole in his body armor. Feeling under the vest, he hit a spot that made him gasp for air again. "OW!! THAT HURT!" he mouthed as he checked for an entrance wound. "I don't feel a hole. I guess that's a good thing, although if it hurt like that getting caught, I can't imagine if the bullet would have actually gone through me," he thought.

Obadiah was returning fire when he noticed Derrick crawling on the ground towards them.

"Move it, Elmo! Someone's shooting at us!"

Derrick was gasping in pain. "I know, one of them hit me!"

Samir dropped his rifle and drug Derrick under the cover of the vehicle. He checked him over and found the hole in his vest. "'E's been 'it, rig't side!" Samir yelled as he tried to check behind the plate for an entry wound.

Derrick reassured, "It's okay! The armor caught it, but... oh... it hurts."

Gunfire erupted from inside the building as well.

"*Snakebite 12, Voodoo 6, have package, taking fire. Prepare exfil!*"

Derrick grabbed his radio and replied through the pain. "*Voodoo 6... be advised... exfil hot.*"

Obadiah and Samir laid down cover fire as the eight-man team exited the building helping Mateo out. As he hobbled up to Derrick, he handed him the hard drive and said, "Guard this with your life!"

Derrick placed it in a pocket on his vest behind his plate armor opposite the side that was hit and ran for the Humvee.

As the team sped away, numerous rounds banged off the outer armor as the gunner returned fire from the 50 caliber mounted on top. Derrick ducked as the sound of a rocket flew by the left side of the truck, followed by an explosion behind them.

"Snakebite 4 hit, Snakebite 4 hit!"

Noticing that their vehicle continued on its original course, Derrick asked, "Are we going to go back and help?"

"A team will, but we must complete the mission and, now that you have the hard drive, YOU are the mission," Obadiah explained.

As they rolled into the base, Derrick was escorted to the IT room, where he secured the hard drive in the IT room safe.

"Now, get yourself to medical," Obadiah ordered.

Derrick looked confused.

Being rather perturbed, Obadiah spelled it out for him, "You were shot, remember? Even though it didn't penetrate your dainty little skin, if you get shot... you go to doc... he make sure you no die. Got it?"

Derrick made his way to the medical tent, where the doctor did a thorough exam. Upon taking off the armor, Derrick saw the large circular bruise on his chest. A few X-rays later, the doctor gave him the good news.

"You're lucky. Looks like you might just have some bruised ribs for a few weeks, but other than that, no major injuries."

Derrick headed back to the command center where the mission debriefing was underway. Obadiah was just finishing up when he walked in.

Chief Henderson stopped Derrick as he entered. "Oh, there you are. I'm guessing you were cleared back to duty since you're here. Is the hard drive secure?"

"Yes, sir. It's locked in the #2 safe in the IT room."

"Very good. I'm awaiting instructions from Headquarters to see how they want the information disseminated. Until then, everybody go get some rest."

CHAPTER 24

It was 3am and Derrick had just laid down after taking a walk around the base to clear his mind.

Just as he had fallen asleep, an explosion rocked the base with a blast strong enough to knock him off the cot he was sleeping on. His radio rang out a brief alarm and then announced, "Mortars inbound!"

Grabbing his rifle, Derrick took off for the muster station where Chief Henderson was already ordering the Ravens to the roof. Seeing Derrick run in, he ordered Obadiah and Samir, "Get Derrick, get the drive and get the...." The chief's voice diminished as Derrick ran for the IT room.

Opening the door, he made for the safe, grabbed the drive, and placed it back into the same side pocket as before.

Obadiah yelled through the open doorway, "Last call, Elmo!"

Derrick was heading out when a chilling broadcast came over the radio.

"Base breached, EVAC to Delta Hotel!"

"*Dat's it, time to go!*" yelled Samir.

Derrick turned around and went to his workbench, where he grabbed a small object that looked like a trashcan with a motor on top. Attached to that motor were two pipes that Obadiah could've sworn to be the missing table legs from the mess hall.

"Stop goofing off, Elmo, we've got to get out of here!"

Setting the device on his chair, Derrick moved it to the center of the room. He then clicked a switch on top to the right twice and ran for the door.

Obadiah and Samir started to move out when they saw Derrick still standing in the doorway, pressing on a TV remote.

"What are you doing? Let's go, you idiot!" Obadiah yelled.

Just then, Derrick heard a beeping from inside the room.

"Uh, oh. MOVE!" he yelled and dove onto the ground to the left of the door.

A second later, Obadiah was knocked down by a white-hot stream of plasma that shot out of the room's door, streaking right past his head. It vaporized the engine compartment of a truck across the street and continued through the building behind it.

"Oops, too much phosphorus," Derrick thought as he admired the sight. Then, he heard the motor whine from inside, and the beam began to move clockwise.

He stood up and yelled, "GO, GO, GO!" and took off running.

The three made for the complex side exit as the sound of AK-47s rang throughout the base. As they approached the side of the mess hall, two combatants ran around the corner. Both Obadiah and Samir opened fire.

Just as the other two were taking their shots, Derrick noticed movement out of the corner of his eye. Looking to this right, he saw a third figure who had just shouldered his rifle. Before Derrick could even think, his training took over, and he fired two quick shots, causing the target to fall to the ground.

Samir spun his head around just in time to see them drop.

"*Dude, Tank you!*"

"Come on! We'll debrief later," Obadiah barked.

Reaching the side exit, Obadiah went through first, and once he gave the all-clear sign, Derrick and Samir followed.

They were heading towards the exfil point as Samir keyed up on his radio.

"*Wite Knigt, this is Rook 12. Sesame Street and Elmo secure. Eading to Otel Delta.*"

Derrick glanced at Samir, only to see a big, toothy grin looking back at him.

Once they ran about a mile, they stopped to catch their breath. Derrick looked back towards the former base to see a large, white glow as bright as a full moon on a cloudless night.

Obadiah, looking rather perturbed, as usual, exclaimed, "Was that your stupid fish assassin juice that shot out of MacGyver's BUTTHOLE back there?!?!"

"I got the idea from one of his episodes. At least they won't be able to steal any of our electronics now."

Obadiah's look turned inquisitive, grabbing Derrick by his plate carrier. He pulled him in slowly until they were nose-to-nose.

"You were the one that stole the remote for the TV in the commons, weren't you?"

Derrick didn't want to answer.

Obadiah snarled at him and, after letting go, said, "Let's head out. We're still vulnerable here."

The three continued north to the meet-up point when they saw lights ahead.

Samir radioed, "*Blue, blue, blue... Rook 12, Tree from de sout.*"

"*Confirmed Rook 12, three from the south,*" came the reply over the radio.

Obadiah moved the last of the overgrowth, and Derrick stopped for a second in disbelief at the scene in front of him. The sun had just broken over the horizon, casting a golden, reddish hue on the Mediterranean Sea, stretching out before them.

The light also revealed three V-22 Ospreys being loaded with evacuees from the base.

Derrick sighed. "Ugh, I hate helicopters."

Still upset after almost being plasmafied earlier, Obadiah snarled, "Your call, Elmo. You can either get in, or hand me that hard drive, and I'll go back and tell Lydia how 'brave' you were when you got cut in half by your own lightsaber."

Derrick hopped into the Osprey, strapping into the first available seat with his radio bag and rifle in his lap. Obadiah and Samir took up rear posts just as the pilot throttled up the deafening blades.

"Man, I could use some headphones," Derrick thought as he watched the city shrink into the distance. He never dreamed he would have been evacuating a post. "Tae will never believe this!"

The Marine sitting beside Derrick nudged him and attempted to yell something, but Derrick heard nothing over the noise of the rotors. Finally, he pointed out the window. Peering out, Derrick saw they were heading towards a ship that looked like a small aircraft carrier with a big white '6' on the island.

After landing, Obadiah motioned for him to follow. Derrick unstrapped and made for the rear loading ramp. Though Obadiah mouthed something, Derrick could still hear nothing but the thumping of the rotors. Obadiah finally pointed towards the island and mouthed, "GO!" Derrick took off running towards the ship's island.

When he approached, the quartermaster stopped him.

"Officer Anderson, I presume."

"Yes, sir! Derrick Anderson, sir."

Grabbing his shoulder, he said, "I have orders to put you and that drive on a flight for Sicily to catch your ride back to the States."

Derrick replied like he had seen in the movies. "Sir, yes, sir!"

The quartermaster led him towards another Osprey that was ready for takeoff, motioning towards the cargo bay. Derrick climbed the ramp into the aircraft.

Inside, nine heavily armed SEALs were already seated around a chair in the middle. One of the SEALs pointed to the vacant seat. Sitting down, Derrick was handed a helmet with a built-in headset.

"Thank you, guys. My ears are ringing!" he exclaimed.

The SEAL that was standing yelled, "Do you have the hard drive!?"

"Sir, yes sir!" Derrick replied as he pulled it out a little from his hidden pocket.

"Load Master, Bravo One. Elmo secure with package. Green for departure."

He then motioned for the SEAL sitting beside Derrick to switch seats.

"Yes sir, Master Chief!" he replied.

The Osprey lifted off the ship and departed to the north towards Sicily.

Derrick finally had time to let his mind drift off to Lydia. He knew she was fast asleep, imagining her lying in her bed all snuggled up with Madeline under her fluffy blanket. He didn't get long to dream when a call came over the headset,

> USS America command, Empire 11, and Empire 18. Stratus 26 under escort.

The reply then came,

> Empire, got Stratus 26 now under escort, USS America command.

Looking at the Master Chief, Derrick asked, "What's he talking about?"

"We picked up two fighters to escort us into Sicily."

He felt a pit in his stomach forming. "Why do we need an escort?"

The Master Chief pointed at Derrick's pocket. "Because of you. The entire Taliban is hunting for that drive... and you... right now."

"Oh, lovely," Derrick groaned. "I kind of liked it better without a headset."

It was a twenty-minute flight from the USS America to the airstrip in Sicily. After touching down, the plane taxied to an awaiting Gulfstream. As the rear door opened, Derrick and the Master Chief exited the aircraft and hurried aboard the small jet. It was much fancier than the Osprey he had just left, with plush, leather seats that could easily fit two people and a big screen TV up on the front wall.

"I could get used to flying like this," he thought as the SEAL closed the door, and they took off on their nine-hour flight home.

Derrick was exhausted from the ordeal he had just survived and finally could relax enough to get some sleep.

...He and Lydia were lying out on a tropical beach. She was sitting in a lounge chair wearing her pink tankini like she had at Virginia Beach. Derrick was lying on his side, watching her soaking up the sun with the breeze blowing across her skin...

He woke up to the SEAL shaking his arm.

"You're nowhere near as cute as the girl I was dreaming about," Derrick joked.

"Man, I sure hope not. Anyway, we've been diverted from Leesburg to Andrews due to some security concerns and have started our descent. Your people have arranged an escort to take you to Langley."

"Thank you, sir," Derrick replied.

The plane taxied up to three waiting black Suburbans with red and blue strobes lighting up the tarmac. The Master Chief led Derrick down the steps and to the open door of the middle SUV.

"It's been a pleasure sir!" as he saluted him.

Derrick shot a quick salute back and climbed in.

"It's good to see you, Derrick," stated the man sitting in the other rear seat.

He was surprised to see the chief had come out to meet him. "Good afternoon, sir. What brings you out today? Needed to stretch your legs?" Derrick casually asked.

"No, Derrick," The chief replied. "I wanted to oversee that hard drive getting to Headquarters personally."

"When Mateo gave it to me, he said it was very important, but nobody ever said what was on it."

"It's a dump of one of the Taliban's servers. It has details of the locations of each one of their leaders. It is also believed to hold their undercover operatives dossiers as well. Our techs are chomping at the bit to get it."

"Couldn't we have just uploaded it and sent it securely?"

"We couldn't risk it. We don't know what tracers are on the data or if it contains malicious code. We have to isolate the drive before we start examining its contents," the chief explained.

`   Derrick could see that something was still weighing on his mind. "That's a good story and all, but I know we have secure ways that we could have just sent the data instead of sending a jet with a fighter escort. You're not telling me something."

The chief's voice grew more serious. "Mateo died in the exfil. He was killed in the Hummer explosion leaving the warehouse. Also, the base invasion was not a random event. They raided it for the drive. Henderson refused to tell them where it was or who had it. He stalled them as you three escaped. When they found out it was gone, they executed him along with the rest of his team."

Derrick hung his head in sadness.

As the convoy turned into the entrance of Headquarters, traffic was stopped in all directions by multiple police cars. Passing the long line of employees trying to leave, Derrick caught a glimpse of a white Beetle. He knew she wouldn't be happy having to sit in that traffic because of him.

They pulled up to the front doors, where two officers awaited them. Derrick and the chief stepped out of the vehicle and headed inside. When they reached the chief's office, a couple of techs were already. Derrick removed the hard drive from the pocket in his body armor and handed it over.

"I know you must be tired, Derrick. Is there anything you need right now? If not, we can head back downstairs, and the guys will take you home. We can do the debrief tomorrow when you are better rested."

Derrick felt so mentally and physically exhausted, he couldn't think of anything but Lydia. "No, sir, I can't think of anything tonight. I just want to curl up in my bed and go to sleep."

"That's fair," said the chief. "We are going to station a couple of officers at your apartment for a few days, just in case. I doubt there will be any trouble. Your name was never spoken, so they shouldn't know who escaped with it or where it is now."

Derrick thanked him as they headed back out front.

The convoy of SUVs pulled up in front of Derrick's apartment. Derrick stepped out, still wearing his desert fatigues, body armor, and with his sidearm holstered on his leg, followed by two officers carrying M4s in full tactical gear. Ms. Lowell happened to be out checking her mail and stood slack-jawed as they walked by.

"Evening, Ms. Lowell." She remained speechless as they entered the building.

"Well, that one is going to be hard to explain. She thinks I work for the Geek Squad."

Derrick was bracketed front and back by the officers as they walked down the hallway to his door. He pondered what Lydia would think as she looked out of the peephole and saw him and two armed TAC officers,

Derrick knocked on their door, and Lydia excitedly opened it, greeting him with a big hug.

"What are you doing home?!?" she asked, her gaze now locked onto the officers.

"I'll explain everything, but Collins and Sullivan will be staying with us for a few days."

Derrick held his breath when he saw Lydia glance down at the hole in his vest. He had traded out the plate, but they didn't have any other vests available. She looked back up at the officers without saying a word about it.

"Well, come on in, guys. You want a coffee? I just brewed up some of Seattle's finest!"

CHAPTER 25

...As Derrick pulled up to the wood mulching plant, he could see a beehive of activity over at one of the huge, industrial wood chippers there. They were paged for an "accident" at the plant with no further details. He grabbed his bag and headed towards the crowd. The foreman met him and told him that one of their employees was trying to clear a jam but forgot to turn the machine off. He walked up to the feeder and looked in...

Derrick jolted awake, screaming. At that moment, Collins kicked his door open and entered with a drawn rifle. Still groggy from sleep, Derrick reached for his sidearm.

"Derrick! Blue! Blue!" Collins shouted as he noticed him reaching for his gun.

It was enough to make Derrick remember the officers that were spending the night. As Collins cleared the room, they both heard Lydia scream. Derrick shot out of the bed and reached her door before Collins. When he entered, Lydia was sitting on the bed, wrapped in her blanket, and one very terrified officer was bent over on the floor beside her. In obvious pain, Sullivan tried to explain.

"We heard you scream. Collins headed for your room and I went to protect her. When I entered, she came out of her bed in a roundhouse kick that landed in a very sensitive area."

Collins started laughing as he grabbed Sullivan and helped him back out into the living room.

"These two are perfect for each other."

Derrick reached down and picked up Madeline, who had fallen off the bed in the scuffle, and then sat down beside her.

"I'm sorry, sweetie. It was another nightmare, and I didn't realize I screamed out loud."

Leaning over, she hugged him.

"It's okay, honey. I'm just glad you are home... and that I wore PJs tonight."

Derrick's imagination started wandering. "Did she mean she doesn't normally?"

His eyes must have been growing because she chimed in, "Calm down, cowboy. I meant a t-shirt and shorts and not a nightgown or something less covering... Well, I just realized that might not have helped the situation. How about you just go back over to your side and get some sleep and we'll talk about this in the morning?"

She grabbed Madeline from him and hugged her. Derrick kissed her on the head and told her good night again.

Collins was looking at Derrick's door when he came back over. It was only hanging by one hinge now and the latch was splintered on the floor.

"Um... the Company will fix that."

"It's okay. I'm just glad you guys are here after the last few days."

"It's our pleasure, although Sullivan told me he would be knocking before he barges into her room again."

***

Derrick had trouble sleeping the rest of the night. After showering and getting dressed, he went out into the living room to find Collins and Sullivan talking with the on-coming crew.

Addressing Derrick, Collins said, "We were just finishing the morning briefing. This is Brady and Watson. They will watch the apartment while you are at work. Sullivan and I will take you in this morning and will bring you back after."

Lydia stepped out to find the living room full of men. She greeted each of them. "Collins, dudes I don't know... Sullivan." She said that last one with a slight grin.

"Ma'am," Sullivan replied sheepishly.

Lydia came over and gave him a peck on the cheek. "Sorry, I kicked you."

Collins gestured towards the door. "If you are ready, we can head for the vehicles."

Lydia looked at Derrick very confused. "Vehicles?!?"

They made their way down the hall, being bracketed by the officers. Derrick was hoping they could get outside without anyone noticing. His hopes were quickly dashed when Collins keyed up.

"*Guardian 4, Guardian 5 on the move with Halo.*"

"*Guardian 5, Guardian 4, Entrance secured, ready for transport.*"

Derrick at least liked his new code name better than his last.

Ms. Lowell poked her head out of her door. "Derrick, what did you do this time?"

Lydia answered her. "It's okay, Mildred. I will get this straightened out."

Derrick glared at her, none the amused, "Why?!?"

They stepped outside of the building to find the same three SUVs waiting for them. The main entrance to the apartment was blocked and officers were securing a small crowd of neighbors that had accumulated trying to leave for work.

"They aren't very subtle, are they? ...Wait, weren't those the same ones I saw speeding into Headquarters yesterday? That was you, wasn't it? I had to sit in that stupid line for thirty minutes!"

"I told Chief you would be mad when you found out," Derrick said grinning.

The convoy merged onto the Dulles Toll Road and sped past the slowed rush hour traffic.

"This is the only way to go to work! We'll be there in like five minutes at this speed," Lydia amazed.

"I think I'd prefer to just close my eyes and not watch," Derrick said while holding on.

Traffic became heavier once they exited onto Dolley Madison Blvd. The convoy tried to maneuver through the stopped traffic, but lights and sirens did little to help their progress.

Lydia was going over her plans for the day to help keep Derrick distracted from the aggressive driving the officers were doing. He got distracted when he saw a new Corvette passing by on the other side of the road.

As he admired the shiny red sports car, the window he was looking out of exploded. Derrick flinched backward as the bulletproof glass caught whatever hit it, but several small pieces still sprayed into his face.

Before Lydia could gasp, her window exploded into a spider web as well. Collins made a sharp left turn, bounced over the median, and accelerated the vehicle into oncoming traffic.

Derrick grabbed Lydia, pulled her head down onto the seat, and covered her. His window took two more impacts, with the second one penetrating the glass, glancing off the back of his head, and embedding into the passenger side door frame.

Sullivan screamed into the microphone, *"Spectre 3 taking fire! Eastbound 123 at Old Dominion in westbound lanes!"*

The other two SUVs caught back up to Collins.

"Overwatch, Spectre 1, suspect in pursuit. Permission to engage?"

"Spectre 1, Spectre 2, Priority is Spectre 3. Sending help your way. Engage as last resort."

The two SUVs dropped in behind Collins, catching multiple rounds into their back glasses as they exceeded 80mph.

They approached the intersection for Georgetown Pike when Collins saw two black SUVs in a V-formation ahead. The officers were positioned behind the hoods of each of the vehicles with their rifles aimed. The convoy raced through the barricade as Derrick heard the officers opening fire on the pursuing vehicle.

"Overwatch, Viper 1. Suspect vehicle neutralized."

"Stay down! Stay down! Are you two hit?" asked Sullivan.

Lydia replied, "I don't know, but my ear is killing me... and why is there blood all over the floor?!?"

When Derrick didn't answer, Sullivan looked back and saw him still covering Lydia... then he noticed the wound track on the back of his head and the blood dripping from his eyes.

"*Overwatch, Spectre 3. Broken Halo. Need medical when we arrive. GSW 2 minutes out.*"

The intersection at Headquarters was once again blocked, but this time it was with armed guards. Incoming traffic to the complex was moved off to the side, and the gates were opened as the convoy sped towards the medical crew, who were just outside the main doors. A helicopter was also circling over the complex, awaiting landing clearance.

The convoy skidded to a stop and the two of them were rushed out opposite sides of the vehicle. Lydia's team quickly examined her. While she had blood all over her blouse, they only found some minor bleeding from her right ear. Upon hearing that, she jumped up and ran around the vehicle to find blood streaming down from several places on Derrick's face. A nurse was holding a soaked trauma pad on the back of his head and over both eyes.

"Overwatch, MedTeam 1. We need the MedFlight to land for transport."

CHAPTER 26

A large medical helicopter slowly made its approach over the Bubble between the tree line and the Headquarters building. The medical team strapped Derrick to a backboard and prepared to move him. Sullivan stood guard, ready to escort them to the helicopter.

Lydia started walking with them when Sullivan motioned to her that she couldn't follow. Angrily, she mouthed to him to get out of the way, threatening to kick him again.

Finally agreeing, Sullivan informed the flight lead that she would be joining as well and provided her with some body armor from the SUV. Lydia was shown to the seat beside the pilot and Sullivan hopped into the back with Derrick as the helicopter picked up off the ground.

It was a short, five-minute flight to Walter Reed. When Sullivan exited the helicopter, he opened the door for Lydia, and they followed Derrick as he was rolled into Trauma Room 2. Sullivan took up point outside of the door with his M4 in patrol position.

Standing outside of Derrick's room, the charge nurse approached Lydia and introduced herself to Lydia. "Hello dear. My name is Pam. You look a little roughed up yourself. Can we check you out too?"

Brushing her off, Lydia replied, "I'm fine. I just want to see Derrick."

Pam put her arm around her. "I know, I know. A lot is going on in there right now, though. How about we get you a room beside his and we can make sure none of this blood is yours? Then when there's less of a crowd in his room, we can take you in. You'll be able to hear if there's any trouble."

Looking at Sullivan, asked, "Is that alright?"

"Yes, ma'am. I can cover both rooms."

After showing Lydia to the room next to Derrick's, Pam started checking her over for injuries as an ER doctor examined her ear. She had a ruptured eardrum from the noise of the impact right beside her head.

"It's just a small hole," the doctor said, "which is where the bleeding came from. It should heal up in a couple of weeks."

Pam brought Lydia some scrubs to change into and then packed her bloody clothes up in a bag.

***

Derrick's doctor examined his entry wound and did a quick x-ray to make sure the bullet wasn't lodged somewhere in his skull.

"You're very lucky. It looks like it skipped off the bone without breaking it. We need to clean it out now and prep it for suturing."

While they were irrigating the long cut, Derrick tried to lighten the mood in the room. "You're new at this waterboarding thing, aren't you?"

The doctor didn't even crack a smile. "You think torture now... wait until we remove that glass from your eye."

Derrick's face quickly turned into a frown.

***

As the doctor was tending to Lydia's ear, she asked for an update on Derrick.

"He's a little roughed up but is stable from what I heard in passing. I did get to talk to Sullivan some, though. From what he told me, if Derrick hadn't deflected it, that last bullet was coming for you."

***

Derrick was wheeled down to a special procedure room where there was what looked like a dentist's chair. After giving him a light sedative, they laid him back to where his head was positioned slightly downward.

"Let us know if you start getting a headache or feel lightheaded. It's not ideal to hang you upside down with a wound like that, but we need to get that glass out," the nurse explained, prepping the instrument tray.

After putting drops of proparacaine in Derrick's eyes to numb them, the doctor put his magnifying glasses on and wheeled over to his head. "Remember that torture comment from earlier?"

Derrick may have been numb, but he could still see everything going on thanks to the medieval torture device they used to keep his eyelids open.

Watching as the doctor's tweezers grew larger and larger in his view, he tried everything he could to close his eyes, but it was futile. One by one, he saw the shards of glass being pulled out of each eye. The doctor was right; He really missed the "waterboarding" from earlier.

After removing the large pieces Derrick's eyes were flushed to remove any leftover pieces.

After the fifteen minutes of flushing was complete, the doctor asked how his eyes were feeling now.

Being overly excited that he could blink again, Derrick replied, "Well, they feel raw, like someone rubbed sandpaper over them for a few hours, but the sharp stabbing pains are gone. I am having a little trouble seeing though. Things just don't look right."

"That's to be expected until they heal completely. If it doesn't clear up in a few weeks, follow up with an optometrist."

***

Lydia was contemplating how Derrick literally took a bullet for her when Pam came in to take her over to his room.

The doctor had just finished bandaging the last row of stitches on the top of his head when they walked in. Lydia noticed that Derrick's entire left eye was a dark red and blood was oozing from its corner, running down his face. He was also trying to hide a large bruise in the center of his chest.

"Hey honey, how are you doing?" she asked.

"I could use a burger."

She smiled, thinking, "That's my Derrick for you—gets shot at three times, flown to a hospital, face bleeding with a head full of stitches, and all he can think about is food."

"Maybe I should be more specific and ask about your head and chest and not your stomach, then."

Derrick tried explaining without too many details. "They pulled a bunch of glass out from all over, including my eyes. Something also scratched me on the back of the head."

The doctor piped in, "Yeah, a bullet, and I didn't use the word 'scratched'."

Lydia looked at Derrick with concern.

Downplaying the severity, he reassured, "It's fine. I'm fine. It's just another cut that they stitched up."

"How many stitches did you need?!?" she asked.

"I think the last count was like twelve or so."

The doctor chimed in again, "Sixty-three... in eight different spots."

Derrick glared at him in disbelief. "Dude! How are you helping?!?"

Turning back to Lydia, embarrassment washed over Derrick's face when he saw how worried she was.

"I'm sorry, sweetie. I never wanted you to be in danger."

Lydia sat down on the bed beside him. "I don't even know how you think any of this is your fault. This is all about that stupid hard drive. It's just what you had to do. If I was there, then I would have gotten it and I'm not sure I would've had the same outcome. You did amazing work over there and just think, we have yet another story we can't tell the neighbors."

After placing a patch over Derrick's left eye, the doctor gave him some final instructions. "Okay, you are all set now. Make sure you keep the bandages clean and change them every day. You can remove the eye patch after a couple of weeks if the redness has gone away."

Still pondering why no one mentioned anything about the large bruise, Lydia asked the doctor about it as he was leaving, "Is that bruising on his chest something to be concerned about?"

The doctor placed his hand on her shoulder. "That injury pre-dated what happened today."

She looked at Derrick as he was putting his shirt on and wondered what else he was hiding from the mission.

Once he had changed into the provided scrubs, Lydia grabbed him by the hand.

"How about we go home and spend some quality time with Collins and Sullivan?"

***

...It was a bright, sunny spring day and Derrick was sitting on a bench in the middle of the park. A small girl came walking up holding a sunflower. As she stood in front of him, the sky turned gray with clouds and the wind picked up. The petals from her flower started blowing away one by one until they were all gone. She looked at him, and through her tears, asked, "Why?" She collapsed into a pile of dust on the ground where the wind blew it away until there was nothing left.

Derrick looked at the clock, which read *3:16am.* The night was taking forever as he was having trouble staying asleep. He wasn't able to lie on a pillow due to all the stitches and bandages, so he was reclined in his chair. Every time he would nod off, the girl would appear in his dreams. It was a different scenario each time, but it always ended with the same question. He thought about going for a walk, but it just wasn't as peaceful, looking like a mummy and having Collins tail right behind him.

After hours of short cat naps, Derrick was relieved when the sunrise started to peak through the window. He walked out into the living room and Sullivan had just started a pot of coffee.

"You read my mind! I guess I will go check the mail while it brews."

Collins grunted as he got up out of his chair. "Good. I need to stretch my legs after Sullivan's marathon game of *Black Ops*."

"Yeah, where you lost!"

"I didn't lose. You used a cheat code!"

"Hey, there's no cheating in war!"

As he and Collins headed downstairs to the mailboxes, they passed Ms. Lowell in the hallway.

"Are you arresting him for beating up that nice floozy that lives with him?" she asked Collins.

"Him? No. It was her that did all that. She even beat up my partner when we were trying to help."

"Oh my! Wait until the bridge club hears this."

After she had gone into her apartment, Derrick turned to him.

"I'm telling her you said that."

"Go ahead. She doesn't scare me. It's Sullivan that's terrified of her."

After they got back upstairs, Derrick slipped off his sandals and headed over to the coffee machine that had just finished brewing. He pulled the pot out and started to pour the steaming hot coffee into his mug. Unbeknownst to him yet, his depth perception was off due to the wounds on his cornea. The coffee missed the mug and landed straight on his wrist, causing him to scream and drop it. Falling onto his bare left foot, the mug shattered.

Lydia ran out of her room to find Collins and Sullivan staring in disbelief as Derrick hopped across the broken glass towards the sink still carrying the pot of hot coffee. He finally reached the sink, leaving a trail of blood on the floor from the multiple cuts that had opened on his foot.

She ran over to where Derrick was now and grabbed the coffeepot from his hand, not realizing it was steaming hot. This caused her to drop the pot, which fell and shattered on Derrick's other foot, flooding it with the burning hot coffee.

Sullivan looked at Collins, who had covered his mouth to hide the laughter he was poorly holding back.

"You think we should go help?"

Shaking his head, Collins replied, "I'm not sure we're trained for this kind of disaster."

Lydia grabbed a couple of ice packs from the freezer while the guys helped Derrick to a chair.

As he picked glass out of his foot with his good hand, Derrick joked, "I guess someone is going to have to make a Starbucks run now since the coffee pot is broken."

Lydia shot into her room faster than he had ever seen her move before and emerged less than a minute later in new clothes, with her wallet and phone in hand.

"You better move it, Sully!" she exclaimed as she was halfway out the door.

"Uh, ma'am, wait up!" Sullivan yelled, grabbing his rifle and chasing after her.

Derrick yelled to Sullivan, "Tell her to make mine iced, please!"

Collins looked at Derrick, chuckling. "I still say you two are perfect for each other."

About thirty minutes later, they heard a quick knock at the door as it opened.

"Blue, Blue!" Sullivan called out as he entered, carrying the drinks.

Lydia followed with a huge smile on her face.

"You happy now that you got your Starbucks, honey?" Derrick asked.

Sullivan rolled his eyes as Lydia sheepishly grinned and nodded her head. "You know that's her second one, right? She downed the first one in the car on the way back." Lydia shot him a glare, which made him flinch a little.

"I'm going to go put my stuff up. I'll be right back," Lydia said as she headed off into her room.

Sullivan sat down next to Collins and passed out the drinks.

"You know she's crazy, right?" he told Derrick.

"Yeah, but she's cute, so it balances out."

Lydia came back out and heard them talking. "What balances out?"

The color on Sullivan's face drained. "Oh, nothing. We were just talking about guns and cars... man stuff... yeah."

***

Derrick showed Lydia how to bandage his foot and hand. He was starting to look more like a mummy every day now.

As she finished up, she could tell something was still bothering him. Hoping that if they had some privacy he'd open up, she suggested they go relax on the balcony. Helping Derrick up, she told Sullivan, "We're going to go out to the balcony for a bit."

Sullivan, kicked back in his chair by the TV, replied "That's fine, ma'am. We can watch you through the window."

She gave him a suspicious look. "That's not creepy at all."

Lydia helped Derrick into one of the padded recliner chairs on the balcony and then looked out at the view.

"It's such a beautiful day, don't you think?"

Derrick saw right through her façade. "You didn't bring me out here to talk about the weather."

She sat down next to him and placed her hand on his leg.

"Back at Walter Reid, the doctor mentioned that the bruise on your chest happened prior to yesterday. I also noticed the hole in your vest when you came home, so I can only assume something else happened on that tour that you're not telling me."

Derrick sighed. "The mission where we went and got the hard drive was where it happened. I was outside with Obadiah and Samir when we started taking fire."

Lydia interrupted. "You were shot?!?"

"Yes, but the armor stopped it. I'm sorry I didn't tell you. I didn't want to make you worry," he said solemnly.

She could tell by his face something else was wrong. "That's not all, is it?"

Derrick's exposed eye filled with tears. "On the mission we went on right before you called, we had an incident with a suicide bomber."

Lydia's heart skipped a beat as she tried to hide the fear that was growing within her.

"I had just gotten back into the helicopter to head to the base when I saw them walking towards us. I fired, and it set the bomb off." He tried unsuccessfully to compose himself. "I took someone's life."

Lydia attempted to comfort him with a hug but couldn't find a spot that wasn't injured.

"You didn't kill them, Derrick. The bomb did. You stopped them," she tried explaining.

"It was a five-year-old girl."

Lydia retracted in horror. "What?!?"

"She was a beautiful, terrified little girl in a sunflower dress," Derrick said through the tears.

Lydia squeezed him harder as tears of her own started welling up.

CHAPTER 27

Sunday morning rolled around, and Derrick was getting ready for church. He still had a patch over his left eye, hiding his bloody sclera, and bandages on his head, hand, and both feet which required him to wear slides instead of his dress shoes. Truthfully, most people wouldn't even have asked about the bandages, knowing how accident-prone he was. He wasn't even really that worried about explaining why Lydia had her right ear covered. What would be harder to explain were the black SUVs and armed escorts.

"Is it possible to not wear the tactical vests for a few hours?" he asked Collins.

"No sir, it's policy, but what we can do is stay toward the back of the room and blend in."

"Blend in," Derrick thought. "Two large military guys in tactical gear carrying M4s will blend in with a group of elderly people in suits?"

While Derrick was trying to figure out a way to get out of this, Lydia came out into the dining room wearing her ankle-length red flower dress. She was able to limit her bandages down to a single cotton ball that hid in her ear.

"Good morning, beautiful," he said to her.

Lydia leaned over and carefully kissed him on the cheek. "Thank you, honey. Why do you look so mopey, though?"

"I called the church building to warn them secretly hoping they would suggest we stay home today."

"I take it from your face they didn't."

Derrick's shoulders dropped and looked even more pitiful. "Noooo. They insisted we come in and assured it wouldn't be a problem."

"Trust me, honey, it won't be that bad."

As Collins sped down the Fairfax County Parkway, Derrick's nerves were in overdrive. He had tried to convince him not to run the strobes, but Derrick was overruled.

"My drive, my ride," Collins smugly replied.

Their replacement SUV had that new car smell, but the memories of the Friday commute were still vivid in his mind.

"I can see it in your eyes," Lydia said, snapping Derrick out of his daze.

"Huh? See what?"

"You're scared it's going to happen again, aren't you?"

He looked down at the floorboard. "Yes, I'm scared. But not for me. I was terrified I was going to lose you. The entire time I envisioned my life without you—having to go to your funeral and then returning to our empty, cold apartment." Derrick started tearing up as Lydia reached down to hold his good hand.

The convoy pulled under the overhang at the entrance of the church building. Sullivan opened the rear passenger door for Lydia and Derrick slid over. Collins had requested that he exit through the same door to limit exposure.

Sullivan led the two of them through the glass doors, where he was joined by Dawson from the third vehicle. When they entered, the entire building fell silent, and all eyes turned towards them.

"Not that bad, huh?"

He and Lydia headed for their seats as if nothing was out of the ordinary when their friend Greg walked up. "Dare I even ask?"

"It's a lot simpler if you don't," Derrick replied.

As the service was about to start, Derrick leaned over to Lydia.

"Everyone is staring," he whispered.

"Oh, come on, no they're not," she said as she looked around the room, seeing all the faces looking back. "Well, not everyone is looking," she added.

"Name one," Derrick replied, glaring.

"Mr. Roberts."

"Lydia... he's not here today."

"Fine, everyone is looking. They're probably just wondering about your bandages."

"Yeah, that's it. Has nothing to do with the SUV convoy parked under the overhang and the army of two standing in broad daylight by the doors. You're right, it's 'how did Derrick blow himself up again?'"

He hoped that with the service starting, people would concentrate on it and not on the less-than-covert show he brought with him. Derrick was wrong. An older gentleman took the podium and said, "Good morning, everyone. The elders wanted to make an announcement."

Looking over at Lydia dejectedly, Derrick groaned, "Oh, no."

The gentleman continued. "You might have noticed a little extra security here today. We wanted to assure everyone that there is no danger. Mr. Anderson just brought some friends from work with him this morning."

Derrick turned into liquid and slid down as low as he could in his pew.

When they finished singing, Derrick went to place his songbook into the rack on the back of the pew in front of him when he missed, and it dropped to the floor with a thud. Instinctively, he lurched forward, trying to catch it, and slammed his forehead on the back of the pew. The lady in front of them let out a scream and Lydia gasped in shock.

Derrick grabbed his head and quietly screamed, "*OWWWWWWWW!*" which made her lose her composure. She had to bite her lip and look away to keep from laughing out loud.

A few deep breaths later, she was able to turn back and check on him. When she did, she was horrified to see blood running down from under his eye patch.

"Derrick! You're bleeding!" she whispered.

Still having a sense of humor after the event, he replied, "I know, but who's Derrick?" as he retrieved his handkerchief from his pocket.

***

The service finally ended, and Lydia stood up to leave. Derrick was still seated on the pew looking straight ahead in a daze.

"Honey, you okay?"

"No. My head hurts. Can we go home?"

As he stood to leave, the preacher walked up and greeted them.

"Hello, Lydia. Derrick... my stars, you look a little worse for the wear. Everything okay?"

"Oh yes. There was just a little accident on the way to work on Friday. We're fine though. It looks a lot worse than it is," Lydia explained.

"Anything we can help with?" as he looked back at the two officers by the front door.

Derrick sighed. "It's a long story..."

"Well, I'm glad you both are safe and if you need anything, let me know."

They headed to the back of the auditorium and met up with Sullivan and Dawson.

"You ready to head out, sir?" Dawson asked.

"Long past... oh, and can we please not leave with the lights on?"

"I doubt it. Collins likes his lights."

Sullivan radioed the convoy, letting them know they were on their way. *"Spectre 3, Guardian 2 on the move with Halo."*

Greg glanced at Derrick who was turning a couple shades of red. "Halo?!?"

"Trust me. It's better than what it was."

***

Back at the apartment, Lydia was making Derrick and their new friends her special chicken and rice concoction when the chief rang his phone.

"Hello Derrick, I have some news about your attacker. The FBI raided his apartment, and they found one of those creepy stalker walls full of pictures. The good news is, you weren't his target. He had the Director's picture plastered everywhere with red circles drawn on her. It appears he had set up waiting for her convoy to come by and thought you were her. We are going to leave the officers there for the night and then tomorrow we will start phasing them back."

"That sounds great, Chief. I'm sure they will sleep a lot better at night knowing Lydia isn't waiting around the corner."

He felt a towel snap him in the butt.

The chief laughed at hearing his yelp. "Derrick, you're supposed to keep those kinds of thoughts in your head. Anyway, stop by my office tomorrow sometime. I want to catch up on everything."

***

Monday morning, Lydia drove them into Headquarters, albeit not exactly by themselves. Collins and Sullivan followed behind in their black SUV.

Feeling more lighthearted than Derrick, she leaned over and whispered, "I think we have a tail."

Derrick rolled his exposed eye.

Lydia had to go to the travel office to finalize her delayed trip to Baghdad which was in a few weeks.

"Chief wanted to see me so I'll catch back up with you outside travel in a bit," Derrick said as they parted and he headed to the elevator.

The elevator doors opened on the 7th floor, and two ladies were waiting to get on. He couldn't help but notice how they took a few steps back when they saw him. It's not every day you see someone walking the halls of Headquarters with a face full of scratches, an eye patch, and half their body bandaged.

Derrick knocked as he entered the waiting area for the chief's office. Rosalyn, the chief's secretary, greeted him.

"Good morning, Derrick. Rough couple of weeks?"

Hearing Derrick, the chief stepped out of his office. "Great Scott, Derrick! I knew you were roughed up a bit, but it looks like you lost a fight with a Wookie."

The chief showed him to a seat in his office. "First off, how are you doing? Looks like things have been a little bumpy since we last talked."

Derrick leaned back in his chair. "Well, you know... a car chase, getting shot at, helicopter ride, a little torture... typical Friday morning."

"I've heard stories from the Ravens about the device you set off. I believe Obadiah used the term 'Magical fish killing juice', for whatever reason."

"He's still mad about that flying fish that smacked him in the face."

The chief looked at Derrick like he just spoke Swahili to him.

"Well, you see, there was an incident with the lake behind the dorms down in Lynchburg..."

"Oh, I read that report, but what does that and Tripoli have in common?"

Derrick detailed how he developed the phosphamite and that he used the legs from a cafeteria table, a motor from an old hard drive, the remote from the common room, and a steel trashcan to put together the machine to spray it out onto the equipment.

"That's ingenious! We were able to get back onto the base and found that the entire contents of the

IT room had melted into a puddle. There was nothing left."

"Well, that was the idea. I guess it worked."

The chief delicately continued, "I've also heard about the first mission; the one with the girl. Are you comfortable going over that one?"

Derrick paused for a bit, reliving the event. "It was a lose/lose situation. We had just loaded the patient onto the other helicopter when I noticed her walk out. Something just didn't feel right. It wasn't that she was approaching the helicopter. I've had that happen several times before when I was flying. Kids are always excited and don't know any better. This girl was terrified... but still walking towards us. It didn't add up. I don't even remember pulling the trigger..."

The girl's face was replaying over and over in his head when he realized he had stopped talking for a bit and the chief was just staring at him.

"Killing someone is hard. Taking the life of a child is probably the hardest. I'd like you to talk with one of our therapists and I don't mean someone from OMS. Let's keep them out of this as much as we can. I'll give you a name. She listens well."

When they were finishing up, Rosalyn's voice came over the intercom. "Sir, she's here."

"I just want to let you know that you did an amazing job. I look forward to seeing where you go from here. There is one more piece of business we need to take care of, though."

The chief led Derrick to the reception area where they found the Director waiting for them.

"Good morning, Mr. Anderson."

Derrick snapped to attention. "Madam Director. I apologize for my appearance."

"At ease, at ease. I've heard about your heroics in Tripoli. Saving your crew from a suicide bomber, keeping the enemy from obtaining our equipment, and returning with high-value intel. We are very proud of your hard work."

"Thank you, Madam Director."

"You could even say you took a bullet for me as well," she said with a grin. "I'm sorry that happened to you. I hope we are giving you the care you need."

"Yes, ma'am. I've received outstanding care. Even during the glass extraction."

"Well, Derrick, let's get down to the reason I am here."

Her assistant handed her a small four-inch by four-inch black velour presentation box. She opened it, revealing a large round bronze medal with the seal set in the center of a five-pointed star.

"I hereby present you, Derrick Anderson, the CIA Intelligence Star. For voluntary acts of courage performed under hazardous conditions and for heroism under conditions of grave risk. The Agency and your nation are forever grateful for your service and sacrifice."

Derrick almost felt a little embarrassed accepting the award. He didn't feel like he did anything beyond what anyone else would have done.

"There were a couple of other good men that deserved this more than me," he said solemnly.

She placed her hand on his shoulder. "I will be presenting Connor and Mateo's families with theirs later today. Keep your chin up."

"Thank you, Madam Director."

Derrick headed back downstairs carrying the box with the medal. He walked by the lobby and noticed they were setting up for the star carving ceremony.

Having still about an hour before they would start, Derrick headed towards the travel office to find Lydia. He could see she was finishing up inside, so he decided to wait on one of their plush benches in the hallway.

Stepping out into the hallway, Lydia smiled when she saw him. "All done with the chief? What did he have to say?"

"He wants me to see one of their therapists to make sure I'm ready to go back out."

Terror filled Lydia's face. "It's not an OMS one, but one of the people on his staff."

"Oh, good!" she said, relieved. "I've heard about those OMS therapists. They will end your career for the fun of it."

She then noticed the box in his hand. "Hey, what's that there? You go to the gift shop?"

Derrick opened the box and showed Lydia the medal.

Gasping, she sat down beside him to get a better look.

"Is that what I think it is?!?"

"It's the Intelligence Star," Derrick said, unemotionally.

"That's amazing! The chief give you that?"

"No, the Director did," Derrick continued nonchalantly.

"THE DIRECTOR?!? As in Director Perrin?!? As in Director of the CIA, Perrin?!?"

"Yep, that would be her."

"Why aren't you more excited?"

Derrick hung his head. "Because those that actually deserved it aren't here anymore to receive it."

Lydia put her arm around him and pulled him closer. "Let's go honor them then."

The lobby was starting to fill with people as everyone was taking their seats for the ceremony. Lydia and Derrick grabbed a few towards the front as the Director was arranging her notes at the podium.

Lydia leaned over and whispered, "As in THAT Director?"

"Yes... her... shhhh."

The ceremony started with the Director giving eulogies for Mateo and Henderson as the master carver started carving their stars. Then, just like she had promised, the Director presented the medals to their widows along with a folded flag.

Derrick was in a daze through most of the observance. He had never been to one of these ceremonies before and didn't realize the memories that would flood back to him. He had only known Chief Henderson for a couple of days and didn't even know his first name was Connor. He had never actually met Mateo before the mission, but he felt like both were lifelong friends that had passed. Looking over at Lydia, who was fighting back tears, he realized how close he had been to almost becoming a third star that day.

★★★

Two stars among many. Two empty spots in a book.

★★★

CHAPTER 28

Lydia was very nervous as they headed to Dulles for her flight. "What if I don't know what I'm doing, and the chief gets mad?"

"They'll just *persona non grata* you and send you home, no worries."

Derrick hadn't stuck his foot in his mouth in a while and forgot how hard Lydia smacked.

"You're not being helpful!"

"You know what you're doing, and you can't be worse than me. I burned my entire base down."

"You're real funny, Mr. Intelligence Star Award."

"Wasn't worth the cost," he replied, solemnly.

Derrick pulled his Mustang into one of the short-term parking spots at the airport. Lydia found that her door barely opened before it reached the vehicle next to her.

"Your car is stupid, you know that?"

"Hey! He can hear you! They just don't know how to make parking spots."

"Mine doesn't have a problem," she quietly said sarcastically, but it was loud enough for Derrick to hear it.

"Yeah… and it looks like a bug!"

She smiled and swatted him a couple of times before leaning in for a hug.

"I'm really scared."

"I know. This part is the hardest. It gets easier once you get there... unless you have Obadiah as overwatch." Feeling there was something more than just nerves, he pushed her out a little so he could see her eyes. "Tell me."

A tear fell from her eye. "I have a bad feeling. Like..."

Derrick pulled her back in close as she broke down.

Through the tears, she finally said, "Like... I won't see you again."

Lydia calmed down after a few minutes and they made their way to security.

"It's going to be okay. It's only 10 days and then I'll be picking you up right back at this same spot. Besides, Madeline and I need some movie time together. We're going to watch the graphic war movies you won't let her see," he said, smiling.

"You better keep her safe or I'm coming for you!"

They kissed, and Lydia headed through the checkpoint.

Derrick was walking through the door of their apartment when Lydia Facetimed him.

"Hi, honey. Miss me already?" Derrick joked.

"LOOK AT THESE SEATS!" Lydia explained as she spun the camera around, showing off her business class seat.

"I told you! They are HUGE!" Derrick exclaimed. "Just wait until you lay them out and actually get to sleep on the flight."

Derrick heard an announcement, and Lydia said, "I'm sorry, honey. They just closed the doors, and I need to turn my phone off. I'll let you know when I'm in Dubai. I love you so much!"

He kissed the screen of his phone and said, "I love you more. I can't wait until the wedding. I've got something planned."

***

Derrick was asleep in bed when the text tone on his phone went off. He rolled over and fumbled around, trying to find it on his dresser. The blinding light made him squint as he focused on the message. It was a selfie of Lydia smiling, holding a Starbucks cup with the "Welcome to Dubai" sign in the background.

She included in the message, "Wish you were here!"

Derrick placed an eye patch over Madeline's eye, wrapped her head with a bandage, and took a selfie with her.

She sent back a text with "ROFL" and "I miss you."

***

Nine days had passed, and Derrick had just finished up his last OMS checkup to renew his overseas clearance. He stopped in at Overwatch to check on Mike. He was still working on getting cleared for his first deployment.

Mike was updating him on his OMS progress when the radio crackled to life, "*Overwatch Command, this is Baghdad, how copy?*"

It was Lydia. Derrick asked if he could answer to surprise her. He picked up the microphone and said, "Polaris, this is Overwatch. We have you loud and clear, but unreadable."

You could almost hear the smile in her voice when she replied, "*Overwatch Command, this is Polaris, we have you loud and clear as well...*"

Then there was some sort of commotion on the radio. A soft voice came back on, "*Derrick... I love...*" And then the radio clicked off.

"Baghdad, Baghdad, this is Overwatch, how copy?"

Waiting a few seconds, Derrick repeated the call. Only silence was heard on the other side.

***

Moments earlier... Lydia was on the roof of the Coms Center, readjusting the satellite antenna. David had tried doing it earlier, but he couldn't get a connection with Overwatch. They were making sure everything worked as Lydia was leaving the next day to go home for the wedding. She checked the strength and received a 70% signal back.

"That should be plenty to get a call out."

She picked up the radio and spoke into it, "Overwatch Command, this is Baghdad, how copy?"

After waiting a few seconds, she received a reply. "*Polaris, this is Overwatch. We have you loud and clear but unreadable.*"

David noticed her face light up. She whispered, "It's Derrick."

She was almost through the scripted radio call when there was a loud crack and something hit her in the chest, knocking the breath out of her.

David instinctively ducked, even though he was behind the roof wall. He then heard Lydia speak, "Derrick... I love...." Her voice faded off, and the radio fell out of her hand.

Lydia's mind flashed back to her and Derrick's first date. How they took a stroll afterward holding hands in the movie and talked until sunrise back at the dorms. Then their trip to Iowa for their first Christmas. How that heart pendant shone in the box and then how their first kiss felt right after she opened that pendant. She flashed to when Derrick gave her Madeline. How she held onto it so tightly when he was in the hospital. Then her mind went to their upcoming wedding. How she imagined him looking as she was walking down the aisle. How he would gaze, lost in her eyes. He always loved her blue-gray eyes.

Yelling for her to get down, David snapped her out of her trance. Lydia dropped to the roof and noticed a large pool of blood forming around her on the ground. David turned white as a ghost. Seeing him, she tried to crawl over to check on him but was stopped by an incredible pain in her right chest area.

David was struggling to speak... "Shot... you're... shot!"

He could see the hole in the front of her shirt to the right of her vest, with blood spreading around it. Lydia looked down inside her shirt and realized the round missed her plate armor and entered her upper chest. With the pain in her back, she could only deduce it went all the way through.

David finally regained enough control to pick up the radio and call for help from the base, although he forgot to change the frequency. In the Overwatch Center, Derrick heard the radio crackle again and lost the strength in his legs when the message that followed was a male voice and not Lydia.

"*Baghdad base, we are taking fire. Man down!*"

Mike jumped back on the radio, seeing Derrick obviously in shock.

"*All stations, all stations. Hold for priority traffic. Baghdad, Baghdad. This is Overwatch, please repeat*".

Realizing he was on the wrong frequency, David switched to the base channel without making another call to Overwatch. "*Baghdad Base, Viper. Mayday! Mayday! Mayday! We are taking fire. Man Down! Need assistance!*"

Mike yelled for one of the other watchmen, "Bring up Baghdad's base radio, now!"

Switching Com2 to the base frequency, they caught a transmission in mid-sentence. "... *tion all stations. Man down! Sniper fire reported from the east. Medics to the roof of Communications, TAC Channel 3. Ravens provide cover for evac, TAC Channel 5. Emergency traffic only!*"

Aaron, the watch supervisor, had walked back in to find Derrick vomiting in the trashcan and several radios stepping over each other.

"What did I miss?" he asked.

"Aaron, we have a priority 1, sniper fire on the communications building in Baghdad," explained Mike.

"Status?"

"One hit... it was Lydia."

Aaron turned around and could see the gray tunnel in Derrick's eyes collapsing in as he began to pass out.

"Derrick! You okay? Stay with us," Aaron said as he helped lower him to the floor." Turning his head to Mike, he ordered, "Page medical."

Seconds later, the overhead intercom rang to life:

<CODE 32 --- Overwatch Center... CODE 32 --- Overwatch Center>

***

The Ravens rushed onto the roof and took up positions, looking for the sniper. Medics then entered, trying to stay below the walls. The first reached Lydia, who was still seated against the outside wall. There was a pool of blood forming around her.

"Lydia, Lydia, Tell me what hurts. Do you know where you are?"

She replied, "Well Tom, this bullet hole hurts the most, but I have this scuff on my knee from last week that still stings a bit."

Tom couldn't help but laugh. "Yep, that's our Lydia."

Turning back into his professional self, Tom said, "I'm sorry, but I'm going to need to take a closer look," as he started to cut off her plate armor straps and carefully removed them. Slitting up the right side of her shirt, he finally exposed the wound. "Okay, we have an entrance in the upper chest and an exit a little lower on the back." Then he checked her heart and lungs. "Heart is good... left lung fine... but I think the right lung has either been hit or the sac is collecting blood. Start her on oxygen. Load and go."

The second medic setup the portable stretcher while Tom grabbed the med card from her plate carrier to check her info.

"Medcenter, Medic 1 on TAC 3."

A voice on the radio replied, *"Medic 1, Medcenter, Status?"*

"We have a twenty-five-year-old female, GSW through and through to the upper right chest, five

degrees downward. Active blood loss. Estimated three pints. BP 90/50. Pulse 84 and strong. Resp. 28 and shallow. Decreased and wet lung sounds on the right. Blood type B+. Started O$_2$. 15 liters per minute, non-rebreather. Wound dressed with trauma pad front and back. Transporting in two."

"Medic 1, Medcenter, TAC 3. Good copy. Trauma team standing by in Room 1."

Turning his attention back to her, "Okay Lydia... this is probably going to hurt some, but we need to get you moving."

They rotated her down onto the awaiting stretcher and strapped her in for the transport.

Lydia saw Tom's face when she winced.

"It's fine, let's just get out of here. I've got a hot date down in the medical building that I don't want to miss."

CHAPTER 29

...*Derrick and Lydia were working on the antenna on the roof of the coms center. She was adjusting it to the coordinates of the satellite when she noticed Derrick had kicked back and was watching her.*

"Mr. Anderson... do you mind? I'm trying to work."

"Oh... I don't mind. I'm enjoying the view," Derrick said grinning.

"You know, you could help," she said to him sarcastically.

"But you look so hot with your hair pulled up and all sweaty."

Derrick jumped as a loud crack reverberated across the valley. He looked up and saw Lydia stationary, kneeling by the antenna. Crawling up to her, he froze when he saw the hole in her forehead still smoking.

"Derrick... I... Love..." she struggled to get out before falling over into his arms. Blood started pouring out the front and back wounds, covering his lap.

"Lydia! Lydia! Stay with me!" he cried.

He stared into her blue-gray eyes as they slowly turned red and then dimmed to black.

Derrick woke, letting out a primal scream that could be heard out into the hallway as the medical team arrived.

While the nurses assessed him, all he could say in between his hyperventilating breaths were, "She's... dead... she's... dead..."

***

The medics slid Lydia over to the trauma table where they removed what clothing she had left on.

Embarrassed a bit, Lydia joked, "I never really was that kind of girl until today."

The doctor glanced at Tom, who said, "Yep, she's been doing that the whole way down."

"Alrighty then, let's begin." The doctor started looking at the wound and spoke the findings into the recorder overhead. "We have what looks to be an in-and-out wound from a bullet. Based on reports, likely a sniper rifle. From the entrance wound, possibly a 7.62. Positive for sig blood loss. Patient placed on 15 liters per minute O_2 prior to arrival. BP and pulse holding for now. Positive for trauma pad presence front and back. Adding second trauma pad and starting blood transfusion, B+, 2 liters."

Lydia was getting lightheaded. She wasn't sure if it was from the blood loss or the fact they found the coldest spot in all of Iraq to put this trauma bed.

"That blood isn't from an alcoholic, is it? Because I'm getting really dizzy."

Lydia's BP dropped to 74/48 and her pulse was getting thready.

"Saline, wide open. Prep a second bag, B+, and call for 2 more," ordered the doctor.

The voices in the room started drifting off into the distance...

Lydia was sitting on Virginia Beach with Derrick by her side. They had made the trip down for the weekend again. It seemed like they were always taking off for the coast as soon as class ended on Friday. They both loved the beach so much. She couldn't think of a time that she had ever been happier than when she was sitting out in the warm sunshine with Derrick. They have spent hours before listening to the waves breaking onto the shore and their legs going completely numb from sitting for so long. She could smell Derrick's cologne. She loved that cologne. She missed that cologne. It was safe for her. She had everything she could ever need if that smell was around her because she knew he was there.

The waves started to be drowned out by the voices in the room.

"Lydia! Lydia! You still with us?" asked the nurse.

"I was on a beach with Derrick, why'd you wake me up?!?"

The nurse glanced at the doctor who sighed heavily. "Too close."

This confused Lydia. "Too close for what? Wait... why are you holding that huge needle full of blood and those paddles?!?"

***

Derrick's legs had regained some strength and he stumbled back onto the operations floor. All of the radios were active and running over each other.

"They were just able to revive her..." Mike updated Aaron who waved the conversation when he saw Derrick.

"Do we have any updates?" his voice cracked as he asked.

"Derrick, why are you up? I told you to stay in my office until we know something."

"I need to know, Aaron."

He placed his hands on Derrick's shoulders and slowly explained, "The base is on lockdown so information is hard to get, but what we did get is, she's alive. They were able to stop the bleeding, but she is in critical condition. That's all we know right now."

Derrick started shaking. "She's alive?"

"Yes... but she's in very serious condition. They will probably be flying her out shortly to a trauma center, but we don't know where. Now, go sit down until we find out more."

***

About an hour after the shooting, Lydia's blood pressure and pulse finally stabilized.

"Looks like we have the bleeding under control and have managed the hemothorax to the right lung," dictated the doctor to the recorder.

He then walked around to Lydia's head and said, "We are coordinating now to get you to a real trauma center. I have one that I trust and am finalizing the transport details." He then excused himself to continue with the arrangements.

"Do you know if anyone was able to get ahold of Derrick?" Lydia asked the nurse beside her.

"Honestly, honey, I don't know, but I can send an aide to find out. Just relax for now."

"He was on the radio when I was shot. I know he heard it. He must be thinking the worst."

The doctor came back into the trauma room about 20 minutes later. "How is she looking?"

Lydia piped up and said, "Anything short of smoking hot is going to be an insult, considering the position I'm currently in."

The doctor finally let out a chuckle at that statement.

The nurse replied, "She's stable... and feisty."

"Great news! I have secured our transport to the trauma center. Normally, I would give you some light sedation to ease any anxiety, but I'm very cautious right now. Are you okay with flying?"

"Oh yes, I love flying. Can you see what they are serving? I assume it will be in first class since I can't sit up right now," Lydia said with a smile.

"Oh yes, most definitely first class. There will be a med crew going with you as well."

"Where exactly will my next passport stamp be?" inquired Lydia.

"Ramstein Air Force Base."

"Germany! She thought. That's nowhere near Iraq."

"I secured a C-17 for the 6-hour flight, and then they will take you by helicopter over to Landstuhl Regional. It's the finest trauma facility in Germany. I did my residency there and know all the surgeons. It's the best place for you."

"I trust you, doc. You've not done me wrong yet. I'd hug you, but I might get blood on your coat." The doctor smiled as he walked out.

***

The door to the watch supervisor's office opened, and Mike came in. "Hey, Derrick. You doing okay?"

"No, Mike... I'm not. Please tell me you have heard something more."

A smile grew on Mike's face. "Yeah... she is getting transferred to Ramstein.

"Ramstein... how do I get a flight to Ramstein?!?" Derrick thought out loud. "I've got to call her parents and fill them in on what's happening. They don't even know she was shot."

Mike put his arm around him. "Go to the bathroom, compose yourself, then head out to your car and give them a call. Aaron told me to make sure you came back in, though, before leaving. He had to make a few calls."

Derrick splashed water on his face, amazed that he still couldn't feel anything. What would he say to her parents? How do you make a call like that? He knew he had to hurry and tell them so he could find a flight to get to somewhere close to Ramstein and maybe drive the rest of the way to the hospital.

He headed outside to his car where his cell phone was and dialed her parent's number.

"Hello, Derrick!" Mary answered. "I'm surprised to see you calling."

Almost breaking down, Derrick finally asked, "Mary, is Jeb there?"

"Why yes, he's sitting over in his chair. Would you like to talk to him?"

"Actually, I'd like to talk to both of you. Can you put it on speaker?"

Derrick heard the phone switch from the headset to the speaker, and then Mary's voice again, "Okay, we're both here. What's up?"

Derrick paused. His voice broke a little again when he said, "Lydia's has been hurt. She was shot two hours ago and is in critical condition. They are getting ready to airlift her to a trauma center in Germany."

Silence. Then distant sobbing.

Jeb spoke up, "What can we do?"

Derrick took a deep breath again. He had no clue what he was going to do, let alone them.

"I don't know. I'm trying to find a flight that will get me close to the hospital. Getting two is as easy as one."

"Do it. I can give you my card if you need it," Jeb ordered.

"I am going to see what I can find. I'll call when I figure something out."

Back inside, Derrick badged into Overwatch. Aaron was standing next to Mike talking but quickly turned to Derrick as he walked in.

"Are you okay to drive?" Mike asked.

"I think so."

"Good. I need you to get in your car, go home, grab whatever items you need, and then hurry over to the Leesburg Executive Airport. Go to the front counter and give them your name. They are waiting for you."

Derrick looked very confused at Aaron.

"I have been on the phone with the chief, who called the director. Chief said she owed you a favor for something about Libya. One of the company jets will be standing by to take you to Ramstein. Everything has been cleared, all we need now is for you to get on that plane."

Derrick was stunned. "I just got off the phone with her parents. I was going to buy them tickets so they could go over as well."

"We'll have the pilot make a pit stop first before you start for Germany. I'll call him and let him know."

"I can never repay you, Aaron," stated Derrick.

"Yes, you can. Bring her home."

***

Checking in on Lydia, the doctor asked, "Hello, dear. How are you doing?"

Smiling at him, Lydia replied, "Well, considering I'm in the Arctic with no clothes on and have not gotten hypothermia, I'm doing well."

"I think we are enough out of the woods for now that we can get you a blanket. The nurse will still need to check for bleeding frequently, but at least you won't be exposed to everyone else who hasn't seen already."

"Did I hear a bit of a joke from you, doctor? I think I did," Lydia said grinning.

The doctor cracked a small smile, shaking his head as he left.

***

Derrick ran back to his car, dropping his keys as he tried to get in.

"Okay, Derrick. Calm down. The plane isn't leaving without you."

As he was heading out of the complex, he tried to make a mental list of everything he would need.

"I'm going to need my suitcase, four to five days' worth of clothes. Do they have laundry services there? I'll need my passport. What will Lydia need? Maybe I should take her a change or two of clothes. Everyone likes fresh underwear. Lydia... I need to grab Madeline! I can't forget her."

Derrick drove as fast as traffic would allow him to their apartment in Reston.

"OH! I should call her parents and let them know!" Dialing their number, Jeb answered, and Derrick gave him instructions.

"I need you guys to grab about five days' worth of clothes, your passports, and get over to the Municipal Airport as quickly as you can. When you get there, someone will be holding a sign with your names on it. They will tell you where to go."

After what felt like hours, Derrick finally arrived at the apartment. Running inside, he almost knocked over their dear old neighbor, but he didn't have time to explain. He yanked his suitcase off the shelf and grabbed 5 shirts, 5 pants, a couple of pairs of shorts, and a handful of underwear and threw them in.

He ran over to Lydia's side and paused for a second when the smell of strawberries overwhelmed his senses.

"Snap out of it. You've got to get going."

He searched through her drawers and grabbed a couple of shirts, shorts, underwear, and some of those fuzzy socks she loved. It occurred to him that this was the first time he ever sifted through her drawers.

"Huh... can't wait to see her in those!"

He put her clothes into his suitcase and grabbed Madeline off the bed.

"Is there anything else I need?!? My laptop is in the car. Phone charger!"

He grabbed it off his nightstand and decided that if he forgot anything else, there was probably a store near there where he could get it. Zipping up the suitcase, he took Madeline and his keys and headed out the door.

***

The doctor poked his head back into the room.

"Lydia, the flight should be here in about two and a half hours. We will load you up as quickly as possible and get you going. The trauma team will be waiting for you when you get there. They will probably do a quick survey of the injuries, take a few x-rays, and then whisk you off to surgery."

***

Derrick raced towards Leesburg. He had only been there once before, and that was to get Lydia some kettle corn from the outlet mall. His GPS took him to the front entrance, but he didn't know where to park. He picked one and hoped for the best.

Grabbing his suitcase, GO bag, and Madeline, he made for the counter.

Being exceedingly out of breath, "Hi! My name...."

"Derrick Anderson, I'm guessing," said the lady behind the counter.

"Yes <breath><breath>, that's me."

"Welcome to the Leesburg Airport. I will take you out to the hangar where we can get you onboard. I hear you will be returning here with your fiancé, so if you leave me your valet keys, I can pull your car into the hangar to keep it safe until you return."

"Wow," thought Derrick. "You don't find this kind of service at Dulles."

He slid his valet key onto the counter, and she escorted him to the side door.

"Your pilots today will be Hank and Amon. They have been flying with the Company for a combined twenty years now. Our head flight attendant, Jennifer, will be with you tonight. When she heard why the flight was going, she insisted on being the one to take it. I hear we have a slight deviation to Bloomfield as well, where we will pick up two more passengers. We've made sure there were additional accommodations onboard for them. We hope you have a safe and pleasant trip and will be praying for Lydia."

Just then, Hank walked up.

"Hello, Derrick. I'm honored to be flying you today. I hear the med-flight is about two and a half hours out of Baghdad and then they will have about six hours back to Ramstein. I think we might be able to beat them there even with the short deviation to Bloomfield. I will do my best, so sit back and relax."

Hank took Derrick's bags and stowed them in the back of the cabin for him. Derrick instinctively took the row with two seats and then realized that Lydia wasn't with him. He strapped Madeline into the seat next to him, so he at least felt like she was there.

A few minutes later, the engines fired up, and they were taxiing out of the hangar. Jennifer introduced herself and brought him a drink before the flight, but exhaustion took over and Derrick was asleep in minutes.

Radioing the tower, Hank called, "Skybird 1, holding short of 3-5 at Alpha with information Echo."

"*Skybird 1, clear onto the active at Alpha. Cleared for takeoff on 3-5 with a departure to the west.*"

With that clearance from ATC, Hank throttled up the engines, and they rocketed into the sky, heading for Bloomfield.

***

The doctor came back once again to check on Lydia.

"We are going to begin prepping you for the transfer to the jet. Once they are fueled, we want to be able to take off right away."

Checking her wounds again, he noticed there was still some blood soaking into the pads, but it was to be expected. Listening to her lungs, he heard the left one was clear, but the right one sounded wet and diminished again.

"Are you having any trouble breathing?"

"A little," replied Lydia, "but I thought it was just par for the course right now."

The doctor looked at the nurse and said, "I think we are going to have to drain it again before they leave. I would hate for them to have to in the air."

***

...Derrick sat on a park bench and watched as Lydia ran over to the swings in the playground. She swung back and forth with the biggest grin on her face. After a few moments of her unbridled delight, Derrick noticed her face suddenly changed to one of horror. He got up and ran for her, but before he could get there, she disappeared into a wispy cloud and blew away.

It was only a little over an hour after they took off when Derrick woke up, and Hank announced they were on final for Bloomfield.

"Wow, that was a REALLY fast flight," he thought.

Bloomfield had a tiny airport that was mostly used by small Cessnas and the occasional charter flight. As they touched down on the runway, Derrick breathed a sigh of relief when he saw her parent's car in the parking lot.

"Well, at least they made it."

Hank taxied the plane up to the only building at the airport, and Mary and Jeb were standing there, waiting. Jennifer lowered the door and went out to address them. Derrick unbuckled and stepped out of the jet as well. To his surprise, her mom came running up in tears and gave him the biggest hug he had ever had in his life… that wasn't from Lydia.

While Jennifer took their bags onto the plane, Jeb walked up to Derrick.

"I'm proud of you. I don't know how you managed this, but you did, and I can't express how grateful I am."

Derrick started to tear up again and, to his surprise, Jeb did as well.

Walking up, Hank said, "The plane has been refueled. How about we head to Germany?"

***

With the transport thirty minutes out, the doctor came back in wearing full surgical garb.

"Oh, this can't be good," Lydia thought.

"We need to drain that lung again before you head out. I am going to numb the area, but it's going to hurt. I can't do much about that, but we have to do it."

Lydia nodded in agreement. Her bedside nurse, whose name she found out was Sarrhi, came up beside her and took her hand. She looked down at Lydia with tears in her eyes.

"Please squeeze as much as you need. I am so sorry."

The doctor then asked, "Are you ready?"

"Yes, let's do it."

***

The sun had gone down. From the looks out the window, they were over the Atlantic Ocean now. The cabin lights had been lowered. Jeb was kicked back in one of the huge captain chairs, snoring away. Mary had sprawled out on the small couch beside him. Jennifer offered to pull it out to a more comfortable bed, but Mary declined.

Derrick now sat alone with his thoughts. It was the first time that he could just stop and think. He thought of how frightened she must be to be going through all of this alone and how much he wanted to just hear her voice again so he could stop reliving the radio call. Their wedding was only supposed to be two weeks away. They were going to go to the Maldives for their honeymoon and he had booked an over-water bungalow. Lydia loved to swim in the ocean. There were supposed to be dolphins that come up to you there as well. He wanted to see her face the first time one swam up to her. He missed her smile.

***

As the doctor stuck the needle into Lydia's side, she screamed feeling like she had a knife made of fire plunged into her. The first time, she was still numb from the shock and blood loss, but this one she felt every tiny movement.

As the blood was being withdrawn from around her lung, she started feeling lightheaded again. As the sound of the hospital room faded into the distance, she was back at her parent's farm.

...It was the first time Derrick had been out to Iowa. Jeb wasn't very fond of this new suitor she had brought home.

"I don't like him. All he wants to do is get into your pants!"

"Daddy, he's not that kind of guy. He hasn't even tried."

"But he wants to. That's the only thing boys think of."

"You were a boy. Was that what you wanted to do with Mom?"

"This isn't about me. Look at his shifty eyes! He's scoping out everything. He wants to rob us."

"Daddy... he works at the same place I do. We are trained to scope out everything... and what would he want with twelve cows and thirty chickens?!?!"

"His kind... the first bump in the road and he will go running to the next skirt. I will never call him my son-in-law."

Lydia grabbed her coat and went outside to where Derrick was on the front porch. She sat down next to him on the swing and laid her head on his shoulder.

"Your Dad doesn't like me, does he?"

"He doesn't like anyone I date. I will always be his little girl..."

The voices started to return as she came back around.

"Are you okay?" the doctor asked. "

Yeah, I'm fine. That was awful, and I drifted off again."

CHAPTER 30

...The viewing was a closed casket, but Derrick just wanted to be near her one more time. He walked in through the doors to find the room full of Lydia's friends and family.

After the reaction Jeb had on the phone, he wasn't sure how his presence would be taken. He didn't have to wait very long.

A deep, booming voice echoed out. "GET OUT! LEAVE US ALONE! OUT!"

"Jeb, can we just talk this out? It wasn't my fault. I just want to say goodbye to her."

Her dad was already storming towards him.

"Please, sir. Can we just talk?" he begged.

Derrick stumbled as Jeb pushed him back towards the front door. Jeb then grabbed him and shoved him again, this time throwing him through the air and out onto the front walk.

"I told you to leave us alone!"

As he was about to slam the doors shut, Jeb noticed the scars on Derrick's wrists.

"Spare the rest of us and try harder next time..."

Derrick jolted awake so violently that he almost fell out of his chair. He stood up to catch his breath and when he turned around, Jeb was sitting there… staring at him.

A scream resonated throughout the cabin that was so loud, it woke Mary causing her to fall off the couch onto the floor. Derrick was plastered against the wall and trying to climb through it when Jeb asked, "Um… you good?"

He carefully slid by Jeb and ran for the lavatory where he promptly locked the door and collapsed onto the toilet seat.

***

Lydia was just nodding off. She finally could relax enough to maybe get some sleep, or so she thought. Just then, six people in flight suits walked in with the doctor.

"Lydia, the transport is here and these fine men are going to be escorting you to Ramstein."

"Well, it's about time you guys showed up. I've just been lying around waiting for you!" Lydia joked.

Sarrhi started tearing up. She came over and gave her a light hug. Lydia whispered into her ear, "Thank you so much! I will never forget you."

The lead flight medic walked up and introduced himself. "Hello, Lydia. My name is Ethan. My team and I will be taking care of you on this flight. We are going to get you transferred to our stretcher and get on out of here if it's okay."

"Yep. I'm ready. I think my Yelp review will be to not recommend vacationing in Baghdad, though.

The people here aren't bad, but their free body piercings kind of suck."

***

After a few minutes, Derrick headed back to his chair to find Jeb was still up and waiting for him.

"Son, I know we haven't seen eye to eye before. Understand that's my baby girl. My only baby girl. I know she's twenty-five now, but she will always be that to me. No man will ever be good enough for her. At least that is what I thought yesterday. The love for her you have shown to me today has made me realize no OTHER man would ever be good enough for her and I would be honored to have you as my son."

Derrick sat stunned for a moment realizing that he had just been called son.

"Thank you, sir. I would be proud to be considered part of the family... oh... and let's pretend earlier didn't happen."

***

The C-17 was sitting on the tarmac with the rear gate open as they wheeled Lydia out of the medical center towards it.

"Wow, that thing is loud!" she thought. They had given her a headset to communicate over the noise, but it was still deafening behind the engines.

Ethan radioed as they approached. *"Loadmaster, Six-team: patient approaching load door."*

The loadmaster replied, "Six-team cleared for patient loading."

"The way the military talks is really dumb," Lydia thought after hearing their radio exchange.

They rolled the stretcher head first up the ramp and into the back of the large plane. Towards the front of the cargo bay, there was an entire setup that looked like the back of an ambulance, overhead spotlights and all.

"Well, you guys went all out for me, didn't yah?" smiled Lydia.

They were finishing up locking the stretcher down to the floor and putting a couple of seat belts on her when Ethan radioed,

"Load Master, Six-team. Package secure. Ready for closure."

The large rear door started slowly closing.

Moments after the door shut, the pilot made the call to the tower.

"Baghdad tower, EVAC 6. Departing ramp, ready for immediate takeoff."

"EVAC 6, you are clear to 3-3L via Bravo. Advise at Bravo, cleared for takeoff with departure to the north."

***

Derrick was having trouble staying asleep. He just kept playing that radio call over and over in his head.

"She sounded so happy to hear his voice and then the very next time he heard it, you could hear her life slipping away," he explained to Jeb.

"You can't think that way, son. I know what you are doing. You can't. I've been there. You may not know, but I was a captain in the Gulf War. I lost a lot of men. Good men. Many right in front of me. You can't go down that road."

"I know, I know," replied Derrick.

"No, son, you don't. Because you are. What happened to Lydia was horrible. That radio call will haunt you for the rest of your life. But there is nothing you could have done differently. It's hard to believe, but this is all part of God's plan. What plan, I don't know, but she didn't give up yesterday. You owe it to her to find out why."

Derrick looked out the window. He could see lights starting to appear. "We must be coming up on Europe now," he said, contemplating Jeb's last statements.

***

Even with the spotlights and the incessant roar, Lydia could finally drift off to sleep for a bit.

...She was walking down the beach alone. It was a cold day, and the breeze was strong. She had forgotten her coat. The sun was going down. She thought about heading back to the house. However, as she watched, the sun stopped setting and hung over the horizon for a bit. Odd enough of a sight, but then the sun started... rising. The surrounding sky changed from a purple twilight to

a bright blue cloudless day. The air around her warmed as well to the point it made her sweat a little. She felt a presence behind her. She turned around. Derrick was standing there in a blue suit...

Waking up, she cried, "No! Come back!" but the dream was gone. "That was odd. The sun changing course. Derrick in a suit. He never wears suits. Especially blue ones! Looked pretty studly, though."

***

Derrick could tell that it was almost dawn as the ground was slowly emerging from the darkness. The eastward travel caused the sun to rise quicker than expected. Before he had a chance to wonder where they might be, an announcement came overhead,

"Good morning, folks. We are on descent now into Ramstein. Please take your seats and we should be on the ground in about twenty minutes."

"I wonder how far along she is in their flight," he remarked to Jeb and Mary.

As if on cue, "Oh, and Derrick, in case you were wondering, your bonny lass is forty minutes till touchdown. We should be on the ground and ready to move when they get there."

Mary let out a small laugh. Probably from the surprised look Derrick had on his face.

***

Ethan leaned over, as if Lydia could have actually heard him over the engines, and said through the mic,

"We have started our descent so we're going to do a quick checkup to make sure everything's good before things start moving quickly after landing."

Lydia nodded.

Ethan pulled the blanket back and carefully started checking the pads for blood. There was a bit more than he had expected, but still within safe limits. He then glanced at the other team member who was doing the checkup with him,

"We will need to monitor that, but I think the best thing would be to get her to the trauma center without delay after we land. They can do a lot more than we could benefit from waiting."

Although her blood pressure had dropped some, her pulse was still good. Ethan would have loved to listen to her lungs, but the noise made it impossible.

Switching his mic to the recorder, Ethan reported, "Checkup complete. BP dropped some. Pulse still strong. Monitor for shock. Green for landing and transfer".

***

Derrick barely felt the wheels touch down on the runway.

"That was a soft landing. I've got to fly like this more often," he thought. "Just not for this reason."

Hank taxied the plane around to a small hangar where two Black Hawks were waiting. Jennifer opened the door and let the stairs down. Amon helped Jeb and Mary down the stairs while Derrick went and got the bags. Joining him in the back, Hank called Derrick's name and placed his hand on his back. "I might have arranged something for you. Do you like helicopters?"

***

"Ramstein tower, EVAC 6 on short final for 2-6 with information Delta." "*EVAC 6 cleared for landing on 2-6, exit bravo and proceed to transfer point.*"

Lydia felt the tires hit the ground a little more firmly than she was used to. Ethan grinned a bit.

"They like planting these things on the runway for some reason."

As they taxied to the hangar where the Black Hawks were, Ethan started moving all of her IVs and monitors back onto the stretcher. He noticed a small puddle of blood on the floor.

"Um... that wasn't there before," he thought. "Vitals are still good. We just need to get moving."

The wheels stop call came over the headsets and Ethan wasted no time in getting the door down,

"Loadmaster, Six-team. Ready for hot offload."

The "hot" call was a coded alert to the team that they needed to move quickly, though he hoped Lydia had not picked up on it.

The giant door started lowering and the noise of the engines was suddenly muffled by the noise of rotors thumping. Ethan took point at the head of the stretcher and the team rolled Lydia out of the plane.

The morning sun flooded the cargo bay, blinding Lydia momentarily as they rolled the stretcher over to one of the waiting helicopters and started loading her. It was a tight fit, but they could get all of their equipment and three of the team members in. For the first time since the incident, Lydia felt a sense of calm wash over her. She was almost at the hospital. Just a few more minutes of flight. But there was something else. Something familiar.

Ethan shut the doors, and the helicopter lifted off.

***

Moments earlier, Hank rushed Derrick into the nearby hangar where two uniformed servicemen met him and instructed him to remove his shoes. As they handed him a flight suit, Derrick looked at Hank, confused.

"I called some of my buddies here and arranged for you to swap out with one of the Six-team members for the flight into the hospital. The guy at the foot of the bed on the left side will swap out with you as they are unloading. There is only one condition. You can only observe… and keep your helmet on. We don't want her blood pressure to shoot up and cause a clot to rupture. They will give you a chance for a smoochiepoo before she heads into surgery."

Derrick had just finished zipping up his navy blue flight suit when the plane pulled up. He raced to put his shoes on and ran out onto the flight line, waiting for the door to open.

Just as Hank had said, as they started rolling Lydia down the ramp, the flight crew member at the foot stepped aside and Derrick grabbed the stretcher and started walking with them. With the combination of the bright sun and his helmet, he was sure Lydia had not noticed.

"Well, her BP might not be going up, but mine sure is," Derrick thought.

Climbing into the waiting helicopter, he helped with maneuvering the stretcher in. This was the hardest part so far.

"She's right there. Like two feet away and I can't touch her or even let her know I'm here."

It was a short 3-minute flight from the airport to the hospital. As they touched down, a trauma crew met them on the pad. The stretcher was maneuvered out of the helicopter, and Ethan motioned for Derrick to follow. Jumping out of the helicopter, he took his position at the foot of the stretcher again. As they entered the hospital, the doctor at the head of the stretcher gave directions to the trauma bay.

Derrick stepped back as they transferred Lydia from the stretcher to the trauma bed. Ethan took the stretcher, and giving him a nod, placed a reassuring hand on Derrick's shoulder.

With the second helicopter circling over the hospital now, Ethan rushed back and secured the door as the Black Hawk lifted off.

The trauma doctor approached Derrick and quietly motioned for him to step outside the room. "We have noticed some increased bleeding, so we are going to need to speed things up with getting her into the operating room. We had planned for you to have a few minutes with her before, but we need to get moving. I'm going to let you help us wheel her back towards the OR and we will stop and let you take your helmet off for a quick hug and kiss before we go in."

"Understood," Derrick replied, slipping back into his less emotional self.

The doctor then went back in and briefed Lydia. "It looks like one of your wounds has opened up again and blood is pooling around your right lung. I know you have had a couple of needles already, so we are going to spare you the next one until you are in the OR and sedated, but we need to head there now."

"Thank you, doc," Lydia replied, graciously.

Derrick came back in just as they were unlocking the bed. The nurse asked if he had time to help them move her. Derrick nodded. He didn't want to say anything as she would surely recognize his voice.

Derrick was pretty sure he was the dumbest looking person in the hospital as he walked down the hall pulling a bed... wearing a helmet with the shield down.

"Just keep walking, just keep walking," he told himself.

They finally reached the operating room, and the doctor had them stop just before a red line on the floor.

"Thank you for helping us, but it's sterile from here on."

Derrick nodded and walked up beside the bed. Lydia looked up at him and said, "Thank you so much for all your work. You guys were amazing!"

He then took his helmet off.

Lydia thought she was dreaming. "What?" Then her eyes lit up! "I knew something was familiar in the helicopter!"

Time stopped for Derrick as he leaned down to kiss her. He had given her many in his life, but this one he never desired more. As his lips touched hers, all the terror of the last 36 hours melted away onto the floor.

He whispered, "I love you," as they wheeled her away.

She replied, "I love you more," as she slipped through the OR doors.

A nurse escorted Derrick back towards the helipad where the second Black Hawk had just landed with her parents. He waited for the blades to stop turning and then walked out onto the pad to assist with their bags. Placing his helmet inside the cabin, he unzipped his flight suit.

Mary came up to him, "Did you get to see her?"

"Yes. She is still as beautiful as always." Derrick then grabbed the bags, and the nurse showed them to the waiting room.

***

Lydia saw the mask being lowered onto her face and then the lights and sounds faded away.

...She stood on a pier that stretched out into the ocean. The sun was a few degrees off the horizon and was lighting up the sky in the prettiest pink, blue, and orange hues she had ever seen. The warm Gulf breeze made her hair blow lightly behind her. She closed her eyes and soaked in the moment. She could hear the waves lightly caressing the snow-white sand beneath the pier. But then an icy breeze blew from behind her. She turned around to find an empty pier stretching back through the twilight towards a small house...

The surgeon exclaimed, "*Crash cart! Two units, wide open!*" as the monitor slowed and then flat-lined.

***

Derrick was squatting in the corner of the waiting room due to all the seats being taken. He was staring at Madeline, being in his own world. It was going on four hours since she went into surgery when the surgeon came out.

"Evans Family?"

Derrick jumped up and joined Jeb and Mary. "Yes, sir!"

"Lydia is finally in recovery after a rough start. The bullet broke off a piece of her rib and it lacerated her brachial artery. The field team stabilized the wound, but one of the times she was moved caused the fragment to dissect the artery, resulting in significant bleeding. The sudden loss of blood led to her heart stopping."

Mary broke down and buried her face in Jeb's chest.

"Luckily, she was here in the OR with a blood supply and a vascular team. We managed to stop the bleeding and restart her heart rather quickly. We are leaving her in recovery overnight on the ventilator as a precaution to make sure there's no further bleeding from the repairs."

Derrick subtly motioned to Jeb, signaling him to move Mary out of earshot.

"What's the prognosis?"

"Her heart wasn't stopped long enough to have caused brain damage. The right arm lost circulation for a bit longer, though, during the repairs. There's no way to gauge if there are any issues until she's conscious and able to move around."

"Can I be there when you wake her up?"

"Of course. We are looking at around 9am tomorrow, so go grab some sleep and I'll see you in the morning."

Derrick walked over and hugged Mary, to which she tightly squeezed him back.

"She's stable, but since they are keeping her in recovery, we won't be able to see her until the morning. The doctor has our numbers if they need us, so let's go grab some rest. It's been a long two days. I have a couple of rooms reserved over at the *Pfälzer Stuben* just down the street."

He led her parents to the transport desk and had the concierge call for the shuttle. Jeb pulled him aside.

"Son, let me take your bag. We both know you are going to come back here right after we get into our room. Let us know if you hear anything."

He handed Jeb his bag and headed back upstairs to reclaim his spot against the wall again. Pulling out his phone, he started watching the video Lydia made for him before the flight to Libya. During the eighth time watching it, he finally nodded off.

***

...Derrick stood in front of the wall of stars in the lobby of Headquarters staring at Mateo's and Chief Henderson's stars. He glanced down at the book and both of their names were there. Then as he watched, another spot appeared under theirs. The name slowly filled in... letter by letter... until it read: Lydia Evans. Tears filled his eyes as a third star appeared on the wall.

Then to add to his horror... a FOURTH star appeared. He looked back at the book to find yet another line filled in with a name, but his eyes were too blurry to make it out from the tears. He wiped his eyes and looked again to find nothing but four empty spaces now...

He jerked awake, gasping for air. That dream felt way too real. Looking around, the lights in the waiting room were dimmed, and all the seats were now empty. He checked his watch. "5am? I MUST have been tired."

The doctor came out just before 9am to escort Derrick back to recovery. Lydia was connected to numerous machines along with a tube going down her throat. He could feel his legs turning to jelly beneath him, either from the sight or not having eaten for three days. They removed the ventilator and checked to see if she was breathing on her own.

"Positive bilateral breath sounds. Let's roll back the anesthesia now and bring her around."

Derrick saw her left arm move a little as she let out a moaning sound, followed by a groggy "Derrick?"

"I'm here, sweetie," he said in a broken voice.

She opened her eyes and smiled. "I'm sorry, honey. I must have slept in."

They transferred Lydia to an ICU room, and a nurse escorted her parents up.

"Momma! Daddy! How did you get here?!?"

"Derrick moved heaven and earth to get us all here," Mary said, tears welling in her eyes.

Jeb put his arm around him. "He did good, honey. He really shined the last few days."

Mary leaned in for a hug when Lydia noticed her arm didn't move like she expected.

Derrick saw her expression and inquired, "You okay?"

His heart sank when she asked, "What's wrong with my arm?"

CHAPTER 31

Jeb walked into her room and exclaimed, "What is that smell?!?"

Lydia glared over at Derrick, who was sitting by the window. "It's his feet! He forgot to pack socks and has been wearing the same ones now for a week!"

Jeb scowled at Derrick. "Son, you need to go find a store and get some fresh ones. You are ruining Frito pies for me."

After being chased out of the room by Mary with a can of Lysol, Derrick searched for a nearby store on his phone.

"Does Walmart not exist here?!?"

Finding a small shop within walking distance, Derrick made his way over to the store. He searched the entire place before finding a small display in the back with a couple of pairs of athletic socks.

As he was walking up to the counter to check out, he noticed a man on the other side of the store who appeared to have taken an interest in him. He pretended to look at some shirts and then headed over to the pants section. As he did, the man paralleled him, glancing in his direction every few seconds.

"Well, this is interesting," Derrick thought as he zig-zagged throughout the store trying to make the stranger trip up and reveal his intentions.

After a minute or two of the cat-and-mouse game, the man waved at a lady who had just entered and greeted her with a kiss.

"Good one, Derrick. The guy was probably freaked out, thinking he had someone tailing HIM."

Heading back to the front to check out, Derrick was lost in thought about the guy he thought was following him. His sleeve snagged one of the shirt racks, causing it to tip over onto him. The rack caught a neighboring one as it fell, sending rows of shirts to the ground in a clang. In his haste to stop the impending calamity, he backed into yet another rack, setting off a domino effect that knocked over five others

After the commotion subsided, Derrick realized he had lost his package of socks and was left with a single empty hanger in his hand.

A short, older lady came running up, screaming at him in German and began ushering him toward the exit.

"Okay! Okay! I get the idea! I'm sorry!" he exclaimed.

She gave him a final shove as he stumbled out onto the sidewalk. Realizing he still had the hanger, Derrick yelled back into the store, "You want this back?" He wasn't sure exactly what she replied, but he was pretty sure it wasn't "Yes".

"Well, that went well," he thought with embarrassment as he checked his maps app to find another store.

While engrossed with his phone, Derrick felt a sudden impact across the back of his head, almost knocking him unconscious. Two men grabbed him, shoved him into the trunk of an awaiting Mercedes sedan, and sped away.

Derrick's head throbbed as he lay in pitch black. The smell of used motor oil and dirt flooded his senses. He felt around to get an idea of where he might be when the car hit a pothole and jostled him about.

"Oh, come on, this old cliché? All I wanted was some clean socks!"

Looking for a way out, Derrick felt for the back of the trunk.

"The emergency handle should be around here somewhere." Finally finding the empty hole where the handle USED to be, "Well, at least they aren't amateurs."

His head still pounding, Derrick laid back down to try to think for a second. When he did, something stabbed him in the back. Reaching around, he found the coat hanger he managed to get out of the store with.

"Well... maybe they are..."

Stretching the metal coat hanger into a handle with a hook on the end, he fed the curved part into the hole where the release was. Feeling it latch, he tugged on it, and the trunk popped open, filling his small space with blinding sunlight. The lid bobbed up and down in the wind as he made for the opening.

"Well, this is going to hurt, but here we go!"

As he crouched down into a ball getting ready to jump, the car hit another pothole and the trunk lid slammed back down with force. It struck him on the top of the head hard enough to make him see stars.

"OWWW! MY BRAIN!" he yelled.

Thankfully, the concussion he just received stopped the lid from re-latching again.

"Tuck and roll! Tuck and roll!" he told himself as he jumped from the speeding vehicle. The impact on the pavement was violent and sent him into a vicious roll.

"Oh, this was a dumb idea," he thought as his skin continuously scraped across the asphalt.

He finally came to a stop, lying flat on his back, looking up at the beautiful, blue German sky. The pain in his head outweighed the numerous spots of fresh road rash all over his body. Even still, he was amazed he survived that stunt.

"I'm alive! I can't believe that worked!"

The growing sound of tires squealing made him realize that he may have spoken a little too soon. Looking to his right, he saw a tanker truck jackknifing down the highway toward him.

Derrick scampered to his feet and started running for the berm.

"Get off the road, get off the road, get off the road!" he repeated to himself, diving into the grass next to the highway and sliding down the hill into a small creek. He cringed at every sound of tires skidding and metal crunching metal.

After a few moments, all the wrecking died down and the road became quiet. "Well, that wasn't too bad..."

He had barely finished the thought when a large fireball erupted over his head as the tanker exploded.

He was covered in mud. Every muscle hurt. The creek water made every abrasion on his body burn.

Derrick lay in the tall grass hiding for a bit, watching to see if the kidnappers would return and look for him. At least that was how the story would be if anyone asked why he lay there for so long. Truth was, he was too worn out to move right then. He watched as the fire burned on the highway and hoped everyone was okay.

...Derrick rushed up to the scene where a dump truck had t-boned a vehicle. Both were on fire and he could hear screaming coming from the car. He grabbed an extinguisher and tried to get to the driver's door, but he never could get close enough. The screaming suddenly stopped...

Catching something out of the corner of his eye, Derrick almost let out an audible shriek. A duck was standing within inches of his face... just staring at him.

"Geez, bird! You almost gave me a heart attack! What are you doing here?!? Do you work for the kidnappers?"

The duck continued to stare.

"Do you understand anything I'm saying? Oh, wait... you're from here. I bet you speak German."

Plugging his statement into his phone's translation app, he played the translation for the bird. *"Bring mich zu Deinem Anführer?"*

Derrick waited for a second.

"Nein?"

The bird never moved.

He slowly reached out his hand and touched it on its side. "Plastic? Seriously? Why is there a plastic duck... on the side of the road... in a swamp... STARING AT ME!?!"

Sirens were now resonating in the distance. Derrick drudgingly pulled himself out of the sludgy water.

"Just one normal trip... just one."

He checked his phone and realized he was over five miles away from the hospital. "It's going to take forever to get back now... and I'm soaking wet!"

Off in the distance, he heard a lady's voice talking to a police officer.

"There was this guy in the middle of the road and I think he ran in that direction," pointing toward the area where he was hiding. Suddenly finding the energy to move, Derrick took off running.

"Time to go!"

Three hours after he had left to buy some socks, Derrick finally made it back to the hospital. Being covered in mud, he was stopped by security when he tried to go through the main entrance.

He sat on a bench staring at an ambulance at the ER. He waited for the medics to go back inside and snuck over to the back where he found a blanket. Grabbing it, he wrapped it around his upper body and fashioned a hood for his head.

Assuming he was a homeless person now, an aide showed him to a seat and brought him a bottle of water. The nurses were rather busy that day triaging, so he slipped away into the hospital under the guise of looking for a bathroom.

Thankfully, he scored the highest in his *SERE* class for evasion.

"You may be good at evading, Derrick, but your anti-kidnapping skills need work," he thought as he snuck down the hall looking for an elevator. His progress was being hindered, though, by his lack of knowledge of the German language.

While he was roaming the hallway, the security guard from the front door saw him. Hearing him yell something in German, Derrick quickly ducked down a side hall. There, he found a sign that vaguely looked like a stairwell next to a door. Slipping through it, he was able to sneak away before the guard came around the corner.

Poking his head out of the second-floor stairwell door, Derrick checked to see if it was clear. There was a cart of linens a couple of doors down. Finding a pair of scrubs, he quickly put them on and wiped down his face the best he could in the hallway sink.

Rushing down the hall towards Lydia's room, he hoped Jeb and Mary had gone for lunch allowing him to get to the shower without many questions. Unfortunately, luck was not on his side. When he entered her room, not only were Jeb and Mary staring at him, but so were the doctor and three students who were examining Lydia's wounds.

Mary exclaimed, "My stars, what happened to you?!"

Jeb had the TV on, and the local news was covering a fiery accident on the A6. He looked at Derrick, then at the TV, and quickly back to Derrick before bursting into laughter.

Derrick finished in the shower and put on the pair of scrubs the nurse brought for him. Stepping back into the room, he found Lydia asleep, and her mom reading a book. Sighing, he sat down next to Mary.

She leaned over and whispered, "Do I want to know?"

Derrick shook his head lightly and said, "Just another normal day."

Mary chuckled and then asked, "Did you find any socks?"

He glared at her out of the corner of his eye.

"I take that as a no…"

***

The next day, Mary and Jeb had gone down to the cafeteria for breakfast. When they re-entered the room, Jeb was taking a sip of coffee but quickly spat it back out onto the floor.

"Sweet bull collars, son!"

Derrick sat by Lydia's bed with a pair of bright pink, fluffy socks on his feet.

"They were cold, and she made me throw out my other ones!" he explained.

Mary rubbed her forehead as she turned around and walked to the nurse's station. "Does there happen to be a store nearby that sells MEN's socks?"

Lydia's nurse laughed, "But he looks so cute!"

Walking back in, Mary ordered Derrick to follow her. "Take those ridiculous socks off and let's go! I'm taking you to a store to get some… but mostly to make sure you don't get into any more trouble."

The taxi pulled up to the hospital entrance, and Derrick and Mary climbed into the back.

"*KiK Landstuhl, bitte,*" she said in German.

Derrick's eyes widened as they pulled up in front of the same store he was at before. Mary noticed his increased level of anxiety when they got out of the car. When they walked in, every employee's head turned and gave Derrick the stink eye.

"How do they know you already?!?"

"I kinda was here yesterday. It didn't go well."

They walked towards the back of the store where Mary picked up a package of socks and turned to show him. Her eyebrows rose when she saw three employees following Derrick, who was trying to appear invisible.

"What did you do this time, honey?"

"I knocked over a rack, looking at a shirt."

One of the employees yelled, "*Neun Racks! Wir haben den Laden gerade wieder zusammengebaut.*"

Looking back at Derrick, Mary shook her head in pity. "Nine racks, really?!? Do you want to just wait outside for me?"

Derrick's discomfort changed to fear. "Nope! No, I don't."

Arriving back at the hospital, they walked back through the main entrance, passing the security guard, who stared intently at Derrick.

"Been making nice with the security guards too, I see?" Mary inquired.

"Well, you know... when you're popular..."

CHAPTER 32

Weeks had passed and Derrick was wheeling Lydia down to therapy when he turned the corner and almost took out a nurse.

Lydia pulled her legs up onto the seat, covered her eyes, and started praying, "Lord... watch over me as I'm wheeled through the valley of the shadow of death. Please don't let Derrick push me down a flight of stairs. You helped me through Baghdad... please don't let it end here in this hallway."

Derrick leaned down beside her face and whispered, "Haha funny girl..."

Since he wasn't watching where he was going, he accidentally ran over the toes of an elderly lady who was seated, waiting.

Aghast, Derrick exclaimed, "Oh I'm so sorry, ma'am!"

Ever since the surgery, Lydia's right arm had been very weak and difficult to move. The doctor had prescribed physical therapy to help re-strengthen the damaged muscles, but every session led to increased frustration.

"Hrrmph!" she grunted in exasperation as she struggled to squeeze the ball in her hand. Derrick couldn't tell if his presence was helping or causing her more distress as he watched her struggle.

She finally broke and screamed out in anger. "JUST MOVE YOU PIECE OF CRAP!!! Grabbing the ball with her left hand, she threw it as hard as she could across the room and cried out in a gut-wrenching scream, "WHYYY?!?

Derrick ran to her side, but she lashed out at him too.

"Get away from me! Why would you want to be around me?!? I'm broken! This stupid arm doesn't work... I have two hideous scars now!" She stopped mid-sentence and broke down into tears.

Derrick refused to leave and wrapped her up in his arms. "Honey... better a scar than a star."

She was trying to fight his vice-like grip but didn't have the strength yet to succeed. "Stop being so dramatic. That was a mean thing to say!"

He pushed her out some so he could look her in the eyes, but not enough to let her escape yet. "Lydia... you died... TWICE!"

Her annoyed and skeptical look made him explain.

"Your heart stopped twice... as in flat-lined... unshockable rhythm... clinical death! Once in the trauma room in Baghdad when they revived you with a pericardiocentesis and then again when you were in the OR here. This time they had to do CPR to bring you back. So, yes... it sucks your arm doesn't work like it did... but you are not some anonymous star on a wall... you're still here... and so am I! I'm not going anywhere... are you?"

Her eyes started to well with tears as she fought back her emotions. She lost. Derrick had never seen her cry so hard in all their time together.

Weeks passed and Lydia's arm grew stronger. Though never fully regaining full strength, she was finally ready to be released back home.

The morning sun glistened off the Gulfstream that was sitting on the tarmac as the shuttle pulled up. A month after Derrick made the whirlwind trip over to Germany... they were finally going home.

"I can't believe we are going home!" Lydia said putting her head on Derrick's shoulder as they walked towards the plane. "Germany was nice, but a month here was far too long."

"Good morning, ma'am! It's nice to finally meet you." Hank said as he met them at the plane.

He helped Lydia up the air stairs and to one of the two plush leather seats beside each other.

"I'm figuring you're gonna want to snuggle up next to that fine gentleman behind me," he said with a grin.

As soon as Mary and Jeb took their seats, Jennifer shut the doors and came around to introduce herself.

"Well, hello Lydia! I've heard so much about you." She gave Derrick a wink. "This guy wouldn't stop talking about you the entire first trip. Is there anything I can get you before takeoff?"

Lydia nuzzled up against Derrick. "Thanks, but I have everything I need now."

Jeb looked at him and smiled a little. His agreeing head nod meant more to Derrick than any words he could have spoken.

***

Derrick was looking out the window as the plane taxied up to the hangar in Leesburg. He figured he would have been excited to see his Mustang shining from inside, but instead, he was met with distress.

"Uh oh," he said under his breath.

Lydia looked a little confused as everything so far was going perfectly with the flight.

"I brought my Mustang to the airport..."

She sat up and looked at him with surprise. "Why?!?!?"

"I don't know. I wasn't thinking when I left. I was just trying to get here as fast as I could, and I don't usually associate the word 'fast' with your car."

CHAPTER 33

Derrick and Lydia sat on the porch, sipping coffee and watching the sunrise when Derrick's phone rang.

"Hey Derrick, how's Lydia?" the Chief asked.

"She's doing great. She's gained most of the strength back in her arm. Her parents have been staying with us since we got back helping out, so she's happy."

"That's good to hear. I'm sorry to bother you, but I'm in a bit of a pickle. We have a tech that underwent emergency surgery last night and isn't doing well. We've been trying to find someone to cover for him for a couple of weeks, but have come up empty. I know Lydia just got back, but do you think she could spare you for a bit?"

Derrick glanced at Lydia, who had a worried look on her face. "Honestly, I think she's a little nervous about me going somewhere dangerous at the moment."

The chief chuckled. "Oh, dear heavens... you are the last person I would send anywhere dangerous right now! No, this is possibly the safest place you could go... and there's even someone there to keep you out of trouble. Since it's short notice, we're also offering a bonus that would easily cover a nice honeymoon. What do you think about Botswana with your buddy Tae?"

A smile grew on Derrick's face. "Please hold," he said covering the phone's microphone.

He leaned over and whispered. "You okay if I go to Botswana for two weeks? They're offering a bonus that will cover our honeymoon."

Lydia's brain started processing. "Isn't that where Tae went?"

"Yep."

"And he'll be there to keep you from being dumb?"

Derrick's shoulders dropped, "Well, yeah, but I'm never really dumb… am I?"

***

Having left Dulles sixty-eight hours earlier, Derrick's flight finally landed at Sir Seretse Khama International Airport, in Gaborone. After grabbing his bag, he walked out of the terminal to find Tae leaning on his car, waiting.

"Hey ya! How was your trip?"

"The lady beside me on the last leg was holding a chicken. It stared at me the whole flight."

"Sounds like she had a thing for you," Tae said, smiling.

"I was talking about the chicken…"

Tae chuckled, "So was I."

It was only a fifteen-minute drive from the airport to the embassy. Derrick was amazed at how modern the buildings and infrastructure looked.

"This is not what I was expecting at all! I figured we would be driving on dirt roads holding a crate of chickens."

Tae laughed. "No, we just save that for the flights."

Derrick was about to send Lydia a text to let her know he made it when Tae suggested FaceTiming her.

"Dude, our phones work better here than back home! Give her a call."

Lydia heard the FaceTime tone coming from her phone and was surprised to see Derrick's name.

"Hey, honey! I didn't figure you would be able to call me from there."

"I didn't know either, but apparently, it's not much different from home. Say hi to Tae!"

He turned the phone and Tae waved as he drove.

"Hey ya!"

Lydia waved, "You have no idea how happy I was to hear you would be there, Tae. He needs someone watching him every minute of the day. Have him tell you the story sometime about trying to buy socks when we were in Germany."

Nudging Derrick, Tae exclaimed, "That sounds like some good conversation to have with our steaks tonight at the cookout!"

Chief was right. This tour was the perfect place for Derrick to stay out of trouble. He and Tae had a couple of hours of work each day and then spent the rest playing video games, waiting for something to break.

"Is this really what your normal day is like?" Derrick asked.

"You betcha! Some days are so slow, I'm able to kick back in the IT room and take a nap," Tae proudly explained.

Derrick shook his head in disbelief. "I've been picking the wrong sites then!"

***

It was Saturday morning, and Derrick was catching up on sleep after a late-night *Call of Duty* party with the Marines at the embassy. The blinds in his room had a small hole in them and the sun outside found just the right angle to shine into his eyes.

"That's so annoying!" Derrick muttered. "The one time I get to sleep in and nature says, 'NO!'"

Rolling over, he stuck his tongue out in triumph. "Bleh! You'll never beat me, Mother Nature!"

As he was drifting back off to sleep, his bed started moving slightly.

"Wow, suddenly I'm really dizzy," he thought.

The slight movement quickly escalated into violent jolting back and forth. Rolling out of bed, he tried to run for the doorway, but the shaking was so violent that he kept losing his balance and running into things.

The world shook for a full minute before suddenly stopping. Derrick's head spun as the fluid in his ears sloshed back and forth.

"Touché, Mother Nature... Touché!"

Derrick stumbled down the hallway as he made his way to the conference room. As he passed Tae's door, he saw his head poking out from under his bed, spastically jerking back and forth.

"Dude, you okay?"

"The ground moved! No one did anything to it! It just moved!"

Derrick extended his hand, helping Tae to his feet.

"Come on, buddy. Let's find the chief; I'm sure he'll want a head count."

They stepped into the conference room just as the chief was hanging up the phone.

"Hey chief, what's the damage? What can we do to help?"

"That was the President's office. The palace has taken significant damage from the quake. We're assembling a team for search and rescue. Do either of you have any experience?"

Tae was quick to volunteer Derrick. "He's a medic!"

"Great, you two grab some radios and make your way to the palace."

Approaching the palace, they finally were able to see the full extent of the damage.

"Oh, wow!" Tae exclaimed.

Derrick radioed the embassy to provide an update. "Chief, we have a partial collapse of the north side of the building, with significant structural damage to both the south and east wings. We are meeting up with command to find out how we can help."

Tae stopped the vehicle in the palace parking lot. "I can't believe they don't have this blocked off. No one even bothered to check our ID."

Spotting the chief of police running by, Derrick stopped him. "Sir, I'm Derrick, and this is Tae. We're from the U.S. Embassy. How can we help?"

The officer pointed in multiple directions and then ran off.

"It's total chaos, buddy. We should probably stay together just to be safe," Derrick suggested.

They entered through the main entrance of the palace, where they found a stream of people evacuating. Overhearing a couple of them talking about the President's family and that they were still unaccounted for, Derrick asked, "Where was the first family when the earthquake hit?"

The lady replied without breaking her gait. "Third floor, east wing. The stairway collapsed."

Derrick exchanged glances with Tae. "Well, that will make it a bit more difficult."

They reached the east wing to find a pile of rubble blocking most of the stairwell.

"You ready to start climbing?" Derrick asked.

Tae cracked his knuckles with excitement. "Like cheese on bacon, man!"

Derrick stopped and turned around with a disgusted look.

Shocked, Tae asked, "What? You never had fried bacon smothered in cheese before?"

"Uh... no. I haven't. Because I'm human," Derrick replied, gagging a little.

"If we get out of this alive, I'll introduce you to it!"

Derrick sighed and whispered under his breath as he began climbing, "Well, there's some motivation."

After an hour of climbing and enduring two aftershocks, they finally reached the third floor. The hallway wasn't in any better condition than the stairwell, which led to difficulty doing room sweeps.

Derrick knocked, and after hearing no response, he slammed his shoulder into the door, popping it open. His momentum carried him into the room... which wasn't there!

Desperately trying to grab the door frame, he found himself slowly tipping toward a three-story fall. Just as he was losing his grip on the knob, he felt a jerk at his belt, and his body flying backward. Landing on surprisingly soft ground, he freaked out when it started to talk.

"Ouch! Dude! Get off me!" Tae exclaimed.

Laying on the ground, they were contemplating the intelligence of searching alone when they heard a faint knocking echo down the hallway. They scampered to their feet and ran for a pile of debris where the noise was coming from. Behind the rubble, they could barely make out a door.

Tae yelled for reassurance. "We hear you! We are trying to find a way in!" while Derrick ran for the kitchen he saw a few doors down.

Tae following behind, said, "Oh, I see your brain working. What can I do?"

Rummaging through the drawers, Derrick found a box of heavy-duty garbage bags. "Fire extinguishers! See if you can find a couple," he exclaimed to Tae.

Derrick was sealing the openings of the trash bags with duct tape when Tae returned with three extinguishers. "This is all they had."

Working the bags into the narrow slot between the wall and the debris, Derrick attached the extinguisher hoses to a tiny opening he left in the first bag. Securing it with more tape, he said, "Here goes nothing."

The white powder began discharging into the bags, slowly inflating them. The rocks groaned, and then started to shift. The bags were able to create just enough space for Tae to slide in and force the jammed door open.

As Tae helped the two girls from the room, the bags began to fail. Derrick scrambled to patch the holes as he yelled for Tae to hurry up. The first lady and Tae squeaked out just in time as they finally ruptured, causing the door to slam shut.

Derrick radioed the chief, instructing him to have the local authorities to be waiting for them in the east wing. Carrying the three-year-old on his back, he then led the group back down the destroyed stairwell.

After handing the first family off, they met up with the police chief to get an update. As they were talking, another aftershock hit and the ceiling started to collapse. They sprinted for the entrance, making it down the front steps just as the ceiling let go, causing the entire east wing to crumble into a heap.

Derrick was sitting with Tae on the bumper of an ambulance, rinsing his eyes out when their radios keyed up, and the chief gave them the good news.

"Hey guys, I just got word that everyone is accounted for at the palace, and they have released you to come back home. See you guys shortly!"

Tae had just started the truck when he paused, staring at the partially collapsed palace.

"To think you were supposed to be staying out of trouble," he giggled.

Derrick's face dropped and he closed his eyes for a second. "Dude... not a word to Lydia."

"I wish I could think on my feet like you do," Tae complemented Derrick as they headed back to the embassy.

"What are you talking about, buddy? You ran right into that room, kicking the door down and all. They wouldn't have gotten out without you. We both did *good*."

They were just about to walk into the conference room for the debriefing when Derrick's phone lit up with Lydia's face.

"Hey honey, I was about to go into a meeting. Can I call you back?"

"Sure dear, but at least tell me you're okay. I saw on the news that Gaborone had one of its biggest earthquakes in history earlier today."

"Oh, it was a doozy. We just finished cleaning up, though," Derrick explained.

Tae walked up giggling, being able to hear the conversation.

"That's good to hear. I was a little worried because they said the Presidential palace had collapsed. It didn't sound good."

Derrick paused, trying frantically to formulate his story. "Yeah, Chief told us about that. I hear everyone escaped, so I guess it all worked out."

Tae looked as if he was going to explode with laughter.

Derrick mouthed the words "Shut up!" to him as Lydia continued. "Funny that you mention the chief because they also said that the first family had to be rescued..."

Derrick cringed as he listened. "That must have been scary, but I'm glad they made it out okay."

Tae ran from the hallway, covering his mouth. In the distance, Derrick could hear him burst out laughing once he went into the conference room.

"Derrick..." Lydia said sternly.

Startling Derrick, he replied, "What?" forgetting he was still on the phone.

"They were rescued by two diplomats... two U.S. EMBASSY diplomats."

Derrick screamed inside. "Oh wow! They sound brave. I bet that's what this meeting is about, then."

Lydia sighed heavily. "I know it was you and Tae."

His heart skipped a beat. "What are you talking about? I was filling trash bags most of the afternoon."

He held the phone away from his ear, waiting for her response.

"You know there were news crews there, right?"

"Oh, crap!" Derrick thought. His brain raced, trying to come up with a reply that wasn't a complete lie. "I'm sure there were, but how would I have known that? We were busy cleaning up."

There was a pause, and then his phone dinged. He looked, and Lydia had sent him a video of her TV screen showing him and Tae jumping out of the building as the floor collapsed.

"That guy doesn't even look like me!" Derrick tried to offer until the second video came through. This one was a close-up of him and Tae sitting on the bumper of the ambulance.

Smugly, Lydia asked, "So... you want to start over?"

CHAPTER 34

Weeks later, Derrick was staring out the window as the aircraft taxied towards the runway.

Laying her head on his shoulder, Lydia asked, "Well, Mr. Anderson... are you thinking about how this is the last time you have to look out the window as a boy scout?"

He chuckled a little. "Actually, I was thinking about how this was my last glimpse of freedom."

She shot straight up in her chair, gasping. "I know you didn't just say that!" pretending to retract as he put his arm around her.

Pulling her in tight, Derrick smiled at her with an evil grin and said, "I was just thinking about what I have planned for after the wedding."

Lydia gasped again, except this time with a smile on her face. "Mr. Anderson! You dirty old man!"

Derrick laughed and said, "Trust me. It will be worth it," as the airplane's tires left the ground.

Derrick watched as the plane landed and traveled down the runway in Kansas City.

"The pilot sure is using all of the real estate today," he mused as he listened to the engines in full reverse.

His demeanor quickly changed when the brakes locked onto the tires hard enough to throw him forward in his seat. Still looking outside, he saw the thousand-foot marker and a large white seven fly by at the end of the runway. It almost felt like they were... skidding.

"Oh, this is gonna hurt!"

Derrick reached down and grabbed Lydia's hand as *"BRACE, BRACE, BRACE!"* rang out over the intercom.

The plane finally came to a stop sideways in the grass beyond the threshold. Derrick looked out the window towards the runway they were just on and could see the flashing lights of the approaching fire trucks reflecting off a sheen on the pavement.

Lydia sat up and asked, "We there?"

"Sort of. We kinda... crashed," Derrick replied in a calm tone.

"Haha, funny guy."

The pilot's voice was then heard over the plane's intercom, *"Okay, folks, from the flight deck. As you can tell, we had a little problem. Please remain calm and stay in your seats with your belts fastened. We are not out of danger just yet, so we will conduct an orderly evacuation once fire services declare the area safe. Buses will be provided for transport to the terminal.*

Lydia's head snapped to look at Derrick.

"Told you."

"Wha... How... What happened?"

"Looks like the runway had ice on it, and we skidded off the end," Derrick explained.

"How are you so calm?!?"

"It's not my first inflight emergency. Besides, if there was something to be worried about, we would have known it by now..."

Just then, the plane began vibrating as it started shifting to the right.

"Are we... moving?" asked Lydia.

A loud crack resonated through the cabin, and the plane erupted in screams as the right side of the aircraft dropped to the ground.

Lydia looked at him wild-eyed as Derrick calmly said, "Landing gear collapsed."

"You think?!?" she yelled sarcastically.

The flight attendants opened the doors on the left side of the plane and deployed the inflatable slides. Being in row one, Derrick and Lydia were the first people out of the front exit. Lydia suggested Derrick lead since he would probably have issues with the height, and she could help by pushing him off.

As he slid down the ramp, Derrick only screamed a little. Lydia followed, and when she cleared the slide, she noticed Derrick had pulled out his phone and was taking pictures.

"What are you doing?!?" she asked, annoyed.

"Tae will never believe this!" Derrick exclaimed.

"He's met you. I'm pretty sure he would."

Taking his arm, she led him to the nearby bus, where, grabbing the first set of seats together, she sat by the window. She was still hugging Madeline when Derrick sat down.

"Are you okay, sweetie?"

Finally able to comprehend the seriousness of the situation, Lydia was starting to feel upset. "No. No, I'm not. Our plane just crashed. I'm not okay."

"Well, technically we just overshot the runway, so it wasn't a 'crash', per se."

Lydia glared at him, eyes full of tears.

"I'm sorry. Come here, honey," he said as he pulled her closer.

It was a short, but surreal ride to a set of outside stairs that led into Terminal C. Upon entering, they heard an announcement being made overhead, *"Attention passengers. Kansas City International has temporarily suspended all flights."*

Derrick nudged Lydia. "Hey! That was us!"

She started smacking his arm repeatedly. "Would <smack> you stop <smack> having so much <smack> fun with this!"

"Ow, ow, ow! Look, a Starbucks!"

Lydia stopped hitting him and spun around. "Where?!"

Derrick took a few steps back. After realizing he was lying, she spun back around, and her eyes could have burnt a hole straight through him.

They made their way to the connecting gate where the screen read "delayed." Lydia's phone rang, and when she checked, her mom's picture appeared."

"Hey, Momma!" she answered with her usual excitement.

"Honey, we were just watching TV, and the news broke in about a plane sliding off the runway in Missouri. They showed someone filming it that strangely looked like... Honey, did your plane crash and Derrick take pictures of it?"

Lydia paused, not knowing how to best answer that question.

"He did, didn't he?"

"To be fair, it wasn't a crash. We just overshot the runway," Lydia explained.

Derrick leaned over and whispered, "Oh, so when YOU say it, it's not crazy?"

Lydia swatted at him. "We're okay. Just had a little adventure. Now we are delayed because of the weather."

Derrick interjected, "And the sideways plane at the end of the runway."

A few hours later, Derrick was sitting at gate 67, gazing at their small airplane. Meanwhile, Lydia was engrossed in a new game on her phone, sipping the coffee she had discovered eleven gates away, and making Derrick pay for because of his "cruel joke" earlier.

"Ladies and Gentlemen, we have received word from the tower that the airport has reopened and flights will resume shortly. Boarding will start in about thirty minutes for flight 2386 to Des Moines."

It was later in the evening when they rolled into Bloomfield.

"You think you can find the house this time?" Lydia asked, laughing.

"Such a comedian," he replied, unamused. Then he realized that he had no idea where he needed to go.

She saw the confusion on his face and chuckled. "You're already lost, aren't you?"

"Well, who wouldn't be?!? This town is laid out so stupidly," Derrick growled in frustration.

Glancing out the windshield as they drove past the town square, Lydia replied sarcastically. "Downtown only has five streets. Even Jimmy manages to navigate his way to the market."

Derrick's mouth dropped open. "You mean the blind guy?!? So rude!"

"Amazing how much different the feelings are this time than last," Derrick said as he stared at the Evan's house.

Lydia leaned over and snuggled up on his shoulder. "I knew you'd like them!"

As they stepped onto the porch, Mary and Jeb opened the door to greet them. Lydia ran up and hugged her mom, while Derrick stuck his hand out to shake Jeb's.

"Evening, sir... Jeb.. sir..." He caught himself mid-sentence.

Jeb glared at him with a rough stare. "Man who's trying to steal my daughter."

It caught Derrick off guard for a split second until Jeb cracked a smile. Derrick felt some of his ribs pop as he tried to survive the bear hug he suddenly found himself in.

"So, this must be what it's like to be hugged by a Wookie," he thought.

Walking in through the door, Derrick leaned over to Lydia and whispered, "Ow."

After hanging up his coat, he was surprised by the twins standing right behind him.

"Oh, come on, already!" Derrick exclaimed.

Caleb asked, "Have you killed anyone yet?"

Derrick paused and then solemnly said, "Yes."

The two boys grew excited.

"Was it the head of some international terrorist ring?" asked Caleb.

"No, I bet it was the leader of some country we've never heard of," William threw in.

Derrick's gaze dropped to the floor. "It was a five-year-old girl."

The twins looked at each other in disbelief.

"Oh, you're just messing with us now."

Choking back his emotions, Derrick explained, "I put two rifle rounds through her chest with the second one detonating the suicide vest her parents put on her to blow up our helicopter."

William looked nervously at Caleb. "He might not actually be lying to us this time."

Derrick sat down at the dinner table next to Lydia. She could tell he was still upset, so she placed her hand on his knee.

"You okay, honey?" she asked.

"I'll be fine."

Leaning closer, she whispered, "You know, I've known you long enough to know when you're lying."

Dinner that night was some of the biggest ribeye steaks Derrick had ever seen. He took one bite of his and immediately recognized the flavor.

"Is this the seasoning I gave you at Christmas?" he asked Jeb.

Mary laughed. "Goodness, no! He had those used up by the end of the week. There's eight bottles now in the spice cabinet!"

Jeb didn't even look up from his meal but slightly grinned. "It's really good."

CHAPTER 35

The next afternoon, Derrick was standing at the front of the church looking at his phone disappointedly. Lydia saw the sadness in his face and walked over.

"What's wrong, honey?"

Derrick looked up and smiled. "Oh, it's nothing. Never been better."

Lydia gave him a look as if to say, "I don't believe you".

"Tae's plane is delayed. He won't make it for the rehearsal."

Lydia was slightly relieved that it wasn't something more disastrous. "Well, at least he will still be here for the wedding, right?"

Looking over at the groom's side and its row after row of empty pews, Derrick somberly replied, "I hope so."

Derrick stood with the minister as they watched Lydia and Jeb walk down the aisle in their final run-through. Handing her off, Jeb said, "Take care of her... son."

Stepping onto the stage, Lydia and Derrick turned to face each other. Lydia's mouth dropped open in surprise. Derrick turned around and saw Jeb just as he was sitting down... on the groom's side of the building. Tears started to stream down Derrick's face as he finally understood Jeb's statement when he handed her off. He stepped down off the stage and buried his face into Jeb's chest, saying through the tears, "Thank you so much... Dad."

***

The small group filed into the *Tequila Grill* for the rehearsal dinner. Derrick took a seat at the end of the table, with Lydia sitting down next to him on his right. Zoey positioned herself across the table, claiming she was going to "keep an eye on him." Unbeknownst to Derrick, Lydia had secretly tasked Zoey with keeping him out of trouble.

Meanwhile, Caleb and William were fighting over who was going to sit by Zoey as each had a crush on her.

She finally stood up and yelled, "FINE! I'll sit in the middle. Would you two just shut up now?!?"

The boys both grinned as Zoey moved into the middle seat. Derrick glared at Caleb as he sat down across from him.

Lydia leaned over and whispered, "Dooowwwn boy."

Up until the entrees were delivered, the meal had been rather uneventful, other than Derrick being stared at the whole time. He tried to ignore him, but Caleb finally broke the silence with yet another round of questions.

"Do you drive an Aston Martin?"

"No. I have a Mustang."

In obvious disappointment, Caleb continued. "Does it at least have ejection seats?"

He was starting to get irritated. "That's not a standard feature, but I would install them if you ever rode in it."

Caleb's eyes grew large. "You're saying you would let me ride in it?"

Picking up his fork and starting to cut his burrito, Derrick replied with a simple, "No."

Caleb was firing question after question at him when Derrick decided to try and ignore him. Reaching for his glass of water, Derrick misjudged the distance, accidentally hitting it instead causing the glass to start tipping over. In a desperate move to catch it before it spilled, he lunged and placed his other hand down for balance. Unfortunately, he put that hand on the edge of his plate, launching his rice and beans into the air… which landed directly on top of Caleb's head. He let out a scream, which silenced the entire table… except for Jeb… who burst into a howling laughter.

***

Lydia drove Derrick up to Oskaloosa to his hotel room at the *Fairfield Inn*. As she put the car into park, she asked, "Now, Tae did confirm he was going to make it, right? I don't want you to be here all alone without a car."

"Yes, he said he had landed and just left the airport on his way here about an hour ago. Don't worry, honey. I will be there tomorrow, waiting at the altar for you."

She leaned over and kissed him. "Only one more night of being Ms. Evans," she said, cheekily.

As she was getting ready to back out, Tae pulled into the spot next to her. Rolling down the window, she yelled, "Make sure my man gets there tomorrow!"

Tae laughed. "I didn't fly almost nine thousand miles just to have him flake out now."

"Hey ya!" Tae greeted him as he got out of the car. "You eat yet?"

Derrick laughed a little. "We had dinner, but it didn't really fill me up for some reason."

"Well, get in! I see they have a Taco Bell down the street. I could crush some burritos right now."

Derrick climbed into the rental car, thinking, "Well if that isn't irony."

He watched as Tae threw back burrito after burrito while scrolling on his phone.

"How do you stay so skinny eating like that?!?"

Tae shrugged. "I always have. Guess it's just in my genes. Hey! There's an arcade just down the street. Want to go there after we finish? That sounds like it would be a great bachelor party!"

Walking in, Tae saw an original Pacman video game console sitting off to the side of the arcade. He ran up to the machine, saying, "Dude, that's my favorite! I'm going to try for the high score."

Derrick watched for the next hour as Tae tore through level after level until he reached level two hundred fifty-five. Grabbing the last pellet, the screen split in two, having nothing but garbage on the right side.

"YES! THE KILL SCREEN!" Tae exclaimed.

Derrick stood behind him, amazed. He had only heard of that glitch in the game but had never seen it outside of YouTube.

Tae turned and asked, "You want to play now?"

Derrick shook his head.

CHAPTER 36

Derrick and Tae pulled up to the church building.

"You ready?" Tae asked.

"Never been more," Derrick replied confidently.

As they were talking, he heard a thud on his car door. Natalie had her face plastered against his window.

"Don't do it! Runaway with me," she begged.

Rolling down the window, Derrick said, "Hello again, Natalie. Have you met my friend Tae here? He's actually available."

"Oh good, you brought someone for Lydia," she replied, trying to pull him out of the car.

Walking up behind Natalie, Zoey smacked her on the arm. "What is wrong with you?!?

Derrick and Tae followed Zoey as she showed them to their changing room. Opening the door to the small room, she stated, "Here you go. Your tuxes are hanging up over there. We gave you two the one with the bathroom because Lydia says you have to stay in here until it's time. Not sure if that is so you don't run away or so Natalie doesn't get ahold of you. Oh, she also had us remove all the trashcans, just in case you got bored."

Having never worn one before, Derrick was trying to figure out all the pieces of his tuxedo.

Tae stepped out of the bathroom fully dressed and looking sharp. "That's called a cummerbund. You put it around your waist."

"Why?!? What's wrong with just a shirt and pants?"

Derrick could hear Tae's stomach growling. "Dude, did you not eat breakfast?"

"I did, but that cheap garbage at the hotel barely tickled my appetite. Maybe I can sneak out and find something in the reception hall," Tae said as he reached for the knob. Sticking his head out, he was met by Hailey who was holding a fly swatter. She whapped him on the head once and yelled, "Back! Get back in there!"

He hurried and shut the door. "They posted a guard... and she's armed. Maybe the windows? I think I saw a McDonald's next door."

Derrick pulled back the curtain, only to find the handles had been removed. "What sadistic person removes the handles from a window?!?" he questioned.

Reaching into his pocket, he pulled out his knife. It was a little slow using the pliers, but he was able to crack it open enough for the two of them to slip out.

Lydia was staring out the window, dreaming about the honeymoon, when she saw Derrick and Tae walking across the parking lot. Sticking her head out of the room, she yelled. "The boys escaped!"

Hailey plowed through the door, only to find the curtain blowing from the open window and the room deserted. "They went out the window!"

Lydia grabbed her forehead, frustration was evident in her voice. "I told you to search them and take his knife!"

The guys found a booth and sat down with their food orders. Derrick stared as Tae placed his tray down with three quarter-pounders on it. "We have food at the reception afterward."

"I know," Tae said, unwrapping his first burger, "That's why I didn't order my usual."

Derrick laughed. "I'm really glad you made it in. I couldn't imagine anyone else being my best man."

"I've watched you two clumsy love birds from day one. There wasn't a chance I was missing this!"

As they were finishing up, Derrick saw Zoey walking across the parking lot in a huff. "Oh no, they're on to us. Remember *SERE* school?"

Quickly dumping their trash, they headed out the side door. They almost made it to the back of the building when they heard, "GET BACK HERE, YOU COWARDS!"

Derrick looked at Tae and said one simple word. "Run."

They took off running into the parking lot and through the drive-thru line as Zoey rounded the corner of the building in a dead sprint.

Tae slid across the hood of Officer Johnson's patrol car, who turned on his outside speaker. "You'll never get away from her, guys! That girl has some fast legs! Even in those high heels!"

Making it back to the building, Tae tried to enter through the window. <WHAP> "Ow! The *Queen of Flies* is back! We need another entrance," he exclaimed, falling back out the window.

Pointing over Derrick's shoulder, he saw Zoey, still making a beeline for them. "Six o'clock! Bandit is still on us!"

"Don't you two dare move!" she yelled.

Derrick and Tae made for the front of the church, and rounding the corner, ran straight into Mary. She had one of those motherly looks on her face as she forcefully stuck out her hand.

"Knife," she demanded.

"Knife, what knife?" Derrick shrugged, innocently.

Derrick sensed a presence behind him. He knew it was Jeb because the ground shook, and an icy wave ran down his spine.

"Oh... that knife," he said as he pulled it out of his pocket and handed it to her.

Glancing over at Tae, who was looking up at Jeb frozen in fear, Derrick introduced them. "Oh, I forgot. Tae, this is Jeb, Lydia's dad."

As Zoey escorted them back to their room, Tae whispered to Derrick.

"Dude, Paul Bunyan just about pounded you into the ground like a spike."

"Who, Jeb? Nah. He's a softie," Derrick joked.

Hailey, who was waiting for them at the door, whapped Tae with the fly swatter again.

"Ow! Why do you keep hitting me?!? It was his idea," Tae cried.

"Because he'll tell Lydia and I'm more scared of her than you."

Tae nodded in agreement. "That's fair."

Pushing them into the room, Zoey barricaded the door from the outside. Tae sat down at the table and stared at the doorway, thinking of Hailey. "You know, she's kinda cute. Violent, but cute."

After about an hour of being locked in their room, Zoey came by and led them to the auditorium. As they exited, Hailey slid something into Tae's jacket pocket. He pulled it out when they stopped at the entrance.

"It's a phone number!" he said, clearly surprised.

"Well, look at you, buddy! That's why she was whapping you. She likes you!"

Tae's smile grew.

The music started, Tae turned to Derrick and said, "Are you nervous? I'm nervous."

"What are YOU nervous for?!?" Derrick asked, confused.

"There are people out there. I don't like standing in front of people."

"Hailey is out there, though. Just look at her."

Tae smiled again.

Derrick sighed with excitement. "No, I'm not really nervous. It's more of the feeling you get when you are about to open that Christmas gift you've been waiting for."

Zoey announced, "It's time," and opened the door for them. They walked out, taking their positions beside the preacher. The wedding march then began playing, and the back doors swung open. Time seemed to stop when he saw her.

Tae leaned over and whispered, "Wow!" as she made her way down the aisle.

Derrick didn't even know Tae was there anymore. Everything else faded away as he locked in on her blue-gray eyes, envisioning their future together.

Jeb handed Lydia over to Derrick and grinned as he let out a short growl.

Leading her up the steps to the stage, Lydia's smile radiated as Derrick whispered, "You are so beautiful."

The preacher asked if there were any objections, and Natalie threw her hand up. Hailey reached from behind and smacked her with the fly swatter she still had.

"Anyone other than Natalie, that is," he reiterated.

Staring into her eyes, Derrick heard nothing the preacher said until he asked for the rings. "Derrick..."

"Huh?" he thought as he snapped out of his daydream.

"The rings?" the preacher asked.

Lydia watched as Derrick signaled down the aisle. The back doors opened again, and there stood Ollie with Larry, both dressed in tuxedos.

She gasped as they walked down the aisle together. Tied to Larry's harness was a small pouch that held the rings.

Turning back to Derrick, Lydia, with tears in her eyes, whispered, "Thank you."

The preacher continued. "Derrick, do you take this woman to be your lawfully wedded wife?"

"I do," he said as he slid the ring onto her finger.

"Lydia, do you take this man to be your lawfully wedded husband?"

"I do."

"By the power vested in me by the State of Iowa, I now pronounce you husband and wife."

Derrick leaned in, and as his lips touched hers, he recognized the familiar flavor of her lipstick: strawberries.

During the reception, after they cut the cake, Derrick disappeared and met up with Tae. They both came around to the front of the hall and stayed just out of sight. The music screeched to a stop, and they walked out, snapping to attention in front of everyone.

Mary leaned over to Jeb and whispered, "This can't be good."

The *Men in Black* theme song started playing, and the two put on their Ray-Bans, breaking out into a clumsy rendition of the MIB dance. Everyone erupted into laughter and cheers.

From across the hall, the words, "YOU TWO, STOP!" boomed over the music. Everything went dead silent as Lydia stood at the head table, glaring at the boys. Tae looked fearfully at Derrick and said, "Oh boy, This is gonna hurt, isn't it?"

Lydia told Olivia, "Hold my bouquet," and removed a pair of sunglasses from it as she started walking towards them. Derrick, feeling rather confused and frightened, glanced at Tae, who was slowly distancing himself.

Strolling up, Lydia took a spot between them. She pointed to the DJ and said, "If you are going to do it, do it right." The music resumed and she dropped right into the sequence, showing them both up.

As they were getting ready to leave, Derrick whispered in her ear. "I have another surprise for you outside." The ushers opened the doors, and as everyone threw birdseed into the air, Lydia saw Fred standing beside their SUV. She looked at Derrick and started crying.

Rushing over to the car, Fred lowered his head. Hugging him, she cried, "I miss you so much, friend. Thank you for coming."

Derrick held the door open and helped her into the SUV. After making sure her dress was fully in, he closed the door, and they headed off towards her house to change.

Derrick went upstairs to the hallway bathroom with his clothes, and Lydia tried to follow.

Grinning, Lydia said, "You know we can change together now."

Stopping her, Derrick replied, "I know, but I want the first time I see you to be in that special moment, and we have a flight to catch."

"A flight?!? But?!?" Lydia exclaimed in frustration.

"Yes, ma'am. Your bag is already packed and in the car, so hurry and change."

When they got back into the SUV, Derrick handed Lydia a small package.

"For me?"

"Well, it's somewhat for both of us," he explained.

Opening the box, she saw a red and white polka dot bikini and gave him an inquisitive look.

Derrick smiled. "I know you don't normally wear bikinis, but you need one and it looked like you. Don't worry, it covers all the right spots nicely."

She still looked a little worried.

"It's your scars, isn't it?" he asked

"I just don't like people seeing them."

"Don't worry. It won't be a problem," he said playfully.

As she pulled the top out, it revealed something blue underneath—their passports.

"We need to hurry if we are going to catch that flight," he said, grinning.

CHAPTER 37

Derrick pulled up to the rental car drop-off, and Lydia couldn't take the suspense anymore.

"Okay! Where are we going? Tell me! Tell me!"

Derrick pressed his lips tight and shook his head.

Leaning over to his ear, she nibbled on it and whispered, "Tell me."

Derrick recoiled. "Down temptress!"

"Fine!" she yelled, sinking back into her seat with a pout. After a few seconds, she added, "Tell me."

Derrick wheeled their luggage up to the American Airlines counter and slid their reservations over to the lady behind it. Lydia tried to look, but he had the paper upside down.

"It's our honeymoon, and she doesn't know where we are going yet, so if you wouldn't tell her..." Derrick politely asked.

"Oh! How sweet. Of course," the lady replied as she checked them in.

"Are you kidding me?!?" Lydia exclaimed, smacking him on the arm.

The agent grinned and handed him back their tickets and bag claims. "Have a pleasant flight, Mr. and Mrs. Anderson."

After clearing security, Derrick was putting his shoes on when he saw Lydia take off running. He looked at the TSA agent standing nearby and said, "Let me guess, there's a Starbucks over there."

The agent laughed and nodded.

Derrick headed over to a nearby column and waited. She walked back over a few minutes later with her drink.

"You know it's 8pm, right?"

"You shush. Now take me to the gate or lose me forever."

Walking up to Gate 3, Lydia finally saw the destination on the screen.

"O'Hare?!? You gave me a bikini to go to Chicago in November?!?"

"You're from Iowa, and complaining about it being cold?!? It's a connecting flight."

"To where?" she asked, grinning.

"To where we are going."

Lydia huffed and plopped down into a chair. Sitting down next to her, Derrick pulled her in close and kissed her on the head. "It's worth it."

We are going to begin boarding flight 1445 to Chicago now at Gate 3. We will start with our First Class passengers.

Derrick stood up and grabbed his bag. Confused, Lydia looked at him strangely. Reaching his hand out to help her up, he said, "Surprise!"

"Seriously?!? We're going first class?"

"We are for this leg" he explained. "I booked us a Qsuite for the rest of the flight."

"Qsuite?" she thought. "Never heard of that before. How did he keep all this a secret?"

Upon boarding the plane, they made their way to the front-row seats. Derrick placed his bag up into the overhead compartments, sat down, and stuck his arm out over the top of her headrest.

"Position assumed," he joked.

Lydia laughed as she sat down and snuggled up against him.

Seeing their playfulness, the flight attendant greeted them. "You two must be newlyweds."

"Is it that obvious?" replied Lydia.

"Nooooo," the flight attendant said, laughing. "Is Chicago your final destination?"

"Honestly, I don't know. He won't tell me."

The flight was only an hour and a half to Chicago, but Lydia was still out cold for most of it. When they were starting their approach, she sat up, revealing her trademark drool spot on his shirt.

Making their way into the terminal, Derrick headed for the bathroom to use the hand dryer, and Lydia went over to Starbucks.

O'Hare is a huge airport, but thankfully their next flight was only ten gates away and it didn't leave for an hour. On their way, Lydia reached down and grabbed his hand.

"I might act like I'm mad, but I really like that you kept where we were going a secret."

Derrick didn't even look over. "I'm still not telling you."

"Oh, come on! I'm going to find out here in a few minutes anyway when I see the board! Just tell me!"

Derrick bit his lower lip and shook his head again. "Nope."

Finally arriving at the gate, the boarding had just begun. Lydia saw the destination on the screen but was even more confused.

"Doha? Isn't that in Qatar?"

"Yes. It's the capital."

"What's in Qatar?"

"2.9 million people," Derrick said, nonchalantly.

She swatted his arm. "No! Where are we going in Qatar?"

"Oh... Hamad International," he replied, cleverly. "Just relax. It's all going to be worth it."

Upon boarding, Derrick gave the flight attendant their tickets, who led them towards the front.

"Here we are, Qsuite 2."

Lydia was taken back at the enormity of the seats before her. They were two business-class seats with no divider that combined to make a full-size bed. She turned around and hugged Derrick.

"Oh, thank you! I was worried we would be separated on our first night."

The flight departed at 11pm, making an already exhausting day feel even longer. Once they reached cruising altitude, Lydia was trying to snuggle into her flight position.

"Why don't we put the seats down and turn in for the night? Derrick lowered the seats and she scooted over with Madeline in her arms, quickly drifting off to sleep on his chest.

"I must be the luckiest man in the world," Derrick thought, pulling the blanket up over Lydia before falling asleep too.

***

Derrick woke up to the overhead announcement that they were beginning breakfast service. He realized he had slept through the night for the first time, nightmare-free. Nudging Lydia a couple of times, she finally lifted her head and looked at him. Her hair was going in all different directions and even part of it was matted to her face.

"You're pretty when you wake up," Derrick remarked.

"Are we almost there?" Lydia asked groggily.

"We have about eleven and a half hours left to Doha."

"Eleven hours! Are there any more flights after this one?"

"There's one more, and it's only five hours."

"Ugh. I'm going to go freshen up then," she said, grabbing a small bag out of her carry-on and heading to the washroom.

While Lydia was away, Derrick tidied up by putting up their blankets and raising the seats back to their normal positions. He asked the flight attendant for a cup of coffee and had it waiting for her when she got back.

"Look at you, Mr. Anderson, being all sweet and tidying up. You sure we aren't almost there?" she teased, giving him a wink.

"Just kick back and relax. I keep telling you, it will all be worth it."

***

A few hours later, Derrick was watching a movie while Lydia lay on him, fast asleep. When she freshened up earlier, she used some of her strawberry perfume, so Derrick was at home.

"If all I did the rest of my life was sit on the couch with this woman snuggled up next to me, I would be a happy man."

Having nodded off as well, Derrick woke as the pilot made their descent announcement.

"Uh… are we there?" Lydia asked, groggily as Derrick tried to wake her.

Derrick stood to stretch his legs as the flight attendant was making their final walkthrough. Seeing the spot on his shirt, she offered to clean up the spill that caused it.

"Thank you, ma'am, "Derrick replied, "but there's no spill." He pointed to Lydia, who was still wiping drool off her face.

***

Lydia was excited because she was about to go into her first airport lounge. They had a four-hour layover in Doha, so they planned on grabbing dinner and a shower before heading out for their final destination. Upon entering the lounge, they found a table to sit at.

"I think it's finally time I can show you where we are going," Derrick said, as he slid her ticket over revealing the destination.

Lydia's eyes grew three times bigger than normal. "The Maldives! Are you being serious, Derrick?"

"Yes. We have a private beach with an overwater bungalow all to ourselves, hence the bikini. You won't have to worry about anyone seeing you in it… except me."

They finished dinner just in time for their shower reservations, with the men's and women's facilities being located on opposite sides of the lounge.

After Derrick finished, he headed back out to try the full-body massage chair he had seen. However, he was mesmerized by the sight of Lydia walking toward him from down the walkway, wearing his favorite sundress. She looked so beautiful in it that he could have sworn she was floating.

"I thought you might like this," she said.

Derrick was at a loss for words.

"I feel like everyone is looking at my scar, though. It's so hideous," she added, trying to cover it with her hair.

As Derrick approached, she expected him to kiss her on her lips, Instead, he went to the left and a little lower, kissing her scar.

"Lydia... I know you think the scar is a flaw, but that scar means you survived and are here with me now, about to fly to paradise. It's not a weakness, but a badge of honor. How many people can say they survived a sniper and came out the other end stronger than ever?"

Derrick pulled her in close as Lydia started tearing up.

It was almost time for the last flight to board, so they made their way to the gate. With all the time zones they were flying through, the flight should put them in Malé a few hours before sunset. Derrick scheduled a shuttle to be waiting for them, and if he planned everything right, they should walk out onto the pier with thirty minutes left before the sun fell below the horizon.

The flight wasn't the only thing that was on time. Lydia's head hit his chest right on schedule. While she slept, Derrick stared at the scar on her back. He was only half telling the truth earlier. Yes, he did love that it meant she was still here with him, but having almost lost her that day, it also scared him. One brief gust of wind and things could have been all different.

During their time in Germany, Derrick had a chance to reflect on their work life and its inherent dangers. He was very good at his job, but it felt like his priorities had started shifting after meeting her.

***

So far, everything was going according to plan. They landed in Malé a few minutes early, and the shuttle was waiting for them. Having a snack on the flight, Derrick expected an undisturbed evening until the next morning when their concierge brought breakfast.

He watched out the window as the shuttle was taking them to the island. Estimating that they would have about 45 mins before sunset, he breathed a sigh of relief.

"Why are you so tense?" Lydia asked.

"There is one more surprise, and I was making sure everything was still a go."

"You're sure a master at that sexy talk there, Cowboy," Lydia joked, patting his leg.

The shuttle pulled up to the back of the island. Derrick helped Lydia out while the driver unloaded their bags, and then led them to their bungalow.

A long, sandy path led them through a grove of palm trees and bushes. Upon reaching the end, the Indian Ocean stretched out before them. To their left, a young man awaited them next to a small bungalow on stilts over the water.

"Congratulations Mr. and Mrs. Anderson! Welcome to the Maldives! My name is Rakin, and I will be your concierge this week. We have your bungalow all set as you requested. Please, follow me."

Showing them to the walkway, he took them out to their hut. "I understand you've had a long flight, so we'll refrain from bothering you unless you call. Should you need assistance, simply press the button on the phone, and you'll reach me directly. Enjoy your stay, and welcome to paradise!"

Derrick took Lydia by the hand and led her out the back door onto a small pier. Taking her to the end of it, he pointed to the setting sun.

"Remember when I said it will all be worth it? This is it. This was the big surprise I wanted you to see. The sunset in paradise on a pier from your very own island."

Lydia stared in amazement at the beautiful colors that started filling the sky and water. They were so vivid that she could almost feel them. They watched as the sun slowly fell below the horizon.

"That was so beautiful! Thank you! You were right; it was worth it. But you were also wrong."

Derrick felt confused.

Taking a couple of steps toward the end of the pier, Lydia turned around, and he suddenly felt like a helpless animal being stalked. With almost a sinister grin, she slid the sundress strap off her left shoulder.

"It wasn't the last surprise."

Her gaze intensified as she slowly pushed the right one off as well. Derrick found it hard to breathe as her sundress fell straight down to the pier, leaving her body surrounded by nothing but the red and orange sunset bathing her skin from behind.

***

...Derrick lay on a blanket in a field surrounded by rows of cornstalks. He stared up into the night sky, watching meteor after meteor streak above. He heard a voice from beside him.

"Did you see that one?!? It was huge!" Lydia exclaimed.

The faint smell of strawberries lofted through the night air as she slid over next to him.

"I can't think of anything I'd rather be doing right now," he remarked.

Lydia rolled over and placed her hand on his chest. "I can," She said as she slowly moved towards him...

Derrick woke, staring at the dark ceiling.

"Ah, man! Are you kidding me!?! Why do I always wake up right before the good part?!?" he thought, feeling frustrated.

As he readjusted in the bed, he felt something snuggle up beside him and an arm fall onto his chest. He was afraid to move, thinking it might still be a dream. Once he realized it wasn't, a euphoric wave of happiness swept over him like none he had ever had before.

***

That morning, Derrick stepped outside onto the porch to find Lydia already standing down at the end of the pier, soaking in the sunrise. The sea breeze blew her hair in the orange sky that was silhouetting her perfect hourglass figure. She was also wearing the bikini he got her.

Sitting down quietly, he watched the beauty before him, not wanting to disturb her. "She's so hot she's stealing thunder from the sunrise!" he whispered under his breath.

She must have heard him thinking because she looked back and gave him a come here nod. He headed to the end of the walkway, and she turned away from the sunrise to him. Taking her head, he started to kiss her but froze when he looked into her eyes. Those blue-gray eyes were now dancing with pink and orange. He got lost in them.

She grinned. "We are on our own beach in the middle of paradise and I'm all yours... your move." She leaped into his arms as Derrick went to pick her up.

Later that day, after lunch, Derrick asked, "How about we go snorkeling? I hear there's an assortment of wildlife around here."

"Yes! But we are taking the slide to get in."

Their bungalow had a waterslide that led from a deck on the roof down into the ocean.

Lydia ran up the open back stairs to the roof deck and noticed Derrick taking his time.

"Hurry up, slowpoke!"

"I'm coming. I'm coming." The open steps were causing his acrophobia to kick in.

When he finally reached the top, Lydia hopped onto the slide and screamed with joy all the way down, splashing into the ocean at the bottom.

Moving to the side, she called back to Derrick, "Come on! That was fun!"

Sighing, he climbed onto the slide. As he started down, he somehow got twisted around and ended up entering the water... backward.

The ocean floor was teaming with life. Numerous exotic fish swam through the brightly colored coral.

"This is SO beautiful!" Lydia muttered through her snorkel.

From underneath their bungalow, three sea turtles swam out into the lagoon. One of them came up and touched her outstretched hand.

A little later, a school of parrotfish came alongside them creating an amazing picture of Lydia with the brightly colored fish.

Deciding to head back in for some lunch, Lydia started up the stairs that led from the water up to the pier. Just as she was almost to the top, Derrick reached out and grabbed one of the strings on the side of her bathing suit and pulled. The knot untied and her bikini bottom fell off onto the pier.

"MR. ANDERSON!" she exclaimed.

"Oh, I'm sorry. Was that attached?" he laughed.

"Yessss... and you missed one" she replied, undoing the bow around her neck.

***

Derrick stared at the clock as it rolled past 3am. He was tired, but just couldn't sleep.

"I guess if I'm going to be up, I might as well go check out the Milky Way."

Making his way to the hammock on the porch, he was amazed at the brightness of all the stars. The night sky here made even Bloomfield pale in comparison.

After a few minutes of counting the satellites he saw, Lydia stepped outside.

"Oh wow! Look how many there are!" she quietly exclaimed as she walked over to the hammock. "Are you admiring the stars or just seeking some alone time?"

Derrick scooted over a little. "Couldn't sleep, so I thought I'd come out and look for aliens. There's an open spot here, no one waiting if you are interested."

She climbed into the hammock and snuggled up against him. It wasn't long before she was fast asleep.

Derrick smiled and whispered, "That's much better."

***

There were only a couple of days left, and they were sitting out in the hammock over the water. Derrick caught something out of the corner of his eye. Grabbing her hand, he pulled Lydia towards the end of the pier.

"Look! Right over there."

Lydia gasped as two dolphins jumped out of the water. "How beautiful!"

"Jump," Derrick told her.

"What?"

This time he was more emphatic. "Get in the water, now!"

Understanding this time, Lydia dove in. Derrick rushed down to the ladder and quietly got in with the camera.

Just as he had hoped, the dolphins heard the splash of her jumping in and came over to investigate. The big one swam right up to Lydia and popped his head out of the water beside her. She stuck her hand out, and the dolphin rolled over exposing its belly. Lydia stroked its stomach a couple of times until it rolled back over.

Before swimming off with the other one, it pecked Lydia on the cheek as if to give her a kiss.

"Thank you, Mr. Dolphin!" she yelled.

It let out a couple of quick squeals, then swam back over to its mate and continued out into the bay.

Swimming over to Derrick. Lydia exclaimed, "DID YOU SEE THAT?!!"

She grabbed him and kissed him. "Thank you so much!!! This place keeps getting better and better!"

***

The sun was rising on the "Island of Paradise," as Lydia called it. It was their last full day on the island. Stepping out onto the porch, she was surprised to find Derrick already out there, lost in thought.

Sitting down next to him, Derrick continued to stare off at the ocean. "Why do we do what we do?" he finally asked.

Being puzzled, Lydia gave him an inquiring look.

Derrick elaborated. "I mean, why are we risking our lives together to take missions that mean nothing?"

That, she understood exactly. Derrick didn't know it yet, but she did a lot of thinking in Germany and had been asking herself that same question.

Lowering her head some, she softly stated, "I keep having that dream where I'm standing on the pier, turn around and you aren't there. It scares me, Derrick."

Pulling her in close, she laid her head on his chest and wept softly. "I don't want any of this if it means you aren't in my future."

Later, as they were still sitting on the porch, a boat appeared from around the island and approached their pier. She watched as it docked and Rakin stepped ashore, addressing them with a chipperness that was only rivaled by Tae.

"Hello, Andersons! I have your boat all ready for you and the items you requested onboard. Is there anything else you will need?"

"Thank you, Rakin. I believe that will be all for now," Derrick replied as Lydia looked quickly back and forth between them.

Derrick helped Lydia down into their beautiful forty-foot-long cabin cruiser with a spot to lay out on the front. Greeting them was a large wicker basket sitting next to a couple of bottles that appeared to be champagne.

"Mr. Anderson! Are you trying to loosen me up?"

"Calm down, it came with the basket."

She gave him a quick peck on the cheek. "I was going to say... you didn't need alcohol to get lucky."

Heading out onto the sundeck, she lay down on the lounge chair and said, "Take me to sea, Captain!" as he pulled the boat away from the pier.

Derrick took her on a tour around the island, where he found a small cove with a crystal white beach. After he dropped anchor, he grabbed the basket and bottles, then headed up onto the sundeck.

"I don't ever want to go back home, Derrick. This is so beautiful. Can we make this ours?"

"Well, I think I've figured out a way that we can."

Lydia sat straight up in her lounger. "What did you say?!?"

"Our dream. The house with a pier into the Gulf. We're close. We can do it."

"But you know what you're saying by that, right?"

Sighing, Derrick replied, "Yeah. I do. It means we would no longer be officers. But it also means we would no longer be voluntarily putting ourselves in mortal danger, and most of all, it also means that your nightmare won't come true."

Lydia paused in thought. "...means my nightmare won't come true..."

CHAPTER 38

Derrick's phone rang at 7:30am. When he answered, the chief was on the other end.

"Good morning, Derrick. I know you just got back from your honeymoon, but I saw a request come across my desk and remembered our conversation earlier. Are you interested in a thirty-day backfill... in London?"

"Well, that does sound amazing, but as you said, we just got back from our honeymoon and I'm not sure Lydia will want me to be gone that long right away."

The chief continued, "I forgot to mention that I actually need TWO. There is a married couple there that is going on home leave and with Lydia's love for London..."

Derrick replied immediately. "We'll take it!"

"Great! I need you both there in three days, so get with travel and they'll get it all set."

Derrick hung up with the chief and went out into the living room, where he found Lydia sitting out on the balcony.

"Hello, my love!"

Admiring the morning, Lydia was amazed at the colors in the sky. "Look at how beautiful the sunrise is from here."

"Not as beautiful as you."

She smiled at him.

Repressing his excitement, Derrick casually said, "So, the chief called. He has a thirty-day backfill available."

"WHAT?!? We just got home, and he wants you to leave for thirty days?"

Pretending to be disappointed, Derrick dropped his shoulders and let a frown fall across his face. "I thought you would be more excited."

Lydia jumped up out of her chair. "You took it?!? Derrick Ichabod Anderson!"

"Well, yeah. I told him yes for you too."

Lydia was visibly upset and had turned her back to him. "I can't... wait, what?"

"There were two spots. We're both going."

"I'm afraid to ask, but WHERE are we going?"

"London."

Lydia spun around to face him. "Say that again?"

Derrick repeated, "London."

Lydia gasped. "As in England?"

"Yes. Big Ben, the Thames, God save the king. That London."

She leaned against the railing, speechless.

"I take it you approve now... oh... and 'Ichabod'?!?"

"That's all I could think of at that moment," she said sheepishly.

"Get dressed because we need to go in to travel and get it set up… we leave in three days."

***

Derrick had always wanted to fly on a British Airways 747-400. Most of them had been retired by now, but he managed to get a flight on one of the last few that still flew. He tried to explain to her how excited he was about it on the way to the airport, but she just smiled and nodded as he was talking.

Unloading their luggage from Lydia's Beetle, Derrick was grumpy that they had to bring hers.

"I still don't understand why we couldn't have brought the 'Stang."

Lydia patted him on the cheek. "Because I had to crawl out of it last time. You'll be fine. You didn't lose any man cards by riding in mine."

Lydia slid her new Diplomatic Passport over along with Derrick's as they were checking in. It was the first time she had used it since her name change.

"It's a pleasure to have you flying with us today, Mr. and Mrs. Anderson."

Lydia giggled a little.

Smiling, the counter agent said, "Let me guess… newlyweds?"

Derrick handed their tickets to the flight attendant as they boarded. "A&C 82. Those are right up those stairs. Make a left and then second from the front."

He headed for the stairs when Lydia tapped him on the shoulder.

"Derrick... why are their stairs on an airplane?"

"I tried to tell you in the car. We are flying over on a 747-400."

Lydia paused for a second and then asked again, "Okay, maybe I wasn't clear enough. Derrick... Why are their stairs on an airplane?"

When they took their seats, he pulled out the information card and showed her that their aircraft had a small upper deck in the front.

"Oh, how cute! How long have they been doing that with planes?"

He rubbed his eyes in amazement. "You don't get out much, do you?"

After takeoff, Derrick pulled out his tablet and headphones to launch into an epic MacGyver marathon while Lydia connected to the Wi-Fi to play games on her phone.

A few hours into the flight, Derrick saw Lydia nodding off. "Honey, why don't you stretch out and get some rest?"

Fiddling with the divider, she couldn't get it to release. "How do I unlock this thing up so I can go to sleep!?"

"It's fixed. Just lay your seat down."

Lydia stared at him in confusion.

"They're lay flats. Like the ones on the flight to Baghdad..."

"But I can't sleep on a plane without laying on you."

Laughing a little, Derrick remarked, "I find that hard to believe. Give it a try."

She lowered her seat to the bed position and tossed and turned a bit before drifting off.

When they were making their approach to London, Lydia kept leaning across Derrick to see out the window.

"Do you see Big Ben? What's it look like? I can't see!"

"Get off me, crazy lady! Here, change me seats." Derrick quickly swapped with her before the flight attendant noticed.

Ecstatically bouncing in her seat, Lydia exclaimed, "I think I see it!"

When she stepped into the terminal, Lydia turned to Derrick. "Did you call me *crazy lady* on the plane?"

"Yeah... it's because you were."

Aghast, Lydia smarted off to him in Spanish as she was walking away.

"*Todavía no has visto loco.*" She didn't think Derrick heard.

He replied back, "*No sabía que sabías español,*" to her surprise and annoyance.

Gathering their luggage from the carousel, Derrick followed the sign that read "Underground - Heathrow Station".

Lydia saw the sign and giggled. "He he, the Underground."

When she started skipping, Derrick finally had to ask. "You going to be okay?"

Smiling from ear to ear, she replied, "Noooooo."

They boarded the Piccadilly line and headed to Acton Town, where they transferred to the District line.

"Do you have any idea where you are going?!?" Lydia inquired. "I'm having flashbacks of Bloomfield."

"Funny... Would you rather 'drive'?" Derrick replied sarcastically.

"*Mind the gap between the train and the platform. This is Westminster.*"

"That's our stop," Derrick said as he grabbed his bags.

They walked up the stairs to the surface, and Derrick couldn't wait for her to step outside. From his research, he knew Big Ben would be waiting for them across the street. He purposely stood to her right so she would tend to look over at him instead of to the left, where it would be appearing.

Topping the stairs, she gasped at the surrounding city. As she panned to the left, her eyes started bulging, and she slowly looked upwards, following the tower up to the clock. She was speechless for a few moments and then only could articulate,

"It's... so... huge..."

The hotel was across the Westminster Bridge, but Derrick thought the short trek was worth her reaction.

As he walked through the lobby of the County Hall Marriott, he realized Lydia wasn't with him. Turning around, he saw her still standing at the front doors with her mouth hanging open.

Going back for her, he said, "Stop being a tourist."

"I can't! Everything here is so... *Londony*."

He rolled his eyes as he walked with her up to the counter. "I wonder why?"

Sliding his reservations over to the front desk clerk, she smiled and greeted him. "Good evening, Mr. Anderson. Welcome to the Marriott London County Hall. I see you are an ambassador level with us. To thank you for your loyalty, we upgraded your room to a suite. Big Ben view still good?"

"Yes ma'am, and thank you!"

Having been admiring the lobby once again, Lydia's head spun back to the counter... "Big Ben view?!?!"

Derrick swiped his card and opened the door. Lydia almost pushed him out of the way, running to the balcony. Outstretched before her were the Thames, the London Eye, and, of course, Big Ben.

"We have to be in the wrong room! We can't afford this room! We don't have to leave, do we?"

Placing their bags down on the floor, Derrick put his arm around her. He smiled as tears of joy rolled down her face. "No, there's no mistake. This is our home for the next thirty days. It's an early Christmas present."

Derrick was unpacking their suitcases as Lydia sat out on the balcony texting pictures to everyone she knew. He overheard her calling her mom as well.

"Momma! It's right there! I can almost touch it!"

They decided to try the steakhouse in the hotel as it was rated one of the best in London. After they were seated, Lydia was going over the menu. "The prices here aren't that bad either. Most of the steaks are only between twenty and forty *quid*."

Derrick had been concentrating on which entrée he was going to choose and shook it off as maybe he just heard her wrong.

The main course arrived and Lydia tried hers. With a sudden and distinctively British accent, she exclaimed, "*Blimey*! This steak is *ace*!"

Derrick stared at her inquisitively.

Meanwhile, the waiter returned to check on them. "How is everything? Is there anything you need?"

Lydia started to reply and Derrick could tell he was going to wish he was invisible.

"I'm *chuffed to bits*! I think we have the *full monty* here, thank you."

Lydia noticed Derrick wasn't eating and was staring at her. "Something wrong?" she asked.

"Have you seen the American girl that I flew here with? I remember she was with me at the airport, but I think I might have lost her on the Tube earlier."

"I was trying to talk to them in their own language so we didn't look like foreigners."

Derrick's head started hurting. "Um... but you already speak their language. They speak English."

"Well, I know he speaks English, but ever since we got here, I feel like I've picked up so much that I can talk to them in their native language of British."

A shocked expression overwhelmed Derrick's face and dropped his fork onto the table. "I honestly can't tell if you are kidding or not on that one."

"Oh, *poppycock*! Don't get your *knickers in a twist* and just eat your steak."

After dinner, they decided to go for a stroll down the Queen's Walk. Along the way, they passed under the London Eye.

"Can we go up?!? Just imagine what the sunset looks like from up there?!?"

Derrick purchased two tickets from the booth and they boarded the next car. Lydia plastered herself against the glass as they started to rise in the air.

"Look at that sunset! It's so beautiful!" she exclaimed.

Looking behind them, Derrick noticed how the sun reflected off the tower and the pink/orangish clouds framing it.

"Honey, behind you."

She turned around and her mouth dropped in amazement. "Get a picture of us with it!" she yelled.

Derrick texted the snapshot to her phone, but she was too busy to notice as she took pictures in all directions. The sunset was nice to look at, but for

Derrick, the sheer excitement, rivaled only by that of Christmas morning, was the most rewarding sight.

The thirty-minute ride was almost over. The sun had long set, and the sky was turning a dark purple. Lydia finally decided to sit down and relax beside him.

"That was so much fun! We should do that every night!"

When they exited their car, Lydia was acting a little more clingy than normal.

"What would you like to do now, honey?" he asked her.

"I'm feeling a little *randy* and you're looking seriously *peng*. Want to go back and *snog*?"

Derrick's head spun. "What in the name of Prince William's left toe did you just say?!?"

She leaned over and nibbled on his ear. Derrick's eyes grew.

She didn't need to say a single word for Derrick to understand what all that meant. "Oh!"

While Lydia was getting ready for bed, Derrick opened the curtains just enough that she could see Big Ben from the bed. As he was admiring the view, he heard a thud and the sound of the shower curtain being pulled off the rod come from the bathroom.

"Honey?"

"I'm good! My shorts tried to kill me, but we're good," she replied, dismissively.

"I told you that for your safety you should sleep in the…"

"Derrick! We talked about that!"

He shrugged and said to himself, "Well, it would be."

Lydia came out and did her signature jump onto the bed and scampered up beside him. As she laid her head on his chest and was wrapping her arms around him, she saw the clock tower through the window.

"OOOOOOH! I can't get over how beautiful it is! I'm not sure I can fall asleep with it being out there."

Three minutes later, her snoring resonated through the room.

***

The next morning was Monday, and Lydia was up early, watching the sun rise behind the Palace of Westminster. As Derrick walked out onto the balcony with her, she turned to him and exclaimed, "I love this view! This has to be on my list of the best places in the world."

They hopped on a double-decker bus outside the hotel and headed for the embassy. Lydia was taking pictures of every *British* building they passed.

"This is SO amazing! Look at all this! It's a British taxi! Hey! Even that old guy on the billboard looks British!"

Derrick laid his face into his hands. "Lydia... that's the King. He looks British because he IS British!"

"Oh, you are such a *wet blanket*, Derrick."

The onsite IT team met Lydia and Derrick in the lobby of the embassy.

"Morning, mates! My name is Wallace and this love here is Genève. I see you found your way alright. Let's go get you two some badges and we will show you around."

Wallace took them on a tour, showing them the facilities and server room.

"And here is where all the fun stuff is going to happen. As you can see, we have a lot of equipment that needs to be refreshed and *organised*."

Derrick was overwhelmed, trying to calculate how many devices were actually in the room. "Let's see... five rows... six racks... three or four per rack... ONE HUNDRED DEVICES?!?"

Wallace nodded in agreement. "Good show, chap. There's one hundred-five, so you have your work cut out for you. Better head back and get some rest. It's gonna be a long couple of nights."

***

They headed in on Monday evening as everyone was going home for the day. They would be breaking the project into four sections with a buffer on Friday for any issues. Since the routers were rather heavy, Derrick would be responsible for the unboxing and installation of the devices while Lydia would run the cables and configure them.

It was around 4am and they both were getting tired enough to be loopy. Derrick heard a commotion from behind one of the server racks and went to check on Lydia. Rounding the corner, he saw her lying on the floor entangled in several cables.

"A little help?" she said pitifully.

***

Tuesday and Wednesday went like clockwork. They found a groove and were able to finish all but one of the rows by the time the day crews came in. Wallace and Genève were amazed at the progress.

"You American chaps work your bums off! Chief is going to be gobsmacked if this is done tomorrow."

Lydia noticed Derrick nodding off on the bus ride back to the hotel. "Honey, you look horrible."

Derrick agreed. "I haven't been sleeping well. Can we go back to the room and take a nap before breakfast? I'd hate to fall face-first into my eggs."

***

Derrick was still exhausted going into Thursday evening. As he removed one of the routers from the top of the rack, the last restraining bolt snapped, causing the device to fall and knock him to the floor. Lydia came running.

Finding him lying on the ground half under the router, she exclaimed, *"What's all this then?"* Derrick smiled and said, "I guess it's my turn to say, 'little help?'"

Lydia lifted the router off of his right arm when she saw his hand. "<gasp> Your... your fingers aren't pointing the same way!"

"Yeah, I think they dislocated as it fell. We need to pop them back in."

"WE?!?" Lydia exclaimed, fearfully.

"It's easier with two, but if you can't..."

"No... no... Just tell me what to do."

Leading her to a table in the office, Derrick directed her on what needed done. "Alright, grab the finger and start pulling steadily, but firmly. Don't stop until it pops back into place. It's also easier if you don't watch."

Lydia shivered in disgust at the thought of what she was about to do. "They do make doctors for this..."

"Yes, but then we wouldn't be able to finish the job tonight. It's really simple. You wouldn't believe how many times it's happened."

"I know you. Nothing surprises me anymore."

Derrick breathed deeply and Lydia took his finger and started pulling it back into its normal position. He could feel the pressure increasing on the joint. Looking into her eyes made the process far less painful this time though. His finger let out a loud pop as it went back into the socket.

Lydia let go and started squirming away. "Eww eww eww eww eww!!!! That was SO gross!!!"

Derrick took a couple more deep breaths of relief and said something which made Lydia cringe. "Okay... now for the other."

The rest of the night didn't go as quickly as before thanks to the limited use of two of his fingers, but Derrick was never one to let a small injury stop him from getting the job done.

They were finishing up the last few cables when the day crew came into the office. Wallace noticed the heavy bruising on Derrick's right hand and asked, "You alright?"

"Of course, why?" Derrick replied nonchalantly.

"You guys did amazing work! Want to grab some brekkie before retiring?" Genève asked.

"Sure, I think that sounds *bangin'*!" Lydia said in her pseudo-British accent.

Back in the room, she crawled into the bed and lifted Derrick's hand to look at it.

"Don't lie to me. That hurts, doesn't it?"

"Yeah, but it will be fine."

She got back up and grabbed some ibuprofen from her bag. "I want you to take these."

He started to object, and she glared at him. "Derrick..."

"Okay, fine. If it will make you feel better," Derrick finally resigned.

Putting the medicine into his hand, "Well, the point is to make YOU feel better, but whatever gets them down your throat."

CHAPTER 39

Derrick settled into his chair as he watched the south England countryside fly by his window. Less than an hour earlier, he and Lydia boarded the TGV and were on their way to Paris for the weekend.

Apparently, it wasn't only airplanes that caused Lydia to fall asleep, as she was already out on Derrick's shoulder. Being rather tired from the long week they had previously, he decided to try to catch a quick nap as well.

...Derrick was returning from an interfacility transfer when he saw a school bus miss a turn and roll into the ditch beside the road. After circling over the site looking for hazards, he carefully lowered the helicopter between the trees and down onto the two-lane road. Emily and Frank exited and made for the bus as Derrick called in the accident. In the middle of his radio call, he heard tires squealing and then a loud bang towards the back of the helicopter. It lunged to the right and then began to spin on the ground, tipping over onto the pilot's side...

He jerked, trying to catch himself from falling out of the helicopter, which also startled Lydia awake. She elbowed him in the stomach and spun around with her fist balled up.

Derrick's eyes widened. "Oh, not again!"

Thankfully, Lydia caught herself before making contact. "Derrick! What the crap?!?"

He apologized while trying to catch the wind that was knocked out of him. "Sorry! I had another bad dream and thought I was falling out of my helicopter."

"Are you okay?!?" she asked, rubbing his stomach.

"I am now that you didn't punch me in the face." Derrick didn't try to nap the rest of the train ride.

Pulling into the station, he opened his Uber app and started looking for a ride to take them to dinner. They gathered their luggage and within minutes, he secured transportation to *Fouguet's*.

The maître d greeted them as they walked up. "*Une table pour deux, monsieur?*"

Derrick grinned at Lydia. "*Oui.*"

She let out a chuckle as they walked to the table. "That's the only word you know, isn't it?"

"What, you're not impressed?"

Lydia was struggling to read the menu as it was written entirely in French. She pulled out her phone to use the translation app when the waiter walked up.

"*Bonsoir, madame et monsieur. Que puis-je te faire boire?*"

She gave Derrick a scared look.

"He asked what you wanted to drink."

"Oh! Water, please."

The waiter didn't speak a word of English from the reaction he gave her.

"Uh, I don't think this is such a good idea anymore," she said regrettably.

Derrick had started to giggle a little, watching her struggle. "I'll take care of it, honey."

Looking at the waiter, he said, "*La dame et moi voudrions commencer avec de l'eau et que recommanderiez-vous en rouge ce soir?*"

Lydia listened in astonishment as they went back and forth spouting words that made no sense whatsoever to her.

When the waiter walked away, she looked at him in disbelief. "What just happened?!?"

Derrick tried to keep from laughing as he said, "I don't know. I guess I picked up on the language like you did British." Seeing her face afterward made him finally break his composure.

Continuing her glare, "Okay hot shot, so you know Spanish and French..."

Derrick interrupted, "Don't forget, I know a little British too."

Unamused, she continued, "Ah, hmm... anyway... what other languages do you know that you haven't told me yet?"

"Russian, Thai, Mandarin and conversational Farsi."

"Conversational Farsi?!? What is that?"

"من پنیر دوست دارم"

She smacked her lips together and glared at him.

"It's when you can speak it, but not write it," Derrick clarified.

Lydia rolled her eyes, but then started glaring at him again. "Wait... did you say Mandarin?"

Derrick grinned. "Wèishéme shì de, wǒ de gōngzhǔ"

"So when we were at *Jade Palace* and I was telling you what each dish was, you already knew?"

Derrick's face dropped knowing he got caught. "You looked so happy explaining them; I didn't want to ruin it."

"Well, that really takes the biscuit!"

The waiter returned with a bottle of *Domaine Pontifical Châteauneuf du Pape 2016* and poured it into the two glasses on the table.

"So you're a wine connoisseur now, too?"

"No, but when you speak their language, they don't try to screw you as bad as a tourist. Do you know what you would like to order?"

Shaking her head, she replied, "How about I let you surprise me?"

Derrick checked over the menu quickly and then ordered. *"Cœur de filet de bœuf pour madame et moi l'escalope de foie gras de canard poêlée."*

"Excellents choix, monsieur."

After hearing the conversation, Lydia was suddenly having second thoughts about letting Derrick order. "You didn't order me any of those snails, did you?"

He laughed a little. "No, I didn't go crazy. I got you the beef tenderloin."

A large smile appeared on her face in gratitude.

After dinner, he took her hand and suggested they go for a walk before going to the hotel. They headed up Champs-Élysées just a bit until the Arc De Triomphe was before them.

"Wow! That thing is so much bigger than I expected!" she amazed.

Lydia noticed that Derrick kept checking his watch. "What are you so anxious about? We are in the city of love! Relax!"

Derrick finally explained his plan. "If we catch an Uber and get over to the Eiffel Tower in the next 20 minutes, we can see it twinkle."

"Twinkle?!?" Lydia asked.

"Oh... you're going to be amazed then."

The Uber dropped them off with a few minutes to spare. Derrick rushed her to the best, unobstructed view he could find and whispered in her ear, "Watch this."

The entire tower went dark and then millions of sparkles started flashing all over it, making it look like a diamond in the jewelry store showcase. Lydia stood speechless for the whole five minutes the display lasted.

When the sparkles stopped and the spotlights came back on, she stood there, staring at it. "I... I have no words."

Derrick smiled and put his arm around her, "I thought you'd like it. Guess what? Our room is right over there, and it has a view of the tower. You can watch it do that every hour."

Lydia sat out on the balcony of their room at the *Résidence Charles Floquet.* She was just finishing recording the sparkle show with her phone for the third time when Derrick joined her on the balcony after getting his shower.

She laid her head on his shoulder. "Mr. Anderson, you sure know how to show a girl a good time."

***

The next morning, Lydia jumped onto the bed, waking Derrick up in shock.

"Guess what I just did?!?"

Derrick glared at her while rubbing his temples. "I'm assuming you mean other than scaring me within inches of my life."

"I booked us tickets to go to the very top of the Eiffel Tower! In thirty minutes!"

Derrick looked out the window in horror. "You mean actually go up that stack of rusty bolts?!?"

Lydia gasped and smacked him on the arm. "It's a beautiful masterpiece!"

"Yeah... that's over one hundred and thirty years old, made of iron, and was left out in the rain too many times."

Derrick stood looking up at the massive structure while they waited in line for the elevator. Lydia put her arm around his waist and squeezed with excitement. "Isn't this so cool?!!"

Derrick didn't move his upward gaze. "Wouldn't you rather go back to the hotel and play 'hide and go seek' in the sheets again?"

"Silly boy. That's a nighttime game."

Finally shifting his gaze to her, "We could turn the lights off..."

Lydia glared at him, unamused, and smacked her lips together.

Derrick's face dropped as he looked back up at the structure, "Can I at least have my eyes closed on the way up?"

Grinning, she said, "Sure. If you want to be locked in a latticework box with me and have your eyes closed, be my guest."

Derrick's face dropped even more.

The elevator doors opened on the top floor and Lydia scampered out to the rail. "This is SO amazing!" she said, looking out at the Paris skyline.

Derrick stayed plastered to the wall of the elevator and motioned for the attendant to take it back down. Unfortunately, Lydia turned around before he could.

"Derrick Methuselah Anderson! Get your butt out here!"

He slowly stepped out of the elevator and onto the shiny metal floor. He could feel himself getting more and more lightheaded the closer he got to the edge.

"Derrick, grab my hand. I'll hold on to you. Do you trust me?"

He shook his head.

Lydia's mouth dropped open in shock. "Well, I never!" Grabbing his arm, she dragged him to the edge. "There's a rail and a netting, you big baby. You aren't going anywhere, so just enjoy this!"

It took a few minutes, but he started getting more comfortable with the situation... albeit... not entirely.

Lydia left to explore the observation deck, wanting to see Paris from all sides. Derrick, content with standing by the elevator, watched as, a minute later, Lydia came running back around, screaming and being followed by a flock of birds.

"Help me! They like my strawberry perfume!"

Grabbing her, Derrick pushed her up against the wall and covered her with his body until the birds got tired and flew away.

"Thank you, honey! You saved me from those killer birds. Uh... you have a little schmutz on your shoulder."

Derrick sighed, "I know. You should see my back."

Just having changed, Derrick stepped out of the men's room at the train station to find Lydia smiling at him.

"I had a fun time this weekend," she said. "You ready to head back and play some hide and seek?"

"Oh sure! Now you want to play!" Derrick overdramatically replied.

Turning towards the train car, Lydia started to climb aboard when she stopped. Turning her head, she gave Derrick a mischievous glance. "You can be 'it' first."

CHAPTER 40

A couple of days went by since their romantic getaway to Paris when Derrick was working late with Winston at the annex. They were re-racking servers and Derrick took a break for some coffee and the bathroom.

After finishing, he stepped back out into the hallway and heard what sounded like glass breaking toward the chief's office. When he went to investigate, he could see a flashlight moving around inside through the frosted window.

Calling security, he asked, "Hey, this is Derrick, up in IT. Is anyone else in the building other than me and Winston tonight?"

"No, sir. No one has come through here. Why?"

"I heard glass break and can see someone in the chief's office."

"Right. Don't do anything stupid. We're on our way."

Derrick hung up the phone and paused for a second. "Ok... I'm going to go do something stupid."

He quietly headed down the hallway until he was right outside the office, where he could hear someone going through the file cabinets and rustling papers.

"The chief is supposed to be bowling tonight," he thought.

The maintenance room was across the hall from the chief's office. Opening the door, Derrick smiled, as it was well supplied. Seeing some items, he had an idea. "Ah! Liquid soap and a tarp... wait a tarp? What could they possibly... ewwww! Come on, Derrick, focus."

Taking the soap, he squirted it under the door and onto the floor. He then unrolled the tarp and held it wide with both hands waiting for his moment.

The light started moving towards the doorway when the person slipped and fell to the ground. Kicking the door open, Derrick jumped onto the victim and wrapped them up securely with the tarp.

The officers rounded the corner and ran down the hallway to the chief's office, finding Derrick sitting on a tarp that was fighting back.

"Derrick, clear right. We've got this now," the first officer ordered.

Derrick stood up as the officers approached. One of them slipped and fell to one knee.

"Be careful, the floor's slick!" Derrick warned a little late.

As they removed the tarp, they revealed a man in a nice suit, which was now covered in bubbles from the soap. "Derrick, you just captured the chief," explained one of the officers, while the other reached down and assisted him to his feet.

Distressed, Derrick apologized. "Chief, I thought you went home. What are you doing here?!? I heard glass break and thought someone broke in."

The chief growled while trying to remove the excess goo from his pants, "I knocked my coffee cup off the desk, you idiot!"

As the officers were assisting the chief, something didn't add up to Derrick. The guards never saw him come in through the entrance. His door was still locked when he kicked it open and one of the windows looked to be slightly cracked.

"I thought you and your wife were going out to dinner since it was her birthday. Isn't she going to be mad?" Derrick asked, testing him.

"I'm running late and was going to meet her at the restaurant, but now my suit is ruined thanks to you."

Walking up beside the chief, Derrick started to profusely apologize again. "I'm so sorry sir, let me HELPPPPP...."

He stomped his heel into the back of the chief's left knee, causing it to give out. One of the officers grabbed Derrick as the chief fell to his knees and swore, "*Ti glupi sine psa!*"

A clanking sound was heard as a flash drive fell out of his pocket and onto the floor.

Crouching down into the guy's face, Derrick bluntly explained. "You aren't the chief. He isn't married. He went bowling with one of his war buddies tonight. What you just called me was in Serbian and I'd bet all my per diem money that we'll find classified information on that flash drive you just dropped."

Hearing the commotion, Winston came running down the hallway. Seeing the guy on the ground, he asked, "What's going on and who's the guy in the chief mask?"

The officer next to him asked, "Mask?"

"Yeah," Winston explained, "That's not the chief. He's a lot skinnier, and the chief has blue eyes. Bright blue eyes."

Both officers raised their rifles as they took the intruder into custody.

***

Lydia left early to go dress shopping. The Marine ball was that weekend, and she wanted to surprise Derrick with the dress she bought. Arriving back at the hotel only a few minutes before Derrick got back, she was scrambling to hide the dress when the door unlocked.

"Hey, honey! How did your day go? Working late tonight, huh?" she asked, trying to hide the panic in her voice.

Oblivious to her suspicious response, Derrick replied, "Oh, you know. Same old, same old," as he hung his coat up on the rack.

***

Security was extra heavy the next morning. As they went through the checkpoint, an officer approached Derrick.

"Sir, the chief would like to see you. Come with us."

Looking at Lydia, he said, "I'm sure it's about some project coming up. I'll meet you in the IT room."

Derrick walked up to the chief's office, where two guards were stationed outside the broken door. Knocking as he entered, Derrick greeted the chief, "Sorry about the door, sir."

He waved Derrick over to his desk, where a video conference was ongoing.

"The Director requested a briefing of the events last night and I'd like you to give her a summary of what happened."

"Sure thing, sir. Do you think we should pull the door?"

Derrick finished the synopsis of what happened and what he saw and then the chief updated their findings from overnight.

"Madam Director, we have determined that they were Serbian and part of the BIA. They compromised one of the windows in my office and made entry. The mask he was wearing was not of high quality, but with the low light, would have been effective against the cameras. The flash drive contained multiple operational documents from our assets in Eastern Europe. We can confirm that none of those documents made it outside my office. We are currently reinforcing the windows and door. I concur on having a team come from Headquarters to certify the site after the upgrades."

***

Derrick adjusted his bow tie while looking in the floor-length mirror in their room. Tonight was the Marine ball, and he was looking sharp in his black tux. A loud thump from the bathroom interrupted his moment.

"You okay in there, honey? Need some help?" he asked.

"No, I'm good! Wait for me in the lobby. I want to see your face when you see this dress."

Grinning, Derrick replied, "I'll meet you outside. Our ride is almost here."

Derrick walked out of the front doors of the hotel to the awaiting black Rolls Royce limousine he rented for the evening. The driver got out and walked around to the passenger side. "Good evening, Mr. Anderson. I will be your chauffeur this evening."

Derrick shook his hand and then admired the car. "That's some wheels you've got there!"

The chauffeur gleamed. "She's a beaut, ain't she?"

A few moments later, while chatting with the chauffeur, the hotel's main doors opened, and out walked Lydia. Derrick's mouth dropped open as she strutted towards him. Her stiletto heels peeked out from underneath the floor-length black velvet gown that had a slit that rose well above her thigh.

All Derrick could get out was, "Wow!"

Even the chauffeur was astonished. Leaning over to Derrick, he exclaimed, *"Blimey! Is that your bird?"*

Giving Derrick a quick peck on the lips, she asked, "You like my dress?"

He was still unable to articulate words and just uttered, "Uhhh. Hmmmm."

Smiling, she said, "I'll take that as a yes," as she gracefully climbed into the limo.

Derrick sat in silence with his gaze fixed on her.

Lydia was starting to get uncomfortable with the silence so tried to start a conversation. "I like the car. It's exactly what I imagined pulling up to my first ball in."

Derrick nodded, "Yeah... yeah... sure."

Noticing his reply was a little off, she checked to see if he was really listening. "I was thinking we could take some of your thermite and see how fast it burns afterward."

Derrick nodded again, "Sure, sure... tomorrow."

"Alright, to be fair, that would be something he would answer," she thought, trying to come up with something more definitive. Then an evil grin grew on her face, "Derrick... I'm pregnant."

Derrick nodded once again, "Yeah, I think I have some of that in my bag."

"Derrick!!" she exclaimed, breaking him from his stupor.

Visibly jumping, Derrick yelled, "What?!?"

"Oh, nothing. I was just making sure you were okay with that."

He had no idea what the conversation was about, but he certainly didn't want to let her know he wasn't paying attention. "Sure, Honey. Sounds good."

Her reply of, "Excellent" with an evil grin scared Derrick.

The limo joined the long line of vehicles queuing in front of the embassy. When their turn came, a Marine in his dress blues opened the rear door. Derrick stepped out and then turned to help Lydia. Flashbulbs lit up the red carpet leading inside.

"I didn't know there was going to be paparazzi here tonight," she remarked.

The two were escorted to their table, where Wallace and Genève were already seated.

"Goodness, gracious mates! You Yanks sure know how to get dressed up!" Wallace exclaimed.

After dinner, Derrick heard the band start playing an instrumental version of "*Can't Help Falling in Love*".

Standing up, he leaned over to Lydia and asked, "Mrs. Anderson, may I have this dance?"

As she laid her head down on his shoulder, she whispered to him as they swayed to the music. "I don't want this night to end. Everything is so perfect."

Derrick couldn't agree more. He closed his eyes and leaned his head onto hers as the music continued in the background.

***

A couple of days later, Derrick and Lydia headed into the annex's large conference room for their final Tuesday group meeting. They arrived a little early, hoping to take seats in the back to avoid being called on.

Derrick did his best to stay awake as the Chief's meetings were very monotone and dry. He started the announcements, which was the last part he had to suffer through before he was free to get some more coffee.

"As for crew changes, since Sergio and Emma will be returning Monday, this is the last week for Derrick and Lydia, who will be heading back to the States. Without their help, the understaffed router upgrade at the embassy would have taken many more months. The ambassador has asked me to share his gratefulness."

Derrick turned a little red and slid down into his chair as the room applauded.

"And finally, as most of you know, we had a foreign intelligence officer make entry into the facility a few weeks back. Derrick, could you please make your way up here?"

Lydia turned to him. "Derrick?"

He only replied with, "Oh, you've got to be kidding me."

Walking up to the front of the room, Derrick stood next to the annex chief. Opening a small presentation box, the chief revealed a silver-colored medal.

"On behalf of the Director, 'for acts conspicuously above normal duties which have contributed significantly to the mission of the Agency', I hereby present to you the *Intelligence Medal of Merit* for your actions on the 18th of December. Your quick reaction and insight saved highly sensitive operational information from making it into the hands of a foreign actor. The Agency is grateful."

As they dismissed the meeting, some officers came forward to congratulate him. After shaking a couple dozen hands, Lydia was next in line. Derrick looked out the corner of his eye at the chief.

"Uh oh."

Lydia put her hands on her hips. "Yeah, uh oh!"

"You didn't tell her?!?" the chief exclaimed, surprised.

"I thought it was classified."

"Let me tell you what happened," the chief started elaborating.

Her gaze switched from the chief to Derrick midway through the story, at which he just grinned.

***

After their nine-hour flight home, Derrick unlocked the door to their apartment and carried their luggage into the bedroom. After dropping them on the floor, he crawled up onto the bed and let out a sigh.

"Oh, fluffy marshmallow from Heaven! I'm having second thoughts about leaving for Kabul next week."

Lydia pulled Madeline out of her bag and snuggled up next to him.

"Well, you can always stay here with me… and Momma and Daddy."

Derrick rolled his head to the side and popped his eyes open. "Say what now?"

Lydia lay there with a big grin on her face. "I asked them to come over and stay with me while you were gone."

Derrick pressed his face back down into the pillow, muffling a dramatic groan. "On second thought… I might need that ticket to Kabul more than ever."

CHAPTER 41

Upon arriving at Dulles for his trip to Kabul and clearing security, Derrick headed to the shuttle that would take him to the hangar where the chartered plane awaited. As he boarded the bus, a familiar voice caught his attention.

"Hey, I didn't know you were heading out to the sandbox, too," Derrick exclaimed.

Richie was sitting in the back with his feet casually propped up on the seat in front of him. "You know me. Anywhere I can lie in the sand and get a nice tan."

The bus headed out towards the hangar where a gray 737-800 with no markings waited for them. They boarded and found instead of the normal rows of seats, there were pods with lay-flat recliners, large TVs, and their own minifridges.

Richie's eyes widened with delight. "Now that's what I call First Class!" he exclaimed.

Derrick sat down in the first pod on the right, and Richie chose the one across from him on the left.

Taking his bag and placing it in the overhead compartment, Richie watched as Derrick struggled to get his stuffed in.

"You know... if you didn't have so much junk..." he suggested, sarcastically.

"It's not junk!" Derrick defended, "You never know when you are going to need something."

"Spoken like a true hoarder," Richie said, reaching into his bag, where pulled out the emitter Derrick gave him as a graduation present.

"You actually brought it?"

"I wouldn't leave home without it. I keep trying to get Chief to make this standard equipment."

Frustrated, Derrick pulled his bag back down to rearrange the stuff inside.

"You don't have one of those lightsaber, go-go juice-emitting things in there, do you?" Richie asked, half-joking.

Derrick looked dejected. "No, TSA took it away from me."

Richie shook his head. "Oh great, I can see the headlines now, 'Dulles Airport closed. Security checkpoint vaporized by lightsaber.'"

Derrick chuckled as he pulled a remote out of his bag. "That couldn't happen. You need this remote to activate it."

Snatching it out of Derrick's hand, he exclaimed, "Give me that!" When he opened the back, he saw the two AA batteries. "You had batteries in it!?! How are you not on the ATF watch list?" Taking them out of the remote, Richie put them into his bag. "I'm keeping these."

Derrick Facetimed Lydia while they waited, wanting to see her one last time before the ten-day blackout. As she answered, he could see her relaxing in the hot tub with her mom.

"Hi, honey! Getting ready for takeoff? I see you're slumming it in coach."

"Just thought I'd call and see your beautiful face again before we lose signal. Richie is here with me, too."

He spun the phone around. "Hello Richie! You take care of my man now, you hear? Don't let him do anything dumb."

Richie laughed. "You know he's a mess, right?"

Defensive, Derrick yelled, "Hey! I'm right here!"

"Yes, Lydia. I will do my best to make sure he gets home safe."

Lydia smiled and said, "Thank you, 'Jack!'"

Jennifer informed them that everyone was on board early, so they were going to close the doors and head out.

"I'm sorry, honey. The mean flight lady is making me get off the phone."

He spun the camera around to Jennifer.

"Mean flight lady!" Lydia said, laughing.

"Hi, Lydia. Glad you're doing better. We'll bring him home."

While they were taxiing, Richie leaned over.

"Why did Lydia call me Jack earlier?"

"You know, as in MacGyver's overwatch. He's always covering Mac's back..."

Richie grabbed a pillow and pressed it over his face, "Good lord, you both are nerds."

Derrick laughed, "Then I should really tell you about her and Larry sometime."

Richie put his headphones in and said, "I'm going to close my eyes, but go ahead, I'm listening."

***

...Derrick is braking hard into the corner. On his left side, he feels something hit him. The nose of his car keeps going left as he turns to the right. The concrete barrier is closing in on him quickly. He hits the brakes, but it does nothing. He feels the violent impact and then the g-forces holding him into his seat. The world around is graying out. Then an incredible noise...

Derrick jerked awake, struggling to catch his breath.

"You okay, dear?" Jennifer asked, walking up.

"Yeah, just a bad dream. I'll be fine. Thank you, though."

"Well, we are starting our descent into Kabul now, so not much longer."

He was still clearing the cobwebs out of his head when a fireball engulfed the left side of the plane, causing it to roll hard to the right and pitch down.

Derrick's phone flew from the tray table, almost hitting Richie in the head before crashing into the overhead compartments and shattering.

Derrick looked out the window and saw most of the wing was missing and what wasn't, was on fire. Glancing towards Richie, he could see the ground coming up fast outside his window.

A section pulled away beside Richie as the plane crashed through the trees, ripping the right wing off, and then everything went black.

CHAPTER 42

Derrick thought he was having another bad dream until the smell of burning jet fuel made him open his eyes. Everything was still black, and he could feel pressure against his face.

He managed to get free of his seatbelt and slide out from under the wreckage that was lying on him. There was fire and mangled metal all around.

He took a step, and the ground gave out from under that foot, twisting his ankle.

"Well, that sucked. Let's not do that again."

Realizing this was not a dream, he started to look for survivors.

Stumbling past what used to be part of an engine, he saw Jennifer trapped under one of the pods. Making his way to her side, he realized it was only PART of Jennifer. He winced in horror.

Over to his left, he vaguely made out another human figure. As he got closer, he realized it was Richie. He had been right beside him on the flight but was now over a hundred feet away in a crater.

Richie was conscious but was losing blood, as his right arm was missing just below his shoulder. Derrick found his bag and used the tourniquet he carried on what was left of Richie's arm.

Off in the distance, Derrick heard vehicles quickly approaching. Knowing that it couldn't be their U.S. friends so soon, he told Richie, "We have to go."

He grabbed both their bags and helped Richie out of the wreckage. For about a kilometer, they headed east, deeper into the forest, until Richie signaled that he needed to stop.

"I think we are okay here for now," Derrick said. "If they would have spotted us, we would have already been captured."

Richie handed Derrick the radio. "Do you think you can reach anyone on this?"

He helped Richie to the ground and then tried a few calls out on the base frequency.

Dejected, Derrick groaned, "I think we are getting blocked by the mountains."

Reaching into his bag, Derrick pulled out a weird-looking contraption and placed it over the antenna.

"Is that your tinfoil hat to keep the government from stealing your ideas?"

"No, it's an amplifier... well, it's supposed to be at least," he explained.

"You haven't tested it?!?"

Derrick tried again. "Mayday, Mayday, Mayday, Kabul base, this is Firebird 12." Nothing but static.

Derrick made adjustments to the amplifier and attempted another call. This time, he heard a response.

"Firebird 12, Kabul base. Received your mayday. What's your location?"

"We are one klick east of the crash site. Look for an IR beam in the sky. Radio silence. Danger close."

Derrick pulled out the emitter from Richie's bag and tried to turn it on, but nothing happened. He took out a small flashlight and examined it.

"Can you tell what's wrong? I mean, with that look on your face, I'm assuming something is wrong with it."

"The battery is cracked. There's no juice getting to it. I'm going to have to find a new power source."

"Can't you just make one from an old speaker and a hairbrush?" Richie said almost mockingly.

"I could if I had some toothpaste."

"Now when you say things like that, I actually think you're being seri... Oh crap, you were."

Derrick checked Richie over again.

"It looks like your tourniquet is holding. How do you feel?"

"Like I just fell out of the sky in a metal tube," Richie replied groaning.

***

The sun started rising and Derrick could finally make out the surrounding area. He was still trying to keep Richie distracted and conscious.

Checking their supplies, he looked for anything he could use to power the emitter but found nothing.

"Do you think there's a building or car nearby that would have something you could use?" suggested Richie.

"Maybe, but I don't want to leave you alone and especially don't want to move you in your condition.

"I'll be fine. Like you said, I'm not losing any more blood. Let's go!"

They made their way along a dirt road, hoping to find a house, a car... anything that had a battery. After traveling a few miles, they saw a light in the distance. It was a small house with a barn. Derrick left his bag with Richie along the tree line and snuck up to the barn using the decaying building to shield his approach.

"There's got to be something in here I could use," he thought as he slid in through the partially opened door. Inside he found a hoarder's paradise! He only had to dig around for a couple of minutes before finding a large, square six-volt battery.

"There's really only one way to know if this has any charge left."

He stuck it up to his mouth, took a deep breath, and touched the terminals to his tongue.

<ZAP>

"Yeeeoowwww!" He quietly exclaimed. "I had to find the only brand new item in this entire garage and stick it on my tongue. Not the brightest move, but effective."

Heading to the door, he listened for a few seconds, then slid out, making his way back toward the woods. As he rounded the corner of the barn, he froze when he saw a kid standing there. Derrick estimated him to be about eight years old.

"Uh... hi. I was just borrowing this to help my friend over there. He's hurt badly and I need to get him some help."

The kid stared without replying.

"Okay. I'm just going to go then," Derrick said.

As he started to walk away, the kid raised a gun and pointed it toward him. Derrick caught a glimpse of it just in time to see the muzzle flash. Time froze as he watched the bullet slowly heading towards him. Derrick instinctively threw his left hand up to block it. The bullet blew through the knuckle of his pinky finger sending his digit flying off in a spray of blood.

There was a second flash. This time, the bullet was heading straight for his face. He tried dodging it but wasn't able to get completely out of the way. When the bullet hit his head, everything went black.

***

Lydia stepped out of the shower and checked her phone again. She was hoping that Derrick had called, and she just didn't hear it ring.

"He should have landed over four hours ago. I would have thought he would have texted by now at least to tell me he got there."

She was finishing getting ready to teach her radio class at Headquarters when her phone finally rang. She ran into the door frame trying to get out of the closet to grab it, but to her disappointment, the caller ID read, "No Name" instead of "Derrick". The Chief greeted her but lacked the usual chipperness in his voice.

"Oh, hey Chief, what's up?"

"You're coming into HQ today, correct? Can you stop by my office before your class?"

"Sure thing, boss. I'm headed out right now. Is everything okay?"

"I'll fill you in when you get here."

She walked into the waiting room for the chief's office and, to her surprise, he was waiting there for her.

"Hi, Lydia. Come on in and have a seat."

As she went to sit down, Rosalyn followed and stood off to the side as the chief closed the door.

"Well, this can't be good," she said.

He sat down in the chair next to her and paused to find the right words. "There's been an accident."

A cold chill ran down Lydia's spine as her face turned pale.

"Derrick's plane went down thirty miles from the airfield into a grove of trees. The base received a short radio transmission by someone using Derrick's distress call sign, although when our team arrived at the location they gave, no one was there."

"Are you telling me he survived, then?"

The chief sighed. "Unfortunately, I've told you everything I know."

She fought back her emotions but finally broke down once the initial shock wore off. Rosalyn came over and held her. Wanting to offer some comfort, the chief added, "If anyone is crafty enough to survive there, it's Derrick."

"I need to get to my class," Lydia said through her tears.

"Don't worry about them. I've already got it covered for the rest of the week. Go home and get some rest. I'll call you as soon as we know something more."

Lydia stood up with difficulty and began to slowly walk towards the door.

The chief offered, "We can have someone drive you home if you would like. Maybe Sullivan, since you know him?"

"Thank you, Chief, but I've got it."

She felt like she was sleepwalking as she made her way to the car. After climbing in, she scrolled through her contacts until she found "Momma," and pressed send.

The ringing of her phone sounded as if it was muffled and off in the distance. When her mom answered, all the emotions she had dammed up broke free, and she cried the hardest her mom had ever heard her.

"Honey, what's wrong?"

She struggled to articulate words through the crying, but managed, "Derrick.... Plane crash... I... Need... You..."

***

Derrick awoke with the worst headache he had ever experienced. Feeling around, he found that the bullet, thankfully, had only glanced off his temple. The smell inside his cell matched the sewage covering the ground.

"Well, this is just great—a real sanitary place to have an open wound," he thought sarcastically.

He slowly walked towards the door and reached up for the bars. Seeing his hands, he realized he was missing a digit, but was having trouble remembering much of what happened.

"Didn't I leave Virginia with ten?!? Wonder where I put that one?" he pondered, still feeling a little loopy from his concussion.

He looked through the bars and could only see an empty concrete hallway.

Not knowing if someone was actually stationed out there, Derrick whispered, "Richie, you there?" He heard only silence.

Saying Richie's name a little louder, this time, he received a reply from the cell next to him.

"Dude, how are you alive? I saw that kid shoot you."

Jokingly, Derrick replied, "Well, I've always had a hard head. Do you know where we are... and have you seen my pinky?"

"First off... ew... but secondly, I don't know where we are at. They took us to some slum hole of a prison. I'm not even sure who *they* are, but I have some guesses."

From down the hallway, they heard a metal door open and the sound of footsteps from multiple people. They walked past Derrick's door, opened the cell next to him, and yelled something in Arabic.

He heard Richie yell back, "You'll never take me alive, you towel heads!" and then multiple punches landed.

The fighting only lasted a few seconds, and then the men left the room. Derrick rushed to the door, but only saw a streak of blood along the floor leading to the direction they had just left.

"Richie! You still there?" he exclaimed in panic, but received no response.

Derrick tore a hole into the fecal-covered mattress in his room and pulled out one of the springs. Unwinding it into an omega symbol, he stretched his arm out the barred window as far as he could, barely reaching the lock.

"This is going to be horribly difficult," he thought. After a good thirty minutes of wiggling the homemade key around, he finally felt the tension and turned as hard as he could. The lock disengaged.

Derrick checked both ways as far as he could see and then slowly opened his door. Once he was sure the hallway was clear, he headed over to Richie's cell. His heart sank as he discovered it was empty. Following the trail of blood on the floor, he made his way to a metal door at the end of the hallway.

"Please be unlocked! I'm not sure I could do that again."

He turned the handle, and to his surprise, the latch retracted. Slowly, he cracked open the old door and peeked around to see what was behind it. There was yet another concrete hallway, but this time it was perpendicular to the one he was in, with exits at both ends. The blood streak went to the right and up to a door with sunlight streaming through the small barred window.

Following the blood trail to the door, Derrick was relieved it was unlocked as well. Sliding out through it, he found himself in a large, open gravel parking lot. The blood trail continued on the rocks but then suddenly stopped. There was a large truck off in the distance kicking up a good bit of dust behind it.

"Richie has to be in that truck!" he thought.

Using the cover of the other vehicles in the parking lot, he made it to the nearby woods unseen.

He followed the road for hours but wasn't making a lot of progress due to his ankle. He stopped to adjust the brace he made out of a couple of sticks and duct tape, as it had started to bruise and swell.

"It would be nice if I just had ONE normal tour."

He trudged for another mile before seeing a compound off in the distance. Noting the guard towers with large rifles, he headed off into the woods again to try to find a less obvious way in.

The sun was starting to set, and he found himself at the base of a fifteen-foot tall fence with multiple layers of razor wire on top. He could see some commotion going on over by one of the tents in the compound.

Five men with guns were pulling Richie from the back of a truck.

"He doesn't look very good," Derrick thought.

***

Returning from one of the searches for Derrick and Richie, Obadiah briefed his sergeant.

"Sarge, we keep getting some weird static on COM4. It's really intermittent. It's not too bad here, but out in the field, it's annoyingly loud and takes over the freq."

"Run it by one of the coms guys. Maybe they can figure out what's causing it."

***

Derrick had an idea that might be able to get him into the complex. Searching the perimeter of the compound, he found what he needed from a rusty car to mix up some makeshift thermite.

"What I wouldn't give for some phosphorus about now."

Waiting until the sun had gone down, he cut a hole into the fence and used the cover of darkness to sneak over to a truck that was left running near a large tent. Inside the truck was a handheld radio.

"Hmm... wonder what would happen if I used lithium instead of phosphorus."

Removing the battery from the radio, Derrick mixed the lithium from it into his thermite compound. He put it in the front seat of the truck and, as he was getting out, tripped over the parking brake, causing it to disengage. The truck started slowly rolling forward.

Sliding over to where he saw Richie being taken, he heard a noise behind him. Derrick turned around as the cab of the truck erupted into a bright red glow. It only took seconds for the metal of the cab to melt and the glow became multiple beams of plasma spraying out in different directions.

Unbeknownst to Derrick, he just rolled his thermite bomb into the munitions depot for the regional warlord. Explosions rocked the compound as mortars fired from inside the tent.

"Yikes! Maybe lithium wasn't a good choice."

***

Obadiah was on patrol around the base when he spotted a red beam shooting up into the sky.

"Alrighty. That's not something you see every day. You know... that looks a lot like..."

Recalling his earlier conversation with the sergeant, he flipped his radio over to COM4 and listened carefully as the static was faint.

"That son of a..."

Obadiah sprinted into the command center and headed straight for the sergeant's office. Holding up his radio, he exclaimed, "S.O.S. It's that muppet from the plane crash!"

The sergeant looked up from his desk, "Can you tell where he is?"

"No, but I just saw an explosion from the direction of the Rashid compound."

"Get your team and get moving," ordered the captain.

***

Derrick remained hidden as he watched everyone running towards the inferno that used to be the ammo depo. When he felt it was safe, he snuck into the tent where he found their bags and some more blood, but no Richie.

Grabbing the bags, he followed the blood trail outside to tire tracks that led to one of the gates out of the compound. He could see tail lights from the same large truck off in the distance. Unfortunately, the gate's guards had not left their post during the commotion, so he had to backtrack.

Derrick crawled out of the hole he had made earlier and watched as they pulled a water hose out to spray on the fire. His eyes grew big.

"Lithium and water... time to go!"

He made his way to a road that led towards the glow of city lights off in the distance when a bright explosion erupted behind him.

Not even having to turn around, Derrick smugly remarked, "That's why you don't put water on lithium."

Derrick pulled the emitter out of Richie's bag and attached it to the top of his own so the beam would have the least chance of getting blocked.

"Man, I sure hope someone sees this."

***

"Magnet 4 departing on PR, TAC1," Obadiah called as he climbed into the Hummer.

The driver, curious, asked him how he knew it was Derrick.

"He made this stupid device in class to burst out S.O.S. on the radio..." He reached for his night vision goggles, "... and he used my DVD laser to shoot a beam into the air."

Looking toward the compound, he saw a faint, green light shining up into the air. "Not bad, Elmo. Not bad."

He handed his goggles to the driver and said, "There! Get us there now!"

***

Derrick was struggling to run along the dirt road toward town when he caught the faint sound of a diesel engine in the distance. He veered into the woods and found some cover. The vehicle pulled up to where he was and then stopped. He could hear some voices.

"Did they spot me? How could they have spotted me?" he thought.

He could barely make out their call, "Blue, blue."

"It's the Ravens! Hopefully," he thought as he emerged from his cover.

"Blue, blue, blue!" Derrick replied excitedly.

A four-person TAC team hurried to his position, flashing a U.S. patch from under a flap on their vests.

One of them began questioning Derrick to verify his identity, but before he could complete it, Obadiah walked up.

"Never mind with the verification; there's only one person on this planet that could come up with something that dumb and yet so genius."

"Seriously?!?" Derrick exclaimed upon seeing him.

"Suck it, Elmo. I just saved your scrawny butt yet again. Lydia is just going to have to deal with the fact that I'm the better man!" Obadiah smugly jested.

"I'm sure she will be rather grateful," Derrick replied, expressing his thanks.

As they were getting into the Humvee, Derrick told them that Richie had been with him earlier and that it looked like they were taking him into town. All Obadiah would say was, "We know," and they sped away from the area.

CHAPTER 43

The team pulled back into the base and Derrick asked again about Richie.

"Talk to Cap. We were the team that was sent to get you," Obadiah replied.

Hopping out of the Humvee, Derrick made his way to the command building. Inside he found the captain on the phone.

"Sesame Street secure. Yes, sir, we saw it. Yes, sir. Right away, sir."

As the captain hung up from the phone, Derrick remarked, "Obadiah came up with that, didn't he?"

The captain showed no emotion to Derrick's joke. "I just got off the phone with the Pentagon. A jet is being sent for your return to DC. Exfil is in 30 minutes."

"Captain, sir, Obadiah mentioned you would have more details about Richie. Where is he? I searched for him, but I lost him after the compound."

Walking over to one of the TV sets, the captain turned it to a local station. On the news was Richie... being dragged into the center of town. Derrick could tell he had been severely beaten.

They tied him to a wooden stand and started yelling something in a language Derrick didn't understand. The scene took a terrifying turn as the man pulled out a large knife and started sawing at Richie's neck, eventually removing his head and holding it up in the air. Derrick couldn't contain his horror and vomited in his mouth.

He was still holding onto the trash can outside of the command center, where he had just relieved himself as the captain stepped out.

"The video is rather grainy so we cannot confirm that this is Officer Turner, but we believe it is likely."

"Sir... I can confirm that was Richie. I put that orange tourniquet on his arm after the crash."

The captain placed his hand on Derrick's shoulder and said, "I'm sorry then, son," before heading back into the building.

Derrick sat on the steps of the command center waiting for his exfil flight. He was crudely trying to re-wrap the stub of a finger on his hand when Obadiah walked up carrying some gauze, tape, and two bottles of water.

Handing him the medical supplies, he said, "I figured you'd know what to do with these."

"Thanks," Derrick replied solemnly, with his head still hung.

Obadiah sat down next to him and offered one of the water bottles.

"I'm sorry about Richie. We were told not to say anything until it was confirmed."

Derrick's confusion grew at this unexpected display of sympathy from his mortal enemy.

Obadiah raised his bottle, toasting, "To Richie." Bumping bottles with him, Derrick felt tears welling up as he echoed, "For Richie."

Growing uncomfortable with the emotional scene, Obadiah stood up and as he walked away, said, "You're still such a wuss. Tell Lydia, if she wants someone with all ten fingers, give me a call."

He kept staring at his wedding ring. "That could have been me. I could have just widowed Lydia today."

Remembering her recurring nightmare, he whispered, "I almost made that dream a reality. Why am I halfway around the globe in a country that means nothing to me when my world is at home?"

He became lost in the image of Lydia standing on that walkway in the Maldives. Everything was perfect in that moment.

He reflected on his tenure at the Agency. When he started, he felt like the work he did made a difference. If he had to sacrifice his life, it would be for the greater good.

"Richie and Jennifer gave up their lives for what? FOR WHAT? No one benefited from their death. No greater good was served. It was just pure, raw evil."

Derrick had been sitting alone, lost inside his head for some time when the captain returned.

"Officer Anderson, your flight is arriving. It's too dangerous for the Company to land their jet here, so we are sending you to Kandahar on a C-130. The Gulfstream will be waiting there to take you the rest of the way."

He stood up and shook the captain's hand. "Thank you, sir," as he headed towards the airfield.

***

Derrick had departed Kandahar International well over eight hours ago. The jet was far nicer than the C-130 he had been on earlier. It even had a satellite phone... unfortunately, it didn't work. He still had another twelve hours left with a refueling stop in Spain.

Derrick had spent most of the time on the flight trying to get the phone to work while reflecting on his life, and career, but mostly about Lydia.

"Here I am. Just survived a plane crash, the deaths of my two friends, and now a twenty-hour-long recall flight with Lydia not knowing anything has happened. Is this the life I want to live?"

Finally fixing the wiring in the phone, Derrick had to wait for at least another three hours before he could call her since it was only 2am in Reston. He knew she wouldn't be able to go back to sleep after he called and told her what had happened.

Realizing he had been awake for over thirty-six hours now, he tried to get some sleep, but every time he closed his eyes, Richie's murder replayed in his brain.

***

Back in Reston, Lydia was wide awake, sitting on the edge of the bathtub. On the counter, two lines showed on the pregnancy test she had just taken. Despite her attempts, she couldn't reach Derrick. They just kept going straight to voicemail.

***

Derrick tried to relax a bit. His mind drifted back to the Christmas trip he took with Lydia to Iowa, recalling the moment he first saw her dad while sitting in the car. He remembered the thought he had at the time: *"I think I'd rather be back on the airplane and have one of its wings fall off instead."*

"Who knew that it wasn't much fun, after all?" he thought half joking.

***

... Lydia stood on a pier that stretched out into the ocean. The sun was a few degrees off the horizon and was lighting up the sky in the prettiest pink, blue, and orange hues she had ever seen. The warm Gulf breeze made her hair blow lightly behind her. She closed her eyes and soaked in the moment. She could hear the waves lightly caressing the snow-white sand beneath the pier. But then an icy breeze blew from behind her. She turned around and saw an empty pier stretching back through the twilight towards a small house...

Her cell phone ringing shook her out of her nightmare. The caller ID read *"No Name"* when she finally found it. Beside the name, the clock read 4:48am.

"At this time of day, why would they be calling unless…"

She answered and heard his voice. She screamed, "DERRICK!!!!!" and started sobbing.

Mary rushed into the room and sat down next to her.

"The chief told me there was an accident."

"Our plane was shot down. Jennifer was killed in the crash. She was cut in t…" Derrick stopped himself.

Regrouping, he continued. "I'm so sorry I wasn't able to call sooner. My cell phone was destroyed when the plane went down and then have been on the run ever since."

"ON THE RUN?!?!" Lydia exclaimed.

"Yes. On the run. They captured Richie. I was trying to save him. They murdered him. They cut his head off live on TV. I couldn't get to him in time."

Lydia felt her stomach go queasy. "Are you okay?"

"I don't know. I survived if that's what you mean. They recalled me back to Washington. I'm on my way home, but I still have another nine hours till we land."

Lydia could hear the pain in his voice. She longed to tell him her news but knew it was not the right time. "I love you, Derrick. No matter what, I will always love you. Can't wait till you get here."

The plane started to lose signal with the satellite. "I'm losing the connection. I love you, sweetie. I just wanted to hear your voice and let you know I'm okay."

The call ended as his phone read *"Signal Lost"*.

Lydia buried her face in her mom's chest and sobbed. She just kept crying over and over, "He's alive!"

***

Derrick had been asleep for a few hours, his body finally succumbing to exhaustion, when the air phone rang. He answered and the chief was on the other end.

"Derrick, I'm so sorry to hear about Richie. How are you doing?"

"Honestly, sir, I have no idea. I feel numb right now, so I can't process much."

"I can only imagine. I'd like to talk to you about everything, but it can wait. I'm going to send a vehicle to pick you up from the airport and take you home."

"If it's okay, sir, I'd honestly prefer it if Lydia came and got me."

"Understandable. Let me know if you need anything. I'll be in touch."

Seeing Derrick awake, Hank informed him of their progress. "We are about an hour out of DC. Customs will meet us when we land, but since it's obvious you didn't bring anything back, it will be quick, and then we can get you into the terminal."

Derrick called Lydia again and let her know he would be landing in about an hour. She grabbed her keys and ran out the door without even telling her parents.

Lydia was waiting impatiently at security. Seeing him, she ran and jumped into his arms. Derrick had never seen her face glow so brightly.

Squeezing him ever so tight, Lydia proclaimed, "I am never letting you out of my arms again."

"You promise?" he replied, tears welling in his eyes.

CHAPTER 44

The next morning, Derrick headed up to the chief's office for the debriefing.

"I have the official report, but that never tells the human side. Can you take me through what you remember?"

Derrick started with the explosion and led him through to when the rescue team picked him up.

"So that device they saw was something you made? From an old iPhone?"

"Yes, sir. I had the idea back in school."

"Richie mentioned this to me a few times. I think it's genius. Any chance we could use it for our future teams?"

Derrick smiled. "I'd be honored, sir. I'll send over the schematics."

As they were finishing up with the debriefing, the chief had one last request. "Medical hit me up. They want to do their standard incident follow-up. I had them set it up in a few minutes so you could be done for Richie's star ceremony."

Derrick headed downstairs and checked in at the front desk. The nurse led him back to an exam room. Within minutes, the doctor came in.

"Good morning, Mr. Anderson. How are you doing today?"

"Well, I just survived a plane crash and watched my best friend get murdered, but other than that, I'm fine."

"Since you brought that up, have you been having any issues from the incident? Anxiety, nightmares?"

Derrick knew better than to answer that question truthfully. These "follow-ups" were nothing but well-orchestrated traps. "No ma'am. I'm fine."

The doctor finished with a physical and suggested he take a two-week break to decompress and then come back for a follow-up.

Lydia was waiting in the cafeteria for him where they were going to get some lunch before the ceremony. Medical had some nice waiting chairs, but she insisted on the cafeteria... mostly because it had a Starbucks. Derrick came and sat down after he finished.

"You lied to them, didn't you?" Lydia asked.

Derrick looked down and didn't respond.

"Honey, you know it doesn't get better if you ignore it."

Derrick nodded his head in agreement. "But they aren't the ones you want to know."

Changing subjects, Derrick pointed to one of the stations. "That stir-fry looks really good today. You in?"

"Sure," Lydia said with a worried look on her face.

Derrick stared as the master carver carefully etched into the white marble wall in the Headquarters lobby. Today, a single, solitary star was being added.

Lydia was alongside with her arm around him while he stood at attention the entire two hours it took the star to be carved. When he finally finished, Derrick saluted goodbye to his friend. He did everything he could not to tear up. He knew if he did, Richie would have made fun of him if he were there. He told Lydia before they left that he would ensure Derrick got home safely, and he did just that. Unfortunately, today, that same good friend became a star on a marble wall.

★★★

One star among many. An empty spot in a book.

★★★

Back at the apartment, Derrick was making dinner. He noticed Lydia sitting on the couch, sniffling as she looked out the window.

"What's wrong, sweetie?" he asked, sitting down beside her.

"Do you know how many times I have almost become one of those stars? I can't keep doing this. That dream has me petrified that one of these times you won't come home and I'll have to look at an empty pier. I can't bear the thought of losing you." Lydia laid her head on his chest and started sobbing.

Stroking her back, Derrick reassured, "I know, I know."

"No honey, you don't. I have something to tell you…"

Derrick sat on the balcony, processing his conversation with Lydia when Jeb came out.

"You mind if I have a seat?" he asked.

"No sir, go ahead."

"It looks like your brain has been running non-stop since you have gotten back."

"It's been a rollercoaster of a week," Derrick explained.

"You sound like this might not be what you want anymore."

"I've had a lot of time to think over the last few days. Lydia doesn't know just how close that mission…" Derrick paused to regroup.

"No, son, I'm pretty sure she does. We all do. Mary and I have been talking. Lydia told us once about the two of your dreams of a house on the Gulf with a pier. Will you let us help you make that happen so you can both be there for your child?"

"Why would you do that?" Derrick asked in shock.

"Call it a selfish request. I can't bear the thought of someone coming to my door telling me something happened to her… or you."

CHAPTER 45

Sitting in the left turn lane waiting for the light to change, Derrick could hear his heart beating over the sound of the signal light clicking.

"I never imagined what it would be like to turn into here for the last time."

Placing her hand on his leg, Lydia reassured him, "I know, honey. This place meant so much the first time I pulled in, too."

The left arrow turned green, and they headed toward the massive complex known as Headquarters.

As they walked into the reception room, the chief was talking with Rosalyn as he waited for them. Showing them into his office, he said, "Derrick, Lydia. Come on in."

Derrick pulled the chair out for Lydia to sit down as he stood behind her.

Sitting on the edge of his desk, the chief asked, "How are you two holding up? It's been a rough couple of months, I know."

"Yes sir, about that. Lydia and I have had some time to talk and we are here to tender our resignations."

The chief visibly sighed. "I was afraid of that. Are you open to discussion? You can always take up to a year of leave if you need it."

"Sir, watching Richie's star get carved into that wall made me realize how close I was to joining him. How close we both have been. Now that Lydia is carrying our first child, we believe it's time to step back and focus on what's really important in our lives."

The chief looked surprised. "Well, congratulations! While I'm sad, I'm also very happy. This job eats families alive, but it's a very hard decision to step away. You two were some of our finest and will be greatly missed. The door is always open if you miss the action."

Derrick shook his hand. "Thank you, sir."

He and Lydia slowly descended the stairs in the lobby and, after giving their badges to the officer at the desk, made their way to the wall of stars.

Derrick found the blank spot that was Richie's. "I'm so sorry I wasn't able to bring you back home. Rest well in Valhalla, my friend."

Taking a step back, he saluted the wall and then turned around to see Lydia standing on the great seal. What his world was and now what his world is.

She reached out and took his hand as they headed for the doors. He stopped, took a deep breath, and then stepped through them one last time.

CHAPTER 46

A couple of years passed when Derrick's phone rang. He looked at the screen to see it was Tae.

Answering, Derrick exclaimed, "How you doing, buddy!?"

"Hey ya! Whatcha doing? I'm passing through town and thought we could catch up."

"Of course! Why don't you come over to the house and we can grill up something on the deck?"

"Grilled meats! You know I'm there!"

A few hours later, there was a knock at the door.

"Hey ya!" Tae greeted, excitedly.

Derrick hugged Tae and showed him in. Mary and Jeb were sitting on the couch playing with a small toddler.

"Tae, I'd like to introduce you to our daughter, Madeline," Derrick proudly proclaimed.

"She's so cute! Are you sure she's yours?" Tae joked as Madeline waddled up to him. Picking her up, he continued. "I didn't know Mary and Jeb were visiting."

Derrick looked over at Lydia in the kitchen and then back at Tae. Making sure she couldn't hear them, he whispered, "They aren't visiting. They sold their land and moved down here after the tornado."

"How's she doing from that?" Tae whispered back.

Shaking his head, Derrick said, "We don't talk about it."

Following dinner, Derrick led Tae out to the rocking chairs on the porch. The sun hovered just above the horizon, painting the sky with a mesmerizing blend of oranges and blues. Lydia stood at the end of the pier, watching the sunset in Derrick's favorite sundress.

"You know, the director asked me to come down and try to talk you into coming back. We could use you again." Tae remarked, glancing towards the end of the pier. "But it looks like you have a better offer."

Toddling out onto the deck beside them, Derrick reached down and scooped up Madeline. "You know, buddy... while I miss the action, I have everything I could ever need now."

Tae smiled. "Yes, you do. Well, pal, I can't wait to get back down here, and go fishing on that boat you got there."

Derrick reached out his hand and said, "It's a standing invitation. You know where we'll be."

As Tae shook his hand, he slipped a piece of paper into Derrick's pocket and then headed back to his car.

Lydia found herself standing on her pier that stretched out into the ocean. The sun was a few degrees off the horizon and was lighting up the sky in pink, blue, and orange hues. The breeze off the Gulf made her hair blow lightly behind her. She closed her eyes and soaked in the moment. She could hear the waves lightly caressing the snow-white sand beneath the pier. A warm breeze started blowing from behind her.

She turned around and saw the pier lead to a house drenched in the orange hue that lit the sky. Derrick was standing there with Madeline in his arms. Having a concerned look on his face, he put a piece of paper into his pocket and made his way down the pier to her side. She leaned her head over onto his shoulder and asked, "Is everything okay?" He put his arm around her as the sun continued to set until it fell below the outstretched water before them.